UNTIL AUGUST AND ONTO FOREVER

THE UNTIL DUOLOGY

RACHAEL OGLE

CONTENTS

UNTIL AUGUST

UNTIL AUGUST

UNTIL SERIES BOOK ONE

AUTHOR'S NOTE

Dear Reader,

    Until August contains themes surrounding pregnancy and miscarriage. These topics may be disturbing or triggering to some readers.

PART ONE

EIGHT YEARS AGO

CHAPTER ONE

JO

The first thing I notice when I step out of the airport is how wide my brother's eyes are. *Guess I really have changed.*

"Okay, what have you done with my baby sister? You are not my Joey." Jay pulls me in for a big hug and steps back to examine my appearance.

Rolling my eyes, I laugh. "Nobody calls me Joey anymore. My roommate is to blame for all of this," I say, gesturing to my appearance. "She made it her personal mission to prove that I am, in fact, a girl."

"Well, remind me to keep you locked up. I'm finally going to have to go big brother mode on all the guys."

I scoff and roll my eyes again. "What guys? There are no guys. Besides, I date now. I'm not a little girl anymore, Jay." Changing the subject, I ask, "Where's Dad? I thought he was the one picking me up."

Jay sighs as we continue walking to the parking lot of the airport. "He's finishing up some stuff for the Christmas block party. He's over at Spence's helping his parents get set up."

Hearing his name automatically makes my pulse beat

faster, but I feign nonchalance. "Oh, really? You think it will be a big party this year?"

He shrugs. "Spence said they've invited the whole neighborhood, not just the houses on the cul-de-sac, so probably. He's in from med school, so we'll probably hang out."

I nod. "It's hard to imagine Spence as a doctor. Or, you as a teacher for that matter. It doesn't seem right."

"Yeah, we're not kids anymore, that's for sure. It's hard to picture you as a writer, but Dad showed me all the articles you've been doing for the school paper. It's impressive, Joey, for a freshman to get a byline."

"It's only a feature every once in a while; it's not a big deal. It's not like I'm writing for the *Times* or anything. Besides, I don't want to write for a paper; I want to write a book. But hopefully, journalism will be a good day job."

"You'll get there. Your stuff's good."

After we finally make it to Jay's car and start to head home, I ask, "How are things with Delia? Are y'all still talking about moving in together?" My brother had met his girlfriend in college and they'd been together ever since.

He smiles. "Yeah, things are good. She'll be there tonight."

"Oh, good. I can't wait to see her. I haven't spoken with her since summer, except through occasional texts and stuff. What time is the party supposed to start?"

"Same time as always, seven. Why?"

I shrug. "I was hoping to see Ruby if she's home and I want to have time to get ready. I can't go looking like this." I'm currently wearing tight jeans and a fitted tee shirt and boots. And while cute, it's not the look I want to project, especially if Spence will be at the party.

"Okay, now I know you've changed. You're talking about 'getting ready'. My baby sister couldn't care less what she looks like and always sits in the corner with a book. Are you ill?" He pretends to check my forehead for a fever and I can't help but laugh.

"Very funny. I'm not a little girl anymore and plan on enjoying myself. I'm quite the partygoer these days."

He shakes his head. "Man, that's weird. Thinking of you with a social life and all that. Not sitting on the sidelines with your glasses and a book."

I feign shock. "You know, they have these things called contacts now. It's amazing. They still allow you to see without making it so you look like a bug. And besides, I think if you saw me at school you wouldn't recognize me. I go out with all the frat guys and you should see me at beer pong. I kick ass."

Jay's expression grows serious. "You're being careful, right? You need to watch out for those frat guys. They're bad news."

I roll my eyes. "I'm fine. There's nothing for me to be careful about. Some things about me haven't changed. I'm not about to sleep around and get myself knocked up. No worries there."

"Okay. Big brother spiel over. I'm glad you're home, sis. I've missed you."

I smile. "I've missed you, too, Jay. I love school, but coming back home is nice."

"It looks to me like you love the beach. You're so tan, Joey."

"I do love the beach, it's great. You'll never hear me complain about being fifteen minutes from the ocean."

Dad is sitting on the sofa when we come in the door around four and he hops up and pulls me into his arms. "Joanna, my girl. Let me look at you." He takes a moment to look me up and down and it's as if he doesn't even know what to say. "You've cut off all your hair. And where are your glasses? What have you done with my little girl?"

I chuckle. "Daddy, I'm still me. I got tired of wearing glasses. Especially going to the beach with them is hard. And my hair was weighing me down. Don't you like it?"

"You look great, honey, I just wasn't prepared to find out you weren't the same little girl I sent to Miami."

Jay interjects as he sets my suitcase down at the foot of the stairs, "Apparently, Joey has a social life now."

Dad looks back at me. "That so? Well, I want to hear all about this Florida life of yours, but it might have to wait. I've got to go help Garrett and Diane finish setting up for the party. Garrett's making a big mess of smoked pork and needs me to supervise."

I laugh. "I'm sure. I bet he needs a taste tester, too, huh? Go, we've got all winter break to catch up. I'll be here for two weeks. Plenty of time."

He kisses my cheek and heads out the door. I take my bag upstairs to my room and see it's exactly as I left it. My bookshelf overflowing with all my favorites. My desk with its single lamp and cup full of pens. My bed with the same quilt I've had since I was fourteen. There's no dust on anything, so apparently Dad comes in to dust at least. I look out my window, to the one that faces Ruby's and pull out my cell phone. She answers on the first ring. "Hey, friend. When do you get in?"

"Look out your window." She looks my way and I wave.

"Get your ass over here," she says excitedly. I laugh and hang up and walk next door. She greets me at the door with a big hug.

"Jo, I've missed you. I want to hear all about Miami." She takes in my appearance and says, "It looks like Florida agrees with you. Shit, girl, talk about a blooming flower. You look amazing."

I blush pleasantly as we make our way up to her room. She's stayed at home while attending art school and her room hasn't changed either, except for the addition of the college textbooks that are stacked next to her desk. We flop down on the bed and I take in my friend. She's changed a lot, too. Her naturally blonde hair is currently a bright red and she sports an eyebrow ring. Her makeup is a dark, smokey gray that makes her brown eyes look almost black. She wears black jeans shredded at the knee and a Nirvana tee shirt that's been tastefully cut in places.

She finally says, "Spill. So you ditched your glasses and you cut your hair and I see that your boobs finally decided to show up. And have you gotten taller?"

I nod. "Looks like it. I've grown three inches since last Christmas, if you can believe it. My roommate, Elise, made me over. We go to all the frat parties and I kick all the boys' asses at beer pong. But because I won't sleep with any of them, it makes me mysterious or whatever." I roll my eyes. "What about you? Any new girlfriends?"

She scoffs. "Not likely. You'd think that going to a liberal arts school, I'd find all these girls who'd want to get their lesbian experimentation phase knocked out, but alas, I'm alone." She eyes me and continues. "Have you seen him yet? And more to the point, has he seen you?"

I don't have to ask to whom she's referring. Ruby is no stranger to my longing for my brother's best friend. I sigh and shake my head. "No. Jay said he'll be at the block party tonight, but I don't know. He normally brings a date to these things. And what if when I see him, I can't even talk to him; I've never been able to talk to him. He's never seen me as anything other than Joey, Jay's little sister. What if he doesn't notice me?"

She shrugs. "You're different now. Look at you, Jo. You're confident; it's all over you. You've come into your own. I've never understood what you see in him, though. He's conceited and shallow."

I give her a pointed look. "Maybe if he had a sister who looked as good as he does, you'd get it."

"Probably. Maybe you need to make him notice you."

"And how am I supposed to do that? It's not like I can walk around in a bikini. That works at school, but it's forty degrees outside."

She laughs. "Well, what are you going to wear tonight?"

I shrug. "I brought a few things, but I was hoping you'd give me your opinion? I know the kind of stuff I wear is not what you like, but you can at least tell me if I look hot."

"Shit, girl, if I thought there was any chance you'd have me, I'd hit on you. You are hot."

I laugh. "Thanks, Ruby. That means a lot. I think."

She stands and walks over to her closet. "What sort of look are you wanting to go for? You've always been a tomboy, but what kind of stuff do you wear now?"

"Mostly sorta feminine and cute? A lot of short skirts and tight tops and strappy sandals. But it's too cold to go that route here."

She considers. "This party is usually sorta dressy casual, so I'd say go that route, with a little more... *oomf.*" She widens her eyes with the last word.

I nod. "Okay. Well, I've got some skirts that might work. And maybe a sweater?"

She flips through some things in her closet and pulls something out. "What size are you now, a ten?"

"Yeah, why?"

She holds out a shimmery black mini skirt. "This is exactly what you need. You've got the legs to pull it off, I don't."

I give her a puzzled look. "Why do you have something like that? It seems a little girly for you."

She rolls her eyes. "I bought it in a moment of weakness when I thought I wanted to be more femme. It's not for me, but seriously, you'll look hot in this. Pair it with some heels and a banging top. What do you have?"

"Will you come over and help me get ready? You can go through the stuff I have and see what will work. I want to do a really smokey eye and red lip, so something that'll go with that."

She nods and comes back over to the bed and picks up my dark hair, currently thrown in a ponytail. "What about your hair?"

I think for a moment. "Probably curls. Apparently, I've got a lot of natural curl, so I'm going to try to encourage it."

Ruby hands me the skirt. "Give me an hour and I'll be over. It won't take me long to get ready and we can walk over from your house."

"Okay. I'll go home and pull a few things for you to look at. I'm so nervous, Ruby. I feel like, at school, I'm a completely different person. Probably doesn't hurt there's beer and liquor at every party and it helps me loosen up."

My best friend's grin widens. "My parents are out of town for a couple of days. I'll bring over some tequila and we'll do shots before we go to the party."

"I don't know. If my dad finds out, he'll flip."

She waves away my concern. "I'll put it in a water bottle and bring it up to your room. He'll never know."

I sigh. It probably wouldn't be a bad idea to take the edge off. "Okay. But I don't want to be sloppy before I get to the party, just enough that I'm not so uptight and make it so I can finally talk to Spence."

"What will you do if you finally get him in front of you? Confess you've been in love with him forever?"

"No. I don't know. I just want him to notice me. I'm not a

little girl anymore and I want him to see that. That I'm a real woman and in his league."

"Babe, you are way out of his league and better than he deserves. Trust me on that."

I roll my eyes. Ruby and Spence have never really gotten along and I don't know why. "Even if it's only for one night, I want to know what it's like when Spencer Jackson has his eye on you; to be on his radar."

She sighs. "Well, if that's what you really want, I don't understand it, but I'll try to help you make it happen. What are you going to do about Jay? Does he still not know you're into Spence?"

I shake my head. "No, I've never let on to him. But I'm not worried. Delia will be there and she'll keep him occupied. I wouldn't be surprised if they don't sneak back to his room halfway through the party. As long as Spence doesn't have a date, I'm not too concerned. My Dad will be hung up with Spence's parents and after the initial greeting and catching me up with everyone, I won't see him until tomorrow. You know how this thing normally goes; old people congregate upstairs while people our age hang out in the basement or out on the patio by the fireplace."

"Well, I'll be over in an hour and we'll get to work."

I hug Ruby and thank her and head back to my house, where I take a long, hot bath and shave my legs and imagine Spence finally *seeing* me.

CHAPTER TWO

SPENCE

"Hey, Spencer, you're still good to work the bar, right?" I nod. I'm still in my sweatpants and tee shirt from my earlier workout and Mom eyes me. "You're not wearing *that* to the party, are you?"

I look down and feign confusion. "What, I thought the party was casual." After she sees I'm joking, she shakes her head and I say, "I know, nice jeans and shirt. Same as every year."

"You could use a haircut, too, son."

I roll my eyes. "I just got one. I like it long."

She sighs. "Okay, well, I guess I'll go back up. Make sure to keep the pours light tonight, okay? Especially with Jay's sister and any kids her age. I'd like that supply to last all night."

I nod. "Got it, Mom."

"All right, well, people are going to start arriving in about an hour, so you probably want to start getting ready."

"I will."

"Thanks, honey. I'm glad you're home, even if it's only for a couple days. I can't believe you won't be here for Christmas."

I shrug. "Yeah, but I volunteered at the hospital to make my internship applications look better. And the only time they really needed anyone was on Christmas, so here we are."

"I know, it just won't be the same without you," she says with a frown.

"I'd say after med, there will be a lot of holidays I have to work until I get some time under my belt. We'll probably have to get used to it."

She walks back up the stairs and I head off to the shower. After I clean up and shave, I stand in front of the closet and settle on a pair of jeans and a black button down with my favorite Converse sneakers. Probably more casual than Mom would prefer, but whatever. I style my hair and roll the sleeves of my shirt up to my elbows and assess my reflection in the mirror. As good as it gets, I guess. I don't suppose it matters anyway, since I'm simply the bartender tonight.

Jay and his girlfriend, Delia show up right at seven when the party starts. I know he's putting in an early appearance because he'll want to make an early getaway so they can spend some time together. I can't begrudge him that; I'd get out early, too, if I had a date to occupy me. But not this year. I haven't had many dates all year, which is unusual for me, but with med school, dating has taken a backseat, so I guess it's just me, myself, and I for now. Still, it'd be nice to at least get laid every once in a while. Probably not tonight though.

I drag my attention back to what Jay's saying, something about Joey. I ask him to repeat it. "I'm sorry, what about Joey?"

"She's apparently gotten really popular at UM, she's writing for the school paper, has a lot of friends. Cut all her hair off, changed up the way she dresses. You wouldn't recognize her. I almost didn't when I picked her up."

"Little Joey, huh? Good for her."

Delia smirks. "Not so little anymore."

Jay gives her a serious expression. "Dee, she's still my baby sister."

Delia shrugs. "Still, did you see her when we were getting ready to leave the house? She looked beautiful."

He takes a sip of his beer. "Joey's always been pretty."

"I'm not saying she hasn't. But she doesn't look like the same girl who left here in August is all I'm saying."

I'm quiet as they go back and forth. Now they've got me curious to see what little Joey's done with herself. All I can picture is the same petite, boyish, squirt with long, brown hair, glasses and braces. People don't change that much in only a few months. Granted, I've not seen her since last Christmas, so who knows?

By eight, the basement is almost full of every person under the age of thirty at the party. It's not a huge crowd by any stretch of the imagination, but I'm busy pouring drinks and manning the stereo when I see my neighbor Ruby coming down the stairs with someone I don't recognize.

My first thought is that Ruby must have a new girlfriend. She looks too hot for her, and they're not well matched. Ruby's always been goth and this girl is... not. She's hot. The light in the basement is not very bright, so I can't make her out from this far away, but there's no mistaking that she's tall with long, toned legs and a great ass under a mini skirt and a low-cut, off-the-shoulder sweater. Her dark hair falls past her shoulders in curls and is pulled back on one side. Her makeup is heavy around the eyes—I can't tell what color, except that they're light —and she has full, dark red lips.

I watch as Ruby whispers something in her ear and she giggles. Definitely a girlfriend. Damn. Ruby approaches the bar and she's dressed in her normal combination of black and angst and I try really hard to not look annoyed when she walks over. "Ruby. What can I get you?"

"Well, hello to you too, Spencer. Can I have two beers?"

I pump the keg and pour two beer and hand them over to her. "Who's your friend? I didn't think you went for the super classy type. I thought you were more interested in my castoffs?"

She gives me a smug smile. "I tend to have better luck with them than you do. They tell me I'm a lot better in bed than you ever are, so I must be doing something right. Thanks for the beer."

She walks away and says something to the hot girl who steals a glance at me over her beer. She bites her lip and then looks pleased about something. Something about her is familiar, but I can't say what. I intend to find out, though.

CHAPTER THREE

JO

Ruby comes back from getting us drinks at the bar and hands me a beer. "Well, you're definitely on his radar. He didn't waste two seconds before asking who you were. I think he thinks we're together, which honestly, gives me immense pleasure for him to think that I have a hot girlfriend when he has no one."

I can't help the smile that pulls at the corners of my mouth at hearing Spence asked about me. I steal a glance at him and he's still looking our direction and I bite my lip. The two shots of tequila I did before we came over and the beer I'm drinking now are definitely helping me feel less nervous.

I frown at Ruby. "I don't want him to think we're together. What if he won't come try to talk to me because he thinks I'm with you?

She rolls her eyes. "Honey, please. He'll come. He won't be able to help himself. A mysterious new girl? He'd love the idea he stole you from me. We have quite the rivalry going."

I look at her, puzzled. "Really? Y'all date the same girls? That's weird."

She shakes her head. "Not really. I've dated a few and give

him a hard time. I tell him they say that I'm better in bed than he is."

I blanch and whisper, "Do they really say he's bad in bed?"

She scoffs. "No. They don't say one way or the other, I just like to give him shit."

I breathe a sigh of relief. Not that I'd have a frame of reference to know if he was bad in bed, but I've always had it in my head that he'd be fantastic. You can't look like he does and not at least be decent, right? I so badly want to find out if my assumption is correct.

Ruby's phone rings and she answers. I hear her talking and her face lights up. I can tell by the way the conversation is going that I'm about to get ditched. She hangs up and gives me a pleading look. "Samantha came into town. Would you hate me if I went to be with her? I know you wanted me to be your wing woman, but I have't seen her in months. And I need get laid. Please don't hate me."

I roll my eyes and laugh. "Of course. I swear, y'all can't stay away from each other."

She shrugs. "It's a perfect arrangement really. We both get what we want, with no strings. Are you sure? I can always go see her later, but since my parents aren't home, it would be nice to not have to hookup in a car."

I hug her. "Go. Get some. At least one of us should tonight."

Her face lights up. "Thank you. I love you. You're the best. We'll get together before you go back to Florida, right?"

"Of course." She waves and heads back up the stairs.

I stare down into my beer, unsure what to do with myself. I don't have beer pong to occupy myself and with Ruby gone, I'm at a loss. I notice the patio outside is pretty empty, but the fire looks nice, so I figure I'll go out there. I finish my beer and drop the red plastic cup into a nearby trash can. As I go out, I steal a glance over my shoulder to see Spence's eyes following me.

I can't help but smile to see he's possibly interested. I grab a blanket from the basket Mrs. Jackson always provides for party-goers who want to get comfy by the fire. I sit on a swing near the fireplace and watch the wood in the fire crackle and I pull the blanket over my lap as the swing sways gently beneath me. I'm feeling pretty loose from the drinks I've had and don't hear anyone approach. "Do you need a refill?"

His voice sends a shiver through me. I look up to see Spence standing a few feet away with two beers in hand. As usual, I'm struck by those moss green eyes and that mop of dirty blonde hair that I've never been able to stop picturing in my fantasies and my heart lurches. "I'm sorry?"

"Oh, I saw that you'd finished your first beer and wanted to see if you needed a refill."

I smile. "Sure, thanks. That's quite the service you offer. Didn't realize you were also waitstaff in addition to bartender."

He gives me a lopsided grin. "Only for the recently abandoned. I couldn't help but notice that Ruby bailed on you."

I shrug. "I can't compete with Samantha. And I'm all right on my own."

After a moment, he says, "If you'd like some company, I'd be happy to join you."

A thrill shoots through me, but I keep my expression neutral. "Don't you have to serve?"

"Eh, by now, everyone's had a couple drinks and my parents won't come down for the rest of the night, so I'm pretty much off the hook." He gestures to the other side of the swing. "May I sit with you?"

I nod. "Sure."

After he sits, he turns to me. "I don't think I've seen you around. Are you visiting from out of town?"

I have to stifle the laugh that wants to bubble up in me. "You could say that."

He eyes me. "That's all you're going to give me?"

I shrug, my tone nonchalant. "You're a smart boy; I'm sure you can figure it out."

He sighs. "I swear, you look really familiar, but I know everyone around here, so I don't know. Have I seen you somewhere before?"

I nod. "Yeah." I'm loving that he still hasn't figured out who I am, so I'm going to let this ride as long as I can before I put him out of his misery.

"Wow, a woman of few words. Okay. Twenty questions? If I guess where I know you from, you go out with me."

I roll my eyes and project indifference. "Well, that's assuming I'd even want to. But sure, I'll play along. I don't think you'll guess, but go for it."

He thinks for a moment and rubs his jaw. "Hmm. Okay, are you related to someone who came to the party?"

"Yes."

"And we've met before?"

I chuckle. "Yeah."

"More than once?"

I nod. "Yes."

He looks mortified. "We've never slept together have we, and I don't remember?"

I snort my beer and sputter. "No."

He sighs with relief. "That's good. Because I would hate to forget someone as beautiful as you."

His words send a pleasant flush down my chest and arms. "That wasn't a question," I say, my tone reprimanding.

"Oh, right. Okay. Are you in college?"

"Yes."

"Okay. Good. So over eighteen?"

I nod. "Yes. I'm not jailbait."

He looks relieved. "Do you go anywhere local?"

"No."

He seems stuck for a moment and then asks, "Boyfriend?"

I shake my head. "No."

"Girlfriend?"

I smile. "No."

"Tattoos?"

I quirk my eyebrow. "That's a strange one to try to figure out my identity, but no. That's ten. Not looking too good for you, Spence, as the last three questions have nothing to do with how you know me."

"So you know my name?"

"Yes. That's eleven."

"Damn." I can't help but laugh. "Do I know yours?"

I nod. "Yes."

"Will you tell me?"

"You'll have to earn it."

He seems to rack his brain and I laugh. "What's so funny?" he asks.

I shrug. "Just the fact it's killing you that you can't figure out who I am. But, I've gotta be honest, I'm kinda loving it. I thought, for sure, you would've guessed by now."

He sighs, frustrated. "Okay. Time to break out the big guns. Do you think I'm cute?"

I scoff. "Again, that's not at all related to the topic of trying to determine how you know me. Try again."

"I'm asking it anyway. "

"You're all right," I reply with a smirk.

"That wasn't a yes or no. Try again."

"Yes. You're at fifteen."

"No, I'm at fourteen."

"No, earlier, you asked what was so funny. That was a question as well. So, you're at fifteen."

He feigns outrage. "You play dirty."

I quirk an eyebrow. "Looks like you'll never know."

He holds my gaze. "Okay, for real, who are you? I would've remembered you if we'd met before."

I shake my head and take a sip of my beer. "That wasn't the deal. You had twenty questions and you are losing, my friend. You're at sixteen."

He asks, "Can I get you another drink?"

I look down into my beer. It's almost empty, and I'm slightly buzzed. If I have another, I'm going to be pretty tipsy, but at this point, I don't care, since it's allowing me to talk to Spence without being so nervous I can't form words. I bring my eyes back to his. "Yes. Seventeen, Spence."

He goes back in and returns with two fresh beers. As he sits, he hands mine over and our fingers brush, making my breath hitch. "Have you known me a while?" he asks. "I get the feeling you know a lot about me."

"Yes."

"Longer than a year?"

"Yes. Nineteen. Two more questions."

"Can I have your number?"

Inside, I'm ecstatic he wants my number. Outwardly, I keep my expression placid. "Yes. One more question."

Since he sat down, his eyes haven't left mine except to dart down to my lips and back, making my heart pound. He quirks an eyebrow. "Wanna get out of here? Go for a drive?"

"That's twenty-one questions and you still haven't figured out who I am. If I'm as unforgettable as you claim, you should know by now."

"You didn't answer the question."

I shrug. "Why, when you don't even know who I am. What would entice me to get in a vehicle with someone who doesn't even know who I am?"

"Well, I know that you're beautiful and confident and sneaky and those just happen to be my favorite qualities in a woman."

I huff a laugh. "First of all, I'm not sneaky. You're a sore loser." I frown and feign compassion. "I know that's a new concept for you. You don't like to lose, but I think, this time, you did. Second of all, I'm not really confident, I'm only tipsy enough to make you think I am."

He smiles. "Are you tipsy enough to go on a drive with me?"

I bite my lip. "Maybe. What's in it for me?"

He looks wounded. "Besides the pleasure of my company?"

"Listen, pal, I've been in your company a lot. I know what that usually entails."

He laughs. "Shit. Seriously, who are you? This is absurd."

"Take me on a drive and find out. You still have your Beamer?"

His eyebrows rise up his forehead in surprise. "You even know what kind of car I drive? But actually, no. I have a Jeep now."

"I know a lot about you."

"Can you at least tell me your name?" he asks, his tone hopeful.

I chuckle. "No, I'm having too much fun. Will your parents expect you to still be here?"

"Nah. Will whoever you're with expect you?"

I shake my head. "I came with Ruby, so they'll probably think I left with her, too."

"So you wanna go?"

"Okay. How many drinks have you had?"

"Only the two. I'm good."

I shrug. "Let's go."

CHAPTER FOUR

SPENCE

I know nothing about this girl who seems to know an awful lot about me, but I'll still take my chances. She's sexy and mysterious and I'll see how far that takes me. I stand and extend my hand and she looks at it and downs her beer before taking it. She starts to go inside and I pull her around the side of the house and up the sidewalk. "We don't need to go through the house. If my parents see us, they'll question where I'm going, but if they can't find me, they'll assume I got bored or something."

"Oh, okay." She follows me, her heels clicking on the pavement. I find my Jeep and thankfully, it's not blocked in by another vehicle. I open the passenger door and she climbs in and I take the half second as she gets in to admire the spectacular view of her ass. I close the door and go around to my own side and start the car.

"Where to?" I ask.

She shakes her head. "You asked me to go on a drive. You have to come up with a destination."

I nod and head toward the mountains. It's a clear night and

the overlooks will be perfect to look at the stars and the lights of the nearby town. As we drive, she suddenly seems nervous. "You okay?"

"Oh, yeah, I just never imagined I'd be in Spencer Jackson's car. Alone. At night."

I laugh. "Well, I'm just me. And you seem to know a lot about me, so you should know I'm not scary."

"I'm not scared of you. I've never been scared of you." She considers. "Well, kinda, but not in a murdery sort of way."

I laugh again. "Yeah, I try to keep all my murderous tendencies under control. We can turn on the stereo. What kind of music do you like?"

"Mostly top 40, but older stuff is good, too. I can listen to just about anything." I turn on the radio and it's on a 2000's station, so I leave it.

After we go down the road a bit with only the radio for sound, I say, "So, if you won't tell me your name, what can I call you?"

She considers. "Ducky."

"Okay. Ducky. And what's that mean?"

"Nope. That'll give me away. You're still a long way from figuring me out."

"Well, you're not making it very easy on me."

"I never said I was easy." Her tone is low and has a playful edge.

"All right, so what are your hobbies?"

"Reading. Writing. Driving all the boys crazy."

"I bet. Okay. What kind of books do you like?"

"Hmm. That's a tough one, because my tastes vary wildly. When I was younger, it was a lot of fantasy; *Wheel of Time*, *Lord of the Rings*. Now, I lean more toward contemporary romance. Jane Green is one of my current favorite authors."

"And what do you write?"

"Eventually, I hope to write a novel, but I mostly write for school."

"An author. Okay. And what kind of books do you want to write?"

"I'd like to write romance or mystery suspense, but I've not had too much romance in my life. So we'll have to see how it goes."

As hot as she is, I find it hard to believe she doesn't have guys lined up around the block begging her to go out with them. "A pretty girl like you, surely you get asked out all the time."

"Yeah, but that's not romance. That's frat guys trying to get laid."

I laugh. "You're probably right. College is a lot of that."

She turns to me. "Is med school like that?"

"So you know I'm in med? Wow, I feel totally exposed. You're not some stalker are you?" I ask the question jokingly, but seriously, how does this girl know so much about me?

She laughs. "Not a stalker. But I do know a lot about you."

I'm curious how much she might actually know and if what she tells me will help me figure out who she is. "And what do you know about me?"

"What do you want to know?"

"A question with a question. Okay. How do I take my coffee?"

"You don't drink coffee. You prefer Red Bull. Give me something harder than that," she replies, a note of challenge in her tone.

I can't help but laugh. "Okay. I guess that was a trick question. What was my number in high school football?"

"Which year?"

"Okay, I really am starting to think you're a stalker. Junior year."

She thinks for a beat, as if searching her memory. "Fourteen. That was the year you joined the varsity team and you had to give up your other number since someone else already had it."

"Correct. Okay, so are you psychic? Is that how you know so much about me?"

"Not psychic. Seriously, you can't even see the forest for the trees, Spence. It's great."

"All right, let's go with a tough one. Do I have any allergies?"

She considers for a moment and I think I've stumped her. "Well, when you were younger, you would have a mild reaction to peanuts, but you seem to have grown out of it."

I'm shocked. Not many people know that about me. "Damn. I feel like this relationship is very one-sided."

She laughs. "Relationship? I wasn't aware you did those. I've never seen you with the same girl more than a few times."

"I'll have you know I had a girlfriend for a few months last year."

"Wow, that's almost like forever for you," she says mockingly.

"Seriously, how do I know you?"

Ducky shrugs. "What does it matter?"

I turn onto the highway to drive up to the mountains. "Because I can't, for the life of me, figure out why I haven't noticed you before, especially if you know me as well as you do. And you're someone I would've really liked to know."

"I guess you'll have to keep trying to figure it out. But if you haven't by now, I don't know if you can. And I'm kinda loving being the mystery woman and want to see how far I can go with it."

"Did I know you in high school?"

"Yes."

"Did we go at the same time, because you can't be older than, what, twenty?"

"Turned nineteen a few weeks ago. So no, we didn't go at the same time."

"But you went to the football games when I was in high school?"

"Yes."

I keep trying to think who this girl could possibly be. I still don't have a clue, but she looks vaguely familiar. And so I drive a bit farther until I come to the first overlook and pull in. Ducky turns to me. "Why did you stop here?"

I shrug. "It's the first overlook. The stars are pretty. We can talk and I can look at you and see if you'll give anything away about who you are."

She grins. "Not going to happen. I dare say you're shit out of luck until I feel like you've earned it."

"And how do I do that?"

Her smile softens and she worries her bottom lip between her teeth. "Talk to me. Have a conversation. It's all I've wanted for years. If I had known how easy you were to talk to, I would've done it a long time ago." She looks down at her hands. "But you didn't see me, so it probably wouldn't have happened anyway."

I lift her chin until she looks into my eyes and I hear her breath hitch. "I see you now. And it looks like I would've really enjoyed getting to know you before now. Why do you say that I didn't see you?"

"Because..." She trails off and huffs out a laugh. "Nope, you don't get that one."

I drop my hand and it lands on hers, but she doesn't pull it away. "Oh, come on. Seriously? I can't even have that?"

"No, that would make it too easy." She sighs and looks out

the windshield. "And I feel like if you knew who I was, it would ruin it."

My brows press together in confusion. "Why do you say that? We're having a great time."

"Yeah, but if you knew who I was, your brain would probably tell you to take me home and I'm not ready yet. I'm enjoying this too much."

My hand still sits on top of hers and I intertwine our fingers. She looks down at our hands. "Is this okay?" She nods and after a beat I say, "You said my brain would tell me to take you home. Are you trying to say that I shouldn't want to be here with you?"

She shrugs. "Probably not."

"Why? I'm very much wanting to be here with you right now."

She sighs. "Again, only because you don't know who I am."

"How long have I known you?"

"Years."

"How many?"

She thinks for a moment and I know she's trying to come up with a cryptic answer. "More than five."

"Wow, really? That long?" I ask, shocked.

She nods. "Yep."

"Then I must have been blind and deaf to not see you."

She chuckles and looks away. "Nah, there were just prettier girls in tiny bikinis." She blanches as if she feels like she's said the wrong thing. But it doesn't mean anything that I can think of, so I don't press it.

I bring her face back to look at me. "No prettier girls here. You're the only one here right now. And you're beautiful."

She darts her tongue out to wet her lips. "You're beautiful, too."

I don't drop my hand and instead bring her face to mine and press my lips against hers.

CHAPTER FIVE

JO

Spence is kissing me. Spencer Jackson's lips are on mine. I'm caught off guard for the split second it takes for me to realize this is actually happening and it's not a dream. And then I'm kissing him back and it's everything I imagined it would be all these years. His lips are soft and his tongue is searching and my hands grip his shirt, wanting to pull him closer to me.

I feel his fingers in my hair and his mouth trails down my neck and it's hot and wet and my heart races and my chest is heaving. I don't want him to stop, but I know if he knew who I was, this would all come to a crashing halt.

His hands trail under the hem of my shirt and inch up my ribs and stop right before he reaches my bra. He pulls back and I'm confused. "What's wrong?"

"I wanted to check in with you. Also, tell me your name."

I shake my head, my breathing still labored. "It's Ducky. And I'm fine. Don't stop." I pull his face back to mine and when we kiss again, it's hungrier and deeper and steals my breath. With shaky hands from nerves, I work to unbutton his shirt and kiss his cheek and neck and inhale the scent of him, never wanting to forget what he smells like. It's a clean scent mixed with something spicy I can't name. I continue to work the buttons of his shirt and kiss down his chest.

He pulls my face back up. "What are we doing?"

I chuckle, surprised by his question. I've never thought he'd be one to take the time to hash things out. "I would think that's pretty obvious."

"But are you okay with it?"

I can't help but laugh. "I wouldn't have thought you'd be one to turn down a hookup. Wasn't this what you were hoping for?" I can see in his eyes I've hit a nerve. "I'm fine. I want this. I've wanted this for longer than you can imagine."

"Seriously, who are you?" His tone is exasperated.

I pull my shirt off over my head. "I'm a girl wanting to hookup with a hot guy. If you want my name after, I'll give it to you. But I never thought you'd be one to turn down a willing lay." His eyes trail down my face to my bra and I can tell he's torn and I don't know what to think about that. The Spencer Jackson I watched growing up never had an issue with casual sex. I've overheard so many conversations about who and when and where, I lost count of how many girls he's hooked up with over the years.

After a moment, I start to feel self-conscious and begin to right my shirt to put it back on and he stills my hand. "Wait."

He thinks for a moment and gets out of the Jeep. "Spence, where are you going?" He goes to the back of the car and opens the hatch and folds down the backseat. He even has a sleeping bag in the back and he takes a second to unroll and unzip it and spread it out. I can't believe this might actually happen. My voice comes out breathy. "Wow, I'm impressed. You're prepared."

He comes to my door and opens it and extends his hand to me. I don't bother putting my shirt back on, because it's dark and no one else is around. I step out of the car and walk around to the back of the Jeep. He lifts me into the back and climbs in after me, shutting the door behind him. I slip off my shoes and toss them in the front.

He's too tall to sit upright, so he leans on his elbow and looks at me. "You seem like a nice girl. Why me?"

I shake my head and scoot toward him. "No. No more questions. I'm done answering questions for now unless it's 'does that feel good.' I'll answer that one or some variation of that. Although, if you have to ask, I'd think you already know the answer." I lift an eyebrow in amusement and honestly can't believe the words that are coming out of my mouth. They can't be mine, but maybe I'm too far gone to care.

I grip the front of his shirt and lower my mouth to his, but don't kiss him. I look into his eyes. "Now, show me what I've been missing all these years." I press my lips to his and he apparently needs no more encouragement, because he pulls me down to him and rolls us so he's on top of me and positions us so we're diagonal in the back of the car. His kiss is deep and possessive and I try to memorize everything. The way his lips feel on mine. The pressure of his tongue. The way he tastes.

Because I know that the dream will end as soon as he finds out who I am. But maybe for the moment, I can pretend it's real and we're together and he wants me. Not a pretty girl who looks familiar and who's confident and sexy. But me, the bookworm little sister of his best friend who's pined for him for seven years. In this moment, I can pretend he's wanted me, too; that I didn't have to fake who I was to get his attention. That I was good enough all along.

His fingers inch up my ribs and caress my breast. His thumb brushes my nipple and it rises to his touch under the thin lace of my bra and my breath quickens. Heat shoots to my core and need throbs low in my belly. I work to finish unbuttoning Spence's shirt and pull it down his shoulders, noticing a tattoo he didn't have last year. And as much as I want to say something, I don't, for fear it will be one more clue to my identity and he'll realize who I am and stop what we're doing. And that's the last thing I want.

Spence rolls me forward a bit and I feel him unhook my bra. I try not to cover myself as he kisses his way down my chest because I don't want him to know how inexperienced I truly am. But he goes about things as if this is entirely normal and his mouth covers my nipple and I gasp with the sensation. I run my fingers through his blonde hair like I've always wanted to and try to savor this moment. Especially because it will probably have to last a lifetime for me.

He lifts his head and bringing his mouth back to mine, kisses me again. I run my fingers down his chest and abs and work to get the buckle of his belt and jeans undone, my fingers no longer clumsy, only determined. Once I do, I slip my hand in and wrap my fingers around his cock, already hard, and I almost moan with the pleasure it brings me to touch him how I've wanted for so long. I stroke him and he lets out a soft groan.

He tugs my skirt down over my hips and my panties come with it and I realize I'm completely naked with a man for the first time in my life and it's Spence. I'm almost giddy, even if a bit scared, because I know it's going to hurt and I feel like I have to pretend like I've done this before.

He pauses and pulls back and simply looks at me in the dim light of the full moon and the car stereo. "What is it?" I ask, wondering if maybe he's somehow figured out who I am and wants to stop.

"Nothing, you're beautiful," he says, his smile soft.

I bite my bottom lip wondering if he knew it was *me*, would he still think that. "Thank you."

He kisses me and trails his hand up my thigh. His fingers slide up my pussy and my exhale is sharp as his thumb finds my clit. I've envisioned this moment so often over the years and I've imagined my hands were his many times, but nothing could have prepared me for the real thing. And when his fingers enter me, I nearly come undone. His thrusts are easy and deliberate, and he works my clit in slow circles until I'm panting. He raises up to look at me while still fucking me with his fingers. His smile is soft and it catches me off guard. I honestly expected Spence would make this about him, but he hasn't. He's being sweet and considerate and trying to make sure that I'm having a good time as well, which, honestly, was all I could ever hope for and confirms what I suspected about what type of lover he is.

After a couple more minutes, I feel my orgasm building, and I grip his shoulders as it crashes through me, his eyes never leaving mine. He kisses me and withdraws his hand. I watch as he opens the console between the front seats and gropes around for something, bringing out a condom. I can feel myself start to tremble with want and nerves in equal measure and as much as I try to hide it, Spence senses the change in me. I curse the lack of alcohol in my system because if I were just a bit more buzzed, I'd be able to pretend.

He shucks his pants and underwear and looks at me, his eyes questioning. My voice is calmer than I feel when I speak. "I said no more questions, Spence."

He rips the foil wrapper and I try to watch as he rolls it down, but it's such a cramped space, and with the angle, I can't. He raises to move in between my legs and I feel his cock against my inner thigh and my heart rate doubles. "I just have one question," he says.

I shake my head. "No."

He takes my chin in his hand and forces me to look at him. "Just one. It's not going to change anything for me. I just want to know so I do this right. This is your first time, right?"

I look away, suddenly embarrassed. "Why do you say that?"

"Because you're trembling," he says, his expression soft. "And I know you want this, and believe me, I do, too. I just don't want to hurt you and if it's your first time, I need to know."

I look at him and nod, heat climbing up my neck. "I'm sorry I didn't tell you. I thought if you knew, you wouldn't want me."

He kisses me. "It's okay. And I very much want you."

Buoyed by his words, I smile and pull his mouth to mine as he enters me. I know he's being as gentle as he can, but it still hurts. I feel pressure and burning and try to breathe through the discomfort. He pauses for a moment, letting me adjust to him. "You okay?" he asks.

"Yeah." He kisses me and begins to piston his hips and I run my hands up his arms and thread my fingers into his hair. After a moment, the pain is less than it was and eventually starts to actually feel good and I rock my hips, unable to not move with him. Because by God, if I only get this once, there's no way I'm not going to be an active participant.

Spence groans and huffs a low *fuck* against the side of my neck. For a beat, I think I've done something wrong, but then he raises his head and looks into my eyes and he's smiling and drops his mouth to mine, his kiss claiming and deep, and I still can't believe this is real. I'm having sex with Spencer Jackson. I'm having sex with Spence and it's *good*. It's better than I could've ever imagined.

He keeps his thrusts shallow and reaches between us to work my clit, and after a few minutes, I feel no pain at all and I can't bite back a soft moan as another climax slowly starts to

build. And when I cry out a moment later, my breath ragged—
and mind racing with shock that I actually got off the first time I
ever had sex—Spence takes that as his cue to be able to finish.
After what is both an extraordinarily long amount of time and
not enough, he shudders with a soft grunt and I know he's
finished.

CHAPTER SIX

SPENCE

I don't relish sex with virgins, not that there have been many, but there's just a lot more pressure to make sure they don't get hurt and there's the emotional aspect as well. But Ducky—or whatever her name is—is beautiful and persistent and her kiss made me want to never stop. I tried to make it good for her and I know she got off at least once, so hopefully, it was a good first experience for her. But for some reason, she seemed determined to have me and who was I to decline? Sex is sex, right?

After, I check in with her. "You okay?"

She smiles and kisses me. "Perfect."

I've had a great time with this girl, even though I still can't shake the feeling that I know exactly who she is; especially from all the clues she's given me. It should be obvious, but it's not, so I guess I'll let it ride.

While we lie in the dark, I simply look at her for a moment. In this light, her blue eyes look almost silver and her lips are still red and full. She notices me staring. "What?"

I shrug. "Just still trying to figure out who you are. I feel like it's right on the tip of my tongue." When she doesn't respond, I say, "You said you'd tell me after. Who are you?"

She sits up and starts to pull on her clothes. "Not yet. When we get back to town. I just want to be in this moment for a little bit longer."

I start to feel anxious. "You really are over eighteen, right?" I have thoughts of my medical career going down the drain because of a statutory rape charge.

She looks at me. "Yes, I told you; I turned nineteen a few weeks ago."

I breathe a sigh of relief. "Okay." I find a napkin in the console and discard the condom and pull on my pants and shirt.

She puts her hand on my chest. "I promise, I'm okay and this was great. You were wonderful. Thank you. Also, the ink is nice. You didn't have that last year, did you?"

"No. I got it after I finished undergrad." She nods and I can't help but feel like I really should know who this girl is and it's bugging me. She climbs over the front seat and I still can't take my eyes off her perfect ass. It is definitely something else. I finish getting dressed, exit one of the back doors of the Jeep, and climb behind the wheel. Before I start the car, I hand her my phone and she gives me a puzzled expression. "You said I could have your number, remember?"

She bites her lip. "You still want it?"

I lean over and give her a kiss. "Yeah, I do. How am I supposed to call you if I don't have it?"

She blushes and puts her number in. I also see that she's sent herself a text from my phone. "So I'll have your number, too."

I nod and she hands my phone back to me. I see she's put it under "Ducky," and I can't help but smile.

We make small talk on the way back to town and about ten

minutes before we get back to my house, Jay calls and I answer on the bluetooth in my car. "Hey, dude. What's up?"

"Hey, man, I was wondering if you'd seen Joey tonight? Dad and I can't find her anywhere and she's not answering her phone."

I consider. "I don't think so. I left a little while ago to go on a drive. Maybe she showed up after I left?"

Jay's quick to respond. "I don't know. She came over with Ruby, but I can't find her either, so I didn't know if they went back to her place." My blood runs cold and I suddenly can't breathe. I look over at the passenger seat and it seems as though she's in the same boat. "Spence, you there?"

I try to keep my tone even although I want to panic. "Sorry, man. I think you cut out. You said she came with Ruby? I don't think I saw her, either. Maybe they left right after they showed up. You know, they're college girls; maybe it's not their scene anymore."

"Maybe. Okay. Thanks. See you later."

"Bye, Jay." I disconnect the call and once I know for sure he's no longer on the line, I yank the car over to the shoulder of the road, struggling to keep my voice calm. "Joey?" I look at her and she can't meet my eye. My chest is tight and I want to scream.

She starts to reach for me and thinks better of it and drops her hands to her lap. "Spence, I can explain."

"Explain what? That the whole reason you didn't tell me who you were was because if I knew, I wouldn't have fucked you?" My words are harsher than I intend and I immediately regret them.

She flinches at my accusation but then straightens and pulls her shoulders back. "Yes. Exactly. I thought if you knew who I was, you wouldn't see me as the beautiful, confident girl you thought I was. The only thing you'd see is Jay's baby sister. But I'm not her anymore."

I'm shocked at how this can possibly be Joey. Joey was always shy and quiet. This girl is confident and sure, but I still can't fight the anger I feel at her deception. "But you lied. You let me think you were someone you aren't."

"Nothing I told you was a lie. I told you the truth about everything. I've known you for years. I've watched you and wanted you since I was twelve, Spence." Her voice breaks and she seems to lose steam. "For just one night, I wanted to be one of those girls you wanted. I knew if you knew that it was me, you would've run for the hills."

She's not wrong. If I had known it was Joey, I wouldn't have gotten within ten feet of her, despite how much she's grown up in the past year. I have to do a double-take to really see that it's her. "Why me, Joey?"

"Nobody calls me Joey anymore. It's Jo or Joanna. I left Joey behind when I moved to Miami. And I've watched you at my house since I was twelve years old, Spence. Even then, I knew I wanted you, as much as a young girl can want her older brother's best friend. I know you never saw me. I wasn't like the pretty girls you brought over to the pool and made out with and slept with. But, if only for tonight, I wanted to be."

She takes a deep breath. "I thought, for sure, you'd realize it was me after a bit. But when you didn't, and the longer I went not telling you, I didn't want it to end. Because I wanted you. Like I said, even if it was only for tonight. It doesn't have to mean anything; I'm not delusional. I don't expect we'll fall in love and get married. I just always wanted my first time to be with you, Spence. I'm sorry."

I can't speak for fear that I'll say something that will hurt Joey. I can't believe she's done this. I can't believe I've done this. Jay's going to kill me. He never had to tell me Joey was off limits because she's four years younger than us; it was a given. I never thought of her that way. Until now. If she were anyone else, I'd want to keep seeing her, at least when she's in town. She's fun and beautiful and our chemistry is something else. If she were anyone else, I'd sneak her back into my room and keep her there all night. But she's not.

I pull back onto the road without responding to her and don't speak the rest of the way to our street. I stop a couple of houses down from mine, pull over, and turn to look at her. I'm still so angry but I try to keep my tone even. "Jay can't find out about this. I'm not about to lose my best friend because you lied to me."

She scoffs. "I'm not going to tell him. You think I have a death wish? How's he going to know?"

I grip the steering wheel and can't meet her eyes because I don't really want to say what I'm about to say. Because despite the fact it's Joey and the fact she lied, I would love to see her again. "And this can't happen again."

I see her nod out of the corner of my eye and she's quiet for a minute before a soft laugh escapes. "I figured I'd only get the once anyway. But can I ask you something?"

I honestly don't know if I can handle any questions from her, but I take a deep breath and turn to her. "Okay."

She's suddenly shy and I can finally see a glimpse of the old Joey and don't know how on earth I missed it. Because now that I know, it's completely obvious. She looks down at her hands. "Was it, you know, okay? I mean, I know I'm probably never going to compare to all the other girls, but it wasn't bad, was it? For you?"

I feel about three inches tall. Because what should have been a special night for her, and was, right up until Jay called, has been overshadowed by the fallout. And if weren't Joey, I'd take her in my arms and reassure her and tell her that it was great. Because it was. But I don't trust myself to touch her again, so instead, I continue to grip the wheel and look down. My voice is soft and I shake my head. "No, Joey. It wasn't bad. It was really good, actually. And if things were different...." I can't finish the sentence because I don't want to speak the words that might alter things between us more than they already have.

She nods. "Well, thank you, Spence. For everything. I promise, Jay's not going to find out. No one has to know. And I know it can't happen again, so no worries there."

"What are you going to tell your Dad and Jay? About where you were?"

"I'll just tell them I was at Ruby's and fell asleep. Tired from finals or something. Ruby will go along with whatever I say, so I'm not worried. Trust me; I can keep a secret." She laughs. "I kept the fact I wanted you for seven years a big secret, so I think we're good."

I nod, unsure how to end things. Before I know what she's done, Joey kisses me on the cheek, steps out of the Jeep, and walks down to her house. And I just watch her as she goes. She pauses on her front porch for a moment before entering the house and when she's inside, I drag my hand down my face and get a sudden whiff of *her* still on my fingers. Jesus Christ, I'm already hard again. *Fuck my life.*

CHAPTER SEVEN

JO

Before I go into the house, I shoot a quick text to Ruby to tell her if anyone asks, I fell asleep at her place. I assess my appearance in my small compact mirror and aside from my hair being a bit mussed and my lipstick being smeared, which I fix, I don't look any different. I check to make sure my skirt and shirt are correct and once I know I look as if nothing has changed, I open the front door.

Jay and Delia are lounging on the couch when I come in and he sits up. "Where'd you sneak off to? I saw you and Ruby come in, but didn't see y'all after that."

I shrug. "Just felt like going back to her house. Didn't really feel like partying this year. I got really tired, probably from finals, and fell asleep. Sorry I didn't hear my phone; I saw all the missed calls when I woke up."

He nods. "Okay. I just thought you were looking forward to the party. Spence said he didn't even see you. I thought y'all went downstairs after you showed up?"

I try not to react to his name. "Never saw him. Maybe he'd stepped away from the bar for a bit. And we didn't stay but a few minutes. Did y'all need something and that's why you were trying to find me?"

Jay shakes his head. "No, I just wanted to see if you wanted to hang out."

I start toward the steps. "I think I'm going to go on up to bed. I'm still really beat. Finals were no joke this semester and I think the fatigue is just settling in."

"Okay. Goodnight, sis," he says with a smile.

"Night, Jay." I walk up the stairs and once I'm in my room and shut the door, I finally feel as if I can breathe. I glance out the window and see Ruby's room is dark. I know she and Samantha must've gone out or they're in bed, so I don't call her, bad as I want to.

I pull the pins from my hair, rub the soreness from my scalp, go into my bathroom, start the shower, and strip out of my party clothes. As I wash my hair and body, I run my fingers along the places that, just an hour earlier, Spence's mouth and hands explored. And as much as I meant it when I told him I knew we can't do it again, that is, in fact, all I want to do. His words play over in my mind. *If things were different...* If I wasn't Jay's sister. If he wasn't Jay's best friend. *If. If. If.*

I don't see him again while I'm home on break. I don't ask where he is, but I overhear Jay telling Dad that Spence had volunteered with a local hospital to help with his resume for after he finishes med school. And I know it's probably for the best, since if I saw him, I honestly don't know if I could keep the want out of my eyes.

Ruby comes over the day before I leave to return to Miami. She's spent most of her time with Samantha and I'm happy they have something that works for them. We're drinking coffee in my room and she finally plain out asks me because I've been quiet about what happened with Spence.

"So, spill, did you talk to him? You've not said a word about what happened after I left."

I sigh. "Yeah, we talked."

"Did he know who you were?"

"Not for a while. It was great. I got to pretend for a little bit that I wasn't Joey. I wasn't Jay's little sister. I was simply a pretty girl at a party who caught his eye."

She eyes me. "I hope you didn't catch anything else from him. So what happened?"

"We went for a drive and he still didn't know who I was, but I guess because I was mysterious, it made it fun for him." I bite my lip and look down. "And he kissed me."

"That look tells me there was a lot more than a kiss." I look up at her and shrug and her eyes go wide. "Seriously, Jo? I knew you wanted to get his attention and talk to him, but I didn't think you'd actually have sex with him. Wow. Did he know who you were when you did it?"

I shake my head with a laugh. "No way. There's no way he would've gone through with it. But apparently, he's easy or I am because we did go through with it. He realized it was my first time, which I really wish he hadn't, but he was very gentle and sweet."

"So, does he still not know it was you?"

I blow out a breath. "No, he knows. We were on our way back home and Jay called to ask if he'd seen me. He said he didn't think so, but then Jay mentioned I'd come to the party with you and he knew instantly."

Her eyes widen in shock. "Shit. What happened?"

"He was pissed, but I think he understood why I did it. I told him I'd wanted him for years and just really wanted my first time to be with him. Of course, we both know that we can't do it again and Jay can never find out."

"So, was it everything you'd hoped it would be?"

I feel the corners of my mouth curl into a soft smile. "Ruby, it was better. And the whole time, I was trying to memorize exactly how it felt and how he smelled and what it was like to have him want me. And even if I never have him again, I think it was a pretty perfect first time."

Ruby feigns disgust and pretends to gag. "Excuse me while I go vomit."

I laugh. "Sorry. I forgot how much you don't like Spence. I've never understood it. What's your deal with him?"

"He's always thought he was the shit and I can't stand how shallow he is and he thinks he's better than everyone else. Mr. 'oh, look at me, I'm going to be a doctor'. He thinks he can't lose. Ever. There's not an ounce of humility in him."

"Wow. Okay. I don't know if I've ever seen that side of him, but whatever."

"You've always had blinders where he's concerned. Just be careful, okay, Jo? I wouldn't want you to get hurt by him."

"Nothing to be careful about. We're never going to see each other again, so there's nothing to worry about."

Just before I get on the plane to return to Miami, I'm scrolling through social media and see a photo of Spence with a medical textbook and a cup of coffee from earlier today. I should leave it, but I can't help myself. I shoot him a text because I don't want Jay or anyone else to see my comment.

> Jo: I thought you didn't drink coffee. Don't tell me I was wrong about the Red Bull. Have you finally crossed over to the dark side?

I honestly don't expect him to respond because I'm sure he's still pissed about the whole thing and would probably rather just go back to pretending I don't exist. And I'm okay with that because I got my dream night with him and if it has to sustain me for the rest of my life, I'll be okay.

My plane is announced, so I stand and roll my suitcase to the gate. While I'm digging out my boarding pass, my phone dings and as I'm walking toward the door of the plane, I pull it out and look at it.

> Spence: The dark side is where all the fun is. Have a good semester, Ducky. Don't get too tan. I'd like to be able to recognize you the next time you come home.

His words are innocent and mean next to nothing, but I still can't fight the thrill that runs through me knowing he responded.

CHAPTER EIGHT

JO — FIVE MONTHS LATER

Spring semester flies by. Classes are a bit more challenging, so I don't go to as many parties. I give myself permission to hook up with some of the guys who were after me last semester, but I don't enjoy it. None of them care about making me feel good at all, and as soon as they're inside me, it's over in what seems like seconds. I finally just gave up and stopped going to parties altogether.

I spend most of my free time at the beach reading and my tan grows really deep. I go to the student health center and get a prescription for the pill so I won't have to worry about getting pregnant if I finally find someone I want to sleep with again. At this point, it's not looking likely anyway, but better safe than sorry.

Spence and I text sporadically, mostly commenting on each other's social media posts. The tones of the texts seem to be completely innocent, but there have been a few where innuendo may be perceived. I have no illusions about what will happen when I return home this week, bad as I would like a repeat of Christmas. Jay is flying down to drive the thirteen hours back home with me and all of my stuff. Dad was going to, but he had to go out of town for a couple of weeks to see an old college friend. I told him I would work at the bookstore while he's gone, so it'll be nice to have something to do this summer.

After I'm done packing up my car with my final stuff, I walk back to my dorm room to ensure I've not forgotten anything. Elise left yesterday, so I'm all by myself and I sit on the bed and look around at the room that literally changed my life. If I hadn't had Elise as a roommate, I'd probably still be the shy, awkward, dowdy girl I was when I arrived. And I couldn't be more thankful for everything that's happened this year. There's not a day that goes by that I don't think about my night with Spence and, oh, what I would give to relive it.

I turn in my dorm key to the RA on my floor and get in my car to head to the airport. As I stop to get a bite to eat, I see I've somehow missed a call from Jay and I'm suddenly confused, so I call him back. He answers on the second ring. "Joey? Hey."

"Hey, Jay. Aren't you supposed to be in the air? I'm getting ready to head to the airport now."

"Yeah, I meant to call you first thing this morning. Delia's mom is sick and she and I are driving to Memphis to be with her. I think we'll be gone a few weeks, from the looks of it."

"Oh, no. I hope it's nothing serious. Okay, sure. I understand. I guess it's just me for the next thirteen hours, then. I'm glad I didn't go to the airport and sit and wait."

"Well, Dad and I didn't want you to drive back by yourself, so I asked Spence if he'd make the drive with you. He didn't have anything going on when he came back into town a couple of days ago, so he said he would. So, you'll still need to go to the airport."

My brain struggles to process Jay's words. I try to keep my voice even, although, internally, I'm freaking out. "Oh. Okay."

Jay's tone is apologetic. "Yeah, Joey. I'm sorry. I know it's not ideal. Hopefully, you won't get too bored driving home. I know you two don't have a ton in common."

Oh, brother, if you only knew. I feign indifference. "I'm sure it'll be fine. It's only thirteen hours." Thirteen hours in a car with Spence. Alone.

"Okay. Well, I'm glad I was able to give you a heads-up. Dad said he might have to extend his trip by a few days, but he'd let you know. Be safe, okay?"

"All right. Thanks. I will. Tell Delia I hope her mother feels better. Bye."

I disconnect the call and have a minor panic attack about what I look like. I'm wearing cutoff shorts and a tank top and my hair is up in a curly ponytail. I did put on some makeup today, but since I was going to be on the road all day, I didn't try with my appearance at all.

It shouldn't matter, but I still would've liked to look decent. Can't be helped now. All my stuff is packed up in the backseat and trunk. I guess I should be thankful the backseat isn't empty; otherwise, I'd probably feel more temptation than I already will by being near him.

I have a momentary thought that I should text Spence and give him hell for not telling me he's the one coming to meet me, but he's in the air and won't get it anyway, so what's the point?

I take a few deep breaths and try to quell the nerves rising in me knowing I won't have booze this time to give me the courage to carry on a conversation with Spence. It will be just me. I'd be lying if I said part of me isn't worried he won't like who I am when I'm not carefree and loosened up by drink. Only one way to find out, I guess.

CHAPTER NINE

SPENCE

I wanted to tell Jay hell no when he asked me to go down to Florida to get Joey. But I was afraid if I said no, he'd wonder why, and I'd already told him the day before I didn't have anything going, so now I sit on a plane headed to Miami.

I should've never responded to the text she sent me when she went back to school. I should've deleted her number and severed all ties. But she's funny and smart and I like knowing she's there.

We've not texted with any sort of regularity, but I see her posts on social media. Most of them are while she's on the beach with a book. I catch glimpses of her legs in the posts and I remember how nice those legs feel wrapped around me and I have to remind myself who she is and what could happen if Jay found out about what we did.

Jay is genuinely the closest thing to a brother I'll ever have. We fight like brothers and don't always see eye to eye, but he was the first person who told me I could make it when I said I wanted to become a doctor when even my parents thought I was crazy. But I'm not willing to give up my best friend regardless of how much I enjoy seeing his sister or how I want to do way more than just see her. Because if he found out, that's exactly what would happen.

As far as I know, Joey didn't date in high school and Jay was in college by that point anyway, so I don't know if he's ever had to be a protective big brother. But knowing how much he loves her, if he knew about the night of the block party, Jay would kick my ass. Mostly because he knows me and who I am and my track record. And I can't blame him. It's not stellar. I leave broken hearts in my wake. And if I broke Joey's? Well, both he and I would probably never forgive me.

I'm anxious the whole plane ride down because I don't know if I know how to be around Joey anymore. Thirteen hours is a long time to be in a car with someone, but will the entire ride be awkward simply because of what happened?

I've been in a car alone with Joey before to pick her up from middle or high school sometimes when Jay or Nick couldn't. But that was before everything happened. When she was just "Joey" and not "Ducky." And anytime I think back on that night, I think of her as Ducky since it's easier to compartmentalize and not feel guilty that I still think about her and the night we shared.

I think about the way she smelled like coconut and vanilla. I think about the way her lips were soft and giving. I think about the way her skin felt under my fingers, soft and smooth. I think about the small sounds she made when I fingered her. I think about the way she trembled just before I entered her, her eyes dark with want. I think about the way her pussy felt wrapped around my cock. Even thinking about it now makes me want her, much as I try not to.

After the plane lands, I take a few deep breaths, hoping I can be strong enough to resist the temptation that will be present with me for the better part of the next day. Once I'm off the plane, I shoot Joey a text to let her know I've arrived.

> Spence: I don't know if Jay told you I would be the one riding up with you. Sorry about that. I didn't feel like I could tell him no without it seeming suspicious. The plane just landed. Are you already at the airport?

Almost immediately, my phone dings with a response.

> Jo: Yeah, Jay called me. It's fine. It's only 13 hours. I'm here now. Out front.

I hoist my backpack over my shoulder. Even though we're supposed to drive straight home, I never fly without a carry-on with a few changes of clothes because you just never know. I walk out the doors of the airport and I'm hit with the oppressive heat of the south Florida summer. I scan the cars lined up along the sidewalk and stop. I catch sight of Joey leaning against the front fender of her car, watching a plane take off. She doesn't see me, so I take a moment to look at her because she's still just as beautiful as she was at Christmas.

She's wearing cutoff shorts and a tank top. Her hair is thrown up into a casual ponytail and sunglasses sit on her face. She's more tan than she was and I can't take my eyes off her. After a second, I know she's caught me watching her and a hint of a smile pulls at the corners of her mouth. I start walking and pretend to be unaffected.

When I reach her car, I stick my hands in my pockets. "Joey."

She rolls her eyes. "I wish y'all would stop calling me that. I'm not Joey anymore." She walks around to the driver's side and opens the door and looks at my backpack. "What's in the bag?"

I take it off my shoulder, shove it in the backseat, and get in on the car's passenger side. "I never fly without a bag with a few essentials. What if the plane had to make an emergency landing? I don't want to get stuck with only the clothes on my back for God knows how long."

She nods and pulls out into traffic. "Smart. How was your flight?"

"Fine, we hit little turbulence over Atlanta, but it wasn't too bad. How does it feel to have your freshman year over with?"

"Weird. It went by so fast. How does it feel to have your first year of med school done?"

"Weird. It did not go by fast. It dragged ass." She laughs. She's focused on the road, so I simply take her in for a moment. "You got more sun this semester."

She shrugs. "We had good weather. I spent most of my time at the beach when I wasn't in class."

"What, no big parties this semester? No beer pong tourneys to win?"

"There were, but not as many as last semester. My class load was heavier, so I had to study more. And it got old, so I read at the beach."

"Yeah, I noticed you read *The Martian*. What did you think about that one?"

"It was great. Funny. Some of the scientific stuff went over my head, but I liked the idea of the guy struggling to survive in the face of no odds of survival. Have you read it? I didn't know you read much, you know, besides school stuff."

I'm surprised. "You mean there's actually something you don't know about me? Well, well. Yeah, I read it last year. I saw somewhere that it's being optioned for film. Hopefully, they don't screw it up."

"Cool. I might have to go see that one. You read anything good lately?"

"No," I admit. "I wish. The only books I've had my head in were the ones for school and if I have to look at another diagram of the human nervous system before August, I'm going to scream."

"I get that. I had to listen to the prose of Shelly's *Franken-stein* all semester. Ugh."

"So, not a fan of the classics?"

"Not too much. I like Shakespeare and Austen. I can do Bronte, too, but I much prefer newer stuff. I feel like it's more relatable and I'm able to really put myself in the character's shoes."

"Is that why you like those contemporary romances? So you can put yourself in their shoes?" I don't realize what I've said until after it's already left my mouth and I want to kick myself. But Joey doesn't seem fazed and continues.

"Well, I also like mystery suspense thrillers as well. I recently read a Karin Slaughter book that kept me up at night. It was terrifying in the best way possible."

"Nice. I might have to try one of those. Send me the name of that one."

"Sure. I can do that." She considers. "I think I might have it in one of my boxes. When I get home and unpack, I'll see if I can find it for you."

After a moment, she blows out a deep breath. I turn to her. "What?"

She huffs a laugh. "I was really scared this was going to be super awkward or that I wouldn't even be able to talk to you since I haven't had a drink."

"You seem to be doing okay. I was nervous it was going to be weird, too. But I guess it doesn't have to be. Only twelve-and-a-half hours left to go."

She laughs. "Yeah. So, can I ask you a question?"

"I don't know. The last time I let you do that, it took a turn."

"Well, if you want to get technical, you were the one asking most of the questions. Terribly, I might add."

I feign injury. "Ouch. They weren't terrible questions."

She frowns. "You asked me if I had a tattoo. How is that relevant to determining who I was and how you knew me?"

I shrug. "Well, if you did have a tattoo, I thought maybe I had seen you when I got mine."

She considers. "Okay, I'll give you that one. But can I ask you a question or not?"

"Well, I'd say it'll make for a pretty boring trip if we don't talk, so sure."

"Why medicine? What made you want to go into it?"

"That's a loaded question. The obvious answer would be that I want to help people and make good money doing it. But can I let you in on a little secret?"

Her lips curl into a smile. "Okay."

"You know when you're in public and there's a medical emergency and someone yells, 'Is there a doctor in the house'?"

She chuckles. "Yeah."

"I want to be able to say, 'I'm a doctor', and come to the rescue."

"So, you have a superman complex?"

"I don't know about that, but I do like to help people."

She nods. "Have you decided on your specialty? Are you going into surgery or anything like that?"

"Probably not, more than likely, I'll do general practice, but we'll see. I do like *Grey's Anatomy* and the idea of performing life-saving surgeries does have a certain appeal. But it's a lot longer program and fellowships and stuff like that. Just knowing I have to finish med and then go do my residency and stuff is enough for now."

"Okay. But do you think *Grey's* is very realistic? All they seem to do is drink at the bar and hook up in the on-call room."

It's my turn to chuckle. "I don't know. It might be fun to find out." She rolls her eyes and I ask, "What about you?"

"What about me?"

"Why writing?"

Joey's quiet for a beat. "That's a loaded question for me, too. I think when most people write, especially if they want to write novels, they think there will lots of fame and success. But I don't think that's it for me. When I think about writing, it's more just wanting to be heard. Having someone read my words and have them be affected by them, good or bad. As long as it's not indifferent."

"Have you written anything lately?"

"Not anything besides papers for classes or the school paper. I'm hoping to get to write some this summer. I haven't really had any inspiration to write anything just for me in a while, so I don't know. We'll see."

"What plans do you have for the summer?"

"Besides working at the store? Nothing really. Ruby and I talked about getting together at the pool quite a bit, so maybe that. You?"

"Nothing at all. I'll mow the yard for my parents and do some other stuff around the house, but I'm going to enjoy my summer."

"What do you do for fun money? Like, to go out on and stuff."

I shrug. "My parents said that as long as I'm in school, they'll support me. So I have a credit card they pay. It has a low balance, but still, it's something."

"So, you have an allowance?" she asks with a smirk.

"I don't like to put it like that."

"But isn't that essentially what it is?"

"I guess."

"Wow, must be nice. Jay and I haven't had that luxury.

Other than food and shelter and, you know, other essentials, from the time I was old enough to work at the store, that was how I had to get spending money. Minimum wage, all the way. How did I not ever know that about you?"

"I guess you don't know as much about me as you think you do," I say, my tone smug.

"Well, I know more about you than you've ever known about me."

I nod. "You're probably right, but I do know some things."

"Like what?" Her question is challenging.

"You don't eat syrup on your pancakes. I remember the first time your dad made pancakes and I was over; you didn't put syrup on them." She seems caught off guard that I'd actually know something about her and I continue. "And when you were, what, thirteen or fourteen, you were obsessed with *High School Musical*."

"Lots of people my age liked those movies; that's an easy one."

"Okay, here's one. When you're reading a book and it gets to a part with action or suspense or whatever, your toes curl in. I can remember you sitting in the living room curled up in that chair by the window and I could always tell if you were to a good part in your book because it would almost look like you were clenching your fist, but with your toes." She's quiet for a minute and I ask, "How's that?"

She nods. "Yeah. It's good."

My voice is low when I speak again. "So, I did see you. Just not like I do now." She swallows and doesn't respond, just turns on the stereo. I feel like I've made the conversation come to a crashing halt and want to kick myself. I shouldn't have said the last part; I know that. Attempting to bring the conversation back, but to a safer subject, I ask, "If you could only take one book with you to a deserted island, what would it be? And don't say *How to Build a Boat* or something like that."

Seemingly happier to be on safer ground, she responds, "Well, shoot, that was totally going to be my answer. Ooh, that's hard. Can I pick more than one? You know, there are so many genres to choose from. And can I pick a series as opposed to a standalone?"

I can't help but laugh at her questions. "Nope. Just one book. Not a series, not more than one genre. One book."

"Damn. That's difficult. You realize you're asking a certified bookworm that question, right? I devour books like air. Let's see. Probably *The Hobbit*."

"Why that one?"

"Well, it's escapism at its finest, which, if I were stuck on an island, I'd probably want." She continues in a voice that's a bit softer, "Plus, it was the first book I read after my mom left, and it got me through that, so if I could survive her leaving, a deserted island should be a piece of cake. What about you? What book would you bring?"

I want to ask her about her mom because I know what Jay says about her, but I'd like to get Joey's perspective, but I don't. "Um, probably something Stephen King. Maybe *It*."

"So, being stuck on an island alone isn't horror enough; you need to torture yourself with clowns? No nightmare fuel for me, thanks." She laughs and I can't help but join in.

"Yeah, why not? Isn't horror its own sort of escapism? Forgetting about your own problems and focusing on those of others?"

"If you say so. I say give me dragons and halflings and wizards over creepy clowns any day."

After a beat, she asks, "If you could only listen to one song on repeat for the rest of your life, what would it be?"

"Wow. That's a good one. I don't know. That's hard.

Because music serves so many purposes. You have stuff you listen to when you're happy. Stuff you need to pump you up, like when you work out. Or when you're sad or angry. But one? Really? Hmmm." I think for a moment. "'Monkey Wrench' by Foo Fighters."

She looks impressed. "Okay, solid choice."

"What about you? You must have one at the ready for you to ask that question."

She nods. "Yeah, I don't know what it is about it, but 'I'm the Only One' by Melissa Etheridge is my go-to. Regardless of my mood. I can be miserable and if that song comes on, I'll just belt it out and it makes me feel better."

"That is a really good one."

"So, do you really drink coffee now? I thought you hated it."

"Probably what I drink hardly constitutes coffee," I admit. "People who actually drink coffee would probably drag me out back and shoot me. Do you still drink yours black?"

"Like my soul."

I laugh. "And you still don't eat syrup on your pancakes?"

"Nope. Too sweet." She projects a totally adorable cutesy face. "I'm plenty sweet enough, didn't you know that?"

"Yeah. I did." Because she is definitely sweet. And beautiful. And smart. And still Jay's baby sister. *Fuck.*

CHAPTER TEN

JO

Talking with Spence has been so much easier than I thought it would be. And hearing him say the things he's noticed about me caught me so off guard. I had no clue what to even say and I was thankful he moved on to easier topics.

Sometime after we enter Daytona, when we've been driving for about four hours, my car starts making a strange noise and then simply dies. I have just enough time to pull over to the shoulder and out of the flow of traffic. But then it just won't go.

I turn my hazard lights on, and Spence tells me, "Pop the hood, and I'll take a look." I do, and we get out and he examines the engine for a few minutes. "I can't readily see anything wrong. Nothing wrong with belts or anything like that. It's not overheated. If I was going to guess, It might be your fuel pump. That'll cause a car to die as it's going down the road."

"Is this something you can fix?" I ask hopefully.

He shakes his head. "No, I'm not a gearhead. I know enough to change my oil and a tire and spark plugs, but anything more than that, and I have to take mine in. We'll probably have to get a tow. And with it being a Saturday, they may not be able to fix it before Monday. It shouldn't be a big job if it is the fuel pump, but we'll be stuck until it's fixed."

"Shit. This sucks. Okay. I'll call my dad. Would you care to call for a tow? We're still in Daytona, right?"

Spence nods and scrolls through Google trying to find a tow company that can take my car into a garage. I dial my dad's number and he answers on the third ring. "Hey, sweetie. How's the drive?"

"Well, Daddy, I'm having some car trouble. Spence thinks it might be the fuel pump, so it looks like we could be stuck for a couple of days while it gets fixed. He's calling a tow now. We're in Daytona, but I'll update you as soon as I know more."

"Oh, no. Well, I'm glad you're not by yourself. You have your emergency credit card, right?"

"Yeah."

"All right. Well, go ahead and get a couple of rooms for you and Spencer to wait it out, I guess. And put the repairs on it as well, okay?"

"Okay, Daddy. I will. I'm sorry I won't be able to run the store for a couple more days."

"It's okay, honey. It'll survive. I'll see you in a few weeks. Hey, can I talk to Spencer for a second?"

"Okay." I hold the phone out to Spence. "My dad wants to talk to you for a minute."

He looks confused but takes the phone. "Mr. Greene? Yes, sir, it looks like it. I'm sorry, I can't fix that myself; otherwise, we'd be on our way." He's quiet for a minute, listening to my father on the other end. With the road noise, I can't make out what he's saying.

"No, sir, that won't be necessary. I've got mine... Well, I appreciate it, sir. We'll be back home as soon as we can... Yes, sir, I will. Do you need to talk to Joey again? Oh, okay. Goodbye."

He disconnects the call and hands my phone back to me. "What did Dad say?"

"He just said he was going to pay for my room and I said he didn't need to do that. But you know your dad. Oh, and the tow will be here in about fifteen. You'll probably want to gather whatever you think you'll need for a couple of days."

I nod and go around to the back, find my suitcase, and then open boxes until I find some shorts, tee shirts, bras, underwear, shower kit, and makeup. I also toss in my bathing suit because, why not? I make sure my backpack has my laptop and a book and call it a day.

We sit in the car and wait for the tow. Spence says, "I sure didn't see this coming, did you?"

"Actually, I totally sabotaged my car so we'd get stuck in a beach town because I don't want to leave Florida." I feign complete seriousness and I can't tell if he thinks I'm joking.

He shoots back, "See, I would've thought it was because you wanted to spend a couple of days with me."

I laugh but can't stop the blush that fills my cheeks. "I bet you'd like it if that was the case." I quickly sober because I didn't mean to say the last part.

He looks out the window. "In a perfect world, yeah."

I sigh. "But our world's not perfect."

He shakes his head. "Nope." He's quiet for a minute. "I'm going to call around and see if I can find us a couple of rooms."

"Okay. Let me know if they need a card to book; I'll get mine."

He nods and clicks through listings on his phone. I hear him call several hotels and motels without success. When he hangs up, I ask, "Still no luck?"

He shakes his head. "There's some kind of big convention

in town, so everywhere is booked up. I'll keep trying." He calls a few more places and then perks up. "Yes, that's fine. I'll take whatever. Thank you so much. The name is Spencer Jackson." He gives a bit more information and verifies the address, then disconnects the call and turns to me. "Okay, so I've good news and bad news."

"Well, I'm assuming the good news is that we got in somewhere?" I ask, my tone hopeful.

He nods, but his expression is less than excited. "Yes, but they only had one room."

Shit. Two-plus days in one room with Spence. I try very hard to keep my mind off the fact that I'll be in the same room as Spence. With a bed. I blow out a breath. "Well, I guess it is what it is. We're both adults, right? No big deal."

Spence nods. "Yeah. Of course. It'll be fine." But I know it won't be fine. And part of me doesn't want it to be.

We sit in silence for the ten more minutes it takes the tow truck to show up. We get out of the car, and Spence talks to the tow truck driver. I hear him telling the driver the plan, which includes taking us to our motel and then dropping my car off at a garage. I internally freak out during the twenty-minute drive to our motel. I pay the tow fee and hand my credit card to Spence to get us checked in as I wait near the door.

For what we could get, the motel's not bad. It's older but clean. Spence comes back over a moment later with the room key. "You ready?"

I nod. "Yeah." We walk down a long hallway, and he gestures to a door and unlocks it. I walk in and flip on a light. While I should be surprised by what I see, it seems par for the course with this trip so far. One bed. *Shit*.

"Well, I guess it could be worse," Spence says.

I scoff. "I don't know how."

He shrugs. "At least it's a king. You'll have plenty of space."

I look at him. "You mean we will."

"No, I'll sleep on the floor."

I roll my eyes. "Don't be stupid, Spence. Like we said, we're adults; we can control ourselves for a few nights, right?"

"Yeah. Right. Adults." He says and nods, but he sounds unconvinced. I can't help but laugh at the absurdity of all of this. Spence looks at me, his expression confused. "What's so funny?"

I turn to him as I set my bags next to the bed. "It's like something out of a rom-com. It's full of all your standard tropes. Brother's best friend, whom the girl has liked for years. There's a mixup and he's forced to come to her rescue and oh, no, there's car trouble and they get stranded in a motel with only one bed. You can't tell me it's not hilarious. All that's missing is a music montage or getting caught in the rain. Quick, check the weather."

He laughs, and it seems to relax us both. After a minute, he says, "Maybe you can use it as inspiration for your book."

I consider. "Not a bad idea. I guess we'll have to see how it all plays out." I check my phone, and it's almost seven and I'm starving.

Spence says as if reading my mind, "I asked the front desk if there was anything within walking distance to eat. She said there are plenty of restaurants, but our best bet might be pizza since they'll deliver. But I can walk to the gas station across the street to get us some drinks and snacks."

I nod. "Pizza's perfect. I can order it. You still like sausage and onions?"

He nods. "Yeah. You all right if I go ahead and go pick up the drinks and stuff?"

"Yeah. I'll probably jump in the shower and wash the road off, but I think it'll take the pizza a while to get here since it's peak time."

"Okay. I'll be right back." He leaves and I lock the door, open my suitcase, and get my shower kit and clothes. I paw through my bag and realize I forgot my pajamas. *Well, shit. There's another box to check for the fucking rom-com.* I think for a minute. I won't be able to sleep in any of the shorts and tees I grabbed and stuffed in my bag. I normally sleep in just an over-sized tee and undies. I pick up my phone and call Spence. "Hey, everything okay?"

I sigh. "Yeah. Um. I forgot my pajamas. Can you see if there's an extra large tee shirt wherever you go get the drinks? Don't most of these tourist places have souvenir tee shirts?"

He's quiet for a moment. "Yeah, I'll see what I can find."

"Thanks. I'll see you soon." I disconnect the call and speak into the void, "What the hell are you doing to me, universe? This is not cool."

I blow out a breath and go shower and shave and wash my face. When I get out, I dry off and wrap one towel around my body and another around my hair. I hear the door open. "Spence?"

"Yeah?"

"Were you able to find a shirt?"

"Yeah. Do you want it now?"

"Yes, please." I stand behind the bathroom door, crack it open, and stick my hand out. He places it in my hand and I pull it in and shut the door. I hurriedly dress and am pleased to see the shirt comes almost to my knees, so that's something, I guess. I hang my towels up and make sure I didn't get water every-where. I tidy up my face wash and moisturizer. I take out my contacts, put on my glasses, and take my birth control pill. When I don't have anything else to do to stall for time that could prevent me from going out, I gather up my dirty clothes and walk out of the room.

I don't look at Spence as I put my things away and sit on

the bed. He looks as though he's going to say something and there's a knock at the door. "Probably the pizza," he offers.

"My card is in my wallet." He waves me off, opens the door, accepts the pizza, and pays the delivery guy before shutting it again. The smell of cheese, garlic, and meat wafts my direction, and my mouth almost waters. He brings the pizza over and sets it on the small table in the room.

"Man, I didn't realize how hungry I was. What did you get to drink?"

"Beer and soda. I figured we'd have beer with the pizza and the sodas for the beach."

I feign shock. "You're going to serve beer to an underaged person? I'm downright shocked."

He chuckles and rolls his eyes. "I'm sure your delicate sensibilities just can't take it, can they?"

"Nope, sure can't. It's too bad we don't have plastic cups and ping-pong balls. I'd kick your ass at beer pong."

He smiles and walks over to the dresser, where a plastic bag sits. He pulls out solo cups and ping-pong balls. "That so?"

I can't help but laugh in surprise. "Shut up. You got beer pong supplies?"

He shrugs. "You kept going on and on about how good you were. I want to see if it's true. You might not know this, but I was quite the pong player in undergrad."

"Oh, it's on. But not right now. I have to get some food in my belly or I'm going to drop." I grab a slice of pizza, sit on the bed, and lean against the headboard. I start to pull my knees up, but I remember I'm not wearing pants and think better of it. Spence hands me a beer. "Thanks."

He sits down on the bed and turns the TV on. "Do you have a preference?"

"No, I'm good with whatever." He flips through the channels and *Armageddon* is on and he flips to the next channel. I reflexively reach for him to signal to stop but pull it back before I touch him. "Wait, go back. I mean, if that's all right. We can keep flipping."

He changes it back. "No, *Armageddon* is fine. And if you touch me, you know I'm not going to attack you, right? You don't have to try to avoid me."

I flush, embarrassed. "Sorry. I just don't know what's okay anymore."

"Yeah, me neither," he admits, "but I think you touching my forearm isn't going to send me into a frenzy or anything."

I laugh. "Good to know." We eat and watch the rest of the movie, and as usual, when I watch Harry sacrifice himself for the good of all humankind, I cry. I dab my eyes with the sleeve of my shirt and Spence turns to me.

"You okay?"

I nod. "Yeah. That part always gets to me. It doesn't matter how many times I've seen it; it sets me off."

"I get that. I can't watch *The Patriot* without crying."

I look at him, surprised. "You're just yanking my chain, right?"

He shakes his head. "No, when Gabriel dies and later when Susan finally talks to Benjamin and tells him not to go? Complete blubbery mess. Don't tell anyone, though; I'll lose all of my tough guy street cred."

"Your secret is safe with me. I'm really good at keeping those, remember."

"So you say. You want another beer?"

"Sure. You trying to get me drunk?" I ask, teasing.

Spence's face falls. "No, Joey, I'm not."

I sober, my tone apologetic. "Spence, I was joking. I promise. Two beers are not going to do me in; you should know that. I had three at the block party and I'd done shots with Ruby before we came over."

He looks at me, shocked, and hands me my drink. "Damn, that's a lot."

I shrug. "I only did a couple of shots of tequila. I was just trying to loosen up and not be nervous."

"Why were you nervous?"

"Seriously?" My tone blatantly asks, *are you stupid?*

"Yeah, why were you nervous?"

I gesture to him. "Um, hello, I was going to see you and I wouldn't have been able to talk to you without some liquid courage."

"You talk to me just fine."

"Now I do. Probably has something to do with the fact that you've seen me naked. That tends to drop a lot of walls."

He blinks and takes a long drink of his beer. "You probably would've been fine then, too," he says after a beat. "I saw you; I was going to come and talk to you. You would have eventually warmed up to me, booze or no."

I scoff. "I think you underestimate how painfully shy I am."

"Not anymore, you're not. Some of the stuff you said the night of the block party, once I knew it was you, I was shocked that you were the one who'd said them."

I give him a sheepish smile. "Yeah, I kinda surprised myself with some of the stuff I said."

He gives me a slow smile. "You didn't hear me complaining." I nod, unsure of what to say. I don't want to veer into dangerous territory and it seems we're headed that way. After a minute, I blow out a breath and Spence asks, "What?"

I shake my head. "It's not fair."

"What's not fair?"

"Life. All of this."

CHAPTER ELEVEN

SPENCE

"Why do you say it's not fair?" I ask her.

Her voice is pained. "Because if I was anyone else or you were, then everything that's happened would be a super cute beginning to something. And if almost anything at all was different, I feel like this would be a date and the fact that we broke down and they only had one bed would be a plus, but it's not. And so it's simply cruel. All of it."

I start to say something about how I agree with her, but she jumps off the bed and starts gathering up garbage and putting it in or beside the trash can. She goes into the bathroom and I hear her brushing her teeth. I sigh, unsure where to go from here. It occurs to me that I could start a fight with her and tell her that if she'd been honest at Christmas before we went on the drive, none of this would be a big deal. Because if she'd been honest, I would've never taken her on that drive and we never would've had sex. But if I pick that fight, she might think I regret having sex with her. And God knows that's the furthest thing from the truth. I regret she withheld information from me, but I don't regret the time I spent with her or what happened that night. God knows I've relived it in my mind enough that there's no way I can regret it. I enjoyed it too much.

So I do nothing and simply dig through my bag and pull out a pair of shorts and boxers and my toiletry kit. Once she returns from the bathroom, she plugs up her phone and pulls the covers down on the bed. I turn to her. "I'm going to take a shower."

She nods and climbs into the bed and takes off her glasses and puts them on the nightstand. "I'm going to sleep. I'm drained from packing my car all morning and everything. Goodnight, Spence."

"Goodnight, Jo." I don't mean to use Jo, but Joey no longer suits her with everything she's said and everything we've done, and I couldn't finish the second syllable. And I find that I like Jo. Both the name and the girl. Way more than I want to admit to myself. Way more than is acceptable for who she is to my best friend. Something flashes in her eyes with the use of something other than Joey, but it passes just as quickly as it arrives.

I turn and walk into the bathroom and shower and when I return, Jo's turned on her left side, facing away from me. She looks to be asleep already, so I take a moment to simply watch her without fear of her catching me. She's so beautiful it hurts. Her dark hair is fanned out behind her and her arm is tucked under the pillow. Her full lips are parted and I ache to run my thumb along her bottom lip. And she's right; all of this is very cruel.

I climb into bed next to her and am very conscious how of close she is, even in this king-sized bed. I'm painfully aware of how if I rolled over, I could wrap my arm around her and pull her to me. But instead, I stay exactly where I am, flat on my back and will myself to go sleep.

When I wake up, I struggle to recall where I am and who's in the bed next to me. And then it comes to me and I remember the flight and Jo and the car and the motel. Sometime during the night, she's scooted closer or I have, because she's stretched out on her stomach, legs splayed, her foot touching mine. I'm rolled onto my side, facing her. Her hand is only inches from mine, definitely close enough to touch, but I resist the urge. I don't, however, resist the urge to lift up the covers and peer at her ass.

Because of how she's sleeping, the tee shirt she wears has hiked up above her hips and her underwear is cute with polka dots and cuts right across her butt cheeks and I can't help but smile. I hear a muffled voice say, "If you're going to stare at my ass, at least buy me breakfast. And coffee."

I flush with embarrassment and drop the blankets as though I've been caught stealing. I look at her head. I hadn't realized that her face was toward me and she gives me a smirk and rolls onto her side, facing me. "Good morning."

"Good morning," I echo.

"See, we are total adults. We've got this."

"Yep. We sure do," I say without much confidence. I really hope she doesn't look down toward the direction of my dick, because the combination of morning wood and seeing her half naked has given me a suddenly painful hard on. "What do you want for breakfast?"

She chuckles and reaches for her glasses and slides them on. "I was just giving you a hard time. I really just want some coffee."

I sit up and roll my neck and shoulders. "Okay. I think there's a fast food place within walking distance. Wanna go?"

She considers. "Okay. Give me a minute. Are you always so get-up-an-go? Don't you ever just lay around after you wake up? That's the best part. Knowing you're awake, but don't *have* to get up."

"Pretty much, I don't usually have a reason to stay in bed."

She wiggles her eyebrows, her expression playful. "Not even when there's a pretty girl in the bed with you?"

I laugh. "Okay. We need a system."

Puzzled, she asks, "For what?"

"For when one of us says something we shouldn't, like you just did. I know I'm just as bad, so it'll be for me, too. If we're going to survive this thing, we're going to have to be more careful, Jo."

Her expression changes, but I can't read it. "You stopped calling me Joey."

I nod. "Yeah."

"Why? I mean, I know I've asked you to, but I didn't ever think you would."

I want to tell her that Joey is Jay's little sister and that's not who she is to me anymore. I mean, she is, but it's so much more complicated than just that. Instead, I simply shrug and say, "Because you asked me to. I get it. I was Spencer all through elementary and middle school, but it felt stuffy and not me anymore, so once I got to high school, I wanted people to call me Spence. And most everyone did, expect for my parents and stuff, so I thought I'd try it out."

"Oh. Okay. Well, thanks."

"Red light."

She frowns, confused. "What?"

"When one of us says something inappropriate, we'll say 'red light'. You know, like a stop light?"

She rolls her eyes. "Oh, right. Okay."

I get out of bed and take my backpack into the bathroom with me and pee and wash my hands and brush my teeth and dress in a pair of shorts and a tee shirt. I wish I had a hat, because my hair is sticking up everywhere, but I wet it and do my best to tame it.

When I come out, Jo is sitting on the bed, dressed in shorts and a tank top and I see the tied string of a bathing suit top peeking out the neck of her shirt. She stands and walks past me into the bathroom and I get a whiff of coconut and vanilla and I'm taken back to Christmas and struggle to breathe. But thankfully, she doesn't notice.

When she comes back into the room, she's ditched her glasses and pulled her hair up into a messy ponytail and has on a bit of mascara. She looks at me. "You ready?"

I nod and make sure I have my wallet and phone and the room key. She grabs her purse and we head out. As we leave, she puts the "Do Not Disturb" sign on the door. She sees the question in my eyes. "I don't want my laptop stolen and they wouldn't change the sheets anyway. If we need more towels, we can get them from the front desk."

I nod and we walk out of the motel. I hadn't noticed last night, but we're in a very busy area with a lot of restaurants and shops within walking distance. I point down the street about a half mile. "Waffle House?"

"Works for me."

As we walk down the sidewalk toward the restaurant, I glance past the hotels to our left and see the ocean. "You planning on getting in today?" She follows my gaze.

"Probably not, I don't like to do more than stick my feet in."

"Really? You pretty much live at the beach now and you don't even get in the water?"

She shrugs. "What can I say? I'm more of a sun and sand girl, not sea."

"And what book did you bring with you?"

"Why do you think I brought a book?"

"Because you're you."

She rolls her eyes, amused. "It's called *Me Before You*. It's about a quirky girl who becomes a caretaker for a paraplegic. He's grumpy and depressed and it's her job to cheer him up."

"Okay. You'll have to let me know how that one goes. Doesn't really sound like my kind of book, but it's an interesting premise."

"So far it's good."

When we get to the restaurant, I open the door and Jo walks in and we take a seat in a booth. It's not very busy, which I think is a bit strange for a Sunday morning, but I'm hungry, so I don't care.

Jo orders coffee and I order a soda and we look at the menu. When the server comes back, we both order waffles with eggs and bacon. While we wait for our food, her phone rings and I can tell it's Nick, checking in.

"Yeah, Daddy, we're good. We're eating breakfast now. Spence talked with the tow truck driver and got the information about the garage. We'll call them first thing in the morning. Hopefully, we'll be out of here by Tuesday, but I'll keep you updated."

She listens to him say something. "Yeah, the motel is fine. We had a bit of trouble finding a place since it's the weekend, but it's nice." She smiles as he says something. "I will, Daddy. Promise. I'll see you when you get home, okay? Love you, too." She disconnects the call and puts her phone away. "Dad said to make sure the garage orders OEM parts. Whatever that means."

I sip my drink. "It just means parts from the manufacturer, not a third party."

"Oh. Okay. Did you bring swim trunks?"

I shake my head. "No, but I can get some at the shop we passed on the way here. I'll totally look like a tourist, but whatever."

"Yeah, I've got to get some sunscreen. I left mine packed up. Will you get in the water?"

I nod. "I love the ocean. I might even spring for a boogie board. I probably won't be able to get away with using one too much longer without people thinking I'm too old, but I enjoy it."

Our food comes and we eat and I notice that Jo doesn't put syrup on waffles either, but she does on her bacon. "So you don't want syrup on pancakes or waffles, but you do on bacon? Explain that one to me."

"Well, bacon is salty and syrup is sweet, so it's a good balance. Pancakes and waffles with syrup is just all sweet, and it's too rich. Too sweet."

"Okay. But I don't think there is such a thing as too sweet. I mean, look at you."

She raises an eyebrow as she brings her coffee to her lips. "Yellow light."

"That wasn't inappropriate, just fact."

"That's why you only got a yellow. Proceed with caution."

I laugh. "Fair enough."

The bill comes and I reach for it and Jo snatches it. "No. Dad's going to check the credit card bill and think I took advantage of you if I don't pay for everything. He already feels like we're inconveniencing you by taking up all your time."

I want to say that I'll be happy to let her take advantage of me, but that's a definite "red light" comment so I keep it to myself and nod. "Okay."

On the way back to the motel, we stop in at a souvenir shop and I pick up some trunks, a beach towel, and sunglasses. Jo gets some sunscreen and her own towel. We pop back into the room so I can change and she can grab her book. I pull everything out of my backpack and she looks at me. "I thought we could just put our stuff in here, so we don't have to carry everything."

"Oh, sure. Thanks." We grab several sodas from the mini fridge and lock up the room and walk across the street to the beach. We find a good spot on the sand and spread out a blanket that we found in the closet of our room. It's hot, but not scorching with the ocean breeze, so it actually feels really nice.

Jo strips out of her shorts and tank top and although I knew she was wearing a bikini under her clothes, I'm in no way prepared to see her in it. Her perfect tits and ass and hips and legs. I'm very thankful for my sunglasses that hopefully hide how much I want her. I try very unsuccessfully to not watch as she slathers sunblock on her face, chest, arms, and legs.

She lays on her belly and opens her book and holds the bottle out to me. "Would you care to put some on my back?"

I take the bottle and put a dollop into my hands and apply the cream to her back and can't stop myself from kneading her neck and shoulders as I rub it in. I don't miss the soft sounds she makes as I touch her and I think to myself, *red light, Spence.*

CHAPTER TWELVE

JO

If I could have done my back myself, I would have. I know it's inviting trouble, but I seriously had no choice. That's not to say that I didn't very much enjoy Spence's hands on my skin, I just keep thinking how unfair this all is.

I know if anyone passed us on the beach, they'd see a couple possibly on vacation, not two people who are fighting a war within themselves. Because I know that as much as Spence and I are committed to trying to keep things platonic, we're both struggling and I hate it so much.

Once he's done putting sunblock on my back, he takes off his shirt and puts some on his own face and chest and arms. I sit up and extend my hand. "Want me to do your back?" He seems to consider it for a long time before handing the bottle over to me. I squeeze some out into my hand and take a deep breath and steel myself to touch him. I rub it in and say, "I should've gotten the spray. Made it easier on both of us."

He laughs. "Yeah, probably. In more ways than one." I exhale and he says, "I know. Yellow light."

"Yep. For sure." I try to enjoy the feel of his skin under my fingers, knowing this is probably the only time I'll get to touch him, so I'll take what I can get. But far too quickly, I'm done and putting the bottle into the backpack and wiping my hands on a towel. "All good."

"Thanks," he says. I lie back down on my stomach and open my book and for a bit, I get lost in the drama of Louisa Clark and Will Traynor and their unlikely and bittersweet connection.

After a while, my neck and shoulders start to ache from reading, and I sit up and stretch. I know Spence is in the water and my eyes automatically search for him, despite my best efforts to the contrary. I find him immediately because I know his body as well as my own—knowledge honed over seven years of watching him at our pool. And I am no stranger to him shirtless, but seeing him walk out of the ocean is an entirely different experience. The water rolls down his abs as he exits the waves and I watch their descent, wishing to follow the droplets with my hands and mouth.

My breath catches when I see him. He runs his fingers through his hair and I'm not the only one who notices him. Several women glance his way as they pass him, but he doesn't look at them. His eyes are trained on me and for a split second, I wish he would look at the other women, because at least then, I could pretend things are the way they used to be, when I was still Joey.

He comes back to the blanket and dries off. "How was the water?" I ask.

"Great. You should get in. It's warm. How's your book?"

"It's getting too serious for the beach."

"That good, huh?" I nod and he sits next to me. He opens the backpack and pulls out a soda for each of us and hands me one.

"Thanks."

After he takes a couple sips, he says, "I don't know how you get any studying done when this is so close every day. I'd never pass my classes."

I shrug. "You get used to it after a while and it becomes like anything else. Don't get me wrong, I love it, but I almost don't notice it anymore."

He looks back toward the water. "I guess it's like that with beautiful things. You take them for granted when they've been around forever."

I should say something about yellow and red lights, but I don't. I simply pull my knees up and rest my chin on them and look out into the ocean and feel myself almost wishing I could go back to before the block party. Because at this point, it would have been easier to never have had him at all than this .

It's like seeing chocolate and knowing it's there. Dreaming of what it tastes like for years and years. But then you get just a sample and you find out how sweet and good it truly is. Then you're told you can never have it again, but it's dangled in front of you for the rest of your life, like some sort of torture. And, again, I think how cruel all of it is. I'm also quick to remind myself that I've done this to myself. I made this choice and I have to live with it.

We finish our sodas and Spence turns to me. "Want to take a walk?"

"Okay." Because really, what else do we have to do?

We rise and walk down to the waterline and the sand is hot. I'm thankful when the water crashes over my ankles, cooling my feet. Neither of us speaks, but there's so much I want to say. I want to tell him I'm sorry I caused everything to change between us. And even though I don't regret any of it, I wish I could go back to before. To tell him to call me Joey again, so I wouldn't have this hope bubbling up in me that he doesn't see me as her anymore. The hope that he sees me as someone he could want to be with. Someone he'd like to be seen with. And if Jay wasn't my brother, it could be that way. But he is.

"You're awful quiet," Spence says after a bit.

I give him a soft smile. "Sorry. What do you want to talk about?"

"Where do you see yourself in ten years?"

"I don't know. Probably with a paper or magazine or some sort of publication. But ideally, I'd have at least one book published by that point. What about you?"

He shrugs. "Hopefully, part of a practice or on my own. I don't know. Hopefully a dog. Maybe married with kids."

I nod. "Good plan." After a minute, I ask, out of sheer curiosity, "What do you think Jay would do if he found out about what happened at Christmas?"

Spence stops walking and turns to me, his expression stricken. "Why, are you thinking about telling him? Jo, you can't. Please." His voice is pleading.

I shake my head. "No, of course not. I just wanted to know what you honestly think would happen? I mean, has he ever told you I'm off limits or whatever?"

He barks out a laugh. "No. He never had to. You always seemed so much younger than us, I don't think it ever occurred to either us you and I might be attracted to each other. But I think if he found out, he'd kick my ass, and I couldn't blame him for it and then he'd never speak to me again."

"What, did y'all think I'd never grow up? That I'd always be a short, skinny, tomboy?"

He sighs and shrugs. "I think he probably will wish that was the case. But, Jo, he can't ever find out. He's my best friend. I don't want to lose him. He'd never blame you for what happened. He would, for sure, think I chased you. And you're his sister, so you automatically take priority in this kind of situation."

"But you didn't chase me. I pursued you. And I'd tell him that."

Spence hangs his head. "He'd never believe that. Jay knows who I am and he'd never, for one second, think I didn't somehow seduce you or make promises to you or whatever to get you into bed. He knows me too well. I'm not a good guy, Jo."

I'm suddenly angry they'd both think I'm still just a little girl. "Well, you didn't make me any promises or anything. And if came down to it, I would tell him you didn't even know it was me when we hooked up. I knew exactly what I was doing."

"It wouldn't matter. To Jay, you'll always be Joey. No matter how much you grow up. Probably not even when y'all are both in your forties and married or whatever. You'll still be his baby sister."

I shake my head in frustration. "It's so stupid. If you were anyone else on the fucking planet, he could care less if I slept with you. For fuck's sake, when he found out about the frat guys I went out with at school, he just told me to 'be careful'."

He touches my arm and his eyes search mine. "But I'm not anyone else, Jo. I'm me. I'm the guy who drops a girl as soon as I've gotten what I want, as soon as I've gotten her into bed. I'm not a guy I would ever trust with my sister. And Jay knows that. He knows all the sordid details of my whole life."

I close the distance between us until our chests are nearly touching and I plant my hands on my hips. "You think I don't?! Mine and Jay's bedrooms shared a wall. You think I didn't hear you talking about every single girl you hooked up with while y'all played video games in his room? All it did was make me wish I was them."

His face falls. "I never knew you heard all that. I wish you hadn't."

"Why? All it means is I'm not blind to who you are. I'd know exactly what I'd be getting with you."

"Which is exactly why you shouldn't want it," he says softly.

"I know. I know exactly why I shouldn't, but I can't help it." I'm suddenly very tired and I heave a sigh. "I'm going to go back to the room and take a nap. I think the sun's gotten to me." He turns to walk with me and I stop him. "I think I need a few minutes alone. Please?" I try to keep the hurt out of my voice, but I don't know if he's convinced I'm fine. I know I'm not. He just nods and lets me walk away.

I manage to make it back to the room before the tears come and for the first time in my whole life, I cry over a boy. In all the years I pined for Spence, I've never cried, but now I do. Huge, racking sobs well up in my chest; honestly, I don't even know why. He's not broken my heart or hurt me in any way, but I think I have. I got exactly what I always wanted. I knew it was a one-time deal, and I was okay with it. I knew I could never have him again, and I told myself that once was plenty. Once was supposed to be enough to last the whole of a life. But I see now I've lied to myself. An entire life of moments with him would never be enough.

CHAPTER THIRTEEN

SPENCE

I watch Jo go and know I'm in so much trouble. All I want to do is chase after her and grab her hand and kiss her. But I stay glued to where I stand and pray for the strength to be strong. After she pulls on her shorts and tank top, and takes her phone, book, and the room key, I go over to the blanket where our things are and pack up the rest of our stuff walk over to a nearby beach bar.

I sit at the bar, thankful for the shade and order a beer. The bartender, an older guy in his fifties with wild silver hair and a scraggly beard in a floral button-down, walks up to me. "Wife or girlfriend?"

"I'm sorry?"

"Only time a guy comes in with that kind of look on his face is when he's got wife or girlfriend troubles. Which is it?"

"Neither."

"Boyfriend, then?"

I shake my head. "No, she's not my girlfriend. She's... trouble."

He considers and nods slowly. "Well, Daytona's good for trouble. As long as it's legal trouble, I say go for it."

"Easy for you to say."

"So what's the trouble with her? Your face says she's the best kind." He wiggles his eyebrows.

I don't have anyone else to talk to, so I figure, why not. "She's my best friend's sister. He was supposed to come down to help drive her home from college and I got roped into coming because he had something come up. We broke down, so we're here for a couple days while her car's getting worked on."

"And she's pretty, huh?"

"Gorgeous."

"So, what's the problem? She doesn't like you?"

"No, apparently, she's liked me for years."

"So, again, what's the problem?"

"If her brother found out, I'd lose him. He's like family. It's too risky. I don't have the best record when it comes to women and he knows it. And it's his baby sister."

The bartender nods. "Tough spot you've gotten yourself into."

"No shit," I say with a huff of bitter laughter.

He wipes down the bar. "At some point, you have to take risks. Otherwise, what's the point to life? What if she's the one girl you want to be different for? What if y'all are here for a reason? You like this girl? You know, for more than just the obvious, although it sounds like that's nice, too."

"She's great. Smart, funny. I've known her since we were kids and until a few months ago, I've never had more than a simple conversation with her, but she's easy to talk to. She knows me, maybe better than I know myself."

"Well, it sounds like you already know what you want." Another customer walks up and he steps away. *Yeah, I do know what I want, but I can't have it. Ever again.*

I order one more beer and nurse it over the next hour, trying to give Jo and myself some time apart to let things die down. Once I can't justify sitting at the bar any longer, I toss some cash on the counter and start walking back to the room. I don't have a key, since Jo took it, so I knock on the door. I wait and a few minutes later, it opens. Her face is red and her eyes are puffy and I know she's been crying and it hurts more than I ever thought it could to know she's in pain.

I walk into the room and drop my bag. I start to say something and Jo holds up her hand, her voice soft. "Don't, Spence. Please. It doesn't matter. It won't change anything. Nothing we say will help either of us. So, it's better if we don't."

I nod. "Okay. If that's what you want."

"It doesn't fucking matter what I want. You've made your choice and I know it's not really a choice at all, because it's Jay. And I'm just me. And that's okay, it really is. I'll be fine. And you'll be fine. And Jay will be fine and he'll never know about Christmas. I promise, I'll never tell him. I meant it then and I mean it now."

She laughs, but it's not a laugh with any humor, but something more along the lines of outrage. "And the fact he's never going to know is the complete kicker of the whole thing. He doesn't know, right this minute, how much I'm fighting with myself over what to do. And he'll never know how much I want you. And it's okay, because it has to be. We'll make it through the next twenty-four hours and we'll go back to exactly the way it was."

She sits on the bed, pulls her knees up to her chest, picks up her book, and opens it. I don't trust myself to sit on the bed with her, so I sit in one of the chairs at the small table and pretend to scroll through social media. I don't hear her turn pages, so I know she's only pretending to read. And I can't help but think how absurd all of this is because we're both torturing ourselves over something that, in all likelihood, Jay is never going to find out about. Because neither of us wants to hurt him.

I have the momentary thought that if it happened again, he'd never find out, either. But I don't let myself dwell on that, because it can only bring us more trouble than we've already got. Because once with her was enough to hook me and make it so she was under my skin for longer than anyone else I can remember. What would a second time do? I don't want to go there.

I go take a shower to clear my head and wash off the ocean and then get dressed before coming back to sit in the same chair as earlier. For almost two hours, we both sit pretending to ignore one another, the air around us thick with tension and unsaid words. My stomach growls and I realize that it's been almost eight hours since breakfast. I finally look at Jo. "Hungry?"

She shrugs. "Not really."

"Well, we've gotta eat. Come on. We'll go find something."

She doesn't say anything, simply puts her book down and rises and grabs her purse. I make sure I have the room key and open the door. We head in the opposite direction of this morning and just walk. The sun is low in the sky and it's humid and warm. Jo's hands are in her pockets and she doesn't look at me. After about a quarter mile, I see a Mexican restaurant. I slow and gesture to the sign. "Tacos?"

"Sure. Hopefully, they don't card. I want a margarita." We enter and are seated after a few minutes and sure enough, they don't try to card Jo when she orders a margarita on the rocks with an extra shot. I order a beer. They bring our drinks, along with some chips and salsa, and I watch her down the shot without making a face, which makes me wonder how much she usually drinks and if I should be concerned.

She nibbles on the chips and finally speaks. "I didn't realize how hungry I was. Thanks for making me get out."

I sip my beer and nod. "I couldn't sit in that room anymore anyway."

"Yeah, it was a bit... tense."

"I thought so, too."

She seems to be loosening up a bit from the alcohol and I know it will probably hit her fast, since she's not had anything since breakfast. She licks the salt off the rim of her glass. "I'm sorry for making it weird earlier. I shouldn't have brought any of that up. Can we pretend I didn't say any of it? Can we start over? Pretend none of it happened?"

"Which part?"

"Any of it. Don't you think it'd be easier if hadn't?" I'm caught off guard because it sounds like she wants to forget about Christmas, too. And even though I probably should, I don't want to do that, so I say nothing and simply study my beer.

The server comes and I order a beef burrito and Jo orders chicken nachos and another margarita. It's only then that I see that her first is over half gone. "Best slow down on those. I don't want to have to carry you back to the room or hold your hair when you start puking."

She rolls her eyes. "I think you underestimate my tolerance. I'm fine. I've never gotten sick. I only tend to make bad decisions when I drink."

"Yellow light, Jo."

Anger flashes in her eyes. "Who said I was talking about you, Spence?"

For the first time since Christmas, I think of Jo possibly sleeping with someone else and jealously grips me. It makes no sense, but I am irrationally mad. It's not like I'm a saint, but I haven't had the opportunity to date or hookup with anyone with my schedule this past semester, so the memory of my night with her is all I've had to keep me going for the past six months.

Neither of us says anything and our food comes a few minutes later and we eat in silence. She goes to order another drink and I tell the server to bring the check instead. "You're not my father or my brother, so you can't tell me how much I can drink." Her tone is petulant and her eyes narrow.

"No, but they're trusting me to make sure you get home safe. You get yourself drunk and walk into traffic, I won't be doing a very good job of that."

"Like you care." She folds her arms and looks away. I open my mouth to say something when the server brings the check. Jo reaches for it and pays for our food and when her card is returned, she doesn't say anything to me, just stands to leave the restaurant. I follow her out and she almost jogs back to the hotel and I nearly have to run to catch up with her.

"Jo, wait up." She doesn't slow and when I finally catch up to her, I grab her arm.

"What, Spence?"

"What is your problem?"

She jerks her arm away from me and keeps walking. "I don't have a problem."

Five minutes later, we're back to the motel and she's still practically stomping to the room. I unlock the door and she flings it open and tosses her purse onto the dresser. I shut the door and lock it and turn to her. "Sure as fuck seems like you have problem."

"Nope. I'm fine." She grabs some things out of her suitcase and goes into the bathroom and slams the door in my face. I hear the toilet flush and the shower start and I pace the floor in a near rage, adrenaline surging through me.

CHAPTER FOURTEEN

JO

After I shower, wash my face, take my pill, and do anything else I can to stall for time, I walk out to the bathroom, don't look at Spence, and walk over to my suitcase and drop my dirty clothes in. I hear him come up behind me. "Jo?"

I pull my hair up in a messy bun and I shake my head without turning to him. "Spence, I'm too tired. I'm going to bed."

"So, it's okay for you to give me speeches all day, but I can't speak my piece in any of it?" he asks, exasperated.

I pivot and raise up to my full height and look at him, my eyes narrowed. "What? What would you like to say?"

His eyes look as though he has a lot he wants to say, but before I know what's happening, he's grabbed my face and is kissing me. It's deep and hungry and angry. My hands instinctively wrap around his waist and pull him closer. I've dreamt about kissing him again for the past six months and now I don't want it to end. I moan into his kiss and much too soon, he breaks his mouth from mine and we're both breathing hard and I know my eyes are wide in surprise.

He spits out, "You think I don't *care?* You think I don't want you? You don't think if I could, I'd throw you on that bed and show you exactly how much I want you? You don't think the thought of you fucking other guys makes me so angry I could track them all down and beat the shit out of them for even touching you? You don't think you're all I've thought about for the past six months? You want to forget it all happened and go back to the way it was before. I can't do that, Jo. I don't want to forget. And part of me rationalizes we could still see each other and Jay would never find out, because I'm not going to tell him and neither are you, but it would only end badly for you."

I can't believe everything he's just said and my voice comes out breathy when I speak. "Why would it end badly for me?"

He drops his hands from my face and takes a step back. "Because I'm not good for you, Jo. I'd only hurt you and I don't want to do that. You're Jay's sister and I'd never forgive myself if you got hurt because of me. I wouldn't even be able to look him in the eye anymore."

I close the distance between us again, but I don't touch him, bad as I want to. "You think I'm looking for anything serious? No. I'm only nineteen. I have no illusions as far as you're concerned. I know who you are, Spence. I've always known who you are. I have no issues keeping it a secret, because I don't want Jay to find out any more than you do. I know it won't go anywhere, because we'll both go back to school in the fall, but I can't make myself stop wanting you. And I know you want me, too. What's the point in fighting it? We're only making ourselves miserable, if yesterday and today are any indication. The only thing I'd ask of you is that if you're sleeping with with me, you don't sleep with anyone else and I won't either. If it stops working, we talk about it like adults and we stop. I'm not stupid, I know you have a shelf life on your relationships."

His expression registers surprise and he seems unsure what to say for a moment, but then asks, "Wait, you've thought about this and how it would work?"

I roll my eyes. "What do you think I was doing while we sitting here not talking to each other. I know you know I wasn't actually reading just like I know you weren't actually doing anything on your phone."

He gives me a sheepish smile. "I know." After a beat he asks, "What about the stuff you said at the restaurant about wanting to go back and forget?"

I let out a frustrated sigh. "I was gauging your reaction and just trying to get a rise out of you. You hadn't really responded to anything I said all day except when we were talking about what would happen if Jay found out, and so I truly thought you didn't care or want me. And then I got mad, because you've flirted with me, but it just felt like you were sending me mixed signals. And if I'm honest, I'd rather you be angry than indifferent. Because at least if you were angry, that meant you felt *something*."

All the fight seems to have left both of us, but I can still see he's unsure; I'm guessing because of Jay. His kiss and his words tell me that he still does want me. I drop to the bed and look up at him and sigh. "Just think about it, Spence. That's all I'm asking. I'm not looking for a commitment beyond us not sleeping with other people. If you get to a point where you're not having a good time anymore, just tell me. We can part as friends and I'll have great memories to look back on. I'm good with that, I promise.

"I already know Jay's not going to be around most of the summer, so it wouldn't be hard to hide this from him, if that's what's holding you back. He's not staying at the house at all this summer. He and Delia got an apartment near the school where he's teaching in the fall and it's over an hour away."

He sits next to me and asks, "Why would you want to do this? To, essentially, let yourself get used all summer?"

I look at him, my expression smug. "What makes you think you'll be using me and not the other way around? Because you're the one who's reluctant to do this, not me. Besides, if we're both clear on what this is, there is no 'getting used', just getting off," I say with a smirk.

He barks out a laugh of surprise. "Jesus, Jo. Who are you?"

For the first time since we came back, I feel vulnerable, but I hold his gaze. "Look, Spence, I told you I've wanted you for years, which is seriously no joke. And, so I'd have you and I'd gain experience so that if and when I find someone else down the road, I'll know what I'm doing. I know you're not going to make fun of me or treat me bad, because the whole time I've known you, you've never been unkind to me. And you know we'll have a good time; we have chemistry and we laugh, so it's win-win, really."

He's quiet for a while and I nudge him playfully. "Were you serious?" I can tell he's not sure what I'm referring to, so I expand. "About the other guys? You really want to track them down and beat the shit out of them?" I have a hard time keeping my smile under control.

He blows out a breath. "No, but when you said that, I got so mad. Because you really should be careful, a lot of frat guys are animals."

I roll my eyes and look down. "Yeah, they got old real quick. They didn't care about me or making me feel good. They only cared if they got off. So, they were less than satisfactory experiences." I can tell he wants to ask something so I press on. "And don't even think about asking me how many, unless you want to talk about your body count, because I'd rather not know. But there were only a few. And although the first time with you hurt, it didn't hurt as much as it probably would've with someone else. You were gentle and still made me feel good. So, I kept comparing other times to that and they just weren't good. At all."

He looks pleased with himself because of what I've said. "Oh, lord, don't go getting a big head, just because I said you were the best I've had so far or anything. It's not really a compliment yet."

CHAPTER FIFTEEN

SPENCE

I can't help but laugh at her comment. She's funny and clever and she's made some impressive arguments about this arrangement. Because that's essentially what this would be. There's not a label, and just one rule, and it has an expiration date, so I can't deny the appeal of that. *Shit. Am I really thinking about doing this? With Jay's sister? Definitely considering it.*

How did we go from "Danger, Will Robinson", to "full speed ahead"? I'm at a complete loss. I was so resolute just this morning; we both were. Is it because we're here together and the temptation is just too great? I know if we had made it home last night, we wouldn't have had any of the conversations we've had today. We would've simply made small talk the whole way home and that would have been the end of it.

I still would've wanted her and she would've wanted me, but we both would have resisted while we were home. If we start this, I won't be able to stop, I can already tell. I'm going to want her for the whole summer. And my body reacts to the thought of having her. Want, like some visceral ache, settles into my limbs and my cock. My heart races at the thought of kissing her and touching her and fucking her.

I blow out a breath, trying to calm myself, because I feel like there are things she's not considered. "I'm not saying yes, but I'm open to discussing the *arrangement* further. If you ever decide to do something other than writing, you might want to consider a career in sales. Because, damn, your arguments in the affirmative were impressive."

She chuckles and I ask, "Are you on birth control? I'm fine with condoms, but I'd just like to know. I got tested right before Christmas, and you're the last person I was with, so I'm clean."

She seems surprised by this, but says, "I've been on the pill since March and got tested when I went to do that. I'm good. The guys I was with after you were before that."

The idea of her with other guys still makes me want to take her to bed right this second and make sure I'm the only one she ever remembers. I don't like how possessive I feel of her. It's not rational, but I can't help it. It shouldn't matter if she was with anyone else. And if *she* was anyone else, I know it wouldn't. But I simply nod. "Okay. So we're good on that."

I continue, "If your dad or Jay or my parents or anyone else is around who knows us, we are strictly Joey and Spence. No touching, no eye prolonged eye contact."

She rolls her eyes. "Well, duh. That was a given."

This last part is probably more for her than me, but it still needs to be discussed. "And if one of us develops feelings that are more than just sexy good time feelings, we have to be honest about it and reassess things."

She bites her lip and for the first time all night, I see a hint of hesitation about all this. But it's gone as quickly as it appears. "Yeah. Okay. Any other conditions?"

"What about dates? Or sleeping over? Thoughts about that?"

She thinks for a minute. "I think dates would be risky. Drinks might be nice every once in a while and probably easier to explain if we ran into someone we knew. But I don't need either. I enjoy just hanging out with you. Sleepovers we can play by ear. Obviously, I'd prefer you didn't kick me out of bed right after or anything, but I know sometimes that might be necessary."

I take her chin in my hand and force her to look at me. "I wouldn't kick you out of bed. I like sleepovers if they're possible, or at the very least hanging out after. I don't mind talking and stuff."

She gives me a soft smile and nods. "Okay. Anything else?"

I consider. "Not that I can think of."

"All right. Want to watch TV?"

I smile. "Sure. I'm going to go change. Find something for us to watch?"

"Okay."

I go into the bathroom and pee and wash my hands and change into my sleep shorts. When I come out , Jo is stretched out on the bed on her stomach, facing the television, her legs bent at the knees. She looks adorable and she's eating some candy. "I see you found the snacks," I say.

She looks over at me and nods. "I love Twizzlers."

I toss my clothes in the floor near my bag and lie down on the bed next to her and prop my chin in my hand. "I know. That's why I got them." Her brows rise in surprise and I ask, "You think you're the only one who pays attention? I've been around you enough when we had movie nights. Twizzlers and Milk Duds. But they didn't have any of those."

"Way better than Whoppers. I don't know how you eat those. They're nasty."

I feign indignation. "Don't be hating on my Whoppers."

"They're old people candy; my dad likes Whoppers."

"Who do you think introduced them to me? What did you find for us to watch?"

"*NCIS.* Do you like crime shows?"

"They're fine." I don't admit I'd rather go ahead and kiss her and forget the TV, but I made such a huge deal of us needing to think all this through, so I want to do exactly that.

During a commercial a few minutes later, Jo points to my tattoo, on my inner right bicep. "What does your tattoo mean? I've been meaning to ask and I just thought of it. It looks like someone pushing a ball up a hill."

I look at it, as if just remembering it's there. "It's Sisyphus, from Greek mythology. He was cursed to push a boulder up a hill for all eternity. Every time he'd get close to the top, it would roll back down." She reaches over to trace it with her finger and I smell her shampoo and have to remind myself to breathe.

"That's a little bleak."

I try to keep my tone even. "Nah, it just reminds me to not give up. I knew I wanted to go into medicine, and after under-grad, I wanted to take a break, but I kept going. And good 'ol Sisyphus reminds me to do exactly that."

"Okay, I can get behind that. Any plans for other tattoos?"

I shake my head. "No, this one hurt like a bitch."

She laughs. "Oh, poor baby."

"Have you ever thought about getting a tattoo?"

"Nope. Maybe if I ever publish, I might get something related to a book, but nothing as of yet."

"Well, I look forward to seeing it."

"I might not ever get one."

"You will. You'll publish and I can't wait to read it and see the tattoo you pick to go with it."

She rolls her eyes. "You've never even read anything I've written."

"Yes, I have."

She looks taken aback. "When?"

"Back in November, when I was home for Thanksgiving, your dad showed me an article you wrote for the school paper about the homeless population of Miami. He was so proud of you. It was great. Really moving stuff. You're a talented writer, Joanna Greene."

She swallows and doesn't seem to know how to take my compliment or my use of her full name. Her voice is soft when she responds. "Thank you. That one's probably my favorite piece so far."

"Well, I can't wait to see what else you do. I'll be in line for you to sign your first book for me."

"Okay. Deal. Hopefully, I'll be able to make that happen."

I nod. "You will. And I'll be there to buy the book from your dad's store when you publish. Promise."

She gives me a shy smile and asks, "When you finish med school, do you think you'll move off, or stay close to home?"

I shrug. "I honestly have no clue. It will probably depend on where I intern and do my residency and stuff. I'd like to stay close to home for my parents since I'm all they have, but I don't know. Do you think you'll move back to Tennessee once you finish undergrad?"

She sighs. "I don't know. I really like Florida. I like living near the beach and to hop on a plane to go see Dad and Jay would only take a couple hours, so I guess it will depend on where I get a job. I'm probably going to apply to all the dailies on the east coast. Who knows if I'll get anything, but it would be cool."

Jo rolls her neck and shoulders and sits up suddenly. "I can't lay like that for very long. It kills my neck and shoulders. Probably all the working in front of a computer at school."

"Want me to rub them?"

She quirks an eyebrow. "You think it's a good idea, while you're still thinking things over?"

I shrug. "Probably not. But I know all the muscle groups, and I can get out those knots. I know you've got them. I felt them while I was putting on your sunscreen earlier."

She seems to have an internal debate with herself for a moment but then sighs. "Okay, yeah. I'm dying."

"All right. You have any lotion?"

"Are you going to ask me to put it in the basket?"

I snort a laugh. "No. I think you're safe."

She jumps off the bed and goes into the bathroom and comes back with a bottle of lotion and sits in front of me. "It might be easier if your lie down on your stomach. Fold your arms under your face."

She doesn't question me, just does as instructed and lies across the bed. I straddle her waist and put some lotion in my hands. *So not shampoo; it's lotion that makes her smell like coconut and vanilla.* I rub the lotion between my hands, warming it up and knead the sides of Jo's neck and up into her hairline.

After a moment, I feel her relax under my touch and I work the knots from her neck before moving down to her shoulders. I'm working into the neck of her shirt for a few minutes and then she rises up and pulls the shirt up in the back until it's over her head and my heart lurches at the thought of her being topless when I'm still undecided about everything. Is she trying to kill me? Jesus.

She keeps it on in the front and gives me a sheepish smile. "You were choking me to death pulling on the neckline."

I chuckle. "Sorry." And although I am still wrestling with indecision, I'm not going to complain about seeing her skin.

I continue to massage her shoulders and find and work out several knots. She wasn't joking; it's no wonder she's in pain.

When I get a particularly large knot worked out, she groans and the sound makes me pause for a moment, so I can concentrate. *Fuck me.* "Sorry, I'll try to be quiet."

"Don't stop on my account." The words are out of my mouth before I can bite them back, and I should probably regret them, but I don't.

"Yellow light, Spence." Her tone is playful.

"Are we still playing that game?" I can't help but ask, even though a flashing red light is shining brightly in my mind, telling me exactly how dangerous this is. I'm probably going to hell and the chariot that will take me straight there will be driven by a horse named In Lust with My Best Friend's Sister.

"Until you decide one way or the other we are."

"Fair enough." I stop rubbing her shoulders to put more lotion on my hands and she starts to raise up and I stop her with a hand on the middle of her back.

"I'm not done."

"But you got all the ones in my neck and shoulders."

"Yeah, but there's still your back. I don't half-ass things. I finish what I start."

"Yellow light."

I can't help but smile as I rub my hands down her back. "What, that was not, in any way, inappropriate."

"Depends on how you look at it."

"Well, you and I must be looking at things from two totally different perspectives. Get your mind out of the gutter, lady." This should not be as much fun as it is and honestly, I don't recall ever having this much fun with my clothes on before.

She laughs. "Fair enough." She exhales when I find another knot under her left shoulder blade.

"You okay? Pressure too much?"

"No, it's good. Really good, actually. I can't promise I won't fall asleep."

"I hope not. You're laying across the whole bed."

She huffs out a laugh. "I guess you'll just have to make sure I stay awake."

"Yellow light, Jo."

"Not inappropriate at all. Although, you know I'm not opposed."

"Ooh, red light."

"Yeah, yeah. Keep massaging, cabana boy." I run my hands down either side of her back and can't help but graze the sides of her breasts. Jo says, "Careful, I might get ideas with your hands where they are."

I want to laugh, but feign total seriousness. "Listen, I am a total professional."

She chuckles. "You don't have to be. Not on my account."

"Wow, you just can't help yourself can you?" My tone is easy and yeah, I'm enjoying this way more than I should. I work down toward her hips and hit a ticklish spot and her body gives under the touch, folding into itself. She giggles and it's adorable, so I intentionally tickle her so I can hear it again.

She squeals and wiggles under me until she's nearly rolled over and our eyes catch and hold and everything stops. I swallows the lump in my throat and plant my hands on either side of her head. Her eyes are the same blue I've always known them to be, but somehow different now, because she's different. *We're* different. They're open and honest and full of want and I have to look anywhere but there after a second. I bring my gaze down to her full lips, slightly parted from where she's been laughing. But she's not laughing now. Now, she worries her lower lip with her teeth and her breath comes out in a soft exhale.

She shifts until she's completely on her back under me and just having her in this position is enough to make my cock jerk.

And I know she feels it, because her right brow tics up ever so slightly, but she doesn't say anything.

Jo brings a hand up and tentatively brushes the hair from in front of my eyes before moving it down to rest on my jaw, her touch both foreign and familiar all at the same time. She doesn't pull me toward her even though I can see in her eyes she would if I gave the barest hint of any indication I'm willing. I dangle on this thread of should and should not; the war between the need to preserve my friendship with Jay and my wanting of his sister.

Then I feel the pendulum swing and the want wins out and I lower my mouth to hers.

CHAPTER SIXTEEN

SPENCE

When our lips collide, it's like giving a parched man his first drink of water in days and I can't get enough. Jo's arms snake around my neck and pull me into her and our kiss is greedy and wanting and drives away any inkling of rational thought I may have still possessed only a moment ago.

I roll us so we're on our sides and I bring my hand to cup her ass like I've wanted to do since I saw her in her bikini this morning. She crooks her leg around my waist and I pull her hips into me and she moans into my mouth and fuck me, I'm never going to be able to unhear her moans.

After a moment, she breaks our kiss and searches my eyes. "Is this just for tonight? I'm fine with that, if it's what you want. If you can't do this once we get back home; if it's too much, I get it. I just don't want to get my hopes up if all I get is tonight."

I roll us again until she's below me and run the back of a finger along her jaw as her knees bracket my hips. "I should say yes. But no, Jo, not just for tonight."

She nods and pulls her shirt off her arms and tosses it onto the floor revealing her gorgeous tits and perfect, dusky rose nipples that I didn't get to fully appreciate the last time we were together. "Okay. That's all I needed to know." She brings my mouth back to hers and I'm overwhelmed with all the sensations I'm experiencing. The smell of her lotion, the taste of her mouth, the feel of her breasts pressed against my bare chest, the sound of her breath quickening under my touch.

I trail my mouth down from her cheek to the hollow of her throat and I feel her pulse race under my lips. When my teeth graze her collarbone, she lets out a soft sigh. I want so badly to simply take her right this second and drive my cock into her. But even more, I want to overwrite the times she was with those other guys, where their hands and mouths and dicks were. I want to make her forget about them, until the only one she ever remembers is me and the times we share. Until sex with anyone else is ruined. Again, I'm struck with the thought that the way I want her to only know my body is irrational and stupid, but there's no stopping it.

I skim my hand up her ribs and cup her breast and the nipple grows taut under my thumb as I roll it between my fingers. I bring my mouth down to draw it in between my lips and Jo gasps and it's music to my ears. Her back arches and she tangles her fingers in my hair and she grinds her hips into me and I can't bite back the groan as she rubs herself against me, only two thin pieces of fabric separating us. "Jesus, Jo."

She brings my face back to hers and our lips crash together. Jo reaches down between us and she slips her hand into my shorts and around my cock, stroking me slowly. My breath comes out in huffs into her mouth and she smiles against my lips. But if she keeps her hand on my dick, I'm liable to blow way before I want to and this will be over sooner than is acceptable to me, a man who prides himself on his stamina. I snatch her hand away and shake my head. "That's enough of that now. You keep that up and I'll embarrass myself."

She huffs an amused laugh and gives me a smug smile. "Hard to believe you'd be undone by just a few pumps of my fist."

I grip her jaw with one hand as I trail my other down her stomach and search out her clit through her panties and she moans and grinds her hips against my hand and I look into her eyes, a slow smile pulling at the corners of my mouth. "You see, the thing is, I've had that sound on repeat in my brain for the last six months and hearing it in real life again has me already wanting to bust. And I don't plan on doing that anywhere but in that sweet pussy." I kiss down her neck and chest and stomach and tug her underwear down her hips and discard them on the floor as I kneel between her legs and simply take her in. "Jesus Christ, you're gorgeous." And fuck, is she ever. All pink and wet and perfect and I need to taste her so bad I can't stand it.

I drop to my stomach and plant my hands on the insides of her knees and dip my head to trail kisses up her thighs when Jo says my name. Her tone is nervous and I immediately stop and look up at her and she bites her lip.

"What is it, Jo?"

"I've never. I mean, no one's ever..." She trails off and flushes with embarrassment I understand what she's trying to say and a satisfied thrill runs through me.

I come back up to her face and cup her cheek. "Good. Then the only memory you'll have is of me and my mouth on your pussy."

Her mouth falls open in surprise and I kiss her mouth deeply before I move back down between her thighs. She's trembling and it feels like the first time again as I lick a hard line up her pussy. She's already so hot and wet and makes my cock ache with want and I can't bite back a groan as the taste of her hits my tongue. Jo gasps and her thighs reflexively attempt to close. I raise my head and look at her. "Relax, I've got you."

Her throat bobs with a swallow and she huffs out a soft laugh and nods. She lets her knees fall open and I settle back in, drawing her clit into my mouth and flicking it with my tongue, working it in languid circles. Jo's breathing becomes ragged and she threads her fingers into my hair and I fucking love it. I bring my hand up and insert two fingers and stroke her upper wall and her hips buck. "Shit, Spence. God." Her words come out in a near whine and after a few more minutes, her pussy clenches around my fingers so tight, I can hardly move them and she cries out and I can't help but smile as I gentle my movements and withdraw my fingers and kiss my way back up her body.

Her chest is still heaving when I drop a kiss onto her lips. She wraps her arms around my neck and deepens the kiss and I know if I'm not inside her in the next thirty seconds, I'm going to lose my damn mind. I pull back and huff a laugh. "Jesus, I need to be inside you right the fuck now."

She laughs and releases me. "Well, don't let me stop you."

I hop off the beed and go over to my bag and dig in one of the pockets for the condoms I keep there. I tug my shorts down and rip the foil wrapper with my teeth and Jo watches me with interest. "What?" I ask.

She shakes her head. "I didn't get to look at you last time because there wasn't room in your Jeep and I just wanted to see you. I've thought about what you'd look like all these years. You really are beautiful, Spence. And damn sexy. Better than I even imagined."

I can't help the flush that creeps into my face hearing her talk like that and quickly roll the condom on. Returning to the bed and between her thighs, I tug her hips toward me. I look down at her and ask, "Do you need me to be gentle? Are you afraid it will hurt?"

Jo shakes her head, her blue eyes heating with want. "No."

I nod and kiss her. "Okay. That's all I needed to know." She smiles at hearing me parrot back what she said earlier. She's about to say something, but I drive into her and whatever it is, dies in her throat and instead, I'm greeted with her sharp exhale. And I have to remind myself to breathe, because she feels so fucking good and I can't finish this quickly.

I take some calming breaths and begin to piston my hips, unable to bite back a low groan as she rocks her hips, moving with me. I try to commit all of this to memory because last time was great, but now that I know it's Jo, it's different. Her eyes are closed, so I just watch her face for a minute memorizing this moment. How her brows scrunch together in concentration and how her cheeks are flushed and how she's biting down on her bottom lip.

I try to remember how her breath hitches with my every thrust. I try to remember how her hands grip my shoulders, how her breasts feel pressed against me. I want to remember every flutter, every sigh, every moan. Because I know we'll have other times, but this one will be special, because there's no deception about who she is. Because even though we'll be together all summer, this is probably the only time we won't have a cloud over us at the possibility of being found out. This is the only time we won't have to be vigilant.

Jo rocks her hips again and I'm driven even deeper into her and I struggle to keep from coming undone. I could let go at any moment, but I don't want this to end. Because as bad as I want the climax, I'm enjoying the feel of her too much.

I grip the back of her neck and bring her mouth to mine and she whimpers against my kiss, sending a jolt of electricity down my spine. I drag my lips to her ear. "Fuck, Jo, you feel so good." I'm not going to last much longer, as bad as I want to so I reach between us and work her clit as I slam harder into her.

She moans my name and it's the sweetest sound I think I've ever heard. "Come for me, Jo," I plead.

A few minutes later, her pussy clenches around me and a strangled cry falls from her lips as she lets go and I watch as she comes undone under me and it sends me over into my own release. I feel it start in my balls and radiate outward until it tears through me with a shudder and a deep groan.

We collapse together in a heap of ragged breaths and shaking limbs. My face is in Jo's neck and after a few minutes, I hear what sounds like crying come from her and I rise up, suddenly alarmed that I've hurt her. But when I look at her face, she's laughing and I'm taken aback. "What?" I ask, alarmed.

"Nothing. I just... I just didn't know it could be like that." She turns her face toward me, her expression relaxed and happy. "Shit, Spence. Glad to know I hadn't hyped it up too much in my head."

Relieved, I can't help but laugh. "I'm happy I could live up to your expectations."

CHAPTER SEVENTEEN

JO

Spence gives me a quick kiss before going into the bathroom. I sit up and find my nightshirt and slip it on, not bothering with underwear and get a beer out of the fridge and sit on the bed, leaning against the headboard and sipping it while I wait for my heart rate to return to normal.

I knew it would be good with Spence, especially after how caring he was the first time, but this was something else. I can't help but wonder if he's like that with all the women he's with, or if it's different with me. But then I don't follow that train of thought, because I don't really want to know what it's like for him with others.

He comes back out a few minutes later and slips his shorts on and sits next to me. I hold the beer out to him and he takes it and sips it for a minute. We're both quiet, seemingly not sure where to go from here. I turn to him. "Do you want to go back to the beach tomorrow?" I'm just trying to make small talk because I don't want things to get awkward and it cause us to end things before they've truly even begun.

He considers and nods. "Sure, we can do that. I'll call the

garage first thing and see what kind of timeframe we're looking at for the repair on your car."

And with that, I'm reminded we'll be going home soon, which, of course, I knew, but it fills me with a sense of loss. Because even though we've said we'll continue this once we get home, there's always a chance we'll be found out or he'll find someone else he would rather see.

Spence runs the back of a knuckle down my arm, his voice soft. "Hey, you okay?"

I nod. "Yeah. Just seems like this is already going to be over too soon. I mean, Daytona anyway. Here, we don't have to worry about anything. But when we go home, we'll have to sneak around. And that's fine, and will probably make it more fun a lot of the time, but this is still really nice."

"Yeah. I thought about that as well." He takes my face in his hands and kisses me and wiggles his eyebrows. "I guess we'll just have to enjoy Daytona as much as we can."

I chuckle. "Yeah, I guess we will." I suddenly feel very tired. "What time is it?"

He picks up his phone and looks at it. "After midnight."

I yawn. "No wonder I'm beat. You got me all relaxed with a massage and worn out with really good sex and it's late."

"Yeah, me too, except the massage part." He winks at me.

I rise and go into the bathroom and pee, wash my hands, and take out my contacts and slip on my glasses. I brush my teeth and turn out the light. I make sure my phone is plugged up and climb into bed and put my glasses on the nightstand next to my phone and turn off the lamp. I snuggle down into the bed on my left side and a few minutes later, Spence pulls me into his arms and brushes a kiss against my neck.

It catches me by surprise, because the gesture is intimate and makes this feel like more than what we've agreed to, but I can't deny that it's nice. I drift off with Spence's arms around

me and can't help but be deliriously happy at how things have
played out.

When I wake, I'm very conscious of Spence's body pressed
against mine. Sometime in the night, I've turned to face him
and my head is on his chest, my leg across his. I've got to admit,
not a bad way to wake up. I press a light kiss against his chest
and start to rise, but he pulls me into him. "Not yet. I'm too
comfy."

I can't help but chuckle. "I didn't know you were awake."

His eyes are still closed. "I'm not. You're still asleep. You're
dreaming."

I laugh and snuggle closer to him. "Which part was a
dream? Because some of it was pretty vivid."

He laughs and kisses the top of my head. "Thankfully, *that*
part wasn't a dream."

"No kidding." We lie there for a bit, Spence's fingers
running up and down my arm and I almost fall back asleep. My
phone rings and I sit bolt upright in bed. I pick it up and see
that it's after nine-thirty and my dad is calling.

I look at Spence and put my finger to my lips and answer
the call. "Hey, Daddy." I affect a chipper tone.

"Hey, sweet girl. I was just calling to see if Spencer had
spoken with the mechanic yet?"

"I'm not sure, I haven't seen him yet. He was supposed to
call first thing this morning, but I've not been up that long. I got
to watching an *NCIS* marathon and stayed up way too late. I'll
check with him when I see him and call you back, okay?"

"Okay, sweetie. Love you."

"Love you, Daddy." I disconnect the call and lie back down
and breathe a sigh of relief.

Spence rolls over and trails kisses along my neck and inches his fingers up the hem of my shirt. "You lie to your dad way too easily."

"None of it was a lie, with the exception of seeing you. There was an *NCIS* marathon, I did stay up way too late, and I hadn't been awake that long."

"Semantics."

I shrug and then sigh as his hand cups my breast. I look up at him, my tone playful. "You have to call the garage. I need a shower and food. I don't have time to satisfy you sexually at this time."

I extricate myself from the bed and he slaps me on the ass. I go into the bathroom and pee and start the shower and while the water heats up, I brush my teeth. I strip and climb into the shower and shave my legs quickly, before washing my hair. While I'm rinsing the shampoo, I hear the shower curtain open. "Spence?"

He asks, "You were expecting someone else?"

"No, just making sure Norman Bates hadn't decided to join us." I hear him laugh as I finish getting all the shampoo out of my hair and open my eyes to see Spence standing in front of me with a smile on a face. "They can't get to your car until tomorrow afternoon. We can pick it up Wednesday morning. I've called your dad and updated him and extended out stay with the motel."

My mouth falls open in surprise. "Really? Two more nights? Well, well, whatever will we do to pass the time?"

Spence lifts my chin and kisses me. "I might have a few ideas."

And for almost the next hour, he proceeds to show me what those ideas consist of.

CHAPTER EIGHTEEN

JO

The following two days and nights pass by much too quickly and before we both know it, we're back in my car headed to Tennessee. Spence and I take turns driving the eight hours home and the closer we get, Daytona really does feel like a dream; three nights and days of fantastic sex and fun—even that game of beer pong that Spence promised, which I totally won. And the closer we get to home, it seems like a cloud descends, and I can't help but wonder how it will change once we're back.

I'm not too concerned about the first couple of weeks, because Dad and Jay will still be out of town, so there's less risk of getting caught, but after that, I don't know how we'll manage it. Because when we're near each other, even when we're not having sex, we find excuses to touch one another and I already feel the loss of that casual intimacy.

When we're about an hour from home, Spence must be able to sense the change in me. He's driving and I'm looking out the window, my knees drawn up and he squeezes my knee. "What's got you in your head?"

I worry my bottom lip with my teeth. "Nothing. Just a bit sad to be out of the Daytona bubble. I'm glad to be going home, I am, but still. It was just nice. I liked not having to think about anytime I touched you, someone seeing something in it. I liked not having to worry about eyes on us."

He nods. "Yeah. It was nice. Are you having second thoughts about everything because it'll be hard?"

I shake my head, for the first time concerned that maybe he is. "No, are you?"

He huffs out a laugh. "Not at all. I'm not done with you yet. I think there's still a lot more experience for you to gain from me."

Inwardly, I breath a sigh of relief. "That so? Well, I look forward to our lessons, Dr. Jackson."

He chuckles. "Not a doctor just yet, Ducky."

The use of the pet name warms me, because we're not official or anything, so "baby" or "babe" or something similar just feels off. But I'll take Ducky.

He takes my hand and intertwines our fingers. "Why did you use Ducky that night? Does it mean anything?"

"Just because I was an ugly duckling, so I figured it was appropriate."

He frowns. "You weren't ugly. You've never been ugly."

I roll my eyes. "Well, if not ugly, I was very plain and needed a lot of help."

"You know, pretty much the whole time we were in Daytona, you didn't wear makeup and wore your glasses a lot. You're still a smoke show, Jo."

"I think you think that because you like me naked."

He smiles. "Definitely a perk, but for real, I don't know how I never saw it before. You're beautiful with or without your glasses or makeup."

"Thanks, Spence. Do you know if your parents will be home when we get there?"

"It'll probably be about four, so not likely. Dad doesn't get home until around seven and Mom gets off at five, but has a yoga class from six to seven, so she usually goes straight there from work."

I can't keep the smile off my face. "So, what you're saying is, no one will be home when we get there?"

He wiggles his eyebrows. "Exactly."

"Well, then, we best get home."

He laughs. "You've got it."

When we get back to my house, I tell Spence to pull into the garage. I unlock the door and tug him inside and up to my room. It feels strange for him to be in here, but I love it.

He looks around and says, "I don't think I've ever been in your room before."

"Yeah, it's a little weird for me, too. But, nice." I walk over to the window and make sure the blinds are closed and Spence gives me a questioning look, so I explain. "Ruby's room is right across from mine. I wasn't planning on telling her about us, so I figured, better safe than sorry."

He nods and looks at my bookshelf, examining the rows of books. "Have you read all of these?"

"Most. Some of the high fantasy are a bit much and I have to be in the right headspace for them, so that doesn't happen very often, but most of the others, yeah."

"And which is your favorite of all the books on your shelf?"

"Didn't we already have this discussion?"

"No, that was to find out what book you'd take on a desert

island. Which of all of these books is your favorite? And you can't say *The Hobbit*."

I examine the shelf, and pull out *The Time Traveler's Wife* and hand it to him. He reads the back and nods. "Sounds good."

"It is. They turned it into a movie a few years ago, too. But the book was so much better."

"Can I borrow it?"

I'm pleasantly surprised and offer him a nod. "Sure. Let me know what you think about it. Then you can watch the movie."

I take the book from him and set it on my desk and tug him over to my bed. He chuckles. "You are insatiable."

He sits and I straddle him. "I blame you. If you weren't so good at it, I wouldn't want it so bad."

He smiles with the compliment and settles his hands on my hips. "To be fair, it's not like you have a lot to compare me to."

I scoff. "Enough to know good from very, very bad." I wind my arms around his neck and kiss him deeply. I still can't get enough of kissing him. It's like a drug I can't kick and I don't want to. I kiss his neck and tug his tee shirt over his head and drop it to the floor before trailing my mouth down to his chest.

Spence pulls my tank top off and it joins his at his feet. I unhook my bra and it slides down my arms and I toss it aside. He kisses my neck and brings my breast to his mouth and when his teeth tug on my nipple, I gasp and feel wet heat pool between my legs. His cock jerks beneath me and I push him back onto the bed and inch my mouth down his chest and stomach until I'm on my knees on the floor.

I start to tug his shorts down and he sits up and stills my hands. I look up at him and he's about to say something, but I get there first. "I want to make you feel good. Will you teach me, Spence? Please."

He brings his face down to mine and gives me a soft kiss. "You don't have to do that to make me feel good, believe me."

"I know, but I want to. And I don't want to suck at it." He smirks and I quip, "And yes, I realize the irony of what I just said."

He releases my hands, so I take that as his go ahead and I unbutton his shorts and he lifts his hips so I can tug them down. My heart is racing, because I don't want to do something wrong, but I've wanted to do this since the first night we were together in Daytona. His cock pops free and I have to stifle a soft gasp at the sight of it, because I'm still not used to seeing him fully. And like he said, I don't have a lot to compare him to, but he's perfectly formed and thick and I know exactly how he feels inside me and my mouth nearly waters as a bead of precum leaks from the tip.

He takes my hand and guides it over his shaft, showing me how to work him and how much pressure so it feels good and after a moment, he lets go of my hand and I continue sliding it up and down. He leans back on his elbows and blows out a breath.

I slide my mouth over the tip of his cock and try to remember the things I've read online and from what other girls have said when they've talked about giving their boyfriends head. I try to use my hand and mouth in the same rhythm and Spence hisses. For a second, I think I've done something wrong and he says, "Shit, Jo. That's good."

I'm buoyed by his praise and my pussy clenches around nothing with his words. I want to bring him the same sort of pleasure he brings me. I run my tongue along the underside of his shaft and flick just under the head and his hips buck and I gag with the unexpected thrust.

"Sorry," he huffs. "That's just really good." I keep going for a few minutes and I think he's going to finish and I try to mentally prepare for what it'll be like, so I don't freak out.

But, instead, he says, "Jo, stop." I rise off him, thinking I've messed up.

He smiles and touches my cheek. "I don't to finish without you." His breathing is heavy as he pulls me to my feet and unbuttons my shorts and slides them down my hips. He brushes kisses along my stomach and tugs my panties down and looks up at me. "Have you missed any pills since you started taking them?"

I think for a second and shake my head. "No."

"Good, because I don't have a condom and I don't want to go to my house and get one. Is that okay?"

I climb onto the bed and pull him down to me. "Fuck, yes. I don't want to wait, either."

He chuckles and settles himself between my thighs. "Such a dirty mouth you've got there."

I smirk. "Probably because it was just wrapped around your cock."

He looks surprised. "Damn, Jo. Looks like I'm going to have to fuck those words right out of your mouth. That's no way for a young lady to speak."

I pull his mouth to mine and kiss him. "Well, fuck away."

"Gladly." He slams into me and I cry out with the impact. I rock my hips to drive him even deeper and feel like I can't bring him close enough to me. How can it be this good? I never thought it was possible. It's just sex, right? Is this the way it's always supposed to be? Probably not, judging by the other guys I've slept with. And if that's the case, I feel like everyone who comes after Spence is going to fall woefully short. He's right, I am insatiable, but it's only because he fucks me so well.

My orgasm starts to build and what seems like seconds

later, I come hard enough to see spots, my hands grasping his hair as I cry out with a sharp rasp.

Spence pounds into me, his thrusts brutal. "Fuck, Jo." And with a final, deep push, I feel him give into his own release before he collapses with a low grunt, spent.

CHAPTER NINETEEN

SPENCE

We lie together in Jo's bed for a bit, and I fight the desire to nod off. Between the last few days of late nights and the drive home, I am utterly exhausted. My forehead touches hers and she's already asleep and I can't help but smile. She's beautiful all the time, but when she is sleeping, her long lashes lay against her cheeks and her mouth is open ever so slightly and I can't stop looking at her.

I brush a kiss across her lips and she rouses and kisses me back, pulling me into her. I reluctantly break our kiss a few minutes later and rise from the bed and go into her bathroom to get cleaned up. When I come out, she's pulled her tank top and underwear back on. Her wavy hair is wild and falling out of its ponytail and she passes me to go into the bathroom and I get dressed and sit on the bed.

It's already different being back home than it was in Daytona, because we won't be able to spend most nights together and probably any time we do get will be moments we steal and sneak around. And while it's fun and hot knowing we could be caught at any moment, it's also less than I'd prefer.

Over the past few days, I've become accustomed to sleeping next to her and enjoy the feel of her in my arms as she sleeps. My parents hardly ever come downstairs at the house, but there's always the chance they will. We could spend the next few nights here, but I'd have to go home at some point in the night and do something with my Jeep. But, I guess this what we agreed to, right? My thoughts are interrupted by Jo sitting next to me. "You okay?"

I nod. "Yeah, it sure is going to be different being back. I'm just thinking about how we're going to make it work."

"You think we can?"

I blow out a breath. "I'd really like it to."

She bites her lip. "Me, too."

She pulls her shorts on and says, "Guess I need to start unpacking."

"Want some help?"

"Nah, I'm all right. It's really only a few boxes. I didn't take that much stuff with me."

I feel like she's trying to brush me off. "You don't want me to stay?"

"No, it's not that. I just don't want your parents to come home and you come out of my house looking like you just got laid." She smirks. "Might raise some red flags."

I smile. "Well, I can still help you bring your boxes up. My mother would be very disappointed if I wasn't a gentleman."

"Okay. Thanks."

When we get her boxes and things brought into the house and put into her room, I don't know how to leave things, which is strange for me. I don't usually have awkward goodbyes with hookups and I know that's essentially what Jo is, albeit a steady hookup, but still. After a beat, she says, "Well, I guess I better get unpacked. Thanks for helping me."

I feel it as a clear dismissal and for some reason, I don't like it, but I don't say anything. "You still good if I borrow that book?"

She jumps up off the floor from where she was kneeling down to open a box and grabs the book off her desk and brings it over to me. "Let me know how you like it."

"I will."

She turns to go back to her box and I grab her arm and pull her in for a quick kiss and she gives me a soft smile when she steps back. "Goodnight, Spence."

I nod. "Night, Jo."

I go down to the garage and get my backpack out of Jo's car and walk out the door to the side of the garage that faces my house. I head down the sidewalk to the back of the house and enter through my entrance to the basement apartment. I go into my bedroom and set the book on my nightstand and pull all the dirty clothes out of my backpack.

I also check the other pockets and find among the various items, the key to the motel in Daytona. I'd forgotten it was there, but I'm happy to see it, as it's the only memento of our time together. I smile and palm the plastic key card, turning it over in my hand. I go over to my desk and find a sharpie and write the on the back: *Daytona Beach with Ducky*. I open my desk drawer and stick it in. I wish I had a photo to go with it, but I guess the memories will have to do.

I toss all the dirty clothes in the washer and go take a shower before fixing a sandwich for supper. I can't help but wonder what Jo ate and if we could've just eaten together, but then I remind myself we can't do that. It unsettling to me how much I miss her, as if the time we've spent together over the past few days has kicked off some sort of addiction in me.

And as much as I hate to admit it to myself, it's not just the sex, although it's phenomenal. Jo is open to trying just about anything and eager to please, but I also enjoy giving her pleasure and seeing it on her face.

It's also the time we've spent together outside the bed. The conversations we've had, discussing our futures, talking about the mundane, the random, the everyday. I look forward to seeing what she thinks about things and I'm genuinely interested in reading the book she lent me, simply so we can have a discussion about it and I can hear her thoughts.

Not for the first time and I'm sure not the last, either, I wonder who Jo is. Because she's nothing like I ever imagined and I can't understand how, in all the years I've known her, I've never *seen* her. But now that I have, I don't ever want to stop.

I'm already thinking about how I don't want our time to end and it's jarring for me, because I've always been one that relishes the end of things, just so I can begin something new, and granted this thing with Jo is new, but after Christmas, I couldn't stop thinking about her.

I mean, who knows, things may fizzle for either of us in the next few weeks and come to a natural end, but I don't see how. And I made the rule about not touching or looking at one another when people are around, but I don't know how easy it's going to be. We had three days where we could walk down the beach hand-in-hand and kiss out in public and it didn't matter, so it's going to be a hard habit to break.

I switch the clothes over to the dryer and grab a beer from my fridge and lie in bed and open *The Time Traveler's Wife*. And before I know it, I'm a third of the way through the book. Jo was right, it's great. The back and forth between Henry and Clare and them stealing moments in the meadow when Clare is younger. And then when Henry meets her for the first time when she's twenty. It's an interesting premise for sure.

I pull my phone out to text Jo, and I see it's after one A.M., but I don't, because I know she has to work at the bookstore tomorrow. So, instead, I get up and grab the hotel key and slip it into the book to mark my spot and fall into a dreamless sleep.

CHAPTER TWENTY

JO

I felt like there was more to be said when Spence left. There was a look in his eyes I couldn't name, and he seemed to be unhappy about something. I don't think it's related to sex, because, at least for me, it's amazing and he seems to be enjoying himself as well.

But all we are is friends with benefits, so I'm not sure how to take the simple gestures he makes, like pulling me close when we sleep and asking to read one of my favorite books. I don't know what it means, if anything.

It only took me about an hour to unpack all of my clothes and books from school. Some of my other stuff I left boxed up and in the garage, because I don't need those things right now, but they'll go back with me to school in August.

I throw a load of clothes into the washer and stick a frozen pizza in the oven before sitting down to watch TV. As I'm flipping through the channels, I come across *The Patriot* and can't help but smile as I watch it, knowing Spence loves this move. I reflexively pick up my phone to text him, but I put it down, because I feel as though if I start texting him things unrelated to our arrangement, it will break some unspoken rule, or he'll grow tired of me. And I don't want that. So, I guess I'll just keep that kind of stuff only for when we're together; after we're spent and sated.

I turn in around ten, since I'll be at the store all day tomorrow and I already know it's going to be a long day, because new releases go on sale on Tuesdays and I've missed it because of the car repairs, so that'll eat up the majority of my day getting them put into the store's system and shelved.

When I wake as my alarm blares way too early, I reach for Spence, but then I remember he's not here. He's at his house. I get up and shower and dress in a comfortable cotton sundress and my favorite Converse sneakers. I put on minimal makeup and pull my hair up into a ponytail and don't bother with my contacts, because my eyes are tired, so I simply slide my glasses up my nose. I assess my reflection in the bathroom mirror, and although I don't look like Joey anymore, Jo may be a stretch for today. I sigh and shrug and walk down to the kitchen to make my coffee before heading out for the day.

As I back out of the garage, I see Spence is already doing yard work in shorts and no shirt, trying to beat the heat. He's obviously been at it for a good bit already, as he's covered in a sheen of perspiration and I have to remind myself to breathe, because he is so damn sexy. When I get to the end of the drive-way, I park and get out to check the mail, still unable to take my eyes off him.

He must sense he's being watched, because his head turns my way and his eyes find mine and he gives me a lopsided grin, but no more, since there very well could be eyes around and we can't get caught this early on. I nod ever so slightly, but he sees it and turns back to his work.

I don't get home until almost seven and I am dead on my feet. I'd spent the entire day cataloging the new books that had come in and dealing with customers who were upset the store hadn't been open for several days as well as packaging online orders to ship out. I'm grumpy and hungry and just want to go take a bath and go to bed.

When I finally get into the house, I slip my shoes off and flex my toes, feeling free for the first time all day. I sigh and walk into the kitchen and open the cabinets trying to decide what I'll have for supper. Dad had gone to the store before he left town, but most of the produce has gone soft and is starting to turn, so I pass on all of it. I don't relish the idea of another frozen pizza, so in the end, I settle on tomato soup and a grilled cheese sandwich. Gourmet it may not be, but it will do.

I'm taking the last couple bites of my sandwich, mopping it through the remains of the soup when my phone dings. I get up and fetch it from inside my purse and check the screen.

Spence: I finished the book.

I have the thought that this must be some kind of code, because I just gave him the book yesterday and it's thick, so maybe he's trying to be covert? But I'm energized by his text and already feel desire settling low in my belly.

Jo: Would you like to come over and discuss
your thoughts about it? I'd love to get your
take on it.

Spence: Sure. Now?

Jo: Give me an hour? I'll leave the back door
unlocked.

Spence: Okay. See you then.

I send him a thumbs up emoji and hurriedly clean up my
supper dishes and run upstairs to shower and shave. About
forty-five minutes later, I'm dressed in a pair of skinny jeans
and a simple white fitted tee shirt. My hair is loose and wavy
and I put my contacts in, so I feel more like Jo.

I hear the backdoor open, even from up in my room and my
breath quickens at Spence's closeness. He calls my name and I
holler down the stairs. "Up here." Every step I hear him take
closer to my room makes me feel more wound up and excited.

Spence stands at my door and leans against the frame, but
doesn't come in. He has the book in his hand and when he
hands it back to me, I ask, "You didn't like it?"

"No, I loved it."

I can't keep the surprise out of my voice. "So, you actually
finished it? I thought you were just trying to speak in code. I
only gave it to you yesterday, how did you finish it so quickly?"

He shrugs. "I don't know, I guess I'm a fast reader." And
then he smiles. "And it wasn't code, I really do want to talk
about the book."

I give him a sheepish smile and sit on the bed. "Oh. Well,
what did you think about it?"

He comes to sit beside me. "It was great. And sad. Henry

and Clare had so much and, yet, so little time. It was unfair, really. The parts about Clare and Gomez made me angry."

I nod. "Yeah, I feel like those parts sort of humanize Clare, though, don't you think? Because through the whole book, Henry is the one with all the flaws; the drugs, the stealing, the violence, and it's a bit creepy how Clare meets him when she's six and he already knows she's his wife, so it's kinda like a chicken and egg thing. Did Clare even have a choice but to fall in love with Henry? He was there all along and part of me wonders if, after he meets Clare, you know, when she's older, does he become who she wants because she's told him things?

"And, although she gets jealous and angry about Henry leaving, which he can't help, she's pretty perfect to him, so the Gomez parts help to prove she is, in fact, very much imperfect."

He nods and smiles. "Wow. You've given the book a lot of thought."

I shrug. "I've read it a few times. Because in spite of its strangeness at times, it's still a beautiful story. And yes, sad. Because a lot of the times and places Henry visits, like when he continually visits when his mother dies, it's like having a wound heal just in time for it to be reopened."

"If you had a choice, which times in your life would you relive?"

I smile and wiggle my eyebrows. "Besides Daytona?"

He chuckles. "Yeah."

I think for a moment and then blush and look down at my knees. "Probably the first time I saw you when Dad brought us here."

I see him try to remember but then he shakes his head. "I don't think I remember when we met."

I shake my head. "Not met, saw. It was when Dad was still looking at houses and he brought us here to see if Jay and I liked it, because I guess it was a contender or whatever. We pulled into the driveway and the real estate agent was waiting on the porch.

"We got out and she and Dad start going over the details. Jay had already gone into the house and I heard him yelling something about the pool. I stayed outside and looked around, because I'd never been to a cul-de-sac before and I thought it would be cool to have neighbors, since we didn't where we lived before.

"I was getting ready to go inside and I saw you come out of your house. It was summer and you didn't have a shirt on, and you were going for a run. You never saw me, but I just stopped and couldn't take my eyes off of you as you went down the street. It was the first time I'd ever felt anything even close to resembling attraction or desire. I mean, I was twelve, so you know, probably not shocking, but you were just so pretty.

"And, I know guys aren't supposed to be pretty or whatever, but 'hot' wasn't something that I thought of back then. Your hair was longer, down past your ears. Your shorts hung low on your waist and your abs would flex as you ran."

I feel myself flush even more deeply. "And that image right there, of you running, fueled so many of my young girl fantasies. At least until you and Jay became good friends and I saw you in the pool."

And then I have the thought that I would like to relive the last time my mom was around and we were all happy. I don't say it, but Spence must see something change in my face and he touches my hand. "Where'd you go, just then?"

I shake my head and smile. "Nowhere."

He lifts my chin. "You can tell me things, you know. You can talk to me. I'm not just a pretty face." He gives me a smirk and I can't help but laugh.

"I know that. What about you, what would you live again?"

"Besides Daytona?"

I huff out a soft laugh and nod. He seems to consider it. "I don't know, maybe the feeling I had when I got my acceptance letter to med school. I remember feeling like I was finally good enough for something, like I'd done something right."

I'm shocked to find out he's dealt with issues of self-doubt. "I've never thought of you as someone who felt like they weren't good enough. I've always thought you were one of the most confident people I've ever met."

He sighs. "Most of that is because I know it's how people see me and it's what they expect, so I fake it. A lot of the time, I'm scared I'm going to screw up my entire life with something stupid I've done and I'm terrified to make a mistake. I know my parents have all these goals for me and put a lot of pressure on me, so I feel like I have to make them proud."

I turn to him and put my hand on his arm. "They are proud of you. When I saw them at Christmas, they couldn't shut up about how well you were doing in med school and how good your grades were and stuff. They're thrilled you're going to become a doctor."

He nods. "Yeah, I guess. I just wonder if they would've still been proud if I'd done anything else."

"Well, what else did you want to do, I'm sure they would have been just as proud."

"Promise you won't laugh?"

"Of course," I promise.

"I wanted to be a singer. Start a band."

I'm surprised. "Can you sing? I don't think I've ever heard you, except maybe with the radio."

He nods, but it's not with any confidence. "Will you sing for me?"

And for the first time in the entirety of the seven years I've known him, he looks shy and unsure and it's adorable and endearing. "I don't really anymore."

"Do you play, too?"

"Piano."

My mouth falls open. "How did I not ever know you can play piano?"

"Probably because I stopped when I was fifteen and started playing football. So that was before you knew me."

"Well, will you play and sing for me? I'd love to hear it. Because, I've gotta be honest, I was truly was obsessed with *High School Musical* partly because Zac Efron could sing and he was cute, so if you can sing and play, well, that's a whole new reason for me to want you."

He laughs. "Maybe. Someday."

I nod. "Okay. I'll hold you to it. Someday."

I notice suddenly it's grown darker and I reach to turn on the bedside lamp. When I turn back, Spence takes my face in his hands and kisses me and I realize this is the first kiss we've shared since he got here. The kiss is tender, without the hunger of our other kisses and I'm caught off guard, because it doesn't feel like it's a prelude, just a sweet kiss.

When he pulls back, he asks, "Do you have the movie?"

I have no clue what movies he's referring to. "What movie?"

"*The Time Traveler's Wife*? Do you have it?"

"Oh. Yeah. Do you want to borrow it?"

"Or, we can watch it together," he suggests.

"Where are your parents?"

His brows scrunch together in confusion. "Why?"

"Just wanting to know what kind of timeframe we're looking at here. If we've only got an hour, there might be better ways to spend our time." My voice has a playful edge.

He chuckles and plants a kiss on my forehead and again, I'm caught off guard, because it's *intimate*. And not that everything else we've done isn't, but it's different and I don't know how to take it.

"They're in for the night. I already told them goodnight. You could come over."

"Do they not ever come downstairs?"

He shakes his head. "Not really. Especially after about nine. They go to bed early. What time do you have to be up in the morning?"

"I have to open the store at ten, so I have to be up by seven-thirty to get ready and be at the store by nine."

He moves my hair off my shoulder as he nuzzles my neck and brushes a kiss below my ear. "I could make sure you get a good night's sleep. Make sure you're up when you're supposed to be."

Goosebumps rise on my arms as his breath plays across my skin. I close my eyes and lean into him and say, "Or, you could stay here. Less chance of getting caught."

"Very true." He looks at me. "You'd be okay with that?"

I nod. "Yeah, why?"

He sighs. "You just seemed a little off last night when we got home, like you wanted me to leave."

I shake my head. "I was fine. I just don't know what's okay, especially now that we're back home. When we were in Florida, we could do whatever and didn't have to worry about things and people. But now that we're home, there are all these logistics and I know neither of us wants to get found out, so I don't know what's 'safe' or whatever.

"I mean, if we're watching a movie and someone comes in, can we justify it? If you come over to the pool to swim and hang out, can we explain it away? I guess I'm just trying to be smart. It's not that I don't want to do that stuff, but I know one of the reasons you were hesitant to do anything was because of Jay finding out. So, where is safe and unsafe territory?

"Can we text about random stuff and it not be deemed suspicious? Like last night, *The Patriot* was on and I watched it and wanted to text you, but thought I better not, because what if someone found your phone and somehow read my texts to you.

"And besides, I'm not your girlfriend, we agreed on not having a label on this, but some things feel like 'girlfriend-boyfriend' territory and I don't know what to do with that, because is it okay?"

CHAPTER TWENTY-ONE

SPENCE

"And besides, I'm not your girlfriend, we agreed on not having a label on this, but some things feel like 'girlfriend-boyfriend' territory and I don't know what to do with that, because is it okay?" Her expression is questioning and she shrugs.

I sigh. "I don't know. I know I don't want Jay to find out, but if it weren't for him, I'd want to take you out and stuff. And, honestly, that's strange for me, because that's not me. I don't do girlfriends. I don't do commitment. You know that."

She nods. "I know and I'm not asking for that. I don't want anything serious, either. I guess I just thought this would be purely physical, which that part is pretty amazing, but I honestly didn't think we'd have stuff in common and want to spend time outside of that. But I like that we talk about stuff. I like that you know things about me and vice-versa. And it makes me feel like we truly are friends with some really excellent benefits." The corner of her mouth rises into a smirk and it makes me smile.

I have a thought. "You know, Jay knows I had to come to Florida to bring you home. He's the one who sent me. But does he know we got stranded in Daytona? Have you spoken with him since you left school?"

She shakes her head. "No. Not unless Dad told him. Have you talked to him?"

"No. I know Delia's mom is sick, so he's probably tied up with that. But what I'm getting at is, we were stuck together for four days with only each other for company while your car was in the shop. It's totally feasible we could develop a friendship, right? Find common ground and talk because we didn't have anything else to do?"

She considers. "Yeah, I guess."

"So, I think we could get away with hanging out because we truly have become friends. We have books and movies in common, so I think we could do it without anyone being suspicious, as long as we're careful about touching and stuff."

Jo sighs. "Maybe. But if we went out somewhere, we'd have to drive separately, otherwise, it looks like a date. And what about if a girl flirts with you? It'd be totally out of character for you to not flirt, especially if you're just with a 'friend'."

I chuckle, because she's not wrong. I shrug. "I don't know about that part, but at least we have some plausible excuses, right? For the time we spend together?"

"Yeah. I guess it could work." She nudges me playfully. "Anyone ever tell you you're pretty smart?"

"You know, I think so. Some even suggest I could become a doctor or something."

She laughs and wraps her arms around my neck and kisses me and pulls me down to her.

A couple of weeks later, I've got Jo in my bed and I'm gripping her hips as she rides my cock, her tits bouncing with every gyration of her hips and her mouth is clamped closed as she attempts to be quiet because my parents are home and there's no way in hell I want them to know I have her here. She's so close and I know I'm not lasting but a few seconds after she gets off.

"Oh, God, Spence," she says with a low whine that has my balls drawing up.

"Fuck, Jo. You feel so good. You going to come for me?" I ask in a hushed voice and buck my hips up into her and she lets out a stilted moan, her pussy pulsing around me. Lifting my head, I suck her nipple into my mouth and give it a gentle tug with my teeth and she cries out, the sound muffled by me hurriedly covering her mouth with my hand as soon as she started clenching around me. Her thighs shake with her orgasm and I'm unable to hold my own release at bay with one final thrust and I groan through gritted teeth as my heart feels like it's going to burst from my chest.

Jo collapses against my chest and I roll us over as I pull out and pepper her face with kisses, making her giggle softly. I stare down at her and Jesus, she's so beautiful. "Will you stay tonight?" The question is out before I can bite it back and she searches my eyes, her expression surprised.

"Do you want me to?"

I don't even think twice before I answer. "Yeah."

"What about your parents?"

I shrug. "They won't come in here, even if they come downstairs and they'll be gone by seven-thirty."

She bites her lip and reaches over to the nightstand where her phone lays and picks it up and taps on the screen for a moment before laying it down again. "Okay."

"Okay," I echo with a grin and lower myself to the bed next to her and pull her into my arms. I don't want to admit to myself how much I miss falling asleep next to her and I know her dad will be home in a day or two, so I want to take advantage of this while I can since it might be the last time I get to wake up beside her. I want to admit even less how much I hate that thought.

———

Over the next several weeks, I see Jo in the evenings after she gets done at the bookstore. We watch movies and she gives me books to read and then we discuss them at length. We laugh and talk and spend time together. And even outside of the sex, which is still fantastic, I wake up thinking about her and what she's doing when we're not together.

Since her dad came back into town, we've had to be more strategic about getting away. We spend a lot more time in our cars, riding through the mountains until we find a backroad and park. It's definitely hot, but there are times when the sex seems like *more;* almost like it's soul deep and it scares me because we agreed we'd discuss things if we started to develop real feelings, but she seems unfazed by anything.

Jo talks about going back to school in a few more weeks and it makes me ache at the thought of what it will be like to not have her around me. I start to have wild ideas about transferring schools so I can be near her and it terrifies me because what does it mean if I have real feelings for her? What would it mean for me, who has never had a serious girlfriend in my life? I've told girls I loved them, but it was simply a means to an end for me to get what I wanted. I've never meant it before.

But for the first time in my life, I start to wonder if I'm falling for Jo. And if so, what am I supposed to do about it? She's got her life and I've got mine and *we* have an expiration date. *But do we have to?* And what if she doesn't feel the same way? What if all of this is purely physical for her?

We truly have become friends. We have a lot in common and it's nice. I don't feel like I have to pretend with her. I don't have to fake confidence and bravado, because she *knows* me. She was like a fly on the wall growing up, always there on the periphery, observing, listening. And truthfully, she probably knows me better than anyone, even Jay, at this point.

Jay. I'm at the point where I'd almost rather he found out about me and Jo. Because I'd love to be able to be with her in the daylight. Walk down the street with her and hold her hand like we did in Daytona. And probably the scariest part of all of this is, that if it came down to losing him and keeping her, I'd almost be willing to make that choice. What does that say about me as a friend if I'm considering that I'd be open to sacrificing my friendship with Jay so I can be with his sister?

He called me yesterday to say that he and Delia were back in town and wanted to see if I could hang out. So Jo made plans to go out with Ruby and we talked about connecting after. But if I know Jay, he'll want to play video games for most of the night and it just doesn't hold the same appeal as it used to. I haven't touched my Playstation since I got back from Daytona. I spend all my time with Jo, or reading and I like it that way.

Unbeknownst to her, I started playing the piano and singing again, because she asked me to sing for her and I want to do it. And so, two weeks ago, I dragged out my old keyboard and dusted it off and started practicing. I put it away when she comes over because I want to be able to surprise her before she goes back to school, and I've been practicing a cover of an Adele song that was on an album we listened to on a ride through the mountains.

I'm not expecting Jay for at least an hour, so I sit down to work on the arrangement and singing. After I've been at it for a bit, I feel a tap on my shoulder and I startle, thinking it's Jo, but I turn to see Jay. I pull my headphones off and stand quickly.

"Spence, I had no idea you could play or sing. Man, that sounded great."

I flush with embarrassment, because he was never meant to know about this. "Oh. Thanks. I used to, and started back a few weeks ago."

"Well, that song was something else. It sounded like there were some real feelings behind it. You have anything you want to tell me?"

Inwardly, I immediately panic. "No, why?"

He nudges me with his elbow, an eyebrow raised. "Come on, man, really? Sounds like there's a girl."

I shake my head, hoping I can keep my voice even. "Nope. No girl."

He gives me a suspicious look and I think for a moment, he knows something. "So, you're telling me you haven't hooked up with anyone all summer? That's not like you."

I shrug. "Just been laying low, I guess. Reading a lot."

"Reading? You don't read."

"Actually, I do. Jo's been lending some books to me."

"Joey? She's been letting you borrow books?" I want to kick myself because I didn't mean to bring her up and I didn't call her Joey. I'm failing miserably at keeping it together. I scramble to try and salvage things.

"Well, yeah. We spent a lot of time talking about different books on the way back from Florida. And, it turns out, we like a lot of the same books."

He looks surprised. "Wow. Okay. I hope it wasn't too much trouble having to go down there. I hated to ask you, but with Delia's mom, I hated to have her go alone."

I wave away his comment. "It was fine. The car actually

broke down in Daytona and we were stuck for a few days, but I'm not going to complain about being at the beach, you know."

"Oh, wow, I didn't know. I'm sorry. I hope Joey didn't give you too hard a time. She can be a bit intense. She probably talked your ear off about all those books."

"No, she was fine. We had a good time."

"Well, good. So, what do you want to do? I could do with a drink, you have anything here?"

I think for a minute. Jo and I drank all my beer last night, so I'm out. "No, sorry."

"Well, I guess we're off to the bar. Maybe we can fix your dry spell, find you a pretty girl for the night."

I don't say anything, just grab my phone and keys. Jay says, "I'll drive."

"Okay." We get in his truck and drive the fifteen minutes to our favorite bar and I'm quiet on the way over, because although I'm happy to see Jay, I'd rather not go out since he's going to expect me to be the same old Spence I've always been, and it's not me anymore. Not since Jo.

When we park, Jay grabs my arm. "Hey, dude, what's up with you? You seem off."

I attempt a nonchalant tone. "Sorry, man. I'm just in my head about school starting back in a few weeks. Definitely not looking forward to those long hours of lectures and labs again."

He nods. "Well, let's get a drink and take your mind off of it, huh?"

"Sure, okay." We walk into the bar and I'm greeted with the live music of an open mic night. I've not been here since before Christmas and the last time was with Jay, so in a way, it feels like old times, but I'm not the old me, so this place where I used to troll for someone to take home for the night doesn't hold the same appeal it once did.

We sit at the bar and order beers. He tells me that Delia's

mom had been diagnosed with breast cancer and they needed to perform a double mastectomy and do aggressive chemo and radiation to try to get it under control. "Man, that's rough. How's Delia taking all of it?"

He shrugs. "Better than she was. The few weeks we were in Memphis helped a lot, I think. She got to spend a lot of time with her mom and be there for her post-op recovery. And Memphis is nice. We had talked about possibly moving, but since I took that job in Cookeville for the fall, it may be a while."

I nod. "Well, I hope everything works out for her mom. Keep me updated?"

"Thanks, I will." He looks around and does a double take toward the back of the bar near the pool tables. "Looks like Joey and Ruby came out tonight, too."

I try to not react, but turn slowly, and sure enough, Jo and Ruby are back at the pool tables. And they're not alone. Ruby is talking to a petite, blonde girl and Jo is chatting with a tall guy with longish black hair and glasses. Jealousy stabs through me. The guy is obviously interested in Jo and she's laughing, leaning against the pool table, stick in hand, drinking a beer. She laughs at something he says and touches his arm and rage fills me. Jay doesn't notice. "Let's go say hi. I've not seen Joey since she got back from school."

I swallow and nod and try to appear calm although I'm angry. We had talked about what would happen if I went out and flirted, but I never expected she would. Not that I didn't think guys would flirt with her, but it didn't occur to me she'd flirt back and it hurts.

We walk over to the tables and I hang back as Jay goes up to Jo and her face lights up at the sight of him. They hug and talk for a minute before Jay gestures to me. Jo's eyebrow tics up at the sound of my name, but other than that, she doesn't react.

And I only see it because I know her face and its subtleties now. I step forward and Jo nods at me. "Spence. Good to see you."

"Joey." Her hand grips her beer tighter at my use of Joey and I hate that I even have to use it. I take a deep breath and look down at my feet, unsure what to do.

I hear Jay say to Jo, "Spence told me what y'all have been up to this summer."

My head snaps up and I see all the color has drained from her face and my heart starts to pound. She glances at me and I give her a subtle shake of my head hoping Jay doesn't see it. Jo's demeanor doesn't change, which I'm thankful for. She simply asks, "Oh, yeah. What's that?"

"The books. He said you've been letting him borrow books. I was shocked. You don't lend out books to anyone."

I slowly start to breathe again. Jo must use all those years that she hid the way she looked at me to keep her expression neutral. Her tone is even and I'm in awe of how cool she's able to be. "Yeah, well, he treats them really well, so I'm not worried about them getting damaged or anything. I'm just glad he's enjoying them."

I feel myself flush, because I know she's not only talking about the books. And I hope the light in the bar is low enough that Jay doesn't see it. Jo's mouth pulls up at the corner and I know she's seen my color change. While Jay's focused on his sister I take a moment to assess her. She's wearing a short red sundress and black sandals. Her hair is loose and wavy and I want to run my fingers through it. I drag my eyes away before I've stared too long and look across the bar. After a minute, I hear Jay tell Jo they'll catch up later. They hug and we start to walk away.

Jo says, "Bye, Spence."

"Bye, Joey."

When we get back over to the bar, I angle myself so it appears I'm facing Jay, but can see Jo out of the corner of my eye. We order another beer and I ask Jay about his new teaching job for the fall. We also order nachos and after they come, I notice the black haired guy is back at the pool table chatting up Jo and again, I'm filled with jealousy.

CHAPTER TWENTY-TWO

JO

Watching Jay and Spence at the bar makes me nervous, because Spence's body language is tense and he keeps glancing at me. He's going to blow this for us and it's pissing me off. He was the one who decided that in public, we had to act normal. And I'm doing that, but he's not. I've watched him for years, and have never seen him so antsy. And every time the guy I went to high school with comes over to talk to me, Spence tenses up. What he doesn't know and I would tell him if I could, is the guy is just a friend and very gay.

I've got to get him alone, so he'll chill. Ruby and Samantha are sitting at a table and haven't glanced at me in a while, so I'm not worried about being missed so I head for the bathrooms. There are two singles for each gender, so I go into the far women's and shoot a quick text to Spence.

> Jo: In two minutes, make an excuse to come to the bathroom. Far women's. Four quick knocks.

I don't get a text back, but a little over two minutes later, there's a knock and I pull him in and lock the door. I whisper, "What the hell, Spence? Jay's going to notice how antsy you are. You've got to chill."

His eyes flash with controlled anger and he stalks toward me. "Who's the guy, Jo? I thought we weren't flirting with other people."

I secretly love that he's jealous, so I lean against the sink and feign ignorance. "What guy?"

He comes to stand in front of me. "Don't give me that shit. You know what guy. Long, black hair, glasses. Are you drunk?"

I stifle a smile, but I'm so turned on that he's upset at seeing me with someone else I can't stop myself from trying to get a rise out of him. "Oh, that guy. He did try to buy me some drinks, but we're not serious or anything."

Spence presses his hips into me and leans down to whisper in my ear, his voice low and seething. "Do I need to remind you what I'd like to do to anyone who'd put their hands on you? To touch what's mine? And last I checked, you're mine until the end of summer."

Heat shoots straight to my core and my breath hitches. I search his eyes and they're dark and hot. I respond, my voice low and husky, "I'd rather you fuck me and make me forget about anyone else."

He crushes his mouth to mine and lifts me up onto the counter of the sink. His kiss is possessive and steals my breath. With shaky fingers, I fumble for his belt and the button of his jeans and dip my hand into his boxers, reaching for his cock, already hardening in my grip. I stroke him quickly and he hisses through gritted teeth and tugs his pants and underwear down below his hips and nudges my thighs apart as he hikes my dress up. He shoves my panties to the side and pushes into me. I bite back the gasp that fights to escape from my lips.

Spence's hands grip my hip as he thrusts into me. He

growls low in my ear, "You're mine, Jo. No one else's. This cunt is mine. You hear me?"

My heart bangs in my chest and my pleasure builds swiftly as I wrap my arms around his neck, my legs hooked around his waist. I look into his eyes and my quiet gasps are punctuated with my words. "Fuck, Yes. Yours, Spence."

I start to orgasm and pull his mouth to mine to stifle my cry as I come violently. His cock jerks inside me as he finishes with a grunt, his face in my neck.

After a beat, I push him back and give him a soft smile and a kiss before hopping down from the sink and straightening my dress. "My friend, Owen, is gay. But nice to know what jealousy looks like on you, Spence. Gotta admit, it's a turn on."

He backs away from me, still angry and rights his pants. "What the fuck, Jo? Are you trying to get us caught?"

I scoff. "You didn't have to follow me in here." Then my voice softens. "You were so tense. I thought you needed to relax. Did it work?"

He clenches his jaw, then sighs. "Yes. But we've been in here too long."

I dismiss his concern with a wave. "I'll go out and text you when there's no one around. Wait three minutes, then come back out. Tell Jay you have stomach problems. I'll offer to take you home, because Ruby is going to go with Samantha and it's on my way."

He shakes his head, his expression amazed. "How do you do that? Come up with plans like that?"

I shrug. "I'm a writer. Stories and scenarios come naturally to me."

"I'll say. Okay."

"Remember, I'll text and you come out three minutes later."

I step out of the bathroom and am thankful no one is

around. When I get back to the pool table, I see that Jay is on his phone, so I quickly text Spence to tell him the coast is clear. I go over to Ruby and Samantha's table and sit and Ruby eyes me. "Where'd you get to?"

I shake my head. "Nowhere." But she looks over my shoulder and sees Spence come out of the bathroom and her eyebrow raises. I keep my tone even. "You're going with Samantha, right? Because I'm not feeling great, so I think I'm going to head out."

She smirks. "Yeah. Sure. Feel better, Jo."

"I think I'll feel fine as soon as I get home."

Her smirk turns into a knowing smile. "I bet you will."

I stand and turn and walk to the bar. I don't look at Spence, but order a glass of water. "Joey?"

I turn at the sound of my brother's voice. "Yeah?"

"I have to go. Delia called. We have to go back to Memphis; her mother's not doing well. Did you drive?"

"Yeah. I'm so sorry. Can I do anything to help? I hate this for Delia."

"Can you take Spence home? I hate to make you cut out early, but I need to get back to Dee."

I nod. "Of course. It's fine. Ruby's going with Samantha, so I was getting ready to head out anyway."

"Oh, good. Okay." He hugs me and claps Spence on the shoulder before he leaves. I feel terrible that Jay and Delia are having to deal with all this.

I turn to Spence. "Ready to go?"

He nods and we walk out to my car. On the way home, we're both quiet in light of what Jay and Delia are going through. Spence takes my hand in his and brushes a kiss across my knuckles. "My parents are out of town. Think you can get away?"

I nod. "Yeah, probably. I can tell Dad I'm staying at Ruby's.

Ruby will cover for me. I'm pretty sure she knows about us anyway, based on her expression at the bar." His eyes go wide and I squeeze his hand. "Ruby's my best friend. She's not going to tell anyone. Not even Samantha. I promise."

He sighs. "Does she know about Christmas, too?"

I nod. "Yeah. I told her. It's not like I thought we'd get together over the summer. I thought it was going to be a one-time thing, so I told her."

"Okay. Well, when we get home, just text me after you're squared away with your dad. Want to watch a movie?"

"Sure, that's fine."

We pull in at my house and I park in the garage. Spence gives me a quick kiss and slips out the side door and I walk inside. Dad's sitting at the kitchen table going over some paper-work. I walk over and plant a kiss on the top of his head. "Hey, Daddy. Having fun?"

He chuckles. "Yeah, loads. What are you up to?"

"I'm going to spend the night with Ruby, just popped in to grab a few things."

I start to walk away and Dad places his hand on my arm. "Hey, sweetie?"

"Yeah?"

"I was going through your credit card statement from when you were in Daytona."

I immediately tense but keep my tone even and project nonchalance as I sit. "Yeah? It was a lot, wasn't it? I'm sorry. I'll work extra at the store over the next few weeks to make up for it."

He waves off my comment. "No, it was actually lower than I thought it would be."

"Oh, well, that's good, I guess."

"Yeah. I was worried the motel hadn't charged for both rooms, so I called them."

My heart starts to race. "Yeah?"

He holds my gaze. "Yeah. They said they were full up and only had one room left, so you took that one."

I nod. "Yeah. There was a big convention in town and everywhere was booked up."

I start to stand and Dad says, "Sit down, Joanna." His tone is serious.

I want to panic, but I keep calm. "What is it, Daddy?"

He takes his reading glasses off and sets them on the table and looks at me. "You know I like Spencer, right?"

"Yeah, of course."

"And there's not a reason I shouldn't keep liking him, is there?"

Heat instantly floods my cheeks. "Why would you say that?"

"You two have spent a lot of time together since you got back from school."

I shrug. "We're friends. We have a lot in common and he borrows books from me."

Dad's expression grows more serious. "Joanna, I like Spencer. He's like family, but you're my daughter, so I want to make sure you're safe. Are you safe?"

My breath catches. "Daddy, I'm fine. Spence and I are friends. He's a good guy."

My father sighs and his tone is exasperated. "Sweetie, does Jay know y'all have been seeing each other? Because if it ends badly for you and him, it won't just be you and Spencer who're affected. Jay will be, too. You know that, right?"

All the color drains from my face and my stomach drops. *My dad knows?* I nod.

"Now, we're y'all fooling around before you turned eighteen? Because as much as I like Spencer, I can't abide that."

I gasp. "No, Daddy. I swear." I look down at my hands. "He

never even looked at me as anything besides a little sister almost. It's not like there was much to look at anyway."

"Until Christmas?" My head snaps up and Dad nods. "Yeah, I know about that. I was out on Garrett and Diane's porch when you and Spencer got back from wherever you went. I saw you get out of his Jeep. I worried something like this might happen when y'all got stranded in Daytona. I know you've always had a sweet spot for him."

My mouth falls open in shock and he rolls his eyes. "I'm old, honey, not blind. Jay and Spencer were apparently oblivious to the way you watched him, but I wasn't."

I look at him, my voice pleading. "Daddy, please, you can't tell Jay. I don't want their friendship to end because of me."

He scowls and shakes his head. "You're not alone in this. Spencer's a big boy."

My words spill out in a rush. "Yes, but I pursued him. At Christmas, he didn't even know it was me when we went for that drive. I chased him. I'm the one who convinced him we could keep things quiet.

"It's only for the summer. I'll be going back to Miami, Spence will be going back to med school. We knew going in we'd have an expiration date. We like each other, but it's not serious. We don't want Jay to feel like he has to choose, when there's no reason for him to do that. But, Daddy, Spence is a good guy. He's kind and sweet to me. I promise. I'm fine."

He squeezes my hand, his expression serious. "And careful? Are you being careful? Not that I don't like Spencer, but I don't want to become a grandpa just yet."

I feel myself flush. "Daddy! Yes, I promise."

He shakes his head. "I'll never understand your generation's need to just 'have fun' or whatever. In my day, you took a girl out and bought her dinner." Sighing, he pinches the bridge of his nose before returning his gaze to me. "I won't tell Jay. I do think maybe y'all should give him a little more credit. You're all adults now. And as much as I hate to see my daughter grown and making her own decisions, I'm not going to get in your way. And let's just drop the whole charade about going to Ruby's, okay? I know she has her girlfriend over most nights, so I would think it would be a bit awkward for you to be there, too, don't you?"

A surprised laugh escapes from me. Dad takes my chin and forces me to look at him. "I wasn't just talking about being careful with your body, Joanna. Be careful with your heart, too, all right?"

I nod. "I am, Daddy. I promise."

He sighs again. "Okay. My speech is done. Go live your life." He turns back to his paperwork and I know I've been dismissed and I rise and go upstairs. I'm still in shock as I pull my phone out of the pocket of my dress and see I have several notifications from Spence checking to see if I'm on my way.

I shoot him a quick text to say I'll be over shortly. I grab a tote bag and shove a change of clothes, my glasses and contact case, my birth control pills, toothbrush, and a book. I look around to see if there's anything I'm forgetting and toss in my phone charger.

CHAPTER TWENTY-THREE

SPENCE

I wait for a text from Jo. I'm anxious and feel like it was too close for comfort at the bar. I know she was right and I was drawing attention to myself, but as bad as it sounds, I hope Jay had too much going on to notice me.

She finally responds to my texts about twenty minutes after we get back and I take a deep breath. I was a bit worried she wouldn't figure out how to leave it with her dad. I see her coming around the house and open the door as she gets to it. Her face is pale and she looks upset.

I take her bag and drop it on the sofa. "Jo, what's wrong? You look upset."

"My dad knows, Spence."

My stomach drops. "Fuck. How did he find out? Is he going to tell Jay?" I can't keep the panic from my voice.

She shakes her head and I tug her to the couch to sit down. She blows out a breath. "Apparently, he's known I had a crush on you for years. And then at Christmas, he was up on your porch during the party and saw me get out of your Jeep when we got back from the drive. And then he was going through the credit card statement from when we were in Daytona and he thought the motel had messed up and only charged us for one room and so he called them."

My inhale is sharp, but she continues. "Yeah, so he suspected. And he knows Ruby has a girlfriend, so he knew I wasn't at her house. He's not going to tell Jay. I told him we were only going to be together over the summer, so there was no sense in hurting Jay, when there's no reason to. And he just wanted to make sure we hadn't hooked up before I was eighteen."

I recoil at the idea that Nick might think I'd take advance of his daughter like that and Jo touches my cheek. "I told him no, of course," she reassures me. "And he just said for us to be careful. He's not going to tell Jay and he's not mad. He loves you. And I told him you're good to me, so it's all good, as weird as it is."

I just try to breathe for a moment while I process her words. "And he knows you're here now? And that you're going to stay?"

She nods. "Yeah, I know. It's weird. I felt so freaked out leaving knowing he knew I was coming over here. But he just said to make good choices."

"Shit. I need a drink. That's a lot."

She huffs out a laugh. "You and me both. I know we drank all the beer last night, but do you have anything else?"

I walk over to the bar and open the cabinet and move things around and find a bottle of tequila. I hold it up. "Look, Jo, your favorite."

She perks up. "Got any limes?"

"No, do you still want some?"

She nods. "Yeah, just a little bit. I'm so freaked out and tense now."

I pour us each a couple fingers of the clear liquor and bring our glasses over to the couch. I hand hers over and sit. She curls into my side and I wrap my arm around her. We sit in companionable silence for a few minutes and Jo asks, "Did Jay say anything to you when you came out of the bathroom?"

"No, I think he was too distracted with everything going on with Delia's mom." She seems to melt into me and I look down and see her glass is already empty. "Jeez, Jo, thirsty?"

She shrugs. "Just still a little freaked out my dad knows I have a sex life. I don't want to think about it. It's weird." She grins playfully up at me. "Want to distract me with sex to take my mind off my dad knowing that I've had sex?"

I can't help but laugh. I down my tequila, feeling the pleasant burn take the edge off of my raw nerves from the revelations of the evening. I set the glass down and tug Jo up off the sofa and into my room. I open the door and freeze. I've completely forgotten to put away my keyboard. Luckily all the sheet music is on my phone and she can't see that.

"Spence, what's wrong?" She peeks around me. "You're playing again?" Her tone is excited. "Will you play for me?"

I sputter. "No. I mean, not yet. I'm not ready."

"Please, I want to hear you."

"I will, Jo. I'm just not ready yet. I will before you go back to school, I promise."

She smiles up at me and nods. "I can't wait."

I pull her to me and brush a kiss over the top of her head. *I can. I'm not ready. Because as soon as I play that song, there's no denying to her how I feel. You can't unring a bell.*

Later, as we lie in bed, I listen to Jo sleeping in my arms. My fingers brush her bare back and I feel like there are not enough days left. Not enough hours. Not enough minutes. Not enough time. As much as I didn't want to start this thing with Jo, I want it to end even less. Because although I've never been in love before, I know I am. At twenty-three, I'm in love for the first time in my life. And I made the rule about discussing feelings, but I can't. Because she'll end it and I'm not ready.

I don't know how I thought I would get out of this unscathed. I mean, I do, I'm me. I've never had feeling for anyone beyond physical. I had no reason to think it would be different with Jo, but it is. And I don't know what to do about that. Do I follow her? Do I ask her to come with me? Could we do long distance? I don't know.

So instead, I pull her closer to me and breath her in, that now familiar scent of her coconut vanilla lotion and pray for the hours to crawl from now until the moment I have to give her up.

CHAPTER TWENTY-FOUR

JO

Once my dad told me he knew about Spence and me, we were able to be more freely at my house. We definitely don't show any blatant affection toward one another, but I don't worry we'll be found out, especially since Jay is still in Memphis.

So we watch TV and read together, eat together, and play in the pool. I can almost let myself believe it's a real relationship, but I know our time is growing shorter and I'm loathe to look at a clock or calendar, because I know it brings me one day closer to goodbye.

This has honestly been the most magical summer and I can't be more thankful for the time Spence and I have spent together. He's opened my eyes to so many things and I almost want to ask if, when I come home over winter break, we can see each other again, but I feel like that's against some unspoken rule about the future. There is no future. Only the now. So I'll enjoy it while I can. For two more weeks, anyway.

A couple weeks ago, I started feeling like I was coming down with some sort of bug. I'd wake up super nauseated in the mornings, but as soon as I ate, it would pass. And then I got really dizzy one afternoon while I was working at the store. And I'd noticed the last time Spence and I had sex, my breasts were very tender.

But I didn't get concerned, until my period was late. The type of pills I'm on make it so I'm only supposed to have four periods a year and the last one I had was at the end of April. I finished my pack of pills and then didn't start. And I freaked out and I thought maybe I'd miscounted, but I knew that wasn't the case and I hadn't missed any pills at all. I was super religious about them, especially because sometimes, Spence and I don't use condoms.

But now, I'm terrified, because I was careful and did all the right things. So I go to a drug store about forty-five minutes away from the house to buy a pregnancy test. I bring it home, shoved in the bottom of my bag like I stole it, thinking for sure someone will be able to see it written all over my face. Dad is gone and I should call Spence, but he's out for the day, getting some books for school or something. I could call Ruby, but she's not super good in a crisis, so instead, I sit on the edge of my bathtub, all by myself and watch as one pink line turns into two and I shatter. Panic grips me and I sit, unable to move for at least an hour, just thinking about how this can't be happening.

I know it couldn't have happened at Christmas, because I've had periods since then and that was almost eight months ago. They tested me when I got my birth control prescription. And that was after the other guys I was with. So sometime between Daytona and now. I think back, trying to figure up the dates. Daytona was early May, and now it's late July, so somewhere between four and ten weeks?

I open my laptop for the first time all summer and google pregnancy symptoms and how quickly can a test show up positive after a missed period. For the next hour, I overwhelm myself with information and I don't retain most of it.

I try to breathe, but I don't know how. *How am I going to tell Spence? How am I going to tell Dad when I was adamant I was being careful? How am I going to tell Jay? Am I going to tell them? I'm not ready to be a mother. I'm still in college. I can't do this.*

I google Planned Parenthood and an ad for a mobile ultrasound bus pops up. It says they're in the area today and they do free pregnancy tests and ultrasounds. I check the time. Noon. And it says they're open until four. I don't think, I just grab my purse and go. When I pull up at the bus that's parked at the bottom of a Walmart parking lot, I pray no one I know sees me enter. Thankfully, I'm the only one on the bus. I'm greeted by a young woman in scrubs and she asks what service I'm interested in and I tell her I think I am pregnant. Although at this point, I know I am already, but I'm not ready to accept it.

She nods and her expression is compassionate. She asks me to complete some paperwork detailing my symptoms, date of my last period, basic medical history. Once I give the clipboard back, she takes it and hands me a cup and directs me to a small bathroom and asks me to pee in the cup and they'll do a test.

After what seems like the longest five minutes ever, a nurse comes to me and takes me to a back part of the bus where there's an exam table and an ultrasound machine. She introduces herself, but I don't catch her name, just that yes, I am indeed pregnant.

I don't even feel the tears start because, honestly, I've been crying on and off all morning. She takes my hand in hers. "You're going to be okay, Joanna. Is there anyone you'd like us to call? A husband, boyfriend?"

Boyfriend. Spence is not my boyfriend, but he is every sense of the word. I shake my head. "No. I'm not sure what I want to do yet."

Her face registers no judgement and she simply gives me a

soft smile and nods. "Okay. Well, if you want, we can do an ultrasound to see how far along you are, to help you determine what you'd like to do." I take a deep breath and nod. She asks, "Do you know how far along you might be?"

I bite my lip. "I'm not sure. The birth control pills I'm on are supposed to make me have four periods a year but I was supposed to start a few days ago, so I honestly don't know. I know it would have happened between May and now. I hadn't been with anyone before that in a while."

"All right. Well, we can narrow that window down a bit for you, okay?" I nod and she gestures for me to lie down on the table and tells me to pull my shirt up and unbutton my shorts. "This gel might be a bit cold, I'm sorry."

But I don't notice that. I only notice that a moment after she puts the ultrasound wand low on my abdomen, there's a definite image of a baby. She toggles a switch and a whooshing sound I know is a heartbeat plays on a set of speakers. I close my eyes and take a deep breath. She says, "Let me do a couple quick measurements." She punches some buttons on the machine and after a minute, she looks at me. "Looks like you're about ten weeks. I can print these out for you." I nod and feel the tears start again. *Fucking Daytona.*

She hands me the printouts and gives me a paper towel to clean off the gel. As I sit up, she says, "You have options. I know this is probably really scary for you. We can set you up with a counselor and they can discuss all your options."

I shake my head. "That's okay. I'll talk to my... friend. He should be a part of the decision."

She nods. "Okay. Well, here are some pamphlets for you to look at. They contain information about the different options you have."

I take them, but don't look at them. I just stumble out of the bus and climb into my car, numb and unsure what to do.

I don't remember the drive home, but somehow, I end up there. I walk up to my room and go into my bathroom and vomit. Not because of the apparent morning sickness, but because of nerves and fear and the feeling that everything I've ever wanted in my life is going down the drain. My college career. My hopes of working at a newspaper. My dream of publishing a novel. Because how am I supposed to do that with a baby?

And Spence. Sweet, kind, beautiful Spence.What about his dreams? He wants to be a doctor; wants it so badly. And I want that for him. But he deserves to know, right? I didn't do this by myself. I don't want to do this, but maybe if he was a part of it? I laugh to myself. Not with any humor, but at the cruelty of it all. At my stupidity.

Adoption, maybe? Because, honestly, I know that I'm not ready to be a mother, but the alternative... I don't know if I can do that either.

I pull the ultrasound photos out of my bag. I sit in the floor next to my bed and examine the images. There are arms and legs and although it's tiny, it's clear. There's no mistaking it for a blob or anything other than what it is. It's a baby. A baby Spence and I made.

I open my laptop back up and research adoption. And again, for the next hour, I overwhelm myself with information. My eyes glaze over and I can't process any more data.

To distract myself, I pull up my school email, because I haven't checked it all summer and I figure it might take my mind off things for just a moment as I go through and clean it out. There are hundreds of emails, many automated ones generated for registration and fees and things. But there's a recent one that catches my eye, from the editor of the school paper marked urgent from two weeks ago.

. . .

To the staff of the University of Miami newspaper:

We look forward to a new school year of great and powerful news stories!

There are some changes you will want to be made aware of that may impact your necessary arrival date to campus for the new school year. All staff or potential staff members of the paper must attend a mandatory seminar regarding reporting policies and upcoming changes to the structure of the paper.

If you are unable to attend, a spot on the staff can not be guaranteed for you, even if you held one in previous years. This year's staff selection will be more rigorous.

We look forward to seeing you on Friday, August 2nd.

August second?! I glance at the calendar, even though I already know the date. It's three days from now. I have to leave in two days.

I thought I had more time. I thought Spence and I had more time.

I call Ruby, because she's supposed to drive down with me because she wants to spend a few days at the beach and she's planning on crashing with me and flying back home. She answers on the third ring. "Jo? Hey."

"Hey, Ruby. I just found out I have to go back to school in three days because of some kind of mandatory newspaper seminar. Will you still be able to go down with me? Or does this screw stuff up for you?"

"Let me check my calendar real quick." I hear her flipping pages, because, of course Ruby has a paper planner, while the rest of the world has gone digital. She comes back on the line a few seconds later. "Yeah, that should be fine."

"Okay, we'll have to leave Thursday morning, by eight at the latest."

"All right. I'll be ready to go whenever. Just call me when you're ready to hit the road."

"Okay. Thanks, Ruby."

After I hang up with her, I call my dad and give him the update and let him know Ruby will still be able to drive down with me so he won't have to close down the store to get me to Miami.

And then comes the hardest call. I know Spence is not home, or I'd just go over and talk to him. He answers on the second ring. "Jo, hey. I'm glad you called. I wanted to see if maybe you'd like to go out of town for a couple days, you know, as a kind of last hurrah before you leave for school."

"I'm not going to be able to do that, Spence."

"Why not? We've got two weeks."

I already feel the tears coming. "No, I found out today, I have to leave in two days. I have to be back on campus by Friday for a newspaper thing." Spence is quiet for a long time and after a moment, I pull my phone away from my face to make sure he's still there. "Spence?"

"Can you come over tomorrow night? I won't be back home until tomorrow afternoon. We can have dinner together, have one last night together?"

I keep my tone even, although the tears begin falling down my face. "Okay, what time?"

"Six?"

"I'll be there."

CHAPTER TWENTY-FIVE

JO

The next day passes agonizingly slowly. I pack my clothes and books into boxes and into my car, along with the things I left in the garage at the beginning of summer.

I lie in bed and look at the clock expecting three hours to have passed and find it's only been ten minutes. I still haven't decided how I'm going to tell Spence I'm pregnant. I have to tell him, but I have no clue how I'm going to do that when I don't even know how to process it myself.

I've already decided I'm going to carry to term, simply because I've seen this baby and heard its heartbeat. And I may not be ready to be a mother, but I just can terminate. And it's Spence. I can make sure this little piece of us and the beautiful summer we shared together has a forever family and Spence and I still get to live our dreams.

In spite of everything, I don't regret my time with Spence. I only wish we had more. And I'm going to miss him so much when I leave. Two days. It's so fucking unfair. I might have been able to prepare myself if I had known the expiration date had changed, but I've cried all day.

And I can probably chalk a lot of it up to hormones, but it's also my heart. I care about Spence so much and don't know what I'm going to do not being able to see him every day. He has so quickly become such an important person in my life.

I've wanted his body since I was twelve. But his mind and his heart are just as beautiful and I love that he's shared them with me. *Love...* I don't know if this can be classified as that, but strong affection that with nurturing could bloom into love? Most definitely.

It's a shame we can't take another person's heart with us places. Isn't there an EE Cummings poem that says something about that? I feel like it's unfair there's not a way to give someone your heart to hold.

Around five, I finally get up and get ready to see Spence one last time. I shower and shave and try to tamp down the nausea. I don't bother with makeup or my contacts, because with the tears, there's no point. I pin my hair up loosely and slip on a casual sundress and sandals.

I go downstairs and see my dad in the kitchen. He takes one look at my face and comes over to hug me and I try not to cry. "I'm going to say goodbye to Spence. I don't know if I'll be home tonight."

He kisses my forehead. "Okay. Will I see you in the morning before you leave; before I go into the store?"

I nod. "Yes."

He searches my eyes. "Are you sure you were careful with your heart, sweet girl?"

Even through the tears I nod again. "I'll be okay, Daddy. My heart's not broken, it just hurts. I knew it was coming, but it's like the end of really good book you want to keep going forever. You know it will end, but it's a bittersweet thing."

He nods. "Okay. Well, I'm here if you need me, all right?"

"Thanks, Daddy." I kiss him on the cheek and head out the

door. I walk around the back of Spence's house and down to the patio and basement entrance. I take a few deep breaths and steel myself as I knock on the door. He answers and he looks just as good as he always has although his eyes are rimmed in red and I feel like I'm not the only one who's shed tears today. I paste a smile on my face as I enter and he pulls me in for a hug. I go into his arms for a long embrace and lay my head on his chest and listen to his heart, and its steady thumping.

We stand there for what seems like hours before he steps back from me. "I ordered pizza. I hope that's okay."

I nod. "Perfect." Because it is. It's fitting it should be the first and last meal we share together. He goes to hand me a beer and I look at it and want to laugh, but I don't. "Can I have water instead? I don't really feel like drinking tonight." He nods and brings me a bottle of water. "Thanks."

We sit on the sofa and he opens the pizza box and the smell makes me want to puke. I try to breathe through my mouth so maybe it won't be so bad. I take a slice and nibble it, but find that I can only eat about half of the piece before I'm done.

"You okay, Jo? It's not like you to not eat."

I shrug. "Just not that hungry. It was good, though. Thanks."

We don't talk, even though it feels like we both have so much we want to say. Several times, I feel the words, "I'm pregnant" form in my mouth, but my body won't let me say them.

After he's done eating, I stand and tug him up and pull him to the bedroom. "Jo, we don't have to do this tonight. We can just talk and hang out. It's really okay."

I turn to him, tears in my eyes. "Please, Spence. I want one more memory of a perfect time with you. Of us. Make it count for the two weeks we're not getting. Please?" I close my eyes and rest my forehead on his chest.

He lifts my chin and brushes a soft kiss across my lips. I

pull him to me and deepen the kiss and the familiar want follows and need begins to coil within me, even through the sadness and tears.

I tug his shirt over his head and kick off my sandals. Spence unzips my dress and it falls to the floor. I unhook my bra and let it slide down my arms to join my dress and I unbutton his shorts and he shucks them.

I climb into bed and pull him down with me. I still feel the tears on my face and Spence kisses the wetness from my cheeks and pulls my mouth to his and our kiss is tender and sweet and full of everything we've left unsaid. His mouth moves down my neck and chest to my breasts and I fight the urge to cry out with the discomfort.

I bring his mouth back to mine. "Please don't stop kissing me, Spence."

And he doesn't. Not when his hands tug my panties down. Not when his thumb works my clit and I'm gasping into his mouth. Not when his fingers enter me and bring me through my first orgasm. Not when he sheds his underwear and drives into me. Not when his thrusts are slow and easy and perfect. Not when we climax together and tears fall down my cheeks afresh, because I know this is the last time. Not after, when I'm in his arms.

He doesn't stop kissing me until he rises from the bed. "I'll be right back."

He slips his boxers back on and goes over to the closet and pulls out his keyboard and a stool. He positions it so he'll be facing me as he plays. I sit up and lean against the headboard with the sheet drawn up to my chest.

He settles in and his fingers move along the keys and it's "One and Only" by Adele. His voice is clear and strong and just as beautiful as he is. I listen to the words and I can't take it, because it's too much. I know what's going to come after he finishes, because by the end, he has tears in his eyes. And I can't hear him say words that sound like "stay" or "future" or "love". I can't take it on top of everything else.

I sit on the edge of the bed and tug my dress back on. Spence comes over to sit next to me. "Jo, I have something I need to tell you."

I shake my head. "No, Spence. Don't. Please."

"Jo, I love you." And even though I knew it was coming it still hits me like a ton of bricks. But he's not done. "I have for weeks. I was afraid to tell you."

I stand, sobs rising from my chest. "You can't say this right now. I leave tomorrow. You wait until the night before I leave to tell me you love me and that you have for weeks? What kind of fairness is that? You made the rule about discussing feelings— you, not me. And we agreed. But you broke the rules, Spence."

"We made the rules, Jo, we can change them."

I look into his gorgeous green eyes. Eyes, that for the past ten weeks, I've looked into with desire and longing. "But you weren't honest. That's not fair to me. You can't spring this on me when I leave in the morning."

"Please? We can make it work. I can transfer schools. We can do long distance. I want to make it work with you. I want us to tell Jay and be together. I want to love you in the daylight. Not just at night, in secret."

I shake my head and search out my shoes in the floor. "I can't do this right now, Spence."

"Jo, please. Don't leave. Stay," he pleads.

"I can't. It's too much."

His voice breaks. "You don't love me?"

"Spence, if we had more time... I want you and I care about you and I know that could grow into love in time. But we're out of time. And it's unfair."

He drops to the edge of the bed, the look on his face

wrecked and he drops his eyes to the floor and I flee, unable to deal with this right now. I hate that I'm not brave enough to tell him everything in this moment, but it's all just too much. The tears start to come as I leave and they don't stop until sometime in the early hours of the morning.

CHAPTER TWENTY-SIX

JO

I wake with a start, and know that I've slept very little. I look at my alarm clock and see it's after seven and I know I need to get up and Ruby and I need to get on the road.

I rise and fight the nausea and brush my teeth, but it only makes me vomit. I slide my glasses onto my face and throw my hair into a ponytail. I pull on a pair of jogging shorts and a tee shirt and pray the nausea stays at bay so Ruby doesn't find out I'm pregnant.

I take one last look around my room and see my copy of *The Time Traveler's Wife*. It breaks my heart to see it, because Spence and I spent a lot of time discussing that book and then the movie after it and it will forever hold the memory of us.

His words last night play over in my mind. *I want to make it work with you. I can transfer schools. We can do long-distance. I want to love you in the daylight, not just in secret.*

Weren't these the words I longed to hear from him my whole life? Every fantasy I had before we became what we are consisted of him telling me he wanted me, that he wanted to be with me. Why am I fighting against it? Is it only because I'm pregnant and I don't know how to tell him? If there was no baby, would I jump at the chance to be with him, however I could?

Yes.

My stomach drops and I realize I've made a terrible mistake. I have to make this right. But there is a baby, and he needs to know so we can decide together what we're going to do. I take one of the ultrasound photos and stick it in the middle of the book. I open the front of the book and write:

I want to relive all the memories with you. However we can. -Jo

I grab my purse and phone and keys, along with the book and run down the stairs. Dad is standing at the coffee maker and I run over and hug him. "I'm sorry, Daddy. I have to tell Spence something before I leave. I love you. I'll call you when I get to Miami, okay?"

He smiles and kisses my cheek and I race out the door and around Spence's house. I knock on the door. A couple minutes later, I knock again. I try the door, and find it unlocked. I stick my head in and yell his name. I set the book down on the coffee table and start toward the bedroom door. It opens and he steps out, dressed only in a pair of boxers. "Jo? I thought you were gone."

My words come out in a rush. "Spence, I was wrong. I was just scared. I'm sorry, I want to do whatever we can to make it work, but there's something we need to talk about."

Spence's face falls. "Jo, please remember that I love you. And I need you to know that when I heard your voice, I was so happy. But, I need to tell you something." Movement over his shoulder catches my eye and my body registers it before my brain does. And suddenly, I can't breathe. There's a girl standing in the doorway of his bedroom in his tee shirt. And there's no other way to interpret what I've seen than what it is, even if my heart wants to try to justify it. My eyes come back to Spence's and his are full of regret.

I immediately begin backing away. "Jo, wait. I can explain." I'm hyperventilating and I turn to run and tears burn my eyes. He chases me and grabs my arm. "Jo, wait."

I spin around and yank my arm from his grip. "Fuck you, Spence." My words are full of venom and he can't hold my gaze.

"I'm so sorry. I was pissed and sad and went to the bar. I got drunk. I'm sorry. I thought you didn't love me. It hurt so bad. She doesn't mean anything. I love you, Jo."

"I said I needed more time, Spence. And you couldn't even give me twenty-four fucking hours?! But, I guess you were right; you said I'd get hurt. That you weren't a good guy. This must be some kind of record for you, huh? Two girls in one night?" I start to walk away and Spence grabs me and kisses me. I don't even realize I've slapped him until I feel the sting in my hand.

My words are cold and full of acid. "Get the fuck away from me. Don't follow me. Don't call me. Go to hell, Spence."

I pull out my phone and call Ruby. She meets me at my house and I ask her to drive, because I am truly crying now and can't see through my tears.

CHAPTER TWENTY-SEVEN

SPENCE — DECEMBER

During the two weeks following Jo's departure, I stayed black out drunk. I didn't eat, I didn't shower. I called and texted and when my texts started being returned as undeliverable, I knew she'd blocked me. I'd held out some minuscule ounce of hope that she'd hear the tears in my voice, the pleading and anguish I felt at the pain I'd caused, and she'd at least pick up the phone. Not so I could explain, because there wasn't any excuses I could offer to make this right, but simply so I could hear her voice.

I returned to school and somehow managed to barely pull C's in my classes, much to my amazement. I lost weight and drank too much and kept checking Jo's social media profiles to see if she ever posted anything, but there was nothing.

I wanted to see how she was, to check up on her, but I couldn't ask Nick, because I couldn't face him and the pain I'd caused his daughter. She must have not told him what happened, because he never looked at me any different. And I can't ask Jay for obvious reasons and I refuse to ask Ruby, because she and I hate each other already.

Nick said Jo was sick and wouldn't be coming home for Christmas, but I knew it was because of me. I knew if I wasn't here, she would be, but the pain of her not being here didn't hurt any less.

I was packing up some stuff to head back to school the day after Christmas, and just happened to look at my bookshelf to see if there were any school books I was forgetting. And I saw something that wasn't there before, something I'd missed. *The Time Traveler's Wife.* My heart stopped, because I didn't know where it came from, but I knew it was Jo's. She must have left it and my Mom put it away after I'd left for school in August.

My hand shook as I pulled the book from the shelf. And it was like it had just happened all over again and I sobbed. I opened the book and saw her note and I wanted to be sick. *I want to relive all the memories with you. However we can. -Jo*

I truly wanted to die in that moment. I know the human body can endure so much pain. The body finds a way to process it through the nerve endings and it sends signals to the brain. Cuts and scraps and broken bones mend over time and the pain is gone. But when the pain is not physical, but damn sure still feels as though you've been stabbed in the gut and the knife has been twisted to reveal a gaping, sucking wound that won't close, what do you do then?

And maybe, it's because I want to forget for a moment. Maybe I want to pretend I'm back in May, when Jo first handed me the book. When everything was perfect. When we were perfect. So I open it and begin again, to read Clare and Henry's story.

I don't devour it like I did the first time, anxious to finish it so I could talk about it with her. I take my time over the next several days, savoring it, feeling it, basking in the story of a beautiful and flawed love. I turn a page toward the middle of the book and see a slip of paper and my heart lurches, thinking maybe Jo wrote a note. But when I flip it over, it's something else entirely.

All the breath leaves my body and my heart bangs against my chest and I don't know anything anymore. And as much as I want think this is some cruel joke or something other than what it is, my eyes catch on the name at the top. *J. Greene.* It's dated for the day before Jo and I shared our final night. The night I fucked it up so royally, there's nothing I can ever do to set it right. Because you can't unring a bell.

Not a joke. Not a trick. Only a very clear image of a baby. *Was she coming to tell me that morning?*

The only thought I have is that I have to talk to Jo. I can't call or text her, she won't get them. I can only go to her. I go into my room and shove clothes and toiletries in my backpack and the book and photo. I can't ask Jay or Nick where her dorm is, they won't know. And then, because I don't have a choice, I'm jogging to Ruby's and I'm thankful to see her car in the driveway. I bang on the door, praying it's her who answers and not her parents.

An eternity later, the door opens and Ruby stands, her hands on her hips. "What do you want?"

"Ruby, I know you hate me, and I know you're going to give me shit, but I need to know how to get to Jo's dorm. I know you took her back to school in August."

"Haven't you done enough to her, Spence?" she asks, her tone full of loathing.

"Yes, but I have to see her. It's important. Please."

"You didn't see her, Spence. How she was the whole way to Miami. She was inconsolable. She cried until she was sick and then she kept crying. You broke her."

My chest heaves as I'm reminded of the pain I caused Jo. "You don't think I know that? You don't think I know I can't ever make this right with her? It's not about that. I have to talk to her. Do you really think I would've come here if I had a choice? Please, Ruby."

My voice breaks at the last and tears fill my eyes and Ruby's expression falters. She must see something in my face that says more than my words have thus far. She closes her eyes as if she's thinking and finally blows out a breath. "Spencer Jackson, so help me, if you make me regret this, I will kill you. How Jo ever saw you for anything other than what you truly are, I'll never know."

She pulls her phone out of her pocket and looks at me. "What's your number, I'll text you the address."

"Thank you, Ruby. Oh, my God, thank you." I give her my number and sure enough, a moment later, a text comes through with a Miami address.

———

The two hour flight takes years off my life and I can only hope and pray the whole way to Jo's dorm she doesn't slam the door in my face. That she'll talk to me. That she's even there.

I walk up to the dorm building and try to think about how I'm going to get into the building, because there's a swipe pad for a key card and I know the door will be locked. But it doesn't stop me from trying the door anyway, just to confirm my suspicion. I sit outside and pray someone will go in or come out so I can get to her.

And, thankfully, I don't have to wait too long. Twenty minutes later, a short redhead comes out of the building and I slip in. Now that I'm in the building, my stomach knots up with nerves and fear. Hope wants to rise, but I don't dare let it take root, because I know there is no hope. Not for *us*. But maybe for the tiny being that we created, there can be.

For a solid five minutes, I stand outside her room, not

daring to knock. Not daring to know one way or the other if she'll talk to me. But then, when I can't stand the not knowing more than the knowing, I raise my hand and knock on the door.

I blow out a deep breath and hear her on the other side as she opens the door. "Belinda, I already told you, I don't want —." And she stops. And now, I think Nick and Jay saying she was sick may be true, because her color is wrong and her eyes are hollow and empty with dark circles. Her hair hangs long and dull, with none of the healthy sheen it had over the summer. She gathers her bulky sweater and wraps it tight around her, and folds her arms across her chest. "What are you doing here?"

Even her voice sounds hollow and I'm instantly worried about her, because she doesn't look well. "I needed to see you, Jo."

"I don't want to see you, Spence. You wasted a trip. Go home. She goes to shut door and I stick my foot in to stop it.

"Were you even going to tell me? About the baby?" My tone is pleading and her grip on the door lessens. She glances around as if she's worried someone will hear and pulls me into the room and shuts the door. I step toward her and she backs across the room, trying to keep distance between us.

"What does it matter?"

"What do you mean, *what does it matter*? You're pregnant? You didn't tell me? I found the ultrasound picture, Jo. In the book."

Her tone is lifeless after a long moment. "I came to tell you that morning."

My stomach drop at the memory. "I wish you would've."

She laughs, but there is no humor in it. "You were a little busy, Spence. How is she, by the way; the blonde? Or do you even remember what color her hair was?"

"Shit, Jo. I told you, I was hurt that I told you I loved you and you wouldn't even hear me. She didn't mean anything to me. I didn't even know her name."

She scoffs. "You're good at that. Fucking girls when you don't know their name."

Despite how I'm trying to recover something—anything— here, I can't keep the anger out of my voice in response to her accusation. "That's not fair, Jo. You lied that night. It wasn't for lack of trying that I didn't know your name."

"Whatever, Spence. I can't do this. I need you to leave. Please go."

"No. Not until we talk about the baby. Figure out what we need to do. How far along are you?"

Her eyes close and she hugs her arms tighter around her middle. "There is no baby, Spence. Not anymore."

Her words hit me and I can't breathe. "Jo, what did you do? We would've figured it out."

Unshed tears sit in her eyes. "You and I both have dreams that don't have room for a baby. I wasn't going to take that away from you."

My chest is tight with sudden loss. "That's not fair. You didn't even talk to me. We could've decided together what to do. I could've been with you when..." I swallow, my voice strained. "You wouldn't have had to be alone."

She looks away. "It doesn't matter now. It's over. Go home, Spence."

She crosses the room and opens the door and holds it. I see now there's nothing I can do. Nothing I can say. No way to salvage any semblance of who Jo and I were to one another.

I feel as though I've been completely gutted. I turn to leave, but stop in front of her, my voice low and filled with sorrow. "I loved you, Jo. I still love you. I'm so sorry I messed us up. I would have wanted it with you. We would've made it work. Our dreams could've made room for this."

A single tear rolls down her cheek, but her voice is steady. "I guess we'll never know, will we?"

PART TWO

PRESENT DAY

CHAPTER TWENTY-EIGHT

JO

After Spence had come to see me at school and I knew he thought I'd had an abortion, I let him believe it, and I didn't see him again. I would go home at Christmas, but conveniently miss the block party every year. I stayed in Florida after undergrad and took a job with a daily in Fort Myers and did a column on crime in the area.

I tried to move on and date, but I feel like damaged goods at this point. My pain over Spence's betrayal and the loss of the baby cut me so deep, it still hasn't scarred over. So I don't do more than hookup randomly. I don't do relationships. I don't do commitment. I don't pretend I'm okay in any sense of the word, even eight years later.

And maybe it's because I never told anyone. I've lived with these losses all on my own for all this time, and I can't help but think of the irony of Spence's Sisyphus tattoo. Because these days, it's me pushing my grief boulder up the hill, only to have to start again every morning without progress.

Jay and Delia got married and I'm thankful they chose to do a simple civil ceremony while they were visiting her mother before she passed. So, I was glad I didn't have to see Spence and pretend I was fine.

Then a couple of years later, they welcomed baby Zoey into the world and it was as if the wound of my pregnancy and the loss were opened afresh and when I held her, I couldn't keep from sobbing. I think they thought it was because I was so happy, but in reality, it was because I was so angry and jealous.

After that, things for me unraveled. I started to drink more and although I've always liked to drink, it became something I needed versus something I wanted. And my performance at work slipped and they presented me with an ultimatum: get help or get out. So I went to in-patient rehab and was forced, for the first time in my life, to face everything; from my mom, to Spence, to the baby.

My counselor advised me to start keeping a journal and write down everything I was feeling, especially after we'd have a session. So I did. And even after I left the rehab and quit drinking, I still saw the counselor to help me make sense of everything.

I wrote in the journals for two years, every thought and feeling I had regarding pretty much every pivotal and mundane moment of my life. And then, I put them away. Didn't touch them or read them, until I was packing to move to a new job in Jacksonville two years later.

I'd almost forgotten about them. But as I reread what amounted to the whole of my life, I realized it read like something out of fiction; drama, love, loss, pain.

So, I turned it into a manuscript, thinking no one would actually read it and it would only be for me and the way I wished things had turned out, because the ending I concocted, was vastly different than the truth.

I changed names, dates, locations, professions. Jo and Spence became Hailey and Wes. Blue and green eyes turned to brown and gray. Blonde and brunette hair turned to red and black. Christmas became the Forth of July. Florida became California and Daytona became Santa Monica. A writer turned into a nurse, a doctor became a musician. And he wasn't a brother's best friend, he was just the boy who lived down the street who she'd known her whole life. Really, I changed any kind of identifying detail that could tell a reader who the story was truly about, unless you lived it. And, honestly, that would only be Spence and me, and maybe Dad and Ruby for parts of it. And I doubted after all these years, he'd even know I'd written it.

When *Bittersweet Summer* was auctioned, it fetched a high enough advance for me to be able to put a down payment on a condo at the beach. My only condition for the book tour, was that I start at my dad's store. It was touted as a coming-of-age new adult romance and was well received by both critics and advance readers alike. And that should have brought me some happiness, but it felt hollow.

Because, if I'm honest with myself, I haven't been happy since the summer I shared with Spence. And no amount of career advancement or accolades or empty sex has come close to the euphoria I felt when I was with him. And I realized as I held our son's tiny body that I had indeed loved Spence, because, otherwise, his betrayal wouldn't have hurt so much. As much as I've tried to stop, I still love him, even after all these years. It makes no sense, but I guess love doesn't care about silly things like sense.

When I did the press for the book, they asked me where I got the idea for the story, I'd tell them a Taylor Swift song took root in my mind and it grew from there. And I've gotten so good at telling the story, the lie slipping off my tongue easily, no one can tell that I touch the small tattoo on the inside of my right wrist when I say the words.

And now, I sit at a table in my father's bookstore where I've seen numerous authors sign books and smile and take photos with fans. I've requested I don't do a reading, simply because I know no matter what passage of the book I choose to read, I'm unable to do so without emotion creeping into my voice, even after subsequent rereads to myself. I hate it, but I don't have alcohol to numb the sharp edges anymore, so I choose to do what I can to limit my own pain.

The crowd is good, and the line is backed out the door and around the building. I sign books and talk to customers and ask them if they want it inscribed with any specific note. And after about an hour, I don't see their faces anymore, I simply glance up and smile before returning my attention back to the book.

Dad comes over several times to check on me and make sure I have a bottle of water. And then, although I knew there was a chance he'd show, I never truly thought he would. I thought after what happened and what he believed I did, he'd hate me and I could understand if that was the case, because I'd hated him a little for his betrayal even if I've forgiven him for it.

He walks in and it's like no time has passed. Except now, we're both older and his hair is shorter and he's dressed nicer, like the doctor he is. And my heart is not prepared, because in spite of everything and all the years that have passed, my body remembers his and when he comes closer, it yearns for his, in a way I've never been able to understand for over fifteen years. And it's a feeling I've never been able to replicate in all the men that have come after him; in spite of how badly I tried to fill the void that Spence and *he* left.

Then, suddenly, I'm cursing myself for even having written the book, because I know if he's here, it means he'll read it, because when I give him a book, he reads it. And I long for those simple days when I would give him a book and he'd read while I'd lay on his chest and he'd read a passage aloud he found particularly interesting or poignant.

And I don't know if I'm ready for him to read my thoughts and know of my love for him. Because he'll know what was true since he lived it, too. And granted, this is only my part of things, but still, he'll know. I don't know if I can stand the thought of him learning how I wish things had worked out, even if certain things couldn't have been changed.

But, in all these years, I've gotten extremely good at schooling my expression. I'm so good at pretending to be happy, only the most constant observer would be able to see the cracks in the façade. So, when he walks up with *Bittersweet Summer* in his hand, I smile and don't let on that I'm dying inside.

CHAPTER TWENTY-NINE

SPENCE

When I left Miami and learned what Jo had done, I became angry. And not the type of angry that makes you want to rage at the sky and tear your clothes. And although I've always had a bit of a temper, this was a whole new type of anger and impotent rage at what I felt like was ripped from me, even though I didn't have a right to feel that way.

I've never been one to fault a woman over their right to choose. It's not my place. But I honestly thought Jo would have spoken with me before she made such a permanent decision. The whole flight home and for many months after, I stared at the ultrasound image and wondered who this little person would have become if they were given the chance. And it just seems so unfair they weren't.

And part of me wanted to hate her for what she'd done, but I've never been able to hate her. I still loved her in spite of it. I can only hope and pray the reason she did what she felt like she needed to do was not precipitated by what *I* did. Because, if that's the case, it feels like it's out of spite, and that somehow just feels even worse.

But I never got to ask her. When I got back, I threw myself into school and then my internship and residency before moving back home to join a practice. And although most of my patients are elderly, I love it. I love taking care of them and listening to them. Because sometimes, they need someone to lend an ear more than prescribe a pill and I'm happy to be someone they can share their stories with and take care of them.

In my final year of residency, I met Lily. And for the first time since Jo, I found myself smiling and laughing again. We were together for almost a year and she was fun and beautiful, but there was something missing. I'd read a book, as I've done more often over the past several years, and she'd read it as well, but she couldn't discuss it with me and she didn't challenge me intellectually. And when she told me she loved me, I couldn't say it back, because deep down, it's still Jo.

It's never stopped being Jo since that Christmas. And part of me hates her because I can't find happiness without wondering what she's doing and what she's reading at any given time. And that's not fair to anyone else, least of all me.

In spite of everything, I still love her. No matter how many woman I've been with since, I've never been able to find one who gets under my skin like she has. I've never been able to dig out from under the wanting of her. And it's not just the sex with her I miss, although I don't fit with anyone the way I did with her, like her body was made for mine, two pieces of the same puzzle. It's her laugh and her smile and her mind and her heart. I miss every inch of her entire being.

I'll be in bed with a woman and go to pull her close after sex and long to smell that coconut vanilla lotion on her skin. And when I don't, my heart aches. Because while they may fill the physical void for a short period of time, no one else has been

able to take up space in my life like her. And I realize it's probably not healthy, but I can't help it.

And so, a few months ago, when Nick came to see me as a
new patient, he mentioned Jo had published and would be
starting her book tour at his store. And God help me if my heart
didn't all but stop at the mention of her name. I've not asked
about her and Nick doesn't offer, and although I think he still
probably doesn't know what I did, he must know things went
south between Jo and me.

I remembered the promise I'd made to her all those years
ago when we were in Daytona and because I couldn't bear not
to keep it, I came. But moreover, I couldn't bear not getting to
see her while she was so close. So, even though I wasn't the first
in line to buy her book, I came as soon as I could to the signing.

She doesn't see me right off, so I simply watch her. Her hair
is shorter, just below her chin and wavy, and colored beyond its
normal chestnut brown. Her makeup is tastefully done and she
looks casually elegant in the sweater and blazer she wears. She
doesn't have on glasses and she says something to a customer
and laughs, but the laugh is wrong somehow; not the bubbly,
carefree laugh of someone who's truly happy. And my heart
aches.

And then, like they would always do when we were in the
same area during our time together, her gaze finds mine. And
there's no malice or anger in her eyes, but her smile doesn't
reach them, in spite of her best efforts. It makes me wonder if
she even truly smiles anymore, and the closer I get to the table, I
watch her body language. When a customer says something,
she glances up, but her gaze doesn't connect with theirs and
I've seen her happy enough, even in the short time we were
together to know that she's not.

Is it only because I'm here, or is it more than that? I notice
she doesn't wear a ring, so I can't help but think she's

unattached and a sliver of an inkling of hope sputters some-where deep within me. And I think maybe, in spite of every-thing that's passed between us and all the water under the bridge, could we try again? I realize this thought is absurd, but honestly, I'd settle for a fucking conversation. Because God, how I've even missed the sound of her voice like I'd miss a limb.

As I walk up to the table, Jo tucks her hair behind her right ear and I see she has a small tattoo on the inside of her wrist, but I can't make it out. Her throat bobs with a swallow, and then she smiles and again, it doesn't reach her eyes fully and I want to ask if she's okay. But, instead, I hand my book over to her. "Spence. I didn't know if you'd come," she replies as she takes it.

I look into her blue eyes, which, without the forced smile, are sad. And it's not a sad that's temporary, like a mood. It's the kind of sad borne from years of it. I know, because I see it in my own eyes most days. I clear my throat to loosen the tightness that's settled. "I promised I would. Your dad told me and he's very proud of you. I can't wait to read it."

Something flinches in her face. It's so subtle, I almost don't see it, but now that I have, I can't help but think it has some-thing to do with me reading the book.

"Thank you for coming." She looks down at the book and signs the first page.

Before I know it, I find myself asking, "How long are you in town?"

She's caught off guard, because I know she wasn't expecting me to ask her any questions or anything. But she says, "I leave tomorrow afternoon."

And I'm instantly thrown back to the time when all we had was one night. I nod. "Would you have time to catch up, maybe get a drink before you leave?" I'm unable to hide the hope in my voice and I'm not sure if I want her to hear it or not. But she's here and I'm here and I can't not ask her to get together.

She bites her bottom lip and her hand grips her Sharpie tighter. "I can't get drinks." My face falls and know it truly is over. But a second later, she says, "I can do coffee. Are you free this evening?"

I nod, hope surging within me again. "Sure. Anytime."

She asks, "Has your number changed?"

I shake my head. "No." I want so badly to tell her I kept it on the off chance she would call or text at some point and couldn't bring myself to change it. But that would make me sound pathetic and I'm sure I don't need any help looking pathetic at this moment. I'm sure it's all over me and I could care less. Especially if it means I get to talk to Jo.

"Okay. Can I get in touch with you when I wrap up here? I'm not sure how late this will go."

"Of course. I understand. Whenever time at all is fine, Jo."

She inhales at my use of her name, as though she hasn't heard "Jo" in a while.

"All right. I'll text you."

I nod and step out of the line to pay for my book. Nick tries to wave away my money and I give him a stern look. "Nick, you're going to take my money. I take enough of yours at the office, so it's like a fair trade, okay?"

He gives me a wide grin and then grows serious. "You get to talk to Joanna?" I blow out a breath and nod. He asks, "Are y'all getting together?"

"Coffee later."

He smiles. "She's staying at the house tonight, in case you need to find her."

I get the feeling Nick is trying to meddle and I wonder how Jo would feel about that. "Does Jo know I bought my parents' house?" My parents decided to retire to North Carolina last year and I bought the house, simply because it's a great house and I've always loved it.

Nick shakes his head. "Nope. I don't get to talk to her much. She's pretty quiet anymore."

"Okay. Well, thanks, Nick. I'll talk to you later." I walk out to my car and take the book and open it. I don't want to read it just yet, because this is a book I want to be able to devote my full attention to. I really only want to read the first page. I run my fingers along the title and her name on the cover. It fills me with such joy for her, that she's done something she's always wanted to. As I open the book and flip through the pages, I come across the dedication and see two.

S - *Sometimes I wonder what it would have been like in the daylight.*
AN - *You'll be with me always. No matter who comes after you.*

My breath catches when I read the first line. Because I'd told Jo all those years ago I wanted to be able to love her in the daylight and I can't help but think she's referring to that. Especially with the "S".

But the second one, I have no way of knowing what that one means. A lover? A friend? I have no clue. The thought of her having a serious relationship hurts. I never thought she'd be single forever, and I wouldn't want that for her, but I still have always hoped she'd be it for me. Whoever "AN" is, they must've left a mark on her.

CHAPTER THIRTY

JO

I'm more than ready to be done with the signing, simply because of the energy I've had to expel to keep up the professional, chipper demeanor has taken a toll. I dread seeing Spence; I don't know why I agreed to go get coffee with him. It's not going to be a good idea, I already know that. But where he's concerned, has it ever been a good idea? Not likely.

By eight, the bookstore is closing and Dad comes over to me. "Sweetie, your signing was tremendous. You should be so proud of yourself, I know I am. I can't wait to go home and read your book."

The thought of my father reading my book sends me into a panic. "No, you don't want to read it. Really."

He looks offended. "I most certainly do. My daughter is a published author. When I recommend it to people, I want to be able to tell them how much I loved it."

"Daddy, trust me, it's not your kind of book. I can write you a synopsis if you want."

"Nonsense. I will read it. You know I read all the new releases that come in."

I know he's being truthful, but the thought of him reading what amounts to my intimate details with Spence terrifies me. Even if some of the details are fictionalized, the parts where Spence and I made love aren't. And again, I curse myself for even writing this book. Dad puts his arm around my shoulder. "Now, what do you have planned for this evening?"

I falter for a moment, because I don't know if I should tell him I'm meeting with Spence, but then I figure what's the point of lying, I'm too old to sneak around. "I'm having coffee with Spence."

His eyes light up. "Wonderful. It'll be good for y'all to catch up." I nod slowly and Dad says, "Well, go on, get out of here. I'll see you tomorrow."

"Daddy, I'll be back home later."

He waves me away. "Don't even worry about it. I'll see you tomorrow. Have a good time with Spencer." My dad is acting very strange and I don't know what to think, but I take a deep breath and text Spence.

> Jo: I'm free if you are. Where would you like to meet?

Not even a minute later, I get a response.

> Spence: Leda's? They have pie also.

It must be a newer place, because I don't know it. I look at my father who is still sorting inventory. "Daddy? Where is Leda's? Is it a new place?"

He thinks for a moment. "Oh, it's just right down the block. You can walk from here." He gestures in the apparent direction of the restaurant.

> Jo: Okay. I'll be there in just a few.

I stop by my rental car and slip out of the blazer I've worn all day. Without it, I feel a bit more casual. I sit in the driver's seat and swipe on some lipstick, hoping it will give me a bit of confidence and I say a silent prayer I'll be able to sit with Spence and talk and not say something that might hurt him more than he thinks I already have.

I walk the two blocks down to the pie shop and through the window, I see Spence already sitting at a table. And because he's looking at a menu, I take a moment to watch him without fear he'll see. He's still beautiful and my heart aches for him. And I know it was risky with the dedication in the book, because as soon as he reads it, he'll know it's for him. But I can't help but wonder how he'll feel when he reads the rest of it. When he does, will he still hate me?

I place one foot in front of the other and finally walk into the shop. When the bell over the door chimes, he turns and our eyes meet and same as it always does, my body reacts, even if I don't want it to. My heart begins to race and my mouth goes dry, but I keep moving forward until I'm at the table.

He stands as I come closer and doesn't sit until I do and I'm reminded he's always been a gentleman. He asks, "Do you still take your coffee black?"

I nod. "Do you still take your cream and sugar with a drop of coffee?"

He smiles. "Actually, I can drink it black now. Residency sort of beat the need for extras out of me. I'll take my caffein anyway I can get it now."

I can't help but smile at that. A moment later, a server brings two mugs and a carafe of coffee over to us. "Can I get y'all some pie? Our special tonight is blueberry."

I consider. "Sure. Can I get it with a scoop of vanilla ice cream, please?"

Spence says, "I'll have the same."

She smiles and nods and walks away.

I take my coffee and sip it. It's strong and bitter and unfortunately, not tequila. I glance up at Spence. "I'm sorry I couldn't do drinks."

He shakes his head. "Honestly, I was shocked you agreed to meet me at all, so I wasn't going to be choosy about what we did."

I bite my lip. "I don't drink anymore. I try to be up front with people about it so they're not surprised."

"Oh, okay. I understand. How long?"

"Four years."

"Wow, Jo. That's awesome." His tone is genuine and I realize how much I've missed having someone who *knows* me.

I look down. "So, how's medicine these days? Dad mentioned you've taken him on as a patient?"

He smiles. "It's great. Your dad is the same as he always was. Except for tonight, anyway."

"You mean how excited he was to hear we were meeting up? Yeah, I caught that as well."

Spence smiles and then sobers again. "You never told him, did you?"

I know without asking what he's referring to and I look down and shake my head. "No. I didn't want that to impact your relationship with him. He's always loved you; he didn't need to know."

His thumb brushes the side of his mug. "I didn't deserve your kindness in that, but I appreciate it." Then he smiles. "You wrote a book, Jo. I'm so proud of you. Truly."

I flush under his compliment. "You don't have to read it. Really."

"Is there a reason you don't want me to?" His tone is serious and I don't know how to respond, so I simply shrug. He holds my gaze. "I've looked forward to reading something you've written for over eight years. Of course I want to read it. How long is your book tour?"

I blow out a breath. "Forty cities in thirty days. It's a tight schedule. A lot of them will be two-a-days. I'm already exhausted, but I guess that's part of it, right?"

He nods. "Right. How are the reviews so far?"

"I try not to read them, otherwise, I get in my own head about stuff. But the ARC reader reviews were positive, and I tend to trust those more than traditional critics."

"ARC readers?"

"Sorry, publishing term. Advanced Reader Copy. Folks who read a book before it's published to get some final feedback and generate buzz before its final printing."

"Wow. I didn't know that was thing. Cool. That's great."

The server brings our pie and I nibble mine as I look at him. "You've cut your hair."

He give me a lopsided grin. "You, too."

I nod. "Yeah, apparently, you have to look the part, too, as a writer."

"Well, it suits you."

"You too, Spence."

He smiles. "So what else has been going on with you? Married, kids?"

My chest tightens at the mention of kids and my hand reflexively goes to my tattoo. "No. You?"

"No. You think you will?"

I shrug. "Who knows?"

He looks at me, truly looks at me and I don't know how to withstand his gaze. "You look sad, Jo."

"I'm fine."

"No, you're not."

My breath hitches. "Sure I am." But even to my own ears,

my voice is hollow, so I know he's not convinced and I hate that even after all this time, he still *sees* me.

"Jo, you've never been one to lie to me. Why start now? When you smile, it doesn't reach your eyes. You try to make it look like it does and most people might not notice, but I know you. I see how sad you are; how deep it goes."

I think to myself that a lie of omission is still a lie, and so, I've lied to him for eight years by letting him believe I did something I didn't. I sigh. "It is what it is. What does it matter?"

Spence's eyes soften. "Jo, really?"

I sip my coffee. "What?" And my tone is exasperated. Because I'm tired and I don't want to hash all this out and drag out eight years of baggage over coffee.

"It matters. It's always mattered. All of it."

My jaw clenches and I can't look at him. But then, I slump in my chair. "Did it, Spence? Really?"

"Yes, Jo. Always."

I blow out a breath and can't help but feel like this was a mistake. Because over the past eight years, I've been able to pretend. And with him, once he finally saw me, I never could. "I should go."

He reaches his hand across the table, but catches himself before he touches me. His eyes are pleading. "Please stay. Eight years and I finally see you, I'm not ready to watch you leave again yet."

I can't bring myself to stand, even though I should, because I, too, don't want to leave him again so soon. I worry my bottom lip with my teeth and tuck my hair behind my ear and his eye flits to my tattoo. I jerk my hand down and pull my sleeve to cover it. "What's with the ink, Jo?"

I shrug. "It's nothing."

"Can I see? Is it related to your book?"

A hot flush fills my entire body. I should have worn a

bracelet or something to hide it. I can't talk about this. Not now. Maybe not ever. I swallow. "It's just an acronym to remind me of a little mantra."

He nods, but his expression tells me he's not buying my explanation. "Okay."

I try to think of something to bring us to a safer topic. "How are your parents?"

"Good. They retired and moved to North Carolina last year."

"Did they sell the house?"

He nods. "Yeah."

"Wow, I didn't know. Do you still play the piano?"

His eyes flash with something, but it's so quick, I can't tell what the emotion is. "No."

The check comes and I reach for it, but he beats me to it. "I invited you." I nod and sip the last of my coffee. "Jo?" Spence's voice is soft and I look up at him. "How long since you were happy?"

It's such a loaded question and I know I can't tell the truth, but if I lie, he'll know that, too. So, instead, I don't answer it at all. "I should go, Spence. Thanks for the pie and coffee. It was good to see you." I rise and turn to leave. I hear him scrambling behind me to pay. I know he's going to come after me, and I try to steel myself to not turn around when he calls my name. A few seconds after I get out of the restaurant, the chime over the door sounds his exit.

I don't stop and just keep walking toward my car. His shoes pound on the pavement as he hurries to catch up with me. He gets to my car at the same time I do and blocks the door. "Jo. Don't run away again, please. Talk to me."

"What is there to talk about, Spence?"

"I don't know, the past eight years? How much I thought about you? How much I missed you? How, even when I met someone who was wonderful, she still wasn't you, so it didn't work."

The idea of him being with someone else hurts more than I want to admit. The idea that he couldn't be happy again after what happened with us hurts even more. Because I always assumed he'd eventually settle down with a great woman and have a wonderful life. But to hear him tell me he still thought about me and missed me? What am I supposed to do with that? I'm barely hanging on by a fucking thread as it is.

"It didn't work with us, Spence. Or, have you forgotten? Too much has happened." My words come out forced and angry but he doesn't look away. His gaze simply drills into mine and God, those green eyes. Why do they have to be so fucking green and perfect and still exactly the same as they always were?

"I know I screwed up and I'll never forgive myself for it. I was so stupid. And I swore to myself if I ever saw you again, I'd at least shoot my shot. Because as hard as I tried to move on and be happy, I'm not. Not since that summer."

My breath catches and I shake my head, not wanting to hear his words. "Spence, don't."

Hell, at this point, if it would work to make him stop talking, I'd shove my fingers in my ears and hum simply so I didn't have to hear him.

He takes my hand and although I should pull it away, I don't. I've never been able to resist his touch, even as casual as this. And even now, all these years later, it's familiar and his hand is warm and large and his thumb brushes the back of my hand and he still looks into my eyes, his expression searching. "You can't tell me you're happy. You can't even tell me the last time you were happy. If you knew, you'd be able to answer the question, Jo."

"It doesn't matter, Spence. It's not going to change

anything." My voice sounds weak, even to myself, and I know if I continue to listen to him, that wall I've built around all my feelings for him is going to crumble. But I can't make myself move.

He leans his forehead against mine. And I want to curse my body for still allowing me to stand here and not back away. "It can, though," he says, his voice full of hope and promise and makes my heart twist painfully in my chest. "I know we're older, but we're still us. And you can't tell me you don't still want me. I can read you like a fucking book, Jo. And yes, I know how corny that sounds."

I can't help but smile in spite of my best efforts to remain unaffected by him but then I sober and shake my head. "Spence, it's never been about wanting or not wanting. I've always wanted you." No truer words have ever left my mouth. For fifteen years, he's the only man I've wanted. In spite of the passing of time and the countless men I used in an attempt to forget him over the last eight years, he is unforgettable.

"Then want me, even if it's only for tonight." His hands cup my face and I can't pull away. He leans down and whispers in my ear. His breath is hot on my skin and it sends a shiver down my spine. "When was the last time someone made love to you, Jo? The way I can? The way you need? I can make you feel good. Let me." He brushes a light kiss down my neck and my knees go watery. Desire I've not felt in so many years pools low in my belly and my resolve is currently doing it's best to resemble a single soldier standing against an oncoming wave of an entire army of enemy combatants. It's a fruitless and point-less stand and everyone knows the single soldeir will go down, but they're currently doing their level best to withstand the onslaught.

Spence says, "Come home with me, Jo. Let me take care of you."

"It's a bad idea, Spence." My argument is feeble and we both know it.

He looks into my eyes again, and this time, they're not searching or hopeful, but determined. "When hasn't it been a bad idea for us to be together? It wasn't a good idea when we hooked up at the block party. It sure as shit wasn't a good idea when we started things in Daytona. But it was the best bad idea ever. And I'd have a million more times of bad ideas with you if you'd let me."

I want to tell him if I gave in and let myself go to that place, I don't know if I could tell him goodbye again, because the last time nearly did me in. Older I may be, but I'm still the same girl who left his house with my heart in a million pieces. Except now, it's more than simply his betrayal that broke me. It was that and the baby and me letting him think I had an abortion and everything that's happened since. And now I'm too damaged.

I don't say any of it, though, because he's kissing me and it's as if all the years fall away and I'm nineteen again. At first, the kiss it tentative, but when I don't pull away, he deepens it and for the first time tonight, I reach for him. And like it always does when we kiss, the wanting beats out the good sense and I don't stop it, even though I should. My hands twist into the front of his shirt and bring him closer, wanting to close the distance of eight years and drive out so much pain.

When he pulls away, my chest is heaving. He brushes his thumb along my bottom lip, his own lips pulled into a knowing smile. "See, Jo, we've still got it. Come home with me?"

I should say no. I should push him away and climb into my car and drive far, far away, because this will not end well. And even knowing that, my body betrays me yet again and I find myself nodding. He doesn't waste a single second and tugs me toward a Jeep. "Spence, I can drive myself."

He doesn't stop walking, my hand in his. "If I let you do that, you'll talk yourself out of it. You'll tell yourself you can't, even though I know you want to. Even though you know you want to. And I can't let you do that, Jo."

He's not wrong. I probably would. But I don't stop him opening his car door to let me enter. I don't stop him when he comes around to get behind the wheel and starts the car. I don't stop him when he pulls away. I don't stop him when we turn down a familiar road and pull in at his parents' house. "I thought you said they sold the house?"

He jumps out of the Jeep and runs around to my side. It's as if he thinks if he leaves me for more than a split second, I'll vanish or run away. And honestly, I'm not sure I won't. "They did, to me."

"Oh." He pulls me toward the front door, which feels strange, because I've come in this way before, but never with him. And it's a bit surreal, because for years and years I always imagined what it would have been like for him to bring me home as more than just Joey. But, as a girlfriend, a fiancée, a wife. But now, I'm just me again, with no label or title. Never a label. Not with Spence, not with anyone else.

When we get inside, I'm struck with how different it is from when his parents lived here. It used to be a stuffy and proper place, where you felt like you couldn't just sit anywhere. But now, it's inviting and he's opened up the room and removed some of the walls. Where once, they were a warm beige, they're a cool gray. The floors used to be stark white carpet that I never could understand how his mother was able to keep that bright. Now, they're a dark gray, weathered wood. The furniture used to be oversized and floral with wooden end tables. They've been replaced with soft, black leather couches and glass and metal tables.

The kitchen, which was once French country, is now something very modern, with sleek stainless appliances and smooth black cabinets and granite countertops.

"Wow, Spence, this is amazing. It doesn't even look like the same house."

He looks around. "Yeah, Mom's taste and mine were quite a bit different. I had some help with the design from the husband of one of the nurses at work, but I'm happy with it."

My eyes drift over to the bar area and like it always does anymore, my mouth waters at the sight of the bottle of tequila. He sees me looking. "I'm sorry, Jo. I can take those away if I need to."

I shake my head. "No, I'm fine. I'll always want it, even if I don't give in. I'm around it a lot. It's hard to avoid. And it's not like I can stop going out to restaurants and parties simply because there might be alcohol. But I've worked too hard to go back to that. And I need it now, instead of just wanting it because it tastes good or using it to take the edge off. So, I just don't."

I huff out a soft laugh. "Although, if I'm honest, tonight was the first time in a long time I actually really felt like I needed a drink. I'm thankful Dad doesn't have any at the house, or I might have given in."

"Why, Jo?" He looks down. "Because of me? Because you didn't want to see me?"

My heart aches at hearing the pain in his voice and I'm quick to reassure him and I tell him the truth. Because apparently, I'm all out of bravado. "Spence, it's not that I didn't want to see you. I wanted to see you so badly, but I didn't know if you'd come and I didn't know if you'd even speak to me after the way we... left things."

He closes the distance between us, his body inches from mine. He lifts my chin and forces me to look at him. "Jo, I've never stopped loving you. Even when I hated you a little. But the love has always been stronger and I couldn't not see you. To find out if you're okay. To look into your eyes."

My breath catches, both at his words and the knowledge that he truly did hate me because of what he thinks happened. "I don't do love. It's not in me anymore, Spence. I'm too broken."

He closes his eyes and leans into me, our foreheads pressed together. "I'm so sorry I broke us. I'm so sorry I hurt you. I want to try again, Jo. Can we do that?"

I shrug. "I don't know. What if it's too late? We had our perfect summer and then it ended. And maybe that's how it should stay. Maybe that's how it was always supposed to be. Because I can't live through that again. I barely survived it last time."

"I know. And I know that's my fault. I've never forgiven myself for that. But can you honestly say we couldn't be happy? I know you haven't been happy in a long time, I saw it in your eyes. I can tell you've gotten really good at hiding it, but you can't hide it from me. I know what you look like when you're truly happy, Jo. And we were happy."

"Spence, I don't know how to be happy. I don't know if I even can be again. I think that part of me has wasted away and shriveled up."

"Well, let me bring it back; make it grow. Let me love you, Jo. I can carry the love for the both of us until you can again. I want to do that."

Part of me wants to give in and say yes, because saying yes to him has never been the hard part. But at this point in my life, I've gotten so used to holding on to this pain, I use it like a shield and don't know how to drop it; not even for him. "And what if I never can? That's not a life I'd want for you. You deserve so much more than that; you deserve everything."

"Jo, half a life with you would be better than any life without you at all. I would take whatever you could give me."

"Plus, how would it even work? I live in Florida. You live here. We have our own lives, jobs."

He grips my face. "I told you years ago, we could always make it work. And at one time, you wrote you wanted to relive all the memories, however we could. Did you mean it?" His voice is so earnest and still hopeful and I want so badly to believe him. I want to pretend I'm still carefree and optimistic, but that's not me anymore.

"I did. But I was so young. And when you're young, things are infinitely easier, because you don't know how the world really works. I do now, though. It's not as simple as all that anymore."

"It can be. I'm not tied down to anything in my life. The only thing I've wanted since that Christmas was you. I would've done anything to keep you. I would have transferred schools to be close to you. I'd set this house on fire right now and walk away if you'd let me follow you." His throat moves as he swallows. "And I know I said you should just want me for tonight, but I don't want that, Jo. It won't be enough for me, I already know that. One night has never been enough for me. I'm not stupid; I know you have obligations. Stay with me tonight and take your tour to think about things. I'm serious, I love you. I want you. I want everything with you. Whatever that means for you."

He takes a deep breath, as if he's in pain and my heart twists seeing it. "And if you can't love me; if you can't be with me, I will respect that and walk away and we'll be friends. I'd rather be your friend and see you happy, even if it's not with me. Even if there's someone else in your future. Because I miss that more than everything else. You became my friend, Jo, not just my lover and I miss you so much.

"I miss our talks. I miss discussing books and movies and music with you and I miss you calling me on my bullshit because I've never been able to pretend with you. You know me too well."

Tears come to my eyes. "Spence, there's never been anyone else. There's only ever been you. Since I was twelve, there's only been you."

"Then have me. Have all of me. Forever. Make love to me. Wake up with me in the morning. Let me hold you and show you love. I swear I'll never hurt you again. I'll spend the rest of my life making up for the hurt I caused you. I'd rather cut out my own heart than break yours again. I love you, Jo."

My heart aches with longing. For fifteen years, I've wanted him tell me these things and I hear them now when I couldn't before, and I wonder if my hesitation is so I can punish myself for what happened. But I still want him. That hasn't stopped. And maybe, I can give myself tonight. For one night, can I drop my guard and let him back in? "Spence, I can't make any promises. I can't say that you'll still want me in a month when you find out how damaged I truly am. Because you might remember what it was like for me to be happy, but I don't know that I do. It's been so long."

His eyes search mine and I can see there's hope and love and desire in his. "Then just promise me tonight. That'll be enough."

But it won't. Not for either of us. It's never been enough. But I can pretend it will be. "Okay. Tonight."

CHAPTER THIRTY-ONE

SPENCE

"Okay. Tonight." And those words send joy straight to my heart. Because even if all I get is this one night; if it has to last the rest of my life, I can carry it with me forever.

I lower my mouth to hers and she leans into me and wraps her arms around my waist and it's like coming home. She pulls me closer and deepens our kiss and moans into my mouth. The sound and all the memories that come flooding back hearing it, send a jolt of electric, hot need to my balls.

Needing her in my bed right the fuck now, thank you, I break our kiss and tug her down the hall to my bedroom. I turn on the bedside lamp and I watch as Jo sees the book that sits on my nightstand. *The Time Traveler's Wife*. It's so well worn, the cover is ragged and torn in several places. She picks it up, her expression one of awe. "You still have this?"

I nod. "Yeah. I've read it so many times, I've probably got it memorized at this point. I read it when I miss you."

Her face crumbles. "Spence, I'm sorry for everything that happened. If I could change things, I would. I've thought about what it would be like to go back so many times. What I would do differently."

I lift her face to look at me. Her blue eyes, always so bright and open, are dull and sad. I want so badly to see the light in them again. "It's okay. I would do a lot differently, too. But you're here now. And if all we have is tonight; if I only get to call you mine for tonight, I want to make it count. Can we do that?"

She nods and kisses me. And it's hungry and greedy, as if she's been starved for years and is sitting in front of a table laden with food. She works the buttons of my shirt and kisses down my neck and my heart pounds so loudly in my chest, I know there's no way she can't hear it. Once she's got all the buttons undone, she pushes my shirt off my shoulders and looks at me and trails her fingers down my chest and abs. "You're still so beautiful; I'll never get over it. When I was just a girl, I wanted so badly to run my finger down your chest. And then, when you were mine for a bit, I thought for sure it had to be some kind of cruel dream after it was all over."

"I'm still yours, Jo. I never stopped being yours."

Her breath hitches and she swallows, obviously still appre-hensive and probably fearful. But when her eyes meet mine again, they're full of want. "Then make me yours, Spence. Even if it's only for tonight, make love to me and make me forget everything. Make me feel like we used to."

Needing no further encouragement, I bring my hand up and grip the hair at the base of her scalp and lower my mouth to her ear. My voice is husky and filled with heat. "You are mine, Jo. Even if you're not with me, you're mine—no one else's. Even if you move on and find someone else, you'll still be mine. Because you were mine first."

Her chest heave against me and I crash my mouth against hers. To show her that she is, indeed, mine. To leave my love on her like a brand. That no matter who comes after me, they'll never be able to love her or please her like I can.

She grips my waist and her nails dig into my hips. I pull back from her to tug her sweater over her head and it's as if any hesitation that remained is gone and a switch has flipped. And for a moment, we're all hands trying to get each other undressed, as if it's a race to see who get there first, our efforts interrupted with sporadic kisses until we're both naked.

I hold her at arm's length to take her in. Her body is different than it was several years ago; more mature. Her breasts are fuller, her hips wider. "God, Jo, you're gorgeous. I've missed the sight of you."

I let my hands graze her breasts as I run them down her body and she shivers. I pull her to me and just the feel of her body against mine makes my cock ache and jerk with need.

She pulls away from me to turn down the bed and climb in, tugging me with her. And we just lie facing one another for a moment, wrapped in each other's arms and I bury my face in her neck and find that she still wears the coconut vanilla lotion that I can only associate with her and I breathe her in. "I've missed this."

I feel her nod against me as she runs her fingers through my hair. "Me, too."

I raise up to look into her eyes and hope she sees how much I love her and with the way the light hits her eyes, I see that doesn't have contacts in. "You're not wearing contacts?"

She shakes her head. "Lasik. I got tired of the glasses and contacts." She smiles. "It's kind of nice to be able to see all the time."

"Well, I bet that is a bit more convenient."

"Yeah, I don't have to remember to take them out anymore and don't have to choose whether I want to look like Joey or Jo anymore. It's just me, Joanna."

"Is that what everyone calls you now?"

She nods. "Yeah, except for Jay, of course. I'll always be Joey to him. I hadn't heard anyone call me Jo since college until I saw you. It was strange."

"I thought you might have been caught off guard by that. It seemed that way, anyway."

"I was. And simply the fact you were there. I knew you had promised, but I didn't honestly think you'd show. I tried not to even let myself hope, because it hurt too much."

I brush a kiss across her lips. "I was just hoping you didn't look at me with hate in your eyes. I knew you'd stay professional because of where we were, but I was praying that your eyes weren't cold when you looked at me. But the sadness I saw gutted me, babe."

She closes her eyes. "You're the only person that saw it. Dad doesn't see it. And I knew you did and I hated you did."

"I always see you. I know I didn't for so many years, but once I saw how beautiful and smart and funny you were, I couldn't unsee all the amazing things about you. And I didn't want to." I blow out a breath. "I told Jay about us."

Her mouth falls open in shock. "What? When?"

"A few years ago. He was visiting and we went out. He's visited a few times a year since he and Delia moved to Cookeville and we go out when he's in town. He noticed I was different. That I didn't flirt anymore, that I didn't look at women anymore. He asked me what had changed and I told him I was in love with you. I told him everything. Well, almost everything. I didn't tell him about the block party, because that's ours. And I didn't tell him about the baby, because if you wanted anyone to know, you'd tell them. But I told him I'd screwed it up. I told him I understood if he couldn't forgive me, but that I still loved you. I told him he'd always be my friend, but if I ever got the chance to be with you again, and you took me back, you'd be the one I'd choose if he gave me an ultimatum."

"What did he say?"

"He was quiet for a long time. He said he'd always wondered if he'd imagined the way I was looking at you that day at the bar, that he saw me watching you. So, I guess I wasn't very covert that day." I huff a soft laugh.

"Was he angry? Because he's never said anything to me."

"I don't know if I'd call it angry. I think he was hurt we didn't tell him. He said if we had, he probably would've gotten over it if we truly loved each other. And then I got so pissed because we snuck around and set an end date on us that summer because we wanted to protect him and apparently, it didn't even matter. And, then, of course, my brain kept going through all the 'what ifs' and I was so sad and angry about how everything ended."

"Spence, I'm so sorry. I thought it was better for you two if we hid it, because I know how important your friendship with him was. And I didn't want you to get hurt."

I nod. "I know. It was easy to justify it back then. I only wish I had known when we started things how important you were going to be to me, because I would have told him from the get go."

"Yeah, hindsight is a bitch. That's for sure," she says, her tone wistful.

"Yep." I take her chin in my hand and force her to look at me so she'll hear my words. "Jo, I'm overjoyed you're here. And I know, for now, it's only for tonight, but I need you to know that I love you and I'll wait for you. I'll wait until you feel like you're whole enough to be with me, if that's what you want. I'll wait fifty years if I have to. Because you're it for me.

"I never thought I would be the guy who falls in love. I

didn't know I could, until you. You made me want be a someone you deserved. You made me want forever."

Tears shimmer in her eyes but she doesn't say anything. I don't know if it's because she doesn't want to tell me she loves me, even though I know she does. I don't know if it's because she truly feels like she can't want us anymore; that everything that's happened has irreparably damaged her beyond what she thinks I'll still love. So I simply kiss her and she pulls me to her and it's sweet and tender until it's deeper and making up for all the time we've lost over the last eight years.

I trail my mouth down her neck to her breasts and when my tongue flicks over her nipple, she gasps and grips my shoulders as she arches her back. I've longed to hear those little sounds she makes during sex for so long, it almost makes me want to weep with happiness to hear them now. I kiss my way down her stomach and over her hips and pause just before I dip my head between her thighs and simply take her in. "Still so fucking perfect. Do you know how many times I've dreamed about your pussy? What I'd do if I ever got you under me again?"

She huffs a laugh and lets her knees fall open. "Why don't you show me? I've had some dreams, too, you know. Why don't you see if you can live up to them."

My heart lifts hearing the playful lilt in her voice and I smile as I kiss and lick and nip my way up her inner thigh, the sweet, earthy smell of her hitting me and making my mouth water. Sliding my thumbs up her pussy, I spread her open and lick a line up the same path, unable to hold back a groan as the taste of her hits my tongue. Jo gasps and her hips buck as I suck her clit into my mouth.

I work it in deliberate circles until she's panting and her fingers are tangled in my hair, the grip almost painful. She grinds her face against me and I thrust my fingers into her and fuck her with my mouth and hand in synchronized, steady rhythm until a few minutes later, she cries out and she's clenching down around my fingers as she orgasms.

She's breathing hard but smiling when I come back up and I roll over to my nightstand and open the drawer and pull out a condom and take a second to put it on before returning to her. She pulls me between her thighs and I hold her face in my hand and look into her eyes as I enter her. Her lips part with an audible exhale, but she doesn't look away. And for that, I'm thankful, because I never want to stop looking into her eyes for the rest of my life.

We move together, slow and languid, both of us seemingly wanting it to last as long as possible. And for a while, we simply enjoy how well we fit together and being back in this familiar embrace. She pulls my mouth to hers and rocks her hips and I drive deeper into her. I whisper words of love and praise and I'll never get over how her soft moans punctuate my every thrust and how it feels exactly the same as it used to. And it makes me see all the more that there was never and will never be anyone but her for me.

Soon, our movements become more desperate, more greedy, and after a few minutes, we're both covered in sweat. I'm already feeling the tale-tell tingle settling in at the base of my spine signaling I'm not going to be able to last much longer and I reach down between us to work her clit and Jo's breathing becomes ragged. Her eyes close and her mouth opens in a near soundless O as she comes undone. I'll never get used to it, as long as I live, the sight of her taking her pleasure. Her body tenses as her climax hits her and she lets out a breathy sigh.

I finally give myself permission to let go even though I never want this to end, and several deep thrusts later, I go over and it seems like I'm never going to stop coming and my cry is a husky rasp that falls from my mouth. My abs cramp and my ears pop and I collapse into Jo, unable to support myself anymore.

When I can finally breathe again, I give her a deep kiss and roll over and climb out of bed and go into the bathroom to discard of the condom. As I come back, I see Jo's crying. I hurriedly climb back into bed next her and pull her to me. I lift her chin to look at her face. "What's wrong, Jo? Did I hurt you?"

She shakes her head. "I love you, Spence. More than you know." Her words make me soar; I've dreamt of hearing her say them for eight years. She pushes on. "But there are things you don't know. And I don't know how to tell you."

I don't know what to make of her statement, so I simply try to be supportive. "Well, you'll tell me when you're ready. It's okay. And whatever it is, we'll deal with it, all right? I promise, nothing you can say or do is going to change the fact that I love you and want to build a life with you."

"Can you promise me something?"

I brush a stray tear off her cheek with the pad of my thumb. "Of course. Anything."

She blows out a deep breath. "Can you wait to read the book until right before I come off my tour? I know it won't take you long to read it because you're such a fast reader, but there are things in the book we need to talk about."

I tense with her words, anxiety settling into my gut. "Why would we need to talk about them?"

"Spence, you'll understand when you read it, but I don't want to discuss it over the phone or through text or anything. I want to be with you in person. Can you come to Florida? There's something I need to show you and we'll need to talk. And you can decide if you still want to be with me. Because, like I said, I'm damaged. You may decide it's too much."

I'm so confused by everything she's said, but I nod. "Okay. I'll put in for a few days off at the end of your tour."

She nods. "I'm sorry I'm not the same girl you were with that Christmas, Spence. I wish every day I was. She was fun and carefree and happy, especially after you. But I'm not her and if, after all this, I'm not enough or if I'm too much, I'm okay with being your friend. Because I've missed that, too."

"Babe," I say gently but firmly, "you are never going to be too much for me and you are more than enough. You always have been. I love you, Jo."

She snuggles closer to me. "I love you, too, Spence."

***

When I wake the next morning and find Jo still in my bed, on her right side, facing me, my heart surges. Part of me honestly feared she'd leave sometime in the night. I notice her right arm is stretched out and I can finally see her tattoo. I glance at her to make sure she's still sleeping because even though she said the tattoo meant something about a mantra, I know she was lying. I look at it and see it's only two letters flanked by tiny wings. *AN.*

I don't have a clue what it can mean. Maybe she'll tell me someday.

CHAPTER THIRTY-TWO

JO

I reach out when I wake up, thinking it was all a dream and I'll be at Dad's in my old bed and I'll find empty space. Instead, I find a warm body. I peek out between barely opened lids and he's looking at me and drinking coffee. "Good morning."

I smile. "Morning. What time is it?" I sit up and take his mug and sip it.

He scoffs playfully. "That's mine, lady. Eight-thirty."

"Well, you love me, so you'll share, right?"

He kisses my bare shoulder. "That I do." He turns and brings over a second mug and lifts it to his mouth and winks at me. And I can't help but laugh. It catches me so off guard and I stop suddenly.

Spence's face registers confusion. "What?"

I shake my head. "I can't remember the last time I laughed. Honestly, I can't."

"Well, then I can't wait to make it happen again. Because you deserve to laugh, Jo." He takes my chin and lifts it. "I loved waking up next to you. I've missed that so much."

I nod. "I thought for sure when I reached for you, I would realize it was all a dream."

"Not a dream, babe. What time do you leave today? What's your next stop?"

"Nashville. I have to be there at five central, so I'll probably have to leave here by two."

He smiles. "Well, then. I have time to make you breakfast."

"You cook?" I ask, shocked.

"You'd be surprised by all the things I can do now."

"Like what?"

He looks sheepish. "I wasn't expecting follow up questions, because I don't really know how to do much more than I did the last time we were together."

I laugh and the sound is foreign, even to my own ears. "But you cook? What do you cook?"

"Lots. But how about some pancakes and bacon?"

"Perfect."

He kisses me and rises from the bed and I watch his perfect, naked body walk across the room and shake my head. Because I've missed seeing his body almost as much as I've missed his heart and mind. He slips on his underwear and pulls a tee shirt out of a drawer and puts it on.

I get out of bed and find my panties and go to his dresser and pull a tee shirt out for myself, because I don't want put my sweater from last night back on. I go into the bathroom and pee and wash my hands and look at myself in the mirror. The ever-present sadness is still there, but I must admit, it looks like it's a bit less.

I grab my coffee mug and walk out to the kitchen and see him putting strips of bacon in a skillet. I look at the interior of the house more thinking how different it looks. Seeing a book-shelf in the corner, I walk over to it and trace my fingers over the titles on the shelf. Mostly sci-fi and mystery suspense. He's also got several movies and I look at those. My eyes land on *The Martian* and I pull it out and look at it.

Arms come around me from behind and Spence kisses the side of my neck and I turn to look at him. "I thought of you when this movie came out."

He smiles. "Did you watch it?"

I nod. "Yeah. They did a pretty good job with it." I put the movie back on the shelf and turn in his arms to face him and wrap my arms around his neck. "I'm glad you came last night."

He gives me a playful smile. "Which time are your referring to? When I came to see you at the bookstore or when I *came?*"

I laugh. "Lord, help. You're supposed to be a grown up. That was a red light statement if I've ever heard one."

He brushes his thumb along my jaw. "I love hearing you laugh. Your eyes light up and it's beautiful." Pleasant heat rises in my cheeks with his compliment. He leans in and whispers in my ear. "I also love seeing you in my tee shirt and nothing else."

"Want to come and take it off of me?" I ask and wiggle my eyebrows.

"What about breakfast?"

"I'd rather skip it and go back to bed. Can you survive until I have to leave?"

He appears to think about it for half a second before jogging over to the stove to turn off the burner. I start walking back toward the bedroom and he takes my hand and practically drags me down the hallway, both of us laughing.

A couple of hours before I have to leave, I put my clothes back on from last night and go next door to get ready to leave.

Spence comes over with me to keep me company while I shower and get dressed to make the drive to Nashville.

On the way to take me back to my rental car, we're both quiet. When he parks in front of the bookstore, he pulls me in for a kiss. "Text me your address and I'll come see you when you get back from your tour."

I look down. "Promise you'll wait until right before I get home to read the book? I was serious, Spence. There are things in there I need to talk with you about."

His brows press together in confusion. "Jo, did you write us into your book? Is that why you're being so cryptic about it?"

I blow out a breath. "Parts. Some are more literal than others, and some much more fictionalized, but yeah."

He thinks for a moment and gives me a lopsided grin. "I guess we were pretty good inspiration for your book after all." I hug him and can't help but hope that after it's all said and done, he still wants to be with me. He pulls back and kisses me. "I promise. I'll probably wait until the plane ride down to read it. It'll give me something to look forward to."

I nod. "All right. I'm going to go in and say goodbye to Dad before I leave."

"I love you, Jo. Let me know when you make it to Nashville safe, okay?"

"I love you, too. I will."

CHAPTER THIRTY-THREE

SPENCE

The following month absolutely crawls. Jo's book sits on my coffee table taunting me, but I promised her I would wait to read it, so I have.

It still doesn't seem real that she's back in my life. I dreamed and hoped for eight years we'd somehow find our way back to one another. And it's almost as if no time has passed.

We talk on the phone and text and share our lives with one another again. We both agree to get tested for STDs to make sure we're in the clear and Jo tells me she got an IUD last year. And a few days after she left, I went to look at engagement rings, because I can't imagine the rest of my life without her by my side. Regardless where we end up; if she wants to stay in Florida, I'm happy to relocate. I want to be wherever she is, because she's my home.

I guessed it would take me about four hours to read her book judging by the size, so I started reading it the morning I was scheduled to see Jo. I opened it up and read the dedication again and smiled knowing that one was for me. When I reread the second one, I was struck with the memory of Jo's tattoo.

AN. I still have no clue what it means, or who it is, but maybe Jo will tell me at some point.

The book is from the perspective of a young woman named Hailey. It starts when she's a young girl and her mother abandons her family and she and her father and sister are left devastated and wondering why. And I know this part Jo must have pulled straight from her life and I'm saddened to read how she felt about her mother's leaving.

As she grows, Hailey becomes acquainted with a boy down the street named Wes and when they're in middle school, she begins to develop feelings for him. He's a popular basketball player who dates all the popular girls, but doesn't see the bookish, shy, sweet girl who's crushed on him for years.

That is, until they come home from college and he doesn't recognize her. She pretends to be someone else to draw him in and seduce him. I can't help but laugh at how Jo wrote our "meeting" and then later, when she describes their first time having sex, my heart races with how she remembers it. It's insight into her mind and heart and almost feels as though I'm reading a personal diary. And I know Jo said some parts of this book were based on us, but this is almost exactly as it happened. I can't help but wonder what else is just as it happened? *What about our break up? And the baby?*

I glance at my phone and realize I've got to go to get on the plane. I stick a slip of paper in the book and put it in my bag, along with the ring box. I only pray Jo says yes when I ask her to marry me.

While I'm waiting for my plane's boarding to be called, I continue reading. Jo's writing is compelling and emotional and *good*. I knew she was a good writer, but this is really great stuff. But I guess if you write what you know, it makes it better. Because that's exactly what Jo's done. She's changed pertinent details, but it's our story.

Her account of "Santa Monica" makes my smile with remembrance of our time in Daytona and the hot and steamy beginning we had to our relationship. Rereading our history makes me want her so much more. And I love reading her feelings and the sensations she experienced.

I laugh again when she describes how "Wes" got jealous when he and "Hailey" were at a bar and they snuck away for a super hot bathroom quickie. I think back on that time and want to recreate the memory with Jo, pronto.

My plane is called, so I stick the book back in my bag and go to board. As soon as I'm in my seat, I pull it out again and continue reading. I'm over halfway through the book and I know it's getting serious because Hailey is talking about the end of summer and how much she doesn't want it to end.

She finds out she's pregnant and I feel my chest tighten as the emotions that are described and the feelings and doubts "Hailey" feels must be exactly how Jo felt and I wish so badly she'd been able to tell me about the baby. That I hadn't fucked it up so she could've.

And when Wes sings to her and tells her he loves her, she says it back and they agree to try and stay together. *If only.* She tells him she's pregnant and although they're both terrified, they decide to put the baby up for adoption because they're both too young and want to be able to provide a good life for their baby and still be able to pursue their dreams.

Did Jo put the baby up for adoption? No, because she would have still been pregnant when I came to see her, and she wasn't. *Was she?* Maybe she was and I just couldn't tell? She didn't look pregnant, but could I have been mistaken? I keep reading.

I'm about three-quarters of the way through the book when my stomach drops and my heart lurches. "Hailey" stops feeling the baby kick when she's seven months pregnant. "Wes" is with her when they find out the baby has passed. She's induced into labor and has to deliver the baby, stillborn, at thirty-two weeks. They hold their tiny baby and see his long, perfect fingers and full lips and never get to hear him cry. They name him Asher Nathan. *AN.*

Was this what truly happened? Did Jo lose the baby? My heart wants to say she would've told me. That she wouldn't keep this from me. I try to think back on our conversation when I went to see her after Christmas and exactly what she said. Because she never came out and said that she had an abortion. *There is no baby. Not anymore. We both had dreams that didn't have room for a baby.* She just let me think she did.

I need to see Jo and find out the truth. She told me there were parts that would make me have questions. And she's right, I have so many questions. My heart hurts at the thought that if the part about the baby is true, she's dealt with this all by herself all these years. It's no wonder she thinks she's damaged. She's carried this immense weight and grief all alone. It's no wonder she's still in pain. I want to take her in my arms and tell her I still love her; that nothing has changed for me.

And because I can't make the plane fly any faster, I keep reading. Losing the baby broke Hailey and Wes. They couldn't survive the loss. *Aren't romance books supposed to have a happy ending? This is depressing, Jo.* They separate for several years and try to move on with their lives. They try to find love with other people, but a chance meeting brings them back together. *That's more like it.* And like magnets, they're drawn to one another and find that they still have all the same feelings they used to and decide to try again. It's sweet and passionate and beautiful.

The epilogue leaves things a bit open-ended in that Hailey and Wes reconcile and fall back in love, and they talk about the possibility of children, but there's not a definite answer for the reader to as whether they did or not.

When I land in Jacksonville, I can't get to my rental car fast enough. I text Jo to let her know I've landed. Moments later, she texts back that she's already at home and she'll be waiting for me.

I make the fifteen-minute drive to Jo's condo and when I get ready to knock on the door, I say a silent prayer that nothing has changed for her in the month we've been apart and I'll get answers to my questions. She opens the door and the look on her face tells me that she's not sure what to expect from me. She gestures for me to come in and I drop my bag and take her into my arms and feel the tension leave her body. I look at her and brush a stray hair from her cheek and give her a soft smile. "Hey."

"Hey," she echos. "Good flight?"

I nod. "Yeah. I had a really good book to occupy me."

At the mention of the book, her expression turns guarded. My heart pounds as I ask the question, "Jo, want to tell me really happened?" I pull away from her and take her right hand and flip it over and brush my thumb across her tattoo.

She looks down and nods slowly. "Can I get you something to drink? I would love to be able to offer you a beer or something stronger, because you might want one after I'm done, but I don't have anything."

"No, Jo. I just want the truth." She tugs me over to the sofa and we sit. I see a box on the coffee table, but I don't mention it. I take her hand and kiss the back of it, hoping to reassure her that no matter what, we're still us.

Jo blows out a breath, seeming to steel herself for the telling. "I came to talk to you that morning. I was going to tell you about the baby so we could decide what to do together. And then, well, you know what happened there." Her words are slow and deliberate and seem to require a lot of mental energy on her part.

"But I knew I'd left the book at your place and I thought any moment, you'd find the it and the ultrasound and come see me. I knew I'd blocked your number, but I thought you'd still find a way to contact me. I'm sorry I did that. I was just so mad and hurt. And when you didn't come, I was even more hurt, because I thought you'd seen the ultrasound and didn't care."

I start to speak to tell her that I came as soon as I found the book and she holds up a hand. "Let me get through this, please. I've only got the energy to get all the way through it once. If you start asking questions or interjecting, I might not make it."

I nod and she continues. "And I'd already decided I wanted to put the baby up for adoption. After I saw the ultrasound and heard his heartbeat, I couldn't terminate. If for no other reason than because he was yours. I'd realized that I loved you, because if I didn't, what you'd done wouldn't have hurt so bad. And I knew he was created in love and so, even if we couldn't raise him, he deserved a future.

"So I had begun to look into adoptive families and agencies and stuff and things were great with the pregnancy. I was able to hide it and wasn't going to tell anyone, unless you happened to show up, but I'd lost hope you would by Thanksgiving, so I tried to focus on being healthy and finding the perfect parents for the baby.

"I knew I wasn't ready to be a mom. And I wasn't going to let you give up your dreams of becoming a doctor. I knew you would have tried to do the 'right thing', but I loved you enough to not let you make that sacrifice.

"I'd told Dad I was sick and had mono and that's why I couldn't come home for Christmas, but really, it's because I was too pregnant."

Shocked, I can't help but interrupt. "You were still pregnant at Christmas?"

She swallows and blows out a slow breath. "A few days

before Christmas, he stopped kicking and I got scared and went to the hospital. I knew before they even did the ultrasound he was gone. And I gave birth on Christmas Eve. I named him Aaron for your middle name and Nicholas for my Dad. I changed it for the book, because I wanted to keep his name in my heart, but honor him nonetheless."

Her hand goes to her tattoo. "They told me that there was nothing that could've been done to prevent what happened. A knot in the umbilical cord formed in utero, and he lost oxygen."

Jo's eyes fill with tears. "He was beautiful, Spence. He had a headful of blonde hair and your long fingers."

"And your full lips?" I ask and she nods. I take a deep breath. "But you let me believe you'd had an abortion. You let me believe you'd done it to spite me. I know you never said it outright, but you know I thought that's what you'd done. All this time, that's what I thought and you let me believe it."

She looks down. "I know. When you came to see me, I was still bleeding from the delivery and in shit ton of physical pain, as well as just being so emotionally raw and devastated. And I couldn't get into it then. I hadn't even processed it all myself yet. I knew if I told you, you would've wanted to stay and comfort me and hash it out and I was still so hurt by what had happened at your house, I couldn't.

"I'm sorry. I'm so sorry, Spence. I thought it would be easier for you to hate me or be angry than to deal with what actually happened. I was okay to carry it on my own to save you the pain. I knew you'd think there was something you could've done and you would've beat yourself up and I didn't want to saddle you with it. So I took it and buried it. And no one knows."

She considers. "I'm sure Dad and Ruby and, I guess, Jay might wonder if that part is true if they read the book, but I didn't want you to have to face the pain." She closes her eyes, as if she can't look at me as she goes on. "Like I said, Spence, I'm damaged. I still carry that day with me every moment of every day. And I don't know if I can bring myself to have more children after that. So I understand if you wouldn't want me. I know you said I was enough, but I can't promise you children and I want you to have them if it's what you want. I love you too much to take that away from you. And I can't tell you that I'll be able do it. I mean, physically I'm fine, but I don't know if I can handle it emotionally.

"And I understand if you hate me for lying all these years. I'm so sorry for that." She shrugs. "I just thought if one of us had to carry it, it should be me. I loved you too much and I didn't want to derail your dreams and plans." She touches my cheek and smiles. "Because I'm so proud of you and everything you've accomplished."

I try to process everything she's said and what's happened. I'm hit with a sense of overwhelming love and compassion for her and everything she's been through. For facing all of this all by herself. And I can't help, as a doctor, but wonder if Jo's ever been diagnosed with depression, because it's clear she has it. And I have the thought that maybe she knows, but doesn't want to do anything about it to, somehow, punish herself. Even though there was nothing she could do.

I take a deep breath and look at Jo and take her hands in mine. "You shouldn't have had to face all this by yourself all these years. I would've wanted to bear that with you. Part of loving someone is letting them share your pain. I understand why you did what you did, but I wish I had known. That wasn't fair to me, Jo."

Tears burn my eyes and I do nothing to stop them. "If you had wanted to put him up for adoption, I would've supported that because it was what you wanted, but I would have been happy to raise him as well, because he was yours; because he was *ours*. I could never hate you. I love you. But I am hurt. I've wondered so many times over the years what the baby would've looked like or who it would have grown up to be, and I thought you'd stolen that away from him because you hated me so much for what I'd done. You let me think that. And it was unfair to me. Because I would have rather known the truth. I would have wanted to be with you when he was born, even if we didn't get to hear him cry, just so you wouldn't have had to face it alone. So we could hold him together and say goodbye."

Tears roll down her cheeks and I'm on the verge of sobbing. I lift her chin and force her to look at me. "I can't imagine what that was like for you. What it must have been like to be all alone and have no one who knew you and knew what you needed in that moment. And you've carried this all by yourself all these years as if it's some kind of ball and chain you've forced yourself to drag along behind you for the rest of your life.

"Someone else should've helped you bear it and it should have been me, Jo. You think you're damaged and broken, but you're not. You have to be the strongest person I've ever met. You faced your entire pregnancy alone. You had to deliver a baby who you never got to hear cry. You've carried all that sorrow all by yourself for all these years. You still managed to finish school. You went to work. You wrote a book. You did incredible things in the face of so much pain. That's not broken or damaged. That is immeasurable strength.

"But I'm here now; I don't want you to carry it all alone. Let me help you." I think about the best way to ask my next question. "Can I ask you something? As a doctor, not as me." Her brows scrunch together in confusion, but after a second, she nods. "Have you ever been diagnosed with depression?"

Jo sighs and looks down. "When I went to rehab, I had to meet with a counselor. She suggested I talk to my doctor about depression, because she suspected I had it and she couldn't prescribe medicine. But I didn't. I felt like I deserved to feel it. And so I have."

I take her face in my hands. "It's one thing to 'feel' it. It's another thing entirely to let it consume your life. To let it impact every single moment of every day. You are depressed, Jo. Clinically depressed. It won't go away on its own. Medicine will help. Because if you didn't have depression, you writing the book would've been this big cathartic thing and it would've helped you, but you're still so sad, babe. I know you are. And not to say you'd be over things by now, because I don't know how you get over losing a child that way, but the hurt would be more manageable, I'd think. Now, I can't give you any meds, but we can find you a good doctor who can help you. It won't be a miracle cure or anything, but it will help. Can we do that?"

"Okay."

"And, Jo?" She looks at me and I continue. "I love you. Nothing has changed for me. I still want you. I still want to build a life with you."

"What about children?"

"I don't need children to have a full life. I only need you. I told you, you're enough. And if that's something that never happens for us, I'll be okay. We'll get dogs." I nudge her playfully with my shoulder and she chuckles softly.

My eyes travel to the small box on the coffee table and Jo lets out a sad sigh. She takes the box and holds it in her lap. "These are some of Aaron's things. I thought you might want to see them."

My heart lurches and my breath catches. I can't speak, but instead, I nod. She blows out a steadying breath and opens it. She takes out two photos and my chest tightens as she hands them to me. "As much as I tried to memorize him, I knew I'd forget small details, so I asked them to take these. Because even then, I'd hoped someday, I'd be able to tell you about him."

I look down at the pictures and there's a tiny baby who appears to be sleeping, even though I know he's not. Jo was right; he was beautiful. And perfect. I trace my fingers along his tiny features and marvel at him—*our son.* The second photo is of Jo and him. She's pressing a kiss to his forehead and I can't hold the tears back. Because even in the photo, it's clear she's crying and I hate that she was there alone; she had to face all of this alone.

"Jo, he's beautiful." She nods and I see tears in her eyes. She puts her hand in the box and pulls out a hat, like the ones they put on newborns in hospitals. It's so impossibly tiny, it fits in the palm of my hand. I lift it to my face, hoping against hope they'll be a trace of that sweet newborn baby smell I remember from my rotation in OB-GYN during med school. But I know, after so much time, it won't be there.

The last thing she pulls from of the box is a brown leather journal. She runs her fingers across the cover. "When I got back to school and I knew for sure that I wanted to put the baby up for adoption, I started keeping a journal for him. With letters and things to him. My hope was, someday, his parents, the ones I chose for him, would tell him about me and give it to him and he'd be able to know me. And you. I wrote letters telling him how we met and fell in love, but we loved him too much to not want the best for him."

She hands the journal to me, but I don't open it. I want to be able to take my time with it. I look at Jo. "Thank you for keeping these things. For showing them to me. Can I hold on to this for a bit?"

She nods. "Of course."

I set the journal on the table and take her face in my hands. "Jo, I love you. I've loved you for years, but knowing everything you've been through, everything you've endured, I love you so much more. Your strength, your perseverance, your ability to turn your pain into something wonderful. Your book is incredible and you are such a talented writer. I loved getting to relive our memories through your eyes. Thank you for documenting all of that. It's beautiful." I brush a soft kiss across her lips and press my forehead to hers. I can't keep the smile off my face when I say, "I especially liked all the sexy bits. You made me look really good."

She huffs out a watery laugh. "I knew you'd like those."

"Yeah, I really liked the bar scene. I'd forgotten how hot it was when we were still trying to be sneaky."

She pulls back and nods. "Yeah, it was pretty hot, wasn't it?"

CHAPTER THIRTY-FOUR

JO

After telling Spence the whole story about Aaron, I was emotionally exhausted and he could tell. We ordered Chinese food and ate on the couch, but I wasn't really hungry, only tired. So he took me to bed and tucked me in and held me until I fell asleep.

When I wake up, I'm curled up next to Spence and he's still asleep. I get up and go pee and wash my hands. While I'm drying them, something on my left hand catches my eye. There's a ring on my left ring finger and my heart stops. It's gorgeous. It's a large oval diamond surrounded by a halo of tiny sapphires set in a band of white gold and the band is inlaid with diamonds. Tears fill my eyes and I turn to go to Spence.

When I come out of the bathroom, he's is sitting up in bed, a mischievous smile on his face. "So, there was something I wanted to ask you, but I can't for the life of me remember what it was."

My voice comes out breathy and tears are falling down my cheeks. "Spence, are you sure? After everything? You still want me?"

He rises from the bed and comes to stand in front of me. He takes my left hand in his and brings it to his lips and kisses my palm. "Jo, I'll always want you, no matter what. I love you. I want to build a life with you, whatever that looks like. I can sell my house and we can live here, or we can keep this place for vacations and still live in Tennessee so you can be close to your dad. Whatever you want, I want. Wherever you are is where I want to be."

Spence brings his hand up to my cheek and brushes my tears away with the pad of his thumb. "I told you I'm not tied to anything in my life except you. I meant that. Marry me, Jo. Have me. Forever. Be my wife. Be happy, babe. It's okay to want to be happy. Let me help you be happy again. Please?"

His eyes are full of love and hope and for the first time in longer than I can remember, I feel a flicker of something that feels an awful lot like happiness and I nod. "Yes, Spence. I love you."

He smiles and kisses me. "Oh, thank God. I already told your dad before I left what I was going to do. I can't imagine having to go back and tell him you'd said no. He was so excited, I'd hate to break the guy's heart. I think he wanted us back together as much as I did."

I can't help but laugh. "Yeah, he thinks you're pretty okay, I guess."

A bit later, after we've had our coffee and simple breakfast of scrambled eggs and toast, we sit on the sofa talking. Spence asks, "I meant to ask you last night, how do you feel like the whole tour went? I know we didn't talk about it much while you were on the road."

I smile. "It went great. It was exhausting, but good. I met a lot of women who'd been through similar situations with miscarriages and things and they said the book said a lot of things they weren't able to and it helped them."

I bite my lip. "I hadn't expected that. Everything was originally just journals I started writing after rehab and I put them away and didn't even open them again for years. When I did, it really read like a good story, so I took a chance. But knowing it might help people, makes me even more glad I did it. Because there were a lot of times I wished I hadn't."

He frowns. "Really? You wished you hadn't published?"

I nod. "Yeah, mainly out of fear. I was terrified you'd read it and hate me or be mad because it is essentially our story and I probably should have discussed it with you, but I couldn't bring myself to do it. And then I thought about my dad reading the sex parts and I almost wanted to vomit. Hopefully, he won't think that stuff was the real deal, I don't know how I'll look him in the eye if he does."

Spence laughs. "Yeah, he might be in for a surprise." His expression grows serious after a beat. "But I'm glad you did it, Jo. Reading your thoughts and feelings made me love you even more. And you painted me in a lot better light than I deserved. And, if you hadn't written and published, I don't know if we would've ever reconnected, and I wouldn't trade that for anything. Over the years, I've wanted so badly to know how you were and see you, but you never come home anymore and I always thought it was because you hated me."

I swallow and shake my head. "I never hated you, Spence. I was hurt by what you did, but I never hated you. Because after I thought about things, even if I didn't exactly understand why, I don't know, but..."

He takes my hand. "What, Jo?"

I blow out a breath and try to find the right words. "You'd never had a serious relationship before. I mean, neither had I, but I knew who you were when we started things. And I knew you'd changed; I saw it over the summer, even if I didn't know how strong your feelings were, I knew you were different. And when you sang to me and you told me you loved me, I knew that was such a huge thing for you, because it had never been you before.

"But I had just found out I was pregnant and then found out I had to go back to school way sooner than I thought I would and so, I was struggling to deal with everything. I was already so overwhelmed and then you sang to me and I knew what was coming. And I know I never said anything, but your playing and singing were so beautiful, Spence. Thank you for that. It was so special. But I couldn't process everything because I was so hormonal and emotional and overwhelmed, I could only run away.

"And I realized later how much that must have hurt you, to take such a huge risk to tell me how you felt and me not be able to hear it. So I could see why you'd want to lash out or whatever and what better way to do that than to go back to your old ways. And so, I forgave you, even if I was still hurt by the betrayal."

Spence's expression is so pained, my heart aches to see it. "Jo, I've wished so many times I could go back. I would've come to you. I would've done anything else except go to the bar that night. I was just so hurt because you were the first person I'd ever loved and I know I didn't know what you were dealing with and that made me feel even worse, because later, I understood why you ran and it made me almost sick. I hated myself so much for what I did."

I move over to his side of the couch and sit in his lap and look into his eyes. I run my hand along his jaw. "Spence, we can't go back. But I love you and I can't wait to be your wife. I can't wait for us to build a life together. I want to move forward. I don't want to dwell on the past."

The corner of my mouth curves into a smile. "You know, except maybe the really, really good parts."

He brushes a stray hair from my face and raises an eyebrow. "You know, I just read a book that had some really, really good parts. Maybe we can recreate some of those scenes."

Heat settles low in my belly as I pull Spence's face toward mine. "Yes, please." Our lips collide and it's as familiar as always with an underlying current of excitement and anticipation. It's hungry and sweet and full of love. I break our kiss to tug his tee shirt over his head and straddle him on the couch.

He wraps his arms around my waist and grips my ass, pulling me closer to him. He kisses my neck and whispers in my ear. "I've missed you so much. One night in eight years is definitely not enough. The past month was the longest thirty days of my life."

He drags my shirt over my head and lets out deep breath. "Man, I've missed these tits." I chuckle and he brings my breast to his mouth and flicks his tongue over my nipple, causing me to let out a soft gasp. He works it between his lips and wetness pools between my thighs.

I reach down behind me and stroke his dick through his shorts. "I've missed this cock."

Spence groans. "My cock's missed you, too."

I kiss him deeply and say, "Show me how much you've missed me, Spence."

"Condom?"

"I have some in my dresser." I get up and we walk to the bedroom and I open the top drawer of my dresser and pull one out and hand it to him. I shed my panties as he pulls down his boxers and rolls the condom on. I start to walk over to the bed and Spence grabs my hand, a mischievous grin on his face. "What?"

He brings me back over to the dresser and turns me to face

it. He comes up behind me brings his mouth close to my ear. "I want you to see what you look like when I fuck you. Your face is so beautiful as you take me, I want you to see it."

My breath catches and desire shoots through me. He places my hands on the dresser in front of me and nudges my legs apart. He smiles at me in the mirror and pulls my hips back and slams deep into my pussy. The breath leaves my body with a huff and my hands scramble for purchase on the smooth surface of the furniture as he thrusts into me. Our eyes connect in the mirror and it sends a jolt through me at seeing him from this angle. He smiles. "Watch you, Jo, not me."

I drag my eyes from his to me and see my breasts swing with the impact each time he drives into me. I watch as a pleasant flush creeps into my face and chest. I see my mouth open, drawing breath, and my chest heaving as my pleasure builds. Spence reaches around me and I see him working my clit in the reflection. Seeing it like this makes everything more acute. "Fuck, Spence. I'm so close." I start to come undone as I watch him make love to me. I begin to climax and watch my eyes go wide and my mouth forms the cry that leaves my throat.

Spence grips my breast as he starts to chase his own release. I watch his face in the mirror, and see it change as he grows closer to his own orgasm. His brows draw together and he takes deep breaths until after a moment, his jaw clenches as he comes with a shudder and guttural grunt.

He brushes a kiss across my shoulder blade and slaps my ass playfully as he withdraws from me and I can't help but laugh. "Well, I guess that's one way to show me you've missed me."

Spence leans down to kiss me. "Don't worry, I'll be happy to show you many more times how much I missed you. We have years to make up for."

"I look forward to it."

CHAPTER THIRTY-FIVE

SPENCE

Later in the afternoon, after we've showered and had lunch, Jo and I take a walk on the beach. It's late-spring, so the weather is good, if a bit hot. We're walking hand-in-hand and it makes me feel like we're back in Daytona when we were younger.

She asks, "How long are you in town for? I forgot to ask when you got here in all the excitement."

"I've got tonight and tomorrow night still. I guess we need to figure out what we're going to do about living arrangements. I know we've got time, but honestly, I feel like we've spent enough time apart already."

Jo chuckles. "Me, too. I've got my job, but I don't know. I like it here, but I also think it'd be nice to have this place as somewhere to come and write or get away. And I'd hate to ask you to give up your practice and my dad would be furious with me if I took away his favorite doctor." She nudges me in the ribs with her elbow playfully

I pull her into my side and kiss the top of her head. "I figured you'd leave your job at the paper so you could focus on writing what you want full-time. Your adoring public is going to want to hear what else you have to say."

She rolls her eyes. "Right. I don't know, that would be nice, but it's scary to think my whole income would depend solely on book sales. Especially when we don't know exactly how well this first one's going to do."

"Hell, babe, don't you know you're going to be marrying a highly sought after general practitioner? I have a waiting list for patients already."

She laughs. "Probably because they see you as some sort of McSteamy; their own personal sexy doctor."

I stop and pull her to me. "I'm only your sexy doctor. Everyone else gets regular old Dr. Jackson."

"You best believe it." She goes up on her toes and presses a kiss to my lips.

"But seriously, Jo, if you wanted to quit and write full-time, we could make it work. My parents paid for my school. I only have my mortgage. We'd be fine."

She looks at me, her expression shocked. "Your parents paid for your entire college and med school? I always knew your family had a little money by the cars and the way your mom dressed and the parties and stuff, but how did they swing that? That's a lot of money."

I shrug. "My dad was an early investor in Apple. And he never took his money out until I got to college. So yeah. Enough to pay for undergrad and med school."

"Shit. I never knew that. Wow. Okay. Well then, I guess I quit my job and move next door to my dad. That's going to be so weird. But, hey, at least we'll have the pool to use, right? You know how fond I am of seeing you at the pool." She gives me a mischievous grin.

"I do. Okay. Well, now that we've got that settled. Wedding?"

She sighs. "I don't know. I feel like I don't need a big wedding, but I want Dad to walk me down the aisle and you're an only child, so your parents probably want to see you get married. Sooner rather than later. And I want to take your name, but I'll keep Greene for writing. I always dreamed about being Joanna Jackson, so I'm not about to give that up."

I smile, pleased. "Sounds perfect to me. How are we going to tell everyone? Especially Jay. I know I told him about us being together all those years ago and I told him that if you'd have me back, I'd jump at the chance. But I don't want to keep it from him this time. I feel like we need to tell him soon."

She nods. "Yeah. Maybe we should call everyone today. Just get it out of the way. We can have a big party or dinner or something over the summer once I get moved. Do you have a preference for a wedding date?"

"Nope. Just so long as it's with you, I don't care when or where."

"Well, do you think your mother would help us plan it? She always throws such great parties and your parents probably have a big list of people they'll want to invite. My dad will want to have some of his friends in the book community, but other than that, I just have Dad, Jay and his family, and Ruby. Do you have a big group of people you'd want to invite?"

I consider. "Mom would probably love it if you asked her for help. Especially since you're the closest thing she'll ever have to a daughter. There may be some buddies from med school and folks from work I'd want to invite, but Jay was really the only close friend I've ever had, so not really."

Jo stops and I turn to her, confused. "What is it, babe?"

Her face lights up and I'm so buoyed by the happiness I see in her expression. "Spence, we're getting married. Oh my God. I can't believe it."

I can't help but laugh. "Well, yeah, I was there when you said yes."

She shakes her head, her face awash with amazement. "Yeah, but I'm marrying Spencer Jackson. I never would've thought when I was twelve this would be my future. I only saw how hot you were and how much I wanted you, but I never knew that you'd be this amazing, deep, intelligent man I'd want to spend the rest of my life with."

I pull her into my arms and look into her eyes. "And I'm marrying Joanna Greene, the most clever, witty, beautiful woman I've ever known. I never would've thought the mysterious girl I met at the block party would be the girl I'd want to change myself for. You made me a better man, Jo. Thank you."

She wiggles her eyebrows. "I think it was just all of the amazing sex we had. You couldn't live without it."

I chuckle. "You're not wrong about that."

I turn us to start walking back toward the condo. "In fact, I could do with some more of that amazing sex right now."

"That so? Well, you'll have to catch me first." Jo takes off running toward her building. She squeals as I chase her and when we're almost back to her door, I grab her and kiss her.

She wraps her arms around my neck and deepens the kiss and then she stops suddenly. She's looking past me and I turn to see what she's looking at. Sitting on the ground next to Jo's front door is a teenage girl. Jo and I exchange confused glances.

She steps a bit closer to the door and the girl sees us and stands and looks at Jo. "Are you Joanna Greene?"

The girl looks to be about fifteen with long, dark hair and brown eyes. She's about five-five and slender.

"Yes, how may I help you?"

The girl looks relieved. "I think you're my sister."

UNTIL FOREVER

UNTIL SERIES BOOK TWO

AUTHOR'S NOTE

Dear Reader,

If you read *Until August*, you will be familiar with the themes of Jo and Spence's story. This book will also deal with elements of miscarriage and stillbirth.

There are also themes related to alcoholism, child neglect, and abandonment discussed.

Some of these scenes and situations may be disturbing or triggering to some readers.

PART ONE

PRESENT DAY

CHAPTER ONE

JO

"Are you Joanna Greene?" the girl who stands next to my front door asks. She's average height and slim, with dark brown hair and brown eyes. She looks to be about fifteen and wears a pair of cutoff shorts, a plain black tee shirt, black Vans sneakers and has a bright yellow backpack slung over one shoulder.

Spence and I exchange confused glances, but I answer, "Yes, How may I help you?"

The girl looks relieved. "I think I'm your sister."

"I'm sorry? I don't have a sister." Spence comes up beside me and place his hand protectively on my shoulder.

The girl doesn't appear to be fazed. "Was your mother Margaret Cole?"

All the color drains from my face. I have't heard my mother's name, albeit her maiden one, since I was eleven. "Who are you?" I can't keep the suspicion out of my tone.

"Harper Cole. My mom is Maggie Cole. She's your mom, right?"

"Maggie hasn't been my mom since I was eleven. How did

you find me? What do you want?" I know my voice sounds strained, but there's nothing I can do to stop it.

Spence interjects, "Jo, maybe we should take this some- where besides the hallway? The coffee shop, maybe?"

Probably smart. I don't want to bring a stranger into my home, even one claiming to be family. I look at the girl— Harper. "Would you like to go get coffee? We can talk. Although, I don't know how I can help if this has anything to do with Maggie."

Harper says, "This isn't about my mom. I mean, not really. But yeah, coffee sounds good."

I gesture for her to follow and Spence takes my hand and pulls me to his side. He whispers in my ear, "You okay, babe?"

I sigh and shake my head. "Not in the least, Spence."

Harper pipes up behind us. "I'm not crazy or anything, I promise. I'm not here to murder you or extort you or anything like that."

"Well, that's a plus, I guess." I look up at Spence and he gives me a lopsided grin.

We walk the two blocks to a coffee shop and I sit at a table. Spence asks Harper, "What can I get for you?"

She considers. "A green tea?"

He nods and walks away to order our drinks and I examine Harper's face. And I guess in a certain light, I could see a resemblance to me, but Jay and I both have our mother's blue eyes. This girl has brown eyes and my dad has gray eyes. "Maggie is your mother?" I confirm.

She nods. "Yes."

"And how old are you?"

"Fifteen."

I do some math, trying to think back. My mother left in the spring, when I was eleven. It's spring again and now I'm twenty-seven. I don't remember my mother being pregnant, but maybe she was? "Who's your father?"

Harper shrugs. "I don't know. My mom's never mentioned him."

Spence brings our drinks over and sits beside me, his arm draped across the back of my chair.

"Okay, so why come find me? What are you hoping to accomplish?"

"I just wanted to meet you. I don't have any other family besides my mom, and well, you know how she is."

I shake my head. "Actually, I don't. Like I said, I've not seen Maggie since I was eleven. How did you find out about me?"

"I read your book. It's great, by the way."

"Thanks, but how did my book lead you to me?"

She sips her tea. "My mom saw the name on the cover and it was as if she'd seen a ghost. She flipped to your author photo, and it was like all the color drained from her entire body. I asked her what was wrong, but she wouldn't tell me.

"Then I saw her going through a shoe box of stuff when she thought I wasn't looking and later, when she went to work, I went through it and saw some photos I'd never seen before." She opens a pocket in her backpack, pulls something out, and hands it to me. It's a photo of Jay, our mother, and me. I recognize it as the Christmas before she left. I flip it over and read the back:

Maggie, Jay, Joanna - Christmas, 2004.

I hand it back to her. "Okay, so, where are you from?"

"We live in St. Augustine. I caught a ride from a friend."

I think about the fact that my mother currently lives less than an hour from me and I haven't seen her in over fifteen years. "And how did you find me?"

"Well, once I figured out who you were, it wasn't very hard to track you down via social media. You really should be more careful with your location services. It made you super easy to find."

I sigh, suddenly freaked out, in addition to frustrated. "Thanks, I'll turn that off from now on. So, what do you want?"

"I just wanted to meet you. I never knew I had siblings. Being an only child is pretty lonely."

Spence chuckles and I shoot him a glare. "She's not wrong, Jo. It sucks being an only child sometimes. Why do you think I spent so much time with Jay at your house?"

I roll my eyes. "It sure wasn't because you were looking at me."

He laughs. "Not then."

Harper says, "Y'all are cute."

I had almost forgotten she was there and I turn back to her. "And what are you hoping to accomplish by meeting me? Money? You think because I'm published, I have some? I can't help you there." Spence squeezes my shoulder as if to remind me to stay calm.

She looks offended. "No, nothing like that. I only wanted to meet you. My mom is, well, she's not good. She drinks a lot and she's angry a lot of the time."

Spence leans forward. "Are you okay? Are you in danger?"

As upset as I am about learning that I possibly have a sister, hearing the compassion and care in Spence's voice for someone he just met makes me love him even more than I already do.

Harper shakes her head. "No, she's not violent or anything like that, she just yells a lot. I stay in my room most of the time. But since she saw your book, she's not been home and I'm worried. She's gone off on benders before, but nothing like this. She's been gone for two weeks."

"I'm sorry to hear that, but I don't know what you think I can do to help. Have you reported her missing?"

"No. If I do that, they'll call child protective services and put me in foster care and I don't want to go back into state custody."

For the first time since she showed up, I'm concerned. "*Back* into custody? You've been in foster care before?"

She looks down into her tea. "Yeah, when I was eight, for about a year."

Spence asks, "So, has your mom been going to work? Have you asked around? Maybe her friends know where she might be."

She shrugs. "She's not been to work. She works at Target, but hasn't been there since the day she left. And the only friend she has hasn't seen her, either."

I nod. "Okay, so what are you hoping I can do?"

She sighs. "Well, if report her missing, and they try to put me in foster care, I was hoping if I tell them I have a sister, they can name you as temporary guardian." My eyes go wide and she puts her hand up. "You wouldn't have to do anything. I'll still stay at my house, but this way, I don't have to go stay with a foster family. I'm fine on my own. I have a part-time job and I can make my own way, I just don't want to have to pack up and move again. My stuff gets stolen and most of the foster parents are only in it for the money and could care less about a fifteen-year-old girl. I mean, there are nice ones, but they're in the minority for teenagers. Most fosters only want to take in little kids."

Spence asks, "If they name Jo as your guardian, wouldn't they expect you to be living with her? How do you expect it to work if you're in St. Augustine? Don't they normally make surprise visits?"

Harper shakes her head. "My caseworker's cool. She knows I'm on my own a lot. She's checked on me every couple months since the first time I went into foster care. I can talk to her. She might go for it."

Spence says, "That's fraud. You can't do that."

She sighs. "Well, it's not like I have any other option, do I? I'm not going back into foster care." Anger flashes in her eyes. *Something probably happened to this girl.*

I look at Harper. "You said Maggie's gone off on benders before?"

She nods. "Yeah, but they usually only last a few days. This is the longest she's been gone."

I have the thought that maybe she read my book and the parts about her set her off. "Do you know if she read my book?" I glance knowingly at Spence.

Harper shrugs. "I don't know, maybe. Why?"

I let out a deep breath. "Because the parts in the book where Hailey's mom left; it's pretty accurate to what happened."

She blanches. "Wow, so your book was based in reality?"

"Parts of it," I confirm.

She glances between Spence and me and smirks. "Which parts?"

I don't answer, but Spence sputters his coffee and I elbow him. "That's not important. I'm not comfortable telling the authorities I'll be your guardian."

Her face falls. "Oh. Okay. Well, thanks for the tea." She starts to rise and I feel like shit. It's obvious this girl's had it rough. Upon closer inspection, her clothes, which I initially thought were stylishly distressed, are simply worn almost threadbare.

She's gathering up her things and I'm hit with guilt. *Shit.* "Harper, wait." She sits back down and looks at me, expectant. I say, "I'm going to step outside with Spence for a minute, okay? Don't go anywhere." She nods and I stand and he follows me outside. I can still see her through the window as I turn to him.

"What the actual fuck? I have a sister? Do you think she's legit?"

Spence blows out a breath. "She looks like you and Jay. She's built like you were at her age."

"I didn't know you knew what I looked like at fifteen," I deadpan.

He huffs out a laugh. "I wasn't that blind, Jo. I know you were a stick and so is she. The hair's the same and her eyes aren't the same color as yours, but the shape is right and her lips are the same as yours. Do you look like your mom?"

I shrug. "I don't know. Dad took down most of her pictures when she left. I only have a couple and I haven't looked at them in years. Maybe?" I look up at him, my expression serious. "What should I do, Spence? If she really is my sister, I don't want her to go into the system. It sounds like she had a bad go of it the last time. But I don't know this girl, what if she's a thief or something? What if she's a con?"

He shrugs. "And what if she's telling the truth? Could you live with yourself if she went into foster care and your mother never came back? She'd be in the system for another three years. If she's family, don't we need to take care of her?"

My eyes go wide and I lower my voice to a whisper. "Are you suggesting I bring this girl home with me? I don't know her. She's not a stray puppy, she's a teenager. And I don't know the first thing about what I'd need to do to take care of her."

Spence rolls his eyes. "It's not like it was so long ago that you were a teenage girl. You feed them, clothe them, make sure they don't get knocked up."

"Shit, Spence, don't even joke like that. That's not funny."

His expression is apologetic. "Sorry, babe. Bad joke, I'm sorry. How about this, we take a drive to St. Augustine, see where she lives. Maybe your mother will be back and all of this will have been for nothing. You might even reconnect with your mom."

Anger, hot and instant, wells up in me. "Maggie isn't my mom. As far as I'm concerned, my mom died when I was eleven. Maggie might be Harper's mom, but she's not mine."

Not a bit surprised or affected by my ire, Spence says, "Doesn't sound like she's much of a mom to Harper, either, Jo. Cut the kid some slack. She sounds smart. She tracked you down. She came to find you. Maybe it wouldn't be so bad for you to bring her home with you."

"Lord, help me, Spence. You and your damn superman complex. You can't help yourself, can you? You're going to be going home in a couple days and I'm going to be left here with this girl all by myself. I was planning on moving home with you in a few weeks after I turned in my notice at work. I'm not going to be able to do that if I have a teenager living with me."

He takes my face in his hands. "We'll be fine. We'll make it work. But if this girl needs help and you are her sister, we probably should help, don't you think?"

"Remind me again why I'm marrying you, when you give me harebrained advice like this?"

He smiles and brushes a kiss across my lips and leans in to whisper in my ear, "Because you love my dick and all the wonderful things it does to you."

I scoff. "You're going to owe me so much for letting you talk me into this."

CHAPTER TWO

JO

We walk back into the coffee shop and I notice Harper is reading. I expected her to be on a cell phone. "What are you reading?" I ask.

She shuts the book. "*The Invisible Life of Addie Larue.* Have you read it?"

I shake my head. "Any good?"

Harper nods. "Yeah, actually."

I look at Spence and he nods. I turn back to her. "Harper, I'm not comfortable telling the authorities you're staying with me if you're actually not. And I know you don't know me that well, but you can come stay with me until Maggie comes back. I have an extra room and you can tell your social worker I'll be your temporary guardian or whatever."

Harper shakes her head. "I don't need to stay with you. I told you, I'm fine on my own."

Spence says, "You said you have a part-time job. How do you expect to pay rent or a mortgage on only a part-time job and go to school and buy food?"

"I'll work more. I'll be fine. School's a joke anyway, I don't need to go. And besides, it's summer break, so no school right now."

"How do you expect to get into college if you don't finish high school?" he asks, incredulous.

She scoffs. "I'm not going to college. How exactly do you think I'd pay for it anyway? I'll be lucky to graduate high school."

I can already tell this is going to be a terrible idea. "Listen, Harper, I'm offering you a place to stay. You can come with me and know that you'll have a roof over your head and your stuff won't get swiped. I'm not much of a cook, but I order really good Chinese food and pizza. Or, you can take your chances with the foster system.

"Because now that I know you're my sister, I can't, in good conscience, let you go back home and live alone not knowing where your mother is. So, it's your choice. I can take you home to get some things and we can leave a note for Maggie with my information and she can call us when she comes back."

She folds her arms and seems to consider, but doesn't look convinced. I sigh. "I'm not a hard ass, Harper. I'm not your mother. If you stay with me, I'm not going to hound you. I have very few rules. You'll keep your room clean, no drugs or drinking. No guys allowed unless I'm home. Take it or leave it."

I glance at Spence and he gives me an approving smile. Harper rolls her eyes. "Fine."

I nod. "Okay. Well, let's go, I guess. I need to go back home and grab my purse."

We all rise and walk the two blocks back to my condo and Spence pulls my keys out of his pocket and hands them to me. I unlock the door and we all walk in. Harper looks around. "Wow, nice place."

I walk over to the kitchen counter and grab my purse. "Thanks, I moved in last year, after I sold my book. Do you need to use the restroom or anything before we go to your house?"

She shakes her head. "No, thanks."

"All right, well, I guess we're good to go. Spence, do you care to drive?" I make sure my front door is locked and hand the keys back to him.

"Sure, you want to take your car?"

"Yeah, unless you'd rather take your rental, what did they give you?"

"It's a Toyota Highlander, so it's bigger than your car. We can take it, if you want."

Harper asks, "Rental car? You don't live here?"

Spence shakes his head. "No, I live in Tennessee."

Her eyebrows scrunch in confusion. "But aren't you guys engaged or married? That's what the big ring is for, right?"

I nod. "Yeah, engaged, as of this morning."

She looks surprised. "Oh, wow. Congratulations."

I smile. "Thanks. We were actually coming back to call our families when we found you."

Spence says under his breath, "That was so not what we were coming back for." I don't think Harper hears, but his comment still makes me blush and I poke him in the ribs and give him a dirty look which only makes him chuckle.

We make it to Spence's rental and Harper climbs in the backseat. When we're ready to go, she gives me the address and I put it into the GPS on my phone to map it. Once we're under-way, Harper asks, "So how long have you guys been together?"

Spence and I exchange glances and I try to think of a way to explain it without making it sound too much like my book. "Well, we grew up next door to one another and Spence and my brother, Jay, were best friends. But we didn't date until I got to college. We broke up for a while and reconnected last month and here we are."

"So, like a month, then?"

Spence says, "Well, we were apart for several years, but we realized during our time away from each other that we still loved one another, so when you know, you know."

He lifts my hand and kisses the back of it and I smile.

Harper asks, "So how much of your book is your story?"

"Just certain parts. Write what you know and all that."

She nods and the rest of the trip is quiet. Once we start getting closer to Harper's house, her body language grows tense and I can tell she's hoping her mother will be there.

As we pull into her driveway and park, her face falls and she sighs. I look at the house. It's a small, gray cinderblock structure that's been decently maintained with some potted flowers on the small front stoop. Spence cuts the engine and we all exit the vehicle. Harper goes over to the mailbox and checks it. Finding nothing, she leads us to the front door and pulls a key out of a pocket of her backpack and unlocks the door.

When we get inside, it takes my eyes a moment to adjust to the dim lighting of the room. The interior of the tiny home is clean with minimal furniture. I can see into the kitchen from where I stand and there are no small appliances on the counter-tops. The floors are industrial-grade tile and the walls are white.

The living room contains one small loveseat, an end table, and table with a small television. Harper nods as I assess the space. "Yeah, I know, it's not much."

I shake my head. "This is nice, Harper. I'm guessing if Maggie's gone a lot, you're the one who keeps things up?"

She shrugs. "I'm going to grab some stuff. Can I bring some of my books and other stuff with me?"

She doesn't add, but it's understood, *in case I don't get to come back.*

I nod. "Of course. Whatever you need."

She takes off down a small hallway and Spence turns to me and says in a low voice, "Well, at least you know she's not a slob. She probably has a lot of issues with wanting to control stuff since her mother is not dependable. This is one thing she can control."

I nod and glance around the room. I notice some photos lined up on the table next to the TV and I can't stop myself from picking one up. It's of Harper and Maggie, definitely a few years old. Maggie's blue eyes—the same as mine—are bright and happy. I can't help but feel a stab of jealousy that my mother has been around and had a daughter and seemed to be happy, at least when this photo was taken.

Spence comes up beside me and puts an arm around me and kisses the side of my head. "You do look like her. You have Nick's nose and chin, but you definitely favor your mother."

I roll my eyes and set the photo back down. I look at Spence and keep my voice low. "I don't know what to make of all this. Apparently, my mother is an alcoholic, which, I guess makes sense about me, but Dad never mentioned she had any issues. He seemed as devastated as we were when she left. And Harper? Maggie had to either have been pregnant when she left or got pregnant right after she skipped out." I take a deep breath. "Spence, what if Maggie never comes back? It wouldn't be the first time she's bailed."

He turns me to him and squeezes my shoulders and levels me with his gaze. "Don't go working up scenarios in your head. I know you're really good at it, but let's be real. In all likelihood, Maggie will come back and Harper will come back home. But with all the issues your mother has, do you think that's good for Harper? It sounds like she's already had a pretty tough go of things."

I nod. "I know. Did you see her face when she talked about going back into foster care? It wasn't happy, that's for sure."

"Joanna?"

I turn to see Harper standing in the hall. "Yeah? Need some help?"

Harper says, "Well, I've got some stuff together, I just want to make sure it's not too much. Will you come tell me if I can bring this stuff, since I don't know how much room I'll have at your place."

I'm hit with a pang of sympathy for this young girl. She's trying to decide out of all of her possessions what is important enough to bring, with the possibility that she may never see the rest of it again. I nod. "Sure."

I walk down the short hall and turn into her room. It's very tidy, with a simple twin bed and dresser, a small desk, and large bookshelf filled to bursting with books. I'm taken aback. Spence comes up behind me and whispers, "I think she's got your book collection beat."

Harper has packed a large suitcase and has a laundry basket full of books. I'm surprised, because from the way she talked, I expected her to want to bring a lot more than only these items. I gesture to the suitcase and basket. "This is all you want to bring?"

She shrugs. "These are the books I haven't read yet, and these are most of my clothes, so yeah. I've already read all the ones still on the shelf, so if I lose those, I guess it's not a big deal."

I'm struck with how accepting she is that she may not be back and it saddens me. "You're more than welcome to bring more than this. You'll have plenty of space for whatever you need. We'll make it work. If you want, we can always come back and get more stuff later."

Harper smiles and I realize it's the first time I've seen her smile. It's really pretty and her brown eyes light up. "Really? Could we?"

"Sure. We'll get you settled at my place and see what else we need to get and go from there, okay?"

She nods. "Thanks."

Spence looks at her expectantly. "Are you ready? I can take that basket." He goes to lift it and grunts. "Lord, Jo. I think she's got your book collection beat in just this one basket. Damn, this is heavy."

I roll my eyes. "I guess it's good we brought along a big, strong man, huh, Harper?"

She chuckles. "I guess so."

Spence takes the basket and walks out to put it in the back of the SUV and I turn to Harper. "Is there anything you need from the rest of the house for now?"

She considers. "No. I've got everything I want that I can think of."

"Okay. Do you want to leave something for Maggie, so she can find us when she gets back? You can leave her my number."

She nods and goes over to her desk and finds a notepad and pen and hands it to me. I jot down my info and hand it back. She writes something else and grabs her suitcase and takes the notepad and lays it on the kitchen table before turning to me. "Okay, I guess that's it."

We walk out of the house and she locks the door.

CHAPTER THREE

SPENCE

I watch as Jo and Harper come out of the house and I'm struck that they do, in fact, look like sisters. Harper's hair is longer and doesn't have the natural wave Jo's does, but the color is the same chestnut brown. And their builds are the same.

This definitely was not how I saw Jo's and my day going. When we found Harper, we were going home to make love and call our families to tell them about our engagement. All that has taken a backseat, I guess.

Harper rolls her suitcase over to my rental car and I lift it into the cargo area. As we're getting ready to get into the car, we hear someone calling Harper's name. She hears it and looks around, trying to decipher the direction where it's coming from. But I see where. There's a guy who appears to be in his late teens jogging over toward us. She notices him and takes off. "Macon!"

Jo and I exchange glances and she shrugs. Harper and the guy—Macon—embrace in a hug that looks more than simply friendly. "Harper, I've been trying to get ahold of you. Where have you been?"

The kid is about five-ten, with darker skin and black hair. He wears athletic shorts and a tee shirt. Harper looks at him. "I'm sorry. My mom is M.I.A. and I found out I have a sister, and I'm going to go stay with her until Mom comes back. I'm sorry I couldn't tell you, I guess Mom didn't pay the bill, and I don't have service right now."

He grips her face. "I was worried. When are you coming back?"

Harper looks down and shrugs. "I don't know. Hopefully soon. Maybe you can come visit me."

Jo and I have been quiet this whole time, but she finally pipes up. "Harper, want to introduce us to your friend?"

Harper turns as if she's just remembering that we're here. She looks at Macon, who I'm guessing is a boyfriend by their body language. "Macon, this is my sister, Joanna, and her fiancé, Spence. This is my boyfriend, Macon Holley."

I step forward and stick my hand out to the boy. "Nice to meet you, Macon."

"Same, man." He shakes it, but not with any confidence and it irks me. It seems like kids these days aren't taught things like good handshakes or stuff like that any more. *Chill, Spence, you sound like an old man.*

He turns back to Harper. "Why do you have to leave? I already told you, you can stay with me."

Jo and I exchange glances.

Harper shakes her head. "I have to report my mom missing. I can't stay with you. They'll put me back in foster care. Joanna said she'll be my temporary guardian so I don't have to go back into the system. You know I can't do that again. I won't go back, Macon."

Macon sighs. "I know. I don't want you to do that, either. Okay. I'll come see you. Where will you be?"

Harper says, "Jacksonville."

Jo pipes up. "Harper, we should probably be going. We'll make sure your phone is working, okay? That way you guys can talk and stuff."

Harper looks back at Jo, a pained expression on her face and nods. "I'm sorry, Macon. I have to go."

They hug and he whispers something in her ear and kisses her. Jo and I wait in the car while they say their goodbyes and she turns to me. "How old do you think he is? Seventeen, eighteen?"

I shrug. "I don't know. It's hard to tell at that age. But she's only fifteen, surely they're not too serious, right?"

She looks at me and raises an eyebrow. "You remember what you were like at seventeen or eighteen?"

I shudder. "Yeah. Hopefully, he's a better guy than I was." We see Harper coming, so we stop talking. When she gets in the car, it looks like she's been crying. I look at her in the rearview mirror. "Ready?"

She nods and turns her head to stare out the window. It's a quiet ride back to Jacksonville and when we're almost to the condo, Jo gestures to a Chili's. "Let's get some supper before we go home. I haven't been to the store since I got back in town and don't have much of anything at my place."

I nod and pull in and Jo turns to Harper. "You hungry?"

She shrugs. "Not really."

We park and get out and walk in and the hostess seats us and hands us menus. A server comes to take our drink orders. I'd really like to have a beer, but order a soda out of respect for Jo. She says, "You can get a beer, Spence, it's fine. I know you'd rather have that with a burger than a soda."

I shake my head. "I'm good, babe."

Jo and Harper both order a sweet tea and once the server leaves, Harper turns to Jo. "You don't drink?"

She shakes her head. "Not for four years." She nods knowingly. Jo asks, "So, how long have you and your boyfriend been together?"

"Two years. But we've known each other since we were five and six."

I ask, "So, he's sixteen?"

She nods. "Yeah."

The server comes back a moment later with our drinks and takes our orders. We all decide to get cheeseburgers. I look at Harper after we're all alone again. "So, Harper, can I ask you something?" She shrugs, so I take it as a yes. "What made you finally decide to track Jo down? You said your mom has been gone for two weeks?"

She nods and sips her tea. She looks at Jo as if she's the one who'd asked the question. "Yeah. After I found the old photo, I looked you up on Instagram and Facebook and found your personal profile from years ago. And I went back and looked through the box and there were a lot more photos—ones of you and your brother and a man. I'm assuming your dad? Your brother looks like him. There were letters she'd written to a guy named Nick saying how sorry she was for everything that had happened and wishing she could go back and all that stuff."

Jo tenses hearing her father's name, but Harper doesn't seem to notice. I reach under the table and squeeze her knee supportively. Harper continues. "So, anyway, I realized you had to be my sister. You look too much like Mom and with the photo and letters and stuff, it wasn't that hard to put things together. And, like I said, I tracked you by your location services. It wasn't that hard to find you. Your Snapchat has your location marked."

She pales and looks at me. "Remind me to turn that off, it's creepy." She turns back to Harper and asks, 'So, have you tried to track your mom the same way you found me?"

Harper nods. "Yeah, like I told Macon, she must've stopped

paying the bill, because I can't find her location. For the past couple of years, I've made sure her location can be tracked with the 'Find my iPhone' feature, so I always knew where she was, but this time, no luck.

"I know this is probably a huge inconvenience to you. I'll try to stay out of your way. I'm not any trouble, I just really don't want to go back into care."

Jo says, "I understand. Sounds like it wasn't a picnic for you."

Harper doesn't elaborate, simply nods. Our food comes and we all eat and Jo and I are only about halfway done with our burgers when we see that Harper has cleaned her plate. I ask my, tone concerned, "Harper, when was the last time you ate? Like, more than a snack?"

She shrugs, "A couple days, maybe. I used my last paycheck to buy food, but it wasn't much, so I couldn't get much. It's mostly been peanut butter sandwiches since my mom left."

I can't help but feel anger for this girl I just met. She's only fifteen and she's obviously had to deal with things she should've never had to. "Are you still hungry, we can get you something else. Dessert?"

She shakes her head. "No, I'm good. Thank you."

Once we're done and the bill is paid, we head back to the condo. I carry the basket of books and Harper and Jo make sure they've got the rest of Harper's bags. Jo unlocks the door and shows Harper to the guest bedroom. I set the basket down on the floor next to the bookshelf. This is the room that Jo uses as an office, but there's a foldout sofa as well.

Jo gestures to the closet and dresser. "Both of those are empty; you can put your clothes there. I'll box up these books on the bookshelf so you'll have room for your own stuff. I'll grab my laptop and take it away so you can use the desk if you'd like. I'll bring some sheets and we'll get the foldout made up, okay?"

Harper nods and looks around. The room is simple, but spacious. "This is really nice."

Jo smiles. "The bathroom across the hall has plenty of soaps and shampoos and stuff under the sink. And there are new toothbrushes as well. If anything is not what you'd like, or you need anything, we can go tomorrow and you can pick out some things. Whatever you need, okay?"

Harper nods. "All right. Would it be okay if I go ahead and take a shower?"

"Sure, Spence and I can make the bed up while you're in the bathroom, that way you'll have some space when you get out. Will that work for you?"

"Yeah." Jo and I are getting ready to walk out of the room and Harper says in a low voice, "Hey, Joanna?"

Jo turns back. "Yeah?"

For the first time since we met her this afternoon, she looks shy. "Thank you for doing this. I know you don't know me and don't owe me anything, but I appreciate it."

Jo seems unsure how to respond, but nods. "Of course. You're welcome here. Make yourself at home."

We walk out and close the door to give Harper some privacy and Jo tugs me into her bedroom and shuts the door behind us. She sighs and says, her voice low, "Spence, am I really doing this? Taking in a teenage girl who I only met this afternoon?"

I sit on the bed and pull her into my lap. "Yeah, looks like it. And you're already doing a great job. She seems like a good kid, maybe just a little damaged. But you're so good with damaged people. Look at me, you turned me from a womanizing player into a perfect gentleman."

She rolls her eyes. "You were always a gentleman, even when you were a player. But, seriously, I don't know what I'm doing here. I want to call Dad and get his input. The dates could work out that Maggie was pregnant when she left us or got pregnant right after, depending on Harper's birthday. Is that why she left? Because she was pregnant? Did my dad know? I have so many questions. And where the hell is Maggie? And what if she doesn't come back?"

I blow out a breath. "I don't know, babe. We'll just have to see how things play out."

"That's easy for you to say. You're going to be back home and I'm going to be here. I don't want to be apart from you for however long this is going to take. We've already spent enough time apart. But I can't move if Harper's here. I don't know much about fostering, but I know I can't leave the state with her. So I'm here. And you're going to be home. How are we going to plan a wedding with us being seven hundred miles apart?"

I take her face in my hands and force her to look at me. "Jo, we'll be fine. We'll make it work. You can take this time to get to know Harper and maybe together, you guys can figure out where your mother is."

She kisses me and wraps her arms around my neck and presses her forehead to mine. "I wish you didn't have to go home yet. I just got you back."

I smile. "Well, we'll just have to make sure the next two nights are enough to last until we're together again. And we can always have sexy FaceTime calls, you know."

She scoffs. "I am not getting naked on FaceTime. You can forget it."

I chuckle. "Well, you can watch me get naked, then."

She huffs out a laugh. "I might be okay with that." The doors to the guest bedroom and the bathroom open and close and Jo sighs. "I guess we better go make up the foldout for her."

CHAPTER FOUR

JO

Spence and I get the foldout in my office made up for Harper and I take my laptop and all my books into my bedroom and stack them on a shelf in my closet. When Harper comes out of the bathroom, she's dressed in plaid pajama pants and a sweat shirt and goes back into her bedroom. Spence and I are sitting on the couch watching TV and I don't want to hover, but when she doesn't shut the door to the bedroom, I tell Spence I'll be right back.

I stand in the doorway to the guest room. "Knock knock."

Harper turns to me. "Hey."

"Everything okay with the shower? Any issues? I know the temperature control can be a little finicky. I meant to mention it before and forgot."

She shakes her head. "It was fine."

"Spence and I are watching TV if you'd like to join us."

She blows out a breath. "I think I'm just going to read if that's okay. I'm kinda tired."

"Sure. Of course. I did want to ask though, are you going to call your caseworker tomorrow? What will that look like, you think?" I tuck my hair behind my ear nervously. "Sorry, I'm really uniformed about this kind of thing."

Harper waves off my comment. "You're fine. Yeah, I'll call her in the morning. She'll probably want to come and do a home study just to make sure that your place is fine. Which it is, trust me. She'll file paperwork with the court naming you temporary guardian until my mom can be located or whatever. It shouldn't be too much of a headache for you."

I nod. "Okay. Well, when we get all that squared away, we can go shopping once you decide if you need anything and we can get your phone squared away. I have wifi so you can use your phone like that until we get it taken care of, if you want. The password is on the front of the fridge."

"Thanks, I will."

I step back. "Well, I'll give you some space. Spence and I will probably be going to bed soon, but if you need me, my room's just down the hall."

Harper nods and I pull the door closed so she knows she's welcome to her privacy. I go back and sit next to Spence on the couch and he pulls me into his side. "How'd it go?"

I shrug. "Fine. I don't know how to talk to a teenager. I don't know her well enough to be super casual, but I don't want to be so stiff, either."

He kisses the top of my head. "It'll get better. Did I hear her say she's going to call her caseworker tomorrow?"

I nod. "Yeah. Hopefully, if she comes over to do the home study, I'll get to talk to her without Harper around to get some insight into this whole situation. I get the feeling Harper's had to fend for herself way more than a fifteen year old should. And that makes me so angry at my mother. You know, even more than I have been since she left. Who does that? Who leaves their teenage daughter to go off and do God knows what?"

Spence sighs. "Addiction is a terrible thing. When it's that bad, the fix is the only thing that matters to them."

Tears immediately come to my eyes. "I can't even imagine it, Spence. I didn't even get to raise Aaron and see him grow up and before he was even born, I would have done anything to make sure he was okay. And my mother abandons two kids, has another one and can't even be there. It's so fucked up."

He pulls me closer to him. "I know. I don't get it either. But you're not your mother. Just the fact that you're showing up for Harper when you don't have to says that. She was right, you don't owe her anything, but you're doing what's right for her. And that already makes you better than your mother."

I look at him. "I'm sad. Take me to bed and make me feel better?"

He gives me a lopsided smile and kisses me. "Happily."

I get up and pull him with me. We walk down the hallway and I stop and knock on Harper's door and wait for her to acknowledge me before sticking my head in. She's sitting on the bed, reading. "Just wanted to let you know that Spence and I are turning in. If you get hungry or thirsty, help yourself to whatever's in the kitchen. See you in the morning."

She nods. "Okay. Goodnight, Joanna."

I pull the door closed behind me and tug Spence down toward my room and lock the door. He starts to pull me over to the bed and I jerk my head in the direction of the bathroom connected to my bedroom and he smiles.

We walk into the bathroom and I turn on the shower. He pulls me to him and kisses me deeply. "I've wanted to do that since we were on the beach earlier this afternoon."

He trails kisses down my neck and I ask, "Was that really just this afternoon? It seems like years ago with everything that's happened."

He nods and tugs my shirt over my head. "Feels like it, huh?"

"Yeah, but I don't want to talk about that anymore." I pull his face to mine. "We have time to make up for and I need this to hold me over until I see you again."

"You've got it, babe." He kisses me and I feel him unbuttoning my shorts and then a second later, they're sliding down my legs. I yank his shirt up and he pulls it over his head. My hands hurriedly loose his belt and the button on his shorts until they join mine on the floor, along with his underwear.

I kiss my way down Spence's chest and stomach and fall to my knees. I push him back against the sink and take him in my mouth. He groans and I pull back from him. "Shh. We have to be quiet. Can't let the teenager hear us."

He chuckles and mimes zipping his lips and I return to pleasuring him. I work my mouth and hand together and flick my tongue around the head of his cock. His fingers tangle in my hair and I run my free hand up his abs. Spence's breathing grows labored after a few minutes and he lets out a soft hiss through gritted teeth. "Fuck, babe. Stop."

He pulls me to my feet and unhooks my bra and tugs down my panties. We step into the shower and he presses me against the wall, the spray raining down on us. He pins me with his hips, his cock hard against me. I pull his mouth to mine, the kiss hungry and deep and it steals my breath.

Spence skims his hands up my ribs and teases my breasts, making me inhale sharply. His mouth descends to draw my nipple between his lips and I can't bite back the moan that escapes. He gives me a smirk. "Shh. Can't let the teenager hear us."

His fingers trails down my stomach to my pussy and searches out my clit, causing me to gasp. "Shit, Spence." He works it in circles and my pulse ratchets up with his movements and when he thrusts his fingers into me, my hips buck reflexively. After a few minutes, an orgasm starts to build deep in my belly. Spence covers my mouth with his as I come to stifle my moans of pleasure as my climax tears through me.

I pull my mouth from his, my breathing labored, and lean my head against the shower wall. He nudges my knees apart with his own and slides his hand around my waist and down my ass before settling it on the back of my thigh and pulling my leg up to crook it around his hip.

He slams into me and I bite down to keep from crying out with the pleasure. I go up on my toes as he drives into me and I snake one of my hands down around his waist to grip his ass, feeling it flex with his every thrust. The angle of his cock entering me causes him to rub against my clit and I already feel another release building in me. My breath is coming in soft gasps and Spence grips my chin and forces me to look at him. "Not yet, Jo. Wait for me."

I try to hold out but know I'm not going to last with the friction and his thrusts. My voice comes out in a soft whine. "I can't, Spence. Fuck." Spence slows down his thrusts and it's like throwing a bucket of ice water on my head and the need immediately ebbs in me. "Not fair, Spence."

He growls low in my ear, "I told you, not yet. You're not coming without me and I'm not done with this cunt yet." Spence continues to fuck me, his thrusts relentless and builds me back up again. And again, just before I'm able to go over into my orgasm, he lets off steam.

After a while, I lose track of time and how many times he lets me get *this* close without finishing me off. And just before I feel like I'm going to pass out from my breathing being so erratic, Spence kisses my neck and whispers in my ear. "Now, babe."

And this time, he does let me come undone and I feel it rip

through me, almost painful from being held back so long. I start to cry out and he covers my mouth with his hand to muffle the sound. My orgasm radiates out through my entire body and I try to remain standing on one leg while Spence's cock jerks within me and he slumps into me with a soft grunt. I'm light-headed and my forehead is laying on his shoulder as we recover and struggle to regulate our breathing.

When I can finally form words, I push Spence back and glare at him. "That was cruel."

He chuckles. "You said to give you something to hold you over. Something tells me you're going to remember that for a while."

I can't help but laugh. "Point taken. In that case, I guess you followed instructions." We take a few minutes to clean up and I cut off the water just as it turns frigid.

When we climb into bed and Spence pulls me into his arms, I ask, "Do you really have to leave the day after tomorrow?"

He sighs. "Yeah, unfortunately. I've got patients scheduled all day that following day. Maybe I can come back in a few weeks. I'll see what my schedule looks like."

"That's asking a lot of you. I hate to make you keep flying back and forth; it's a waste of money."

He shrugs. "We don't really have a choice, Jo. With Harper, you're kinda stuck. And it's not like you can leave her, especially after you made the point of her not being on her own."

"I know. But I still don't have to like it. I'm going to miss you. You're still here and I already miss you."

He pulls me tighter to him. "I know, babe. Me, too."

CHAPTER FIVE

JO

When I wake up, I reach for Spence and find his side of the bed empty. I look over at my alarm clock and see it's a little after seven. I sigh and get up and make the bed before walking into the bathroom to pee and brush my teeth.

I slip into a pair of jogging shorts and a teeshirt before padding into the kitchen. A pot of coffee is made, but I don't see Spence. "He said he was going for a run."

I startle and turn to see Harper sitting at the kitchen table reading. "Jesus. You scared me."

She chuckles and lifts her own coffee mug to her lips and raises an eyebrow. "I must say, well done, Joanna. That Spence is... Wow. Has he always looked like that?"

It feels weird to hear a fifteen-year-old girl talk about a man over twice her age, but I remember what it was like to be fifteen, so I simply nod. "Yeah. For as long as I've known him."

"And how long is that?"

"Since I was twelve."

"How old was he then?"

"He was sixteen."

She looks impressed. "Damn. Macon's good looking, but Spence is something else."

I pour my coffee and bring it over to the table and sit across from her. "Did you sleep well?"

"Yeah, except can I say something?"

I feel my brows go together in inquiry. "Okay."

"You may want to rethink sex in the shower, because I think the vent in your bathroom is connected to the one in my room."

I flush with embarrassment and sputter my coffee and she cracks up. "I've got headphones. I'll make sure to put them on when y'all go to bed. Sounds like you pulled a lot of your real life into your book." I struggle to breathe and Harper rolls her eyes. "Joanna, it's fine. I'm not a prude. I say, good for you."

I'm still trying to breathe when the front door opens a couple minutes later. Spence comes in, shirtless, his upper body glistening with sweat. And in spite of what Harper just called me out for, my pulse begins to race at the sight of him. He comes over to lean down and give me a kiss. I don't look at Harper and instead ask him, "Good run?"

He nods. "Yeah, I'm going to go take a shower. Want to come keep me company?"

If possible, I blush even more and Harper bursts out laughing. His expression turns confused and I just shake my head. "No, I think I'm good here. I'll start breakfast. Pancakes?"

He nods and walks back to the bedroom. I turn to Harper, finally feeling like I can speak without being flustered. "Spence goes home tomorrow, so you won't have to worry about anything. I'm sorry about all...that."

She dismisses my apology with a wave. "Don't worry about it. Mom's had tons of boyfriends. I've heard a lot of things I would've preferred not to." I can't hide the shock on my face and Harper rolls her eyes. "She's an alcoholic. Lots of late nights at bars."

My chest tightens knowing this is just one more thing Harper's had to endure because of Maggie. "I'm sorry you've been through all that, Harper, but I prefer to keep my private life private. I'll make sure to be more considerate in future."

"I said it's fine, Joanna. Let's not make it big thing. I was just giving you a hard time." After a beat she asks, "You said pancakes for breakfast?"

I nod. "Yeah, I should have the stuff to make them. I know I have a pack of bacon. You want to help?"

She looks surprised and nods. "Okay."

A bit later, once the bacon is almost done and I'm finishing up flipping the last couple of pancakes in the skillet, I see Spence come into the kitchen dressed in khaki shorts and a tee shirt. He pours himself a cup of coffee and leans against the counter and sips his mug. "Smells good in here. Jo, please tell me you have syrup. I know you don't eat it, but I can't eat my pancakes without it."

I roll my eyes. "You know I eat it on my bacon. Of course I do."

Harper's head snaps up. "You don't eat syrup on your pancakes?"

I shake my head. "No. Too sweet."

She smiles. "Me, neither."

I nod and smile. "Cool. Spence, looks like most of the syrup is all yours."

We enjoy our breakfast and Harper tells us about the current book she's reading, which sounds good. She offers to help me clean up and Spence tells us he'll do it since we cooked. I excuse myself to go get ready for the day and turn to Harper. "Have you called your caseworker yet?"

"I'll call her now. Is there a specific time you want me to see if she can come?"

I shake my head. "No, we'll be here all day, so whenever is fine."

"Okay. I'll let you know what she says."

While I'm putting on my makeup, Spence comes into the bathroom and sits on the sink. "What was all of that earlier? With Harper? You looked like you wanted to die." I glance up at the vent in the bathroom. I tug him in the bedroom and make sure the bedroom and bathroom doors are both closed. "What's with the secrecy?" he asks with a smile.

I blow out a breath and keep my voice low. "Apparently, Harper heard us in the shower last night. All of it. The vent in the bathroom is connected to the one in her bedroom."

He snorts a laugh. "Oh, shit. Oops, I guess."

"Yeah, but Spence, I apologized and told her we would be more considerate, because I don't want to broadcast my sex life to my fifteen-year-old sister. But she said it wasn't a big deal because Maggie apparently brings lots of guys home and she's heard a lot of things." My eyebrows rise suggestively.

His expression grows serious. "Wow, babe. That's terrible."

"Yeah. I really hope I get some one-on-one time with her caseworker so I can talk to her and get some information. The more I hear about Maggie, the less I like."

Spence considers. "How about this, when the social worker comes and gets settled, I'll see if Harper wants to go for a walk on the beach or to the grocery store with me. You think she would?"

I shrug. "Maybe, I don't know."

CHAPTER SIX

JO

Harper connects with her caseworker and schedules for her to come at three. I make sure the condo is picked up and the guest bathroom is clean and make a pitcher of sweet tea. I don't have a reason to be, but I'm nervous at the thought that someone is going to come in and judge my home for the suitability of housing a teenager.

And right at three, there's a knock at the door. Harper jumps off the sofa and puts her book down on the coffee table. I answer the door and see a black woman in her mid-forties, dressed in a pair of dark jeans, a white blouse and black blazer, in spite of the heat. She has a large tote bag slung over her shoulder and when her eyes connect with Harper, she smiles. I gesture for her to enter. "Hi, I'm Joanna Greene. Please come in."

She enters and shakes my hand. "Hello. I'm Cori Lipscomb, very nice to meet you. Thank you for agreeing to meet me on such short notice."

"Of course, it's not a problem at all." I gesture to Spence.

"And this is my fiancé, Spencer Jackson." They shake hands and we all sit at the kitchen table.

After we sit, Cori turns to Harper. "Harper, would you care to give Joanna and me a bit of time to ourselves to chat."

Harper doesn't seem fazed. "Sure."

Spence says to Harper, "I need to go get a few groceries and Jo said you might need a few things. Want to ride along?"

She shrugs. "Okay."

Once they're gone, and we're alone, Cori opens a large notepad, pen poised to take notes. "So, Joanna, Harper says you're her sister?"

"It appears so. We have the same mother. But I didn't find out about her until yesterday. She read my book and apparently, her mother found it and Harper found some old family photos of her and my brother and myself. She tracked me down. She's a smart girl."

Cori smiles warmly. "She really is. You said Maggie is your mother?"

I sigh. "Maggie left our family when I was eleven and I've not heard from her in sixteen years. We assumed she'd died, honestly."

She nods and makes a note on her pad. "I see. But you're willing to be Harper's legal guardian until Maggie can be located? Why would you agree to do that if you only met her yesterday?"

"I know I don't know her that well, but I know she's adamant about not returning to foster care. Can I ask why she might feel so strongly about that?"

Cori looks pained. "There was an incident with a boy at the foster home she was in for several months. He was quite a bit older than her and there may have been some inappropriate behavior."

My chest tightens and protective anger instantly surges

through me. "Inappropriate how? Are you saying she was abused? Or molested?"

Cori lays her pen down. "No, nothing like that. He was abusing animals and forced Harper to watch. But she was traumatized."

I feel a bit better, but not much. "I would imagine so. She was only eight, did she receive any kind of counseling for the trauma?"

She nods and offers me a small, reassuring smile. "Yes, of course. Now, how much has Harper told you about Maggie's absence?"

"That she hasn't seen her in two weeks, but has been afraid to report her missing because she was afraid to go back into foster care. That Maggie is an alcoholic with a tendency to bring home random men since who knows when. And that Harper has heard Maggie and these strange men having sex on many occasions. That this isn't the first time Maggie's gone off. I'm sure there's probably a lot more, but this is only day two." I can barely keep my rage for what my mother has put Harper through contained.

Cori lets out a breath. "Yes, Maggie is troubled and Harper's been on my case list for many years."

"So how does Maggie still has custody? It sounds like she's unfit."

"The courts are hesitant to remove a child from the care of its mother without cause. Maggie always goes through the necessary steps to make sure that she's able to retain custody of Harper. She loves her, she just has a hard time."

I can't help feeling like this is a load of bullshit. "Do you know anything about Harper's father? I asked Harper who he is, but she says she doesn't know."

Cori shakes her head. "No, we've never known who he was. Hasn't ever been in the picture as far as I know. You said

Maggie left your family sixteen years ago? Is there a chance that your father could be Harper's father?"

I shake my head. "I don't think so. And if my father had known Maggie was pregnant, he would have done everything in his power to make her stay. If she was pregnant, it wasn't his or he didn't know. But I also haven't called my dad to get his insight on any of this. We haven't discussed Maggie in many years."

She nods, taking in what I've told her. "Well, when Harper called me this morning, I put a call into the local police department to see if they'd picked up anyone matching Maggie's description, but they haven't, so she's still out there somewhere, hopefully."

"If they find her, will she be charged with neglect?"

"It's probable. That would be up to the district attorney."

"And what happens if Maggie doesn't come back? Legally, I mean, with Harper?"

Cori sighs. "If Maggie is not located within sixty days, the state of Florida can and will terminate her parental rights. Especially given her history."

I can't hide my shock. "Sixty days? Then what happens?"

"Harper would become a ward of the state and placed up for adoption."

I blow out a breath. "And what happens if Maggie comes back on day fifty-nine?"

"She'd mostly likely be charged with neglect, but her rights would remain intact to see if reunification would be possible. Harper would be in foster care during that time. Or, if you're willing, with you."

"I'm supposed to move. I don't have any dates set in stone, but I'm getting married. My fiancé is a doctor with a successful practice in Tennessee, where we're from. I wouldn't be able to move while Harper's in my care, correct?"

Cori shakes her head. "No. She must stay in the state of Florida. If—and I know this is probably a scary prospect—Maggie's rights were to be terminated, and you adopted Harper, she could move at that point."

I hadn't considered I'd be the one to adopt Harper if Maggie never came back, and I'm unable to hide my surprise. "Wow, I don't know. That's… Wow. That would be something I'd have to discuss with my fiancé."

The other woman nods, her expression neutral. "Of course. But I do want you to know, if Maggie doesn't return, you are considered the next of kin, so you would have the option to adopt Harper if that becomes necessary. And Harper is a wonderful girl. She's been through a lot, but she's bright and if she was encouraged, she would thrive and have a wonderful future.

"And even if Maggie does come back, which at this point, I don't know. After this long, I can't honestly say I've seen a lot of cases where the parent does come back. But if Maggie comes back, I would hope you'd stay in Harper's life to be a good influence. You seem as though you'd be a steadying presence in her life. Which for teenage girls is important."

I nod. "Yeah, I know. I have a great dad and older brother who kept me grounded." After a beat, I say, "Harper mentioned you might need to look around; make sure this is an okay place for her to live?"

Cori nods. "Yes, if that's all right. Would you care to show me where Harper will be staying?"

"Of course. Now, because everything was such short notice, I had to move some things around, but Harper's in my office, which doubles as a guest room." I walk down the hall and open the door to see Harper's left it spotless and folded up the sleeper into a sofa. I gesture to the couch. "The sofa folds out into a queen bed. Like I said, short notice."

Cori smiles. "This is perfectly adequate. You have a lovely home. Does your fiancé live here as well?"

I shake my head. "No, ma'am. He has a house in Tennessee. We'll be living there full-time once we're married. He was just coming to visit me for a few days after I came off my book tour. We hadn't seen one another in about a month. And we just got engaged yesterday, so the wedding plans are in the very early stages."

"Well, congratulations." We make our way back to the kitchen table and retake our seats. "So, here's how things will go. I'll file an emergency order of guardianship on your behalf with the state. You'll still have to complete some paperwork and you and your fiancé will both need to be fingerprinted and background checked and go through the mandatory parenting classes, but all that's only a formality. Harper is free to continue staying with you while all this is underway. If Maggie gets picked up, I'll be notified. If she contacts Harper or you, please call me at once. The police will have to be notified as well."

I nod. "Okay. So in the meantime, we do nothing?"

"Pretty much. Just sit tight. I'll leave the paperwork with you. I'm out this way a couple times a week, I can swing by and pick it up. You can go to any police department to be finger-printed. You'll want to do that as soon as possible, as well as the parenting classes."

I nod. "Of course. So, is that everything? Do you have any additional questions for me?"

Cori eyes the pitcher of tea. "Is that sweet tea? May I have a glass?"

I flush with embarrassment. "Oh, my. I'm a terrible hostess. Of course. Please forgive me." I pour her a glass and hand it over.

She thanks me and asks, "So, how long have you and your fiancé been together?"

I laugh. "It's a bit complicated. I've known him since I was twelve. He was my older brother's best friend. He came down to help me move home from college after freshman year and we got stranded for a few days in Daytona with car trouble. We got to know one another better and fell in love over the summer.

"We ended up splitting at the end of the summer because I was in Miami and he was in med school, and then we didn't see each other for eight years. But he came to my book signing last month and we realized we still had feelings for one another. And as they say, the rest is history."

Cori's eyes grow wide. "So, was it really like your book?"

"You've read my book?"

She nods. "Yes, when Harper told me your book was what lead her to you, I read it this morning. It was wonderful and moving. Was it inspired by your real life?"

"Parts," I admit. "I wrote about Maggie as well. I can't help but wonder if what I wrote may have been the catalyst for her leaving again. Maybe guilt or something?"

Cori considers. "You can't blame yourself in Maggie's leaving. She's an alcoholic. She may just be past help at this point. We can't know with these things sometimes. I hope regardless of what happens with Maggie, you'll stay in Harper's life."

I nod. "I plan on it."

CHAPTER SEVEN

SPENCE

While Harper and I are killing time and grocery shopping, I try to make small talk. "What do you think you'll do after high school? Any particular interests?"

Harper shrugs. "I like to read, but I don't know if there's anything I could do in that."

"Sure there is. There's editing, publishing, writing. Just ask Jo. She's always loved reading and from a young age, she wanted to be a writer."

"Joanna said she's known you since she was twelve."

"Yeah. She knew me better than I knew her."

"How's that possible?"

I consider, not wanting to share too much of our history with her. "Well, I was friends with Jay for years. And Jo's four years younger than us, so she was just Jay's sister until she grew up and we got to know each other better."

"So the parts in the book where Hailey had a crush on Wes for years and he never knew, is that accurate?"

I nod. "Yeah." I immediately want to change the subject, because I don't feel comfortable answering questions that might follow that one. "So, Macon? You guys have been together for two years?"

"Yeah."

"That's a long time for someone your age, isn't it?"

She shrugs. "He's my best friend. He's always been there for me when my mom goes off, he makes sure I'm okay. When Mom brings someone home, I'll usually go stay at his house just so I don't have to be there."

"How are his parents?"

"They're good. I love them. They treat me like family."

I smile. "Jo's dad has always treated me like family, too."

She looks down. "Does Joanna think that her dad is my father?"

I shrug. "I don't know. Her dad has gray eyes. She said the dates could work out, depending on your birthday, but it's unlikely."

Harper nods. "I figured it was a long shot anyway."

"Do you like staying at Jo's?"

She smiles. "Yeah, it's great. I had the best night sleep in a long time. I like having a sister. I know she didn't really want to take me in and you talked her into it. So, thanks."

"That didn't have anything to do with you. I think it probably had more to do with your mother. That part of Jo's life is still tough for her."

"Well, thanks anyway. I know y'all took a big chance having me come and stay. But I promise, I won't be any trouble."

We come to the cereal aisle. "What's your favorite?"

"I don't know, we don't really eat cereal, it's one of those luxury foods."

"Well, pick one. Whatever kind you want. And don't even think about going with some boring corn flakes or anything like that. If the box doesn't have some sort of animal or cartoon character on the front, it's not worth it."

She laughs and takes off down the aisle, examining the boxes. She comes to the Lucky Charms and looks at me. "If that's what you want, go for it." She puts the largest box in the cart and we continue gathering items.

When we get to the health aisles, I gesture to the feminine hygiene items. "You need anything that way?" Harper blushes and shakes her head. "Okay, well, if you need anything, I'm sure Jo can get you taken care of."

She just nods. "Joanna said you'll be going back to Tennessee tomorrow?"

I nod. "Yeah, I have patients I have to get back to."

She perks up. "Patients?"

"Yeah, I'm a doctor."

"Wow. That's cool that I have a doctor in the family. Good thing to have."

I chuckle. "Yeah, I guess. Most of my patients are older folks, so I don't usually get a lot of excitement in my daily work life. But that's all right, I'll leave the excitement to the ER."

I confirm there's not anything else she might need and nothing else I can think of Jo might need and we head to the checkout. While I'm loading things onto the belt, Harper asks, "Why did you become a doctor?"

I smile. "Jo thinks I have a superman complex. That I like to save people. But I like to figure out problems, too. I've always liked puzzle video games and medicine is, a lot of times, like a big puzzle to figure out, so I like it."

"Was med school hard?"

"Just long. Sometimes boring. A lot to memorize. But I enjoyed it."

"When do you think you and Joanna will get married?"

I shrug. "We've not set a date. We want it to be soon, but nothing is set in stone yet."

She nods. "And she's moving when you get married?"

"That's the plan. But as long as you need her, she'll be here. We've already talked about it."

"Do you think you guys will have kids?"

Although Jo's pretty sure she doesn't want kids after what she went through with Aaron, I decide to be vague. "We're not sure yet. We're still young, we've got plenty of time to decide that."

Harper nods. "Cool. Y'all will make good parents someday."

"Thanks. How can you tell? We don't even have a dog or anything."

"Well, it's obvious you guys love one another and if you're willing to take in a teenager you don't even know, that's next-level parenting already."

I can't help but smile. "I'll keep that in mind."

By the time we make it back to the condo and get everything carried in, the social worker and Jo are sitting at the table, laughing like old friends, which makes me feel like the meeting must have gone well.

Harper and I set the grocery bags on the counter and Cori rises from her chair. "Harper, will you walk me to my car? We can chat for a minute."

Harper looks at me. "I can help put this stuff away when I get back."

Jo waves her off. "Go ahead, we'll get it."

Cori shakes Jo's hand and then mine. "It was lovely to meet y'all. I'll be by to pick up that paperwork in a few days. You have my number if you need it, Joanna."

Jo nods. "Yes, ma'am. Thank you for coming today. Have a safe drive."

Once Cori and Harper step outside, I turn to Jo. "How did things go?"

"Good. She said that Maggie's not been picked up by the police yet or anything, so at this point, they don't know if she'll be back. But Cori said if Maggie's gone for more than sixty days, the state will terminate her parental rights and Harper will go up for adoption. And as next of kin, I'd have the option to adopt her before she's placed in the system, once I pass all the background stuff and all that."

I feel my eyes go wide. "Sixty days? That's it?"

Jo looks surprised as well. "That's what I thought. And I don't know, Spence. At this point, that's forty-five days from now. Six weeks. You and I would definitely have to talk about that. Because honestly, I can't see letting someone else who's not family take her if we can. I know that's asking a lot of you. And if that's not something you'd want, we wouldn't have to —."

I cut her off. "Jo, of course. She's your sister. She's family. If Maggie doesn't come back, we'll take care of her. Do I exactly relish the idea of parenting a teenager at the age of thirty-one, not so much, but I'd do it. I wouldn't be able to live with myself if we turned her out and someone treated her bad."

Jo breathes a sigh of relief and her eyes soften. "You are the best man, you know that?"

I shrug. "That's what you tell me. But Harper's a good kid, it seems like."

She nods. "Yeah, the social worker loves her. I don't know if she cares for Maggie so much, just based on history, but she said Harper's smart and mostly well-adjusted and in the right environment, she'd thrive."

We start putting the groceries away and I tell Jo, "When we were at the store, we'd gone down the feminine hygiene aisle and I asked if she needed anything and I think I might've embarrassed her for a second. You might want to check with her."

Jo chuckles. "Can you blame the girl? A super handsome man asks her about period supplies? Did you really expect that to go over well?"

I shrug. "I'm a doctor. It's natural. It does't bother me."

"Yeah, but to a teenage girl, that kind of stuff is so embarrassing. I'll talk with her and take her out myself if she needs anything."

Once we get everything put away, I pull Jo into my arms and lift her chin to brush a kiss across her lips. "I'm sorry I have to leave tomorrow."

She deflates and leans into me, her head on my chest. "I know. What time is your flight?"

"Early. I have to be at the airport by seven."

"That early? I don't like it. And we still haven't told everyone we're getting married. You want to tackle your parents and I'll take Dad and Jay? Although, I guess Dad probably already knows since you told him what you were up to before you left."

"We can do that." I kiss her deeply and back her up against a counter and trail kisses down her neck. "We'll have to make tonight count, Jo. It may be weeks before we see each other again."

She pulls my mouth back to hers and nods. We don't hear Harper come back into the condo until she says, "Y'all realize you have an impressionable teenager living here now, right?" Jo and I jump apart suddenly and when we both look at Harper, she has an amused expression on her face. "Don't worry, I'll wear my headphones tonight."

I look at Jo and she flushes and shakes her head.

CHAPTER EIGHT

JO

After supper, the time seems to go by too fast. I know I only have a few hours left with Spence before he goes back home and it feels like the end of that summer all over again. Even though this is nothing like that, it still feels like it will be years before I see him again.

Harper is in her room talking to Macon on the phone when Spence and I sneak off to bed. And even though I know Harper knows what we're doing, it still feels wrong to broadcast it. When we undress, it's not hurried, both of us wanting to savor what will be the last time we're together for at least a few weeks.

Our movements are slow and deliberate, his eyes never leaving mine. He enters me and I let out a soft sigh, barely louder than a whisper. And when we come, it's together, with a tear on my cheek. Spence kisses it away and reminds me that we'll be back together before we know it.

I fall asleep in his arms, but all too soon, he's waking me with a kiss to say goodbye. And when he leaves, I keep my tears held back until the door closes behind him. And although everything inside me knows he'll be back, it still feels like even if he were only gone for five minutes, it would still be too long.

I crawl back under the covers and when I wake again, it's late. Harper doesn't attempt to get me out of bed, sensing I need time. But when I roll over, I see a steaming cup of coffee and toast with jam on the nightstand and I can't help but smile at her attempt to make me feel better.

I dress and take my empty mug and plate into the kitchen and set them in the sink. She's sitting on the couch with her knees drawn up watching daytime television. I go to sit next to her on the sofa and say, "Thank you for the coffee and toast. You didn't have to do that."

She shrugs. "I know how much I miss Macon and he's only forty-five minutes away. I figure you miss Spence more."

"Well, thank you. Yeah, I do miss him. We were apart for eight years and I just got him back, so I feel like anytime without him is just too much anymore."

I look down at my hands, not sure how exactly to word my next statement. "Harper?" She switches off the TV and turns to me, her expression expectant when I bring my gaze to hers. "I'm calling my brother—*our* brother—today to tell him about Spence's and my engagement, and my dad, too. I'm also going to tell them about you, if you're okay with that. Because Jay deserves to know about you and I want to ask my dad some questions about when Maggie left. I don't know if he'll tell me anything, but I'm still going to ask." Harper nods slowly and opens her mouth to say something, but then closes it again. "What is it?" I ask.

She bites her lip. "Do you think that your dad knows who my father is?"

I shrug. "I don't know, honestly. I don't know if Maggie was pregnant when she left. I don't think I've asked, when is your birthday?"

"August fifteenth."

I do some quick calculations in my head. Maggie was already pregnant when she left us. I nod. "Yeah, she was pregnant. She left us in April."

Harper's expression is pained and she looks away. "I'm sorry I broke up your family, Joanna. If I wasn't here, Mom maybe would still be with your family."

My breath catches that she'd think any of this is her fault. I take her hand in mine and give it a squeeze. "No, honey, none of this is on you. Maggie made decisions. She's still making decisions. Addicts hurt people. It's unavoidable." I bring her face around to look at me. "I know I didn't react the greatest when you showed up. I'm really sorry about that. It didn't have anything to do with you. That was all about Maggie. I'm so glad to know I have a sister. I'm glad you're here."

"What will happen if she doesn't come back?" I see fear in her eyes for the first time since I've met her and it nearly guts me.

"She's got time to come back before any decisions have to be made. Hopefully she will and hopefully she can get some help. But no matter what, I'm here for you, okay? Now that I know you're family, you're stuck with me, kid." I nudge her with my elbow and she gives me a soft smile.

"But what about when you move back to Tennessee?"

"Spence and I have plenty of space. You're welcome to come visit us. He bought his parents' house when they retired and moved, so he still lives next door to my dad, who has a great pool. But I'm not going anywhere right now, okay?"

She nods. "Can Macon come visit today?"

"Sure. He can come for the evening, but y'all have to hang out in the living room, All right?"

"Okay. Thanks, Joanna."

"You can call me Jo or Joey, if you'd prefer. Jay calls me Joey. Spence is the only one who calls me Jo anymore, but that's what I went by in college. Joanna's more professional and my dad is really the only other person who calls me that."

"Jo. Okay. I like that." She smiles and I excuse myself to call Jay.

I go into my room and shut the door so I can have privacy. I make my bed and sit leaning against the headboard and click the FaceTime icon next to his name. As a teacher, I know he's not working, so I don't even bother to check the time. He answers after a moment. "Joey, hey. Long time, no see."

"Jay, how are you? How're Delia and Zoey?"

"They're good. We miss you. Are you coming up any this summer?"

I shrug. "I'm not sure. I'll have to see how things go. So, the reason I'm calling is to tell you a couple things. First off, I know Spence told you about us being together all those years ago. I'm sorry we hid it from you. I realize in hindsight we should've just talked with you and it would've saved us a lot of heartache."

Jay nods slowly. "Yeah. I never expected you'd be single forever, Joey. I mean, I didn't expect that you and Spence would get together and I don't know if I would have preferred that knowing him the way I do, but I noticed he was different after that summer and once I found out why, I could see he'd changed."

"Yeah, well, the thing is, he came to my book signing last month and we realized we still have feelings for one another and we're getting married." I hold my hand up so he can see the ring. "I know this seems really fast, but neither one of us was able to move on after our break up and we've both spent the last eight years still in love with each other. So we hope you'll be happy for us. It would mean a lot to us to have your blessing."

My brother blows out a breath. "Wow, Joey. Okay. Well, of course. I want you to be happy and if you and Spence are happy together, of course you have my blessing. I love you both."

I can't keep the happy tears from my eyes. "Jay, you don't know what it means to hear you say that. Thank you. I love you, too." I dab my eyes with my shirt. "There's more."

His eyes go wide. "Are you pregnant?"

"No! Nothing like that. We don't even know if we want kids. Um, wow. I don't know how to say this."

"What is it, Joey? I figured telling me about you and Spence would be the hard part. What's got you rattled?"

"We have a sister, Jay."

All the color drains from his face with his shock. "What? How's that possible?"

"Her name is Harper. She's fifteen. Maggie was pregnant when she left us. I'm almost positive she's not Dad's, but she tracked me down after she read my book. Apparently, Maggie saw my book and when she realized it was me, she freaked out.

"She's an alcoholic and abandoned Harper. She hasn't seen her in over two weeks. She said Maggie's gone off on benders before, but nothing like this. But she was afraid to report her missing because she'd have to go into foster care. And, Jay, this girl has been through a lot. She's already been in foster care in the past. She's a sweet girl and way more mature than she should be for her age. But I'm her temporary guardian until Maggie can be located."

He blinks as he absorbs the tale. "Shit, Joey. A sister? That's wild. But you've got her? She's living with you?"

I nod and blow out a breath. "Yeah. Her social worker says if Maggie doesn't come back within sixty days, the state will terminate her parental rights and Harper will be put up for adoption. And Spence and I have already decided if that's the case, we'll take her. She's family, Jay. I can't, in good conscience, not be there for her. Especially given everything she's been through. I know we were screwed up because Maggie left, but it honestly seems like we had it a lot better than Harper has. At least Dad was good to us and we didn't have to worry he wasn't going to be there."

Jay swallows, processing my words. "Wow. This is crazy, Joey. So, tell me about her. What's she like?"

I smile. "She looks like me, except she has brown eyes. She's smart. She reads, maybe more than I do. And in spite of everything she's gone through, she's a good kid. You'll like her."

"I can't wait to meet her. Maybe Dee, Zoey, and I can make a quick trip down for a few days. I can't believe we have sister. And that she's half my age. That's crazy to me."

I nod. "Yeah. Well, I'm going to call Dad. He knew Spence was going to propose, but I haven't told him I said yes, so I should probably give him the news. And I want to ask him questions about Maggie. I don't know if he'll tell me anything; he's always been so tightlipped about her."

Jay nods. "Yeah. Let me know what he says. Tell Harper I said welcome to the family. I should probably call Spence and give him shit. I'm really happy for you, Joey. Congratulations. We love you."

I disconnect the call and take a couple of breaths before FaceTiming Dad. He'll probably be at the store, but he'll most likely take my call if he's not busy. He doesn't answer, so I set my phone down. A few minutes later, he returns my call. When I answer, his smiling face fills the screen. "Joanna, sweet girl. Do you have news for me?"

I huff out a soft laugh. "Yes, Daddy. Spence and I are getting married."

"I knew you'd say yes. That's wonderful, I'm so happy for you two."

"Thanks, Daddy. But listen, that's not the only reason I called. I need to ask you a few questions if you have time. Could you go somewhere a bit more private for a minute?"

"Of course, honey. Let me step into my office." I see him walk into his office and close the door before settling in the chair behind his desk. "All right, what's up?"

"Daddy, what can you tell me about when my mother left?"

"What do you mean? You remember, don't you? You were eleven. She was here and then she wasn't."

"Did you know she was pregnant when she left? And that she's an alcoholic?"

Color rises in his cheeks and I realize he did know and my breath catches. "Why are you asking about this, Joanna? All that was so long ago."

"You knew she was pregnant? You've known this whole time? I have a sister, Daddy. She tracked me down. She lived about forty-five minutes from here and I never knew. Maggie left her. Harper, that's my sister, put two and two together when Maggie saw my book and author photo. She saw her going through some old photos and figured things out."

Dad swallows. "Maggie told me she was pregnant, but I knew it couldn't be mine. I had a vasectomy after you were born, but I hadn't told her. She already had issues with alcohol at that time and I didn't want to have any more children knowing if she got pregnant it could harm the baby and you and Jay were more than enough for me.

"But she tried to pass the pregnancy off as mine until I told her it wasn't possible. She never would tell me who the father was, but I was so upset by what she'd done, I asked her for a divorce. She tried to say she'd leave, but she'd take you and your brother with her, and I wasn't going to let that happen. She'd tried to pick you guys up from school and I went because I thought she might run with you and even called the police because she showed up at the school drunk."

He looks down, as if the next part pains him. "The police took her in for driving under the influence. They held her for thirty days, hoping it would dry her out since she was pregnant. I filed for divorce and she didn't contest it, but after her thirty-day hold was up, she'd tried to come back to the house and take you and Jay away. I wouldn't let her in the house and she finally gave up and left. I honestly kept waiting for her to come back and try to take you guys away again, but after that, she didn't come back."

I'm quiet for a while trying to take in his words. "I'm sorry you went through that, Daddy. Having to find out she cheated and then trying to pass off a baby as yours? That's unbelievable."

He shrugs. "She may have really hoped it was mine, for all I know. If I hadn't had the vasectomy, I would have had no reason to suspect it wasn't. So, you said Maggie abandoned this girl?"

I nod. "Yeah. She's been gone for over two weeks. Harper sought me out so she wouldn't have to go back into foster care. She's had a hard life, Daddy. This isn't the first time Maggie's left her. So she's with me now. And if Maggie doesn't come back, Spence and I will take her if the state terminates Maggie's parental rights. Now that I know about her, I wouldn't be able to leave her. She's a great kid. Way tougher than she should have to be."

"Wow, Joanna. That's a lot. How old is she, about fifteen?"

I nod. "Yeah."

"That's a hard age for a girl."

"Yeah, I remember. Okay, well I'll let you get back to work. Harper wanted to know if you had any idea at all who her father might be. And I couldn't wait to tell you about Spence and me. Love you, Daddy. I'll talk to you in a few days, okay?"

He disconnects the call and I shake my head. I feel bad for bringing all this back up to my dad. And I wish so badly I could go into the living room to tell Harper that I have an idea about who her father is, but I can't do that. So I simply sit in the quiet of my room for a bit before going back out to join her on the sofa.

CHAPTER NINE

JO

Over the next few weeks, Harper and I develop a routine. We spend time at the beach and cook together and read independently. We share books; we watch TV. It really is like having a little sister, I guess.

I submit my resignation to the paper and spend at least a couple of hours each day working on ideas and chapters for a new book, another romance novel with some suspense elements. Not having Spence around makes it easy to distract myself by working.

We still haven't heard from Maggie. Cori said she still hasn't been picked up or anything. Harper and I have gone back to her place a couple of times and there's no evidence Maggie's come back at all. Except the last trip we made that way, there was an eviction notice taped to the front door, so Harper got the rest of the things she thought she'd miss, mainly books, which I can get behind. Every time the phone rings and it's Cori, I see Harper's eyes grow hopeful, only to have her hopes dashed.

She's only cried once that I know of. When she'd been here

about two weeks, she broke down and wondered if she'd done something to make her mother not want her anymore. I held her as she cried and fought to keep my own emotions in check. It was the first time in my life I can truly ever remember feeling like I hated my mother. Not even when she left us did I hate her. But I had Dad and Jay to fill in the gaps she left. Harper only has herself. And me, I guess.

By the time Maggie's been gone for forty-five days, I almost hope she doesn't come back, as bad as it sounds. Because Harper is doing very well, and it's clear to me that Maggie can only hurt her by coming back into the picture.

Spence has been able to come back and visit a couple of times and we're slowly planning our wedding for the fall or winter. He and I both agree we want to see how things play out with Harper before we get married.

He's coming tonight and I can't wait to see him. He managed to somehow get away for a whole week this time and we've decided before he goes back to Tennessee, we're going to talk to Harper together to see if she'd be interested in us adopting her if the state terminates Maggie's parental rights.

I went to the grocery store to gather some things for when Spence comes, and had asked Harper if she wanted to come along, but she said she had a headache. By the time I get back from the store and running a few other errands, I'm cranky because I got a flat tire and had to change it in the heat of the day and I'm now covered in grease and sweat and trying to carry as much as I can to minimize the number of trips I make to the car.

I fumble my keys trying to get them in the lock and drop them. I curse under my breath and struggle not to drop the bags as I stoop down to pick the keys back up. When I finally get inside, I breath a sigh of relief and set the bags down on the kitchen table. I don't see Harper on the couch so I start back toward her room. "Harper, you're never going to believe what happened to me on the way home. I got a flat—." I enter her room and stop in my tracks.

My blood run cold and anger grips me. Harper and Macon are both half dressed and it's obvious they were scrambling to put their clothes on, as Harper's hair is mussed and Macon's shirt is only halfway on. In spite of the fact I want to scream, I calmly go sit on the sofa. Harper comes after me. "Jo, it's not what it looks like. We were just—."

I cut her off and try to keep my tone even. "We'll discuss it in a minute." Macon comes out a moment later fully dressed and has the good sense to look abashed. I level him with my gaze. "Macon, I think you better go. Harper can call you when she's ungrounded."

He nods. "Yes, ma'am."

Anger flashes in Harper's eyes and she starts to speak and I hold up my hand. "I said we'll discuss it in a minute. Tell Macon goodbye."

They both seem unsure how to take my calm tone and I think it frightens them a bit because they don't kiss, and I hear Macon making a hasty retreat. I don't know how I'm so calm, when all I want to do is lock Harper in her room until she graduates college. But I keep reminding myself I'm not her mother and I have to be delicate with her.

Once I know Macon is gone, I gesture for Harper to come sit beside me. She reluctantly comes and sits on the far end of the sofa with her knees drawn up and she doesn't look at me. I take a deep breath. "Harper, I only gave you a few rules for staying with me. And I was very specific that you couldn't have guys here when I'm not home. So you're grounded for a month."

"A month! That's totally unfair."

"I understand you feel that way, but there are consequences when you break the rules. And it's not that I don't like Macon, he's a nice guy, but what you all did was disrespectful to me. You lied and snuck around. I trusted you.

"I've not kept you from seeing Macon anytime you wanted and I know you probably think I'm old fashioned or whatever, but it's only because I want you to be smart and safe. Sex has real consequences. It's a great thing, believe me, but it can also be scary and lead to things you're not ready for. At fifteen, it's easy to only see the thrill and the fun of it, and you can lose sight of what can happen."

"Jo, I'm fine, I promise. Macon loves me and I love him. He wouldn't hurt me or anything like that."

"I'm not saying he would. How long has this been going on? Do you sneak him in here every time I go out? And think real hard before you try to lie. I'm not angry, I'm just upset because I trusted you."

Harper looks down at her knees. "He's come over a few times. But this was the first time we ever…"

Inwardly, I breathe a sigh of relief, but also a pang of fear grips me. "Were you smart? Were you careful? Are you on birth control?"

"We were careful."

I level her with a gaze. "Define careful, Harper."

She blushes and says in a low voice, "He used a condom."

I blow out a breath. "The fact you're blushing when you talk about protection tells me that although you made a very adult choice today, you might not have been ready for it.

"Believe me, honey, I know what it's like to want to share that part of yourself with someone. It's special. Trust me, it wasn't that long ago for me. I remember how exciting it is when it's new. But adult choices can have very adult consequences. I know that as well."

I sigh. "I'm not mad at you. I'm not judging you. Lord

knows I am definitely not the poster child for making perfect decisions. But fifteen is really young, and although physically, you're mature enough to handle sex, there are so many emotional and mental implications that go along with that decision."

"How old were you?"

"I was nineteen."

She seems surprised. "Really?"

I nod. "Yeah, I was in college."

She smirks. "Was it with Spence?"

Now it's my turn to blush. "We're not talking about me, Harper. You're still grounded. I'm not Maggie, I'm not trying to be your mother, but you are my responsibility, so I just want to keep you safe. I know you love Macon. And I'm not going to stop him from coming over here, but you're grounded for a month simply because you broke my rules and my trust. And that was disrespectful."

She bites her lip and nods. "Come on, Jo. Tell me, was it like in the book? Did you not tell him your name and he didn't know it was you?"

I huff out a laugh. "I'm not discussing this with you."

Her expression seems to say that she's impressed. "Wow, that was pretty clever of you."

I roll my eyes and then can't stop myself from asking, "Harper, are we okay? I don't know how to do this teenager thing. I'm your big sister and I don't want to have to put on the guardian hat, but this time, you didn't leave me a choice."

She sobers. "Yeah. I'm sorry. I just love him and wanted to show him that."

I have the thought that maybe Macon pressured her. "Did he pressure you into this? Because that's not okay, Harper."

She shakes her head, her expression adamant. "No. We'd been planning this for weeks, we just hadn't had any time to ourselves. And I didn't call him to come over, he happened to just stop by, and it seemed like the perfect opportunity."

"Okay. Well, we'll talk more about all this over the next month while you're on house arrest, all right?" I stand and blow out a deep breath. "Can you come help me get the rest of the groceries?"

She nods and we troop out to my car to get the remainder of the groceries. Once everything is put away, I come to stand in front of Harper. I lift her chin and brush a stray hair off her forehead. "I didn't ask earlier, are you okay? Do you want me to run you a warm bath? It can help with the pain."

She flushes and shrugs. "I'm okay."

"All right. And Harper, just because you do it once, doesn't mean you have to do it again, especially if you feel like you're not ready to do it again. It's okay to change your mind. Are you on birth control?"

She shakes her head. I ask, "Is that something you want to do? I'm not saying you have to, and it would be in no way saying that I support you having sex, but if you're going to do it, you should be smart. Sometimes things get heated and condoms get forgotten and then... things can happen. Even when you're very careful, things can happen." I can't help but think of Aaron and my chest tightens.

She must see something in my eyes and she straightens. "What happened to you, Jo?"

I swallow. "Nothing. I was just speaking hypothetically. Just giving you things to think about, okay?"

She doesn't look at all convinced by me, but simply nods. "Okay."

And then the most unexpected thing happens and Harper hugs me. It's the first time she's done it and I'm caught off guard. "Thank you for not freaking out and going apeshit on me. You're a great big sister. I love you, Jo."

I struggle to keep my emotions in check as I hug her back. "I love you, too, kid. Don't break my trust again, though, okay? I can't promise the next time I won't lose my shit. I was trying very hard to be a cool, understanding big sister, not crazed guardian."

She laughs. "I promise."

CHAPTER TEN

SPENCE

When I get to Jo's, there's a palpable tension in the air. Harper is lying in front of the couch reading and Jo is cooking supper. She doesn't immediately come over to me and throw her arms around me and I know something's up. I take my bag to the bedroom and come back into the kitchen and stand next to her. "Hey, babe. Everything all right? Looks like I missed some fun around here. I don't even get a hello when I come in the door?"

Jo stops what she's doing and sighs. "Sorry. I've just got a lot on my mind." She lowers her voice. "I'll fill you in later."

I take the utensils from her hand and put them next to the stove and pull her into my arms and she seems to melt into me. I raise her chin and brush a kiss across her lips. "I missed you."

She smiles. "I missed you, too. You have no idea."

I raise my eyebrows suggestively. "I bet I do have an idea." I kiss down her cheek and neck, but then Jo pulls away, which is not like her. "Jo, what's wrong?"

She waves me off. "It's not you. I'll tell you later. Some stuff happened, and it's been handled, but I'm a little on edge." Her eyes dart to the living room and I quirk my head in Harper's direction and she nods.

"Do we need to talk about it now?" I whisper, "Did Maggie make contact? Is she back?"

Jo shakes her head. "No, nothing like that. Like I said, I don't want to get into it now. I tell you everything here in a bit. I promise. It's fine."

"Well, you seem like you're in a bad mood. I just want to help."

She brings her hand up to my face and rubs her thumb across my cheek. She keeps her voice barely above a whisper. "I am, but it has nothing to do with you and later on, I fully expect you to fuck it out of me. But it can't be helped for now. So just give me a kiss and go hang out with Harper while I finish up supper. It should be done in about fifteen minutes."

I give her a deep kiss before dragging my mouth to her ear. "Sounds like you very much need an attitude adjustment. I look forward to providing it to you."

She chuckles. "I can't wait." I turn to go into the living room and she slaps me on the ass as I leave.

I sit on the couch and Harper closes her book. She seems down, but asks, "Did you have a good flight?"

"Yeah, pretty good. I feel like as many times as I've made the same trip back and forth, I could almost fly the plane by now. How are things? I thought maybe we could do some driving lessons while I'm in town. They gave me a Charger for a rental this time. Could be pretty sweet to take on a drive."

She shrugs. "Don't know if I can. Didn't Jo tell you, I'm grounded. For a month." She's matter of fact, and her tone contains no trace of anger.

"Really? I wasn't aware of that. Want to talk about what happened? That's a pretty stiff punishment."

She shakes her head. "I'm sure Jo will tell you all about it."

"Okay. So, what book is it right now?"

She holds it up. *Red Queen*. I ask, "What's it about?"

"Mainly racism and politics set in a dystopian future. It's sort of like *X-Men* meets *Game of Thrones*. At least, that's what they say. I've never read or watched *Game of Thrones*."

I nod. "Sounds cool. Let me know how you like it. Might be an interesting read."

"Do you read a lot, like Jo?"

"Don't know about that. I think between you and Jo, all the book stores will never have trouble staying in business with how many books y'all buy and read. Jo usually reads one and if she thinks I'll like it, she'll let me read it. We used to spend a lot of time reading together."

"What's your favorite book?"

"Well, that's hard, because the first one Jo lent me will always be special. It was *The Time Traveler's Wife*. But otherwise, I don't really have a favorite. I tend to gravitate to sci-fi or mystery suspense more often than not. I like to figure out who done it before the end.

Harper nods. "Isn't *The Time Traveler's Wife* supposed to be a romance? You don't really strike me as the romance book type."

"It is, but it's also pretty gritty in parts. And I read Jo's book, so I'm not opposed to romance. I can read just about anything."

Jo hollers from the kitchen to say that supper is done so Harper and I go wash up and come sit at the table. She's made meatloaf, mashed potatoes, and green beans and I give her a smile as I sit. "Smells great, babe."

"Thanks, Spence. Hope it's alright. You know I'm not much of a cook."

We dig in and after a few bites, Harper says, "It's really good, Jo."

"Thank you. After supper, if you do the dishes, you can call Macon and talk to him for ten minutes."

Harper's eyes go wide. "Really? I thought I couldn't talk to him the whole time I'm grounded? Not that I'm complaining, believe me."

Jo swallows her bite. "Don't mistake my charity for condoning what happened. Ten minutes a day. That's it. And he can't visit until you're ungrounded."

"Deal!" She jumps up and throws her arms around Jo's shoulder. "Thank you. Thank you. Thank you."

I'm utterly confused and give Jo a *what the hell* expression. She just shakes her head and I know it means, *tell you later*.

True to her word, after Harper does all the supper dishes, she's allowed to call Macon. Once her time is up, she surrenders her phone to Jo without being asked. I have to admire her for taking her punishment with maturity, whatever she did. I'm beginning to wonder if I even want to know.

Once Jo and I turn in for the night, we're lying in bed and I can't stand it anymore. "What did Harper do? A month seems like a lot. She's a good kid."

Jo sits up and turns on the bedside lamp. "I caught her and Macon having sex today. I had gone to the grocery store and when I got home, they were in her bed."

Disbelief and rage fill me in equal measure. "Are you shitting me?"

She sighs. "No. And I stayed a whole lot calmer than I felt. I actually surprised myself. I sent Macon away and he still had all of his appendages intact, I might add. But I had a serious conversation with Harper. She said they were careful, but when I said, 'define careful', she got all shy and blushed. I told her since she wasn't even mature enough to talk about protection without being embarrassed, she's probably not mature enough to be having sex.

I'm having trouble breathing. "I'm going to kill that kid. It's too bad he's not eighteen, I'd kick his ass."

Jo places a hand on my arm, attempting to calm me. "She's fine, Spence. He didn't pressure her. I honestly believe they love each other, but I tried to convey the importance of being smart. I almost wanted to tell her about what happened to me, but I don't want to trot that story out as a scare tactic. It seems like a cheap trick. But I told her just because she did it once doesn't mean she has to do it again if she decides she's not ready to go there."

"So this was her first time?"

"That's what she said. She told me he's been over before when I wasn't here, but today was the first time they'd had sex. And I tend to believe her. She's not lied to me to this point as far as I know. But yeah, she's grounded for a month."

"Wow. I'm kinda glad I missed all the excitement. I probably would've pummeled him and gone to jail."

"And I told her I don't like having to pull the guardian card; that I'd much rather just be her big sister, but that she left me no choice. I told her I was upset because I'd trusted her and she'd broken one of the very few rules I'd given her." Jo sighs. "Oy vey. 'Raise a teenager', they said. 'It will be fun', they said. But I didn't enjoy this part of it, Spence. All I could think was, 'please don't get pregnant'. I was terrified. I mean, I felt a little better when she said they'd used a condom, but not by much.

"I told her if she wanted to get on the pill, we could talk about that. I told her that I, in no way, support her having sex at her age, but I can't stop her. She'll find a way if it's what she wants to do. We know that all too well. But I told her she should be smart, because sometimes things get heated and condoms get forgotten."

I can't help but chuckle. "Yeah, they do." I cup her face and look into her eyes. "Sounds like you did real good today. I'm proud of you, Jo."

She sighs. "I'm proud of me, too. And Harper hugged me and thanked me for not freaking out. And she told me she loves me. Spence, I wanted to cry. She's such a good kid. Seriously good. As bad as it sounds, I almost hope Maggie doesn't come back. I don't know if I can watch her go back with everything I know about what she's been through."

I sigh. "I know. But we'll just have to wait and see, I guess. What day are we on?"

"Forty-five. Fifteen days. But I'm not getting my hopes up. I feel like if I do, it'll jinx it and Maggie will miraculously appear. I mean, I don't know what would happen, especially if she's charged with neglect, but she'd still retain her rights, even if she's in police custody. And I just want Harper to be safe and happy."

"I know, babe. Me, too. We'll just have to hope for the best, I guess."

Jo leans over and kisses me. "I'm glad you're here. I'm sorry I was in such a bad mood earlier."

I can't help but smile. "Totally understandable, given the circumstances."

She kisses my cheek and her mouth trails down my neck. "You know, I think I still have a bad attitude, though. I might be in need of an adjustment."

"That so? Well, we can't have any bad attitudes while I'm town." I slide my hand up the hem of Jo's nightshirt and skim her ribs with the tips of my fingers, hitting a ticklish spot, making her giggle, before moving up to cup her breast.

And like she always has under my touch, she lets out a soft sigh. It's a sound I've come to love and look forward to since the first time we were together. My thumb grazes her nipple and it rises to meet me and just like that, I'm instantly hard.

Jo pulls her shirt over her head and she wraps her arms around my neck and moves her mouth back to mine for a hungry kiss. I bring my hand around her waist and pull her closer as I lower us back to the bed. I'll never get used to the feel of her under me, the way her skin feels against mine, the way she fits perfectly with me.

She wraps her legs around me and grinds herself into me and whispers, "I've missed you so much, baby."

My heart races with need, but we never have enough time together with us being apart so much and I try to make the most of the time we do have. I try to slow down and enjoy it as much as possible. I pull back from her and grip her jaw and search her bright blue eyes. I run my thumb along her bottom lip. "I'm here now. And I'm all yours."

I lower my mouth to hers and simply kiss her for a moment, our lips giving, our tongues exploring. She moans into me as our kisses become more fervent, more needy.

Jo's hand slides down between us and into my boxers and she wraps her fingers around my cock, stroking leisurely. I have to breathe for a minute to not come undone under her touch. I can't bite back the soft groan that leaves my throat and she smiles against my lips.

I work my mouth down her neck and chest, licking and nipping as I go. I bring her breast to my lips and tug the nipple between my teeth causing her to gasp and arch her back. I flick the tight peak with my tongue before moving to the other.

Jo lets out a soft moan as I reach down to work her clit through her panties and I shove the fabric to the side and slide my fingers into her and find that she's already so wet, so hot. It still brings me so much pleasure to know that she's wet for me. That she's always been wet for me. I stroke the upper wall of her pussy and her hips buck. "Spence, I need you. Shit."

But I keep going, working her tits with my mouth and fucking with my hand until after just a few moments, she's clenching around my fingers and gripping the back of my neck as she comes, a low raspy sigh falling from her lips.

After I gentle my movements as she comes down, I plant a kiss on her shoulder and rise from the bed to go over to the dresser and grab a condom. I shed my boxers and rip the packet with my teeth and I've got it rolled down before I climb back into bed and settle between Jo's thighs.

Her eyes slide closed as I thrust into her and she smiles. I could watch her face as she takes me all day long. It's a sight I committed to memory long ago and I still can't get over it. We move together and Jo rocks her pelvis against me, her nails digging into my back as I slam into her and it's a mix of pain and pleasure and just enough to stave off my need to finish.

Shifting slightly, I bring her legs up and brace the backs of her knees against my biceps. The change in the angle causes Jo to bite down on her bottom lip to stifle a loud moan as I drive deeper into her. We're both breathing heavy and she grips my face and I hold her gaze as I watch her go over a second time, a pleasant flush coloring her cheeks and her mouth is open in a slight O as her pussy clenches around my dick, sending me into my own climax. I feel it start low in my abs and radiate down my legs as I come, my orgasm seeming to rip through me, my cries falling as ragged gasps and I slump into her.

When I rise to go dispose of the condom and come back to the bed, slipping my boxers back on, I ask, "So, attitude properly adjusted?"

Jo chuckles, her voice breathy. "Ask me again when I can breathe." She gets up a few minutes later and I hear the toilet flush and the water running in the bathroom. As she climbs back into bed, I pull her into my arms, the familiar scent of her coconut vanilla lotion hitting my nose as I fall asleep.

CHAPTER ELEVEN

JO

Spence wakes me with a kiss on the cheek. "I'm going to go for a run, be back soon."

I reach for him. "No, stay in bed with me. You're on vacation. Take the day off."

He chuckles. "Nope. Can't do it. I'll bring back breakfast. Love you." He brushes a quick kiss across my lips and I roll back over.

Sure enough, when I wake up and pad into the kitchen, there's a box of pastries on the counter. Spence is sitting on the sofa with a cup of coffee. I'm surprised to see he's already showered and changed. "I must have been out if I missed you coming back to shower and everything."

He pulls me into his lap. "Yeah, you were sawing logs. Super adorable, by the way."

I can't help but laugh. "Is Harper up yet?"

He nods. "Yeah, she came out and got coffee and a danish and went back into her room. I take it she's not much of a morning person, either. Y'all are so much alike it's scary."

"Yeah, but she usually beats me out of bed. I'll go check on her, see how she's feeling today." I give him a raised eyebrow. "You know, after yesterday."

He blows out a breath and nods. "Want me to fix you some coffee? And do you want an apple or cherry danish."

I kiss him. "Bless you. Apple please." As I rise from his lap, he gives me an affectionate swat on the behind. I go down the hall to Harper's room and knock on the door. "Harper?"

A moment later, I hear her answer softly, "Come in."

I open the door and see her sitting on her bed, legs pulled up. "Hey, kid. How you doing today?" She shrugs and I sit down on the edge of the bed. When I get a good look at her, I can see she's been crying. "Harper, what's wrong? Did something happen?" She shakes her head and I brush her hair off her face. "Do you want to talk about it? Big sister hat on. Not guardian. You can talk to me."

She bites her lip. "My mom's been gone for six weeks. I don't think she's coming back, Jo. I can't help but feel like it's my fault. Like, if I hadn't had your book in the house, she would've never seen it and it wouldn't have stirred all this up and she wouldn't have left."

Although I understand where she's coming from, it still hurts to hear her say the she'd rather still have Maggie than found me. But I don't react, because I know none of this is about me. "You can't blame yourself; her leaving is not your fault. Don't even think that way. Maggie needs help. Addicts and alcoholics can't stop on their own. I know, I've been there. A lot of times, they have to get to their lowest point before they can see they even need help. I had to do that. I almost lost my job when my drinking got out of control."

"Do you think she'll get help? Do you think she'll come back?"

"I'm not going to to lie to you, Harper. I don't know. I wish I did. But I can tell you that no matter what, you're not alone.

I've been right where you are. But there's a chance she might not. I'm here, though. I know I'm not her, and I could never fill her shoes, but I'm here for you. Spence and I love you and we'll make sure you're taken care of. Okay?"

Harper wraps her arms around me and I feel her start crying. I return her embrace and pat her back, and want to cry right along with her. I want so badly to be able to take this pain from her. Because I know the not knowing is worse than finding out the truth and how much it can haunt you.

After a few minutes, her crying turns to sniffles. I say, "Oh, I forgot to tell you, Jay and his family are coming down for a few days this week. So you'll get to meet him and his wife and our niece, Zoey."

She pulls back. "Really? I have a niece? That's so cool. What's Jay like?"

"He and Spence are a lot alike. They're both athletic and tall. Jay is more serious and straitlaced. He's a teacher. He and Delia, his wife, met in college. She's great, too. Jay's a great big brother; he excels at it. The whole time I was growing up, he never treated me like I was a pest. He always made sure if he and Spence were watching a movie, they included me." I nudge her playfully. "But I didn't spend a lot of time watching the movies. I was too busy watching Spence."

She chuckles and I touch her cheek. "There's that pretty smile. Now, did I overhear Spence ask you if you wanted to go do a driving lesson?"

Harper wipes her eyes and nose with the hem of her shirt. "Yeah. He said something about it yesterday, but I didn't known if I could with me being grounded."

"It'd be a shame to waste that sweet rental car, don't you think? Besides, driving lessons are educational, so therefore, are excluded from groundings."

She hugs me. "You're a great big sister, Jo. Jay must have set a really good example for how to be an older sibling, because you excel at it, too."

"You're a pretty great little sister, kid. Want me to go ask Spence if he'll take you on a drive?"

"Would you? I'll get ready."

"Sure. I know he's already had a shower and stuff, so it shouldn't be a problem." I walk out of her room and pull the door closed behind me and return to the living room to sit next to Spence.

He hands over my coffee and danish. "You were in there a while, everything okay?"

I blow out a breath. "Not really. Harper feels like it's her fault Maggie left, because she had my book. And I think it's setting in with her that she might not come back. I hate seeing her in pain. And I've been there. I want to be able to tell her it gets easier, but part of me knows it doesn't. Maggie left me over fifteen years ago, and I still don't know if I'm over it sometimes. By the way, I told Harper you'd take her on a driving lesson. I hope that's okay."

He kisses the side of my head. "Oh, yeah, it's fine. I offered yesterday. Might take her mind off things for a little while."

"Exactly my thinking. Thank you for the coffee and danish."

He winks. "Don't worry, you can thank me later."

I smile. "I look forward to it."

Later in the afternoon, while Spence and Harper are gone on a driving lesson, I take some time to clean up a bit around the condo. Jay and his family won't be staying with us since I only have the two bedrooms, but we'll hang out here a lot since I'm right on the beach and want to make sure we're ready for their arrival. I also lay out some chicken to make for supper tonight.

Once I have everything done, I spend some time writing, because I know I won't have time later in the week once Jay comes into town. My phone dings and I check to see that Spence has taken a photo of Harper behind the wheel of the car and she's laughing. It makes me happy to see her smile after how sad she was this morning.

I swear, if Maggie ever comes back, I'm going to kick her ass. How anyone could leave this girl, I'll never know.

When they get home, they're laughing and carrying iced coffees. Spence hands me one and leans down to give me a kiss. "Welcome home. Did you all have a good lesson?"

Harper hops up on the kitchen counter. "Oh my gosh, Jo. That car is amazing—so much power. I felt invincible. We had a blast."

"Harper's a natural. She's already mastered honking and giving people the finger when they cut her off."

I can't help but laugh. "Well, best to use that particular skill sparingly. I'm glad you guys had fun. We're going to have chicken for supper, but I haven't started it yet. Are y'all hungry right now, or can you wait a bit? I'm kind of on a roll with this chapter and would like to get a little further before I shut down for the day."

Spence squeezes my shoulder. "I'll fix dinner, you keep writing. Harper can help me, right, kiddo?"

She nods. "Sure."

I keep writing and every once in a while, I'll glance over into the kitchen to watch as Spence and Harper cook together. They laugh and talk and he shows her the best way to keep from crying while cutting an onion. I'm struck that someday it could be our kid he's teaching in the kitchen. *He's going to be a great dad someday.*

The thought makes my breath catch. Because for the first time since Aaron, I find myself thinking about having kids. It's scary, and although I'd told Spence I didn't want kids, watching him with Harper and seeing how protective he is of her makes me love him even more. And I wonder if I could do it again. Could I let myself want that? Risk what happened before to give him that? Give *us* that?

CHAPTER TWELVE

SPENCE

I watch as Jo gets more attached to Harper by the day. I see it in her eyes and the way she watches her. I'm worried what will happen if Maggie comes back in the next two weeks and what it could do to Jo. Especially if I'm not here with her if, and when, Harper has to go home. She had to survive losing Aaron all alone. I'm not going to let her go through that again. Not when the sadness that has plagued her for so long finally seems to be lifting.

Jay, Delia, and Zoey arrived yesterday and they fell in love with Harper immediately. She just fits in so well with all of us and if I'm honest, I'll be devastated if she has to go back to Maggie. I've not been able to spend as much time with her as Jo, but I love her, too. I never had a little sister, unless you count Jo, but that makes things weird when I think about it, so I don't.

But Harper is great and I love being a big brother to her. And she's a great little sister. She is smart and has been asking me more and more questions about going into medicine and it makes me think that might be something she wants to do when she grows up. It's hard to believe this is the same girl who, only weeks ago, said she wouldn't be going to college. Is she finally letting herself dream? Does she feel safe enough to be able to do that now? I hope that we—more Jo than me, but still—have made her feel like it's okay to want a successful future.

We all went out to the beach today and Jay and I were throwing a football and we were showing Harper how to throw it and put some spin on it. Then we played two-hand touch, Jay and Harper versus Jo and me. The girls both held their own, but not surprisingly, Jay and I both carried our teams.

In truth, like Jo, I'm praying we make it through the next two weeks without a call, text, email, smoke signal, or carrier pigeon regarding Maggie. Because I don't want to give Harper up any more than Jo does.

The morning Jay and his family leave to go home, he gives Harper his information and tells her to call him if she needs anything. She hugs everyone and when they leave and it seems a bit bittersweet. We're sitting at the kitchen table drinking coffee while Jo writes in the bedroom. "It's really cool I have siblings. And they have people who love them and Zoey is so cute."

"Yeah, I've always felt like it would've been nice to have a brother or sister, and I guess I kinda did, but you're part of an amazing family, Harper, let me tell you."

She nods. "I know. Y'all have been really good to me and I'm really glad I found Jo."

"We're glad you found us, too, kiddo. Want to go for a drive? I have to leave the day after tomorrow, so the car will go back, too. Get it while you can."

Her eyes light up. "Yes! Can we? Can we also get iced coffees?"

"Of course. Let me go tell Jo, see if she wants to come along. She'll probably want to stay and write, but I'll check with her anyway."

When I walk into the bedroom, Jo is on the phone, her expression tense. I shut the door and her eyes snap to mine and I see it in her face before she's even hung up. My heart stops. She continues her call. "Thanks for letting me know, Cori. I'll call you in the morning."

Jo disconnects the call and bursts into tears and I rush to her side and sit next to her on the bed. "Where is she? Where did they find her?"

"They picked her up outside of Atlanta for possession the day before Harper came to find me. They didn't know until yesterday she was wanted in Florida for child neglect, so they shipped her back down here. Spence, it's so unfair. We were so close."

I wrap my arms around her and rest my chin on the top of her head. "I know, Jo. I'm so sorry. What happens now?"

"I asked Cori if I could see Maggie before we tell Harper she's back. I have a lot of things I want to say to her and I won't be able to do it in front of Harper. I'm going to see her today. I'm going to ask her to surrender her rights and let me adopt Harper."

I'm shocked, although I shouldn't be. It's the right move. "Really? Wow. You think she will?"

"I don't know, but I can't not do anything. Of course, even if she won't, she'll have to go through the process of getting out of jail and reunification, so it could still be months before Harper would go back to her. And she'd have to find a place to live and a job. And I know this puts our wedding and me moving on the back burner, Spence, but Harper's more important right now."

I lift her face and brush her tears off her cheek with my

thumb. "Of course she is. All that can wait. I want Harper to be safe and happy just as much as you do. If we can keep her with us, even for a little while longer, I want to do that. I just hate I'm not going to be here during all this."

Jo leans her head on my shoulder. "Thank you, Spence."

"For what, babe?"

"For having your superman complex. Without it, I wouldn't have taken Harper in and gotten to know her and I love her so much. So, thank you."

There's a knock on the door and Jo hurriedly wipes her tears. Harper enters with her eyes covered. "Y'all better not be naked in here."

Jo and I both start laughing. I say, "You're good, kiddo. I was just telling Jo we were going to go do a driving lesson. She said she'd love to join us, but she has an errand she needs to run."

Harper shrugs. "Want us to pick you up an iced coffee on our way back?"

Jo smiles. "Thanks, but I'm good. I'm not sure how long I'll be gone. But y'all have fun and be safe, okay?" She turns to me. "I'll call you when I start to head home and we can decide what we want to do for supper."

I plant a kiss on top of her head. "Sounds good." I rise from the bed. "Okay, Harper, today's lesson is going to be the proper execution of donuts in the Kroger parking lot."

CHAPTER THIRTEEN

JO

I knew when I saw Cori's name on my phone screen what it was going to be about. I could feel it in my bones. And now, I sit in a metal folding chair at the county jail behind a plexiglass partition with one of those phones you see in the movies. I've left my engagement ring at home, because I don't want Maggie to know anything about me. If I weren't coming for Harper, Maggie could rot in here for the rest of her life and I wouldn't think twice.

Instead, I wait. I wait what seems like an eternity for my mother to come and sit in her own folding chair. I wait to see if she recognizes me, but then I remember she saw my author photo, so I know she will. I wait to see if she offers any explanation or any type of valid excuse. And part of me waits to see if she'll even apologize for leaving Jay and me all those years ago.

The woman who sits in front of me in an orange jumpsuit doesn't look anything like the woman I remember my mother to be. She's rail thin, with close cropped dark brown hair shot through with gray. But the eyes and mouth are the same, so I know it's her. Her skin is sallow and she has dark circles under her eyes. I don't say anything, but pick up the receiver as she does.

She swallows and in a voice I've not heard in well over a decade, she says, "Joanna, my sweet girl. It's so good to see you." I want to laugh at the absurdity of her comment, as though it's only been a few days since she last laid eyes on me, not sixteen years.

"Maggie. I won't pretend it's good to see you. I can't do that. My sobriety requires that I'm honest with people. What about yours, or are you not sober, so you can lie?"

"I know you're upset and probably have a lot of questions. I'm sober. I have been for twenty-eight days. Where's Harper? I thought she'd come see me."

"She doesn't know you're here. I wanted to see you first."

"I'm glad you came. I've thought a lot about you and Jay over the years."

Her tone is flat and void of emotion and I don't know what to think about it except that I feel like I want to vomit or punch someone; I am so irrationally angry. But then I remember why I'm here. "Well, we've not thought about you much at all. Not after you up and left."

"I wanted to bring you all with me." Again, her voice sounds robotic, as if she's only saying what she thinks I want to hear, not really what she feels.

I narrow my eyes. "You wanted to take us from Dad and run. He told me what happened. You tried to pass Harper off as his baby and then came to my school drunk while you were pregnant to try to run away with me and Jay. What is wrong with you? How could you do that to Dad? To Jay and me? Do you know how devastated we were? For years, Maggie. Do you even know who Harper's father is? Or were you too drunk to know who you'd slept with?"

I honestly didn't mean to get so emotional but apparently, I'm still bitter about her leaving. She at least has the good sense to look ashamed and I know I'm probably right about her not knowing who Harper's father is. I take a few deep breaths and try to calm down. "I came to ask you to do right by Harper. Haven't you put her through enough? Surrender your parental rights and let me adopt her. Let her be happy. She's happy and loved and she can have a future. I'll make sure she goes to college. She deserves more than what you can provide her."

Anger flashes in Maggie's eyes. "I'm not going to do that. She's my daughter. Mine. I'll be out in two weeks. I already have a place to live when I get out. I already have a job lined up. She'll come home with me as soon as I go through all the channels. You think you know what's best for her because you're some fancy writer now? You know nothing about being a mother. I'm her mother."

"I know that a real mother doesn't do what you did. A real mother doesn't abandon her children. A real mother does right by them. If you want to be a good mother, let Harper go. It shouldn't be too difficult for you, you've done it before." The words are out of my mouth before I can bite them back and I mentally chide myself again for being emotional. I know none of it will help my case and if Spence were here, he'd remind me to calm down and try to be rational.

I blow out a breath and attempt to reason with my mother. "You know I can provide a better life for her than you can. I have resources. Did you know she's talking about wanting to go into the medical field? When I first met her, she wasn't even sure she was going to graduate high school. If she stays with you, she's going to squander her potential. You didn't do right by Jay and me. Do right by Harper. I'm begging you. I've never asked you for anything in my whole life. But I'm asking you for this."

"I'm not going to let you have her. She's the only person who's ever truly loved me. I'm not going to give that up. I'll get out of here and she'll be back with me."

Her phrasing strikes me as strange. "You know, Maggie, in everything you've said, you never once asked how Harper was, only *where*. You haven't even said you missed her. You only want her for the validation she gives you and that may be the worst thing of all in this. That's not love."

"Of course I love her. She's my daughter." But her tone is flippant, as if she can't be bothered with any genuine emotion.

Angry tears well in my eyes. "I was your daughter too, Maggie. And Jay was your son. But you only cared about yourself. Just like you're doing now. If you truly loved Harper, you'd want what's best for her. And you know that's not you." I hang up the phone and turn to leave. Part of me hopes Maggie will bang on the glass or do something to get my attention and tell me she's sorry, but she doesn't. And I don't know why, but it still hurts, even after all these years.

As I sit in my car in the parking lot of the jail, I finally allow myself to cry. I cry for the little girl I was when my mother was around and I thought my life was perfect. I cry for the girl whose innocence was stripped away when her mother left. I cry for Harper and the fact she's probably going to have to go back to Maggie and how angry and sad and helpless that knowledge makes me feel.

I start the car and for the first time in longer than I care to remember, I have to force myself to keep driving instead of stopping at a liquor store. I turn my blinker on at two before changing my mind. I know if I give into that, I'm no better than Maggie, so I go home. When I get back, I notice Spence's rental car is in the parking lot and I shoot him a text.

> Jo: I just pulled in at home. I'm sorry I didn't go get food. Can you take Harper out for supper? I don't want her to see my face right now. I need to calm down and collect myself.

> Spence: Of course. Will an hour be enough time for you? Or do I need to go for ice cream, too?

In spite of my mood, I can't help but laugh and love Spence even more than I already do.

> Jo: Ice cream. Yes. Can you bring me some back?

> Spence: You've got it. Love you. Call me if you need anything else, okay?

I send him a thumbs up emoji and pull my car to a different spot so Harper won't see me. Once they come out and leave, I pull into my assigned spot and go inside.

I go into my bedroom and drop my things and climb into bed, not even bothering to remove my clothes. I'm so sad and angry and emotionally spent, I fall asleep almost immediately.

Some time later, I feel Spence shaking me. When I sit up, he pulls me to him and I can't hold the tears back again. "Spence, it's not fair. It's so wrong."

"Can you tell me what happened? What she said?" he asks gently.

I try to compose myself and breathe. "She didn't even apologize for leaving me and Jay. She asked where Harper was. But not once during our conversation did she ask how she was or say she was sorry for leaving her, either. When I asked her to let me raise Harper, she said she couldn't do that because Harper is the only person who's ever really loved her and she wasn't going to give that up.

"She doesn't care about her, she only wants the validation Harper gives her. She said she's already started the reunification process. She's already lined up a job and a place to live. Spence, we're going to have to watch Harper go back to her."

He wipes my tears, but I don't miss the ones sitting in his eyes. "We knew this was a possibility, as much as we didn't want it to be. If Maggie goes through all the legal channels, there's nothing we can do. We can make sure Harper knows we're here for her, no matter what happens, we can visit her and still try to be a positive influence on her. We can make sure if Maggie screws up again we're here to pick up the pieces." He lifts my chin. "I know this hurts, babe. I'm so sorry. I hate it so much and if I could take this pain away, I would."

I nod. "We have to tell Harper. Cori's coming in the morning to take her to see Maggie. I don't want that sprung on her. I want her to have time to prepare. I need to tell her now, before I lose my nerve."

He sighs and his throat bobs as he swallows thickly and I know I'm not the only one devastated by this. I know he loves her just as much as I do. We stand and he takes my hand and we walk into the living room. Harper is lying on the floor watching TV, oblivious to how much things are getting ready to change for her again. Spence says her name softly, his voice filled with emotion and my heart twists.

She looks up at us and she sees my face and turns off the TV. She stands, her eyes darting between Spence and me. "What's wrong? What happened? Jo, have you been crying?"

I sit down on the couch and pat the seat next to me and Harper joins me, her expression full of apprehension. I take her hand and blow out a deep breath. "Harper, they found your mother."

Her eyes fill with tears. "She's dead, isn't she?"

I shake my head. "No, honey, she's in jail. They found her outside of Atlanta about a month ago and when they discovered there was a warrant out for child neglect, they sent her back here. Cori is going to come get you in the morning to go see her."

"Can you come with me to go see her?" Her voice is pleading and sounds more like a little girl than the mature teenager she is and again, my heart twists painfully.

I wipe her tears away and try to stay strong for her. "I can't. I wish I could. But Cori will be with you. And you'll come back here after, okay? We can talk about things if you want. Whatever you want to do."

"Did you see her? I figure you must have. That's where you went earlier, right?"

I huff out a soft laugh. "You're too smart, kid. Yeah, I saw her. I had some things I wanted to say to her. I'm sorry I didn't tell you before I went."

She shrugs. "How was she? Is she clean?"

"She said she has been for four weeks. She said she's started the reunification process and that she's already lined up a job and place for you two to live. She'll be out in two weeks, but I'm not sure how long after that she'll be through the process."

Harper looks down and nods slowly. I take her hand in mine. "Harper, listen to me, okay? No matter what happens with Maggie, Spence and Jay and I are your family now, too. And when you go back, if you need me, I will be there. Whenever at all. Got it? You can come and visit us anytime you want. Spence and I are here for you, day or night.

"And when you get ready to go to college, we'll make sure that happens for you. You're too smart to not follow whatever dreams you have. You're my sister and I'm not giving you up, all right?"

Large tears roll down Harper's face. "I think I'm going to go to my room for a little while."

I nod. "Okay, honey. If you want to talk, we're here, okay?"

CHAPTER FOURTEEN

SPENCE

We have Harper for six more weeks. I come down every weekend to see her and Jo to soak up what time we have left with her. None of us talk about the calendar and the fact that she'll go back home the day before her sixteenth birthday.

Jo puts on a brave face, but at night, I hold her as she cries. The condo has become a tomb and on her last night, we go out to eat for her birthday and we give Harper a gift card loaded with money to buy a ton of books. We joke it'll get her through the next month.

Probably the hardest thing about all this is that Harper has almost completely shut down since she learned she'll be returning to live with Maggie. She still hasn't told us what happened when she went to see her mother in jail, but Cori told Jo the reunion was not exactly happy. Maggie made it clear to Harper she'll be going home with her. She's stopped talking, stopped reading, stopped sleeping, almost completely stopped eating. She spends most of her time sitting on the beach, staring out into the ocean.

It breaks my heart to see it because I can see she's already crawling back into herself and what her life will be like again. I'd give anything to see her smile. If it hurts this much to lose a child who's not even yours, how much more must it have hurt Jo when she lost Aaron? I can't help but feel like she's losing a child all over again. And it's just not fair.

The morning Cori comes to get Harper and take her to Maggie, we fix pancakes and try to pretend it's a normal day. But all too soon, Cori knocks on the door and we all troop out to her car with Harper's things. I load her belongings into the back of the vehicle while Jo says her goodbyes. She pulls Harper into her arms. "Memorize our Tennessee address, okay? If you ever, ever, ever, need me, I'll come running. I love you, kid. This is not goodbye, okay? Anytime, anyplace, I'm there, got it?" Harper nods and comes over to me.

I pull her in for a hug and rest my chin on her head. "Keep up the driving lessons. No donuts, you suck at 'em. Watch your blind spots, okay?"

Harper says, "How am I going to get better at donuts if I don't practice?"

I can't help but laugh, even as my heart breaks. "You're a good kid, Harper Cole. We love you. You're the best little sister I've ever had."

"You're a good big brother, Spence. Thank you for everything. I love you both." Harper climbs in the car and drives away and we watch, both of us in tears.

Over the next two weeks, Jo and I pack up her clothes and books to take back to Tennessee. We try to reach out to Harper, with no response, which Jo takes hard. My theory is that Maggie took her phone away or had her number changed. Jo even reached out to Cori, but she couldn't tell us anything other than Harper is okay.

When we make the drive to Tennessee, Jo and I are both quiet. After a while, she asks, "Spence, why does it hurt so bad? It shouldn't hurt this much, right?"

"I think it should. It reminds us how much she meant to us. It reminds us that love can hurt and be beautiful. But she's a tough kid. She'll be okay. And, I think, eventually, we will be, too."

"I don't want to be okay, Spence. I want her back. She should be with us. It's not right. Maggie doesn't care about her or what's best for her, if she did, she would have let us raise her. We could've stayed in Florida so Maggie could still see her, but she would've had a better chance with us."

I squeeze her hand and swallow the lump that's formed in my throat. "I know, babe. It sucks."

When we pull into the driveway at the house, we don't unload Jo's things, opting instead to go into the house and climb into bed. We're both sad and I wrap her in my arms and we both pretend we'll be okay, even though we know we're a long way from okay.

During the weeks and months that follow, we fall into a routine. I go to work and Jo writes. Although, I think the theme for her next book has changed to reflect the sadness she's currently dealing with. We spend time with Nick and have dinner with him at least once a week.

Jo and my mom plan the wedding, scheduled for the week after Thanksgiving. I tell Jo I would have been happy eloping, because I truly just wanted to be married to her, but I know it's important to have her dad walk her down the aisle. And, besides, my mom loves to plan a party.

She calls Cori once a month to check in on Harper, who insists she's still doing okay, but that she can't give us any information about how to get in touch with her. Jo and I have both scoured social media to see if Harper has a profile, but Maggie must keep a tight leash on her, because we've not been able to find anything, which we both feel is strange. What sixteen-year-old doesn't have any social media profiles?

Jo even went as far as reaching out to Harper's boyfriend via Instagram, but he told her Harper isn't allowed to see him anymore because Maggie found out that they'd slept together. I know it's killing Jo that she can't do anything and has no way to find out any information about Harper.

Our wedding day comes, and we're married at the same church where my parents got married, even though Jo and I aren't catholic. But it made my mother happy, so we were okay with it. And it was a beautiful service. The only thing missing was Harper. I know Jo would've had her as her maid of honor had she been here. Instead, it was Delia. And Jay was my best man.

When Nick walked Jo down the aisle, I couldn't keep the tears out of my eyes. She looked so beautiful. Her dress was strapless and flowed out from her hips. It was ivory and made of satin with some beading around the waist. I'll never forget what she looked like as she walked toward me, happy tears in her eyes.

We honeymooned at the condo in Jacksonville, but we were both so reminded of Harper during our time there, it was a bit sad.

About six months after Harper went back to Maggie, Jo called Cori to check in and she said Maggie had moved and she didn't know where they'd relocated, so she wasn't sure how

Harper was doing. It broke Jo's heart, as she'd lost the last remaining tie to Harper and truly had no way of knowing if she was okay.

She isolated herself in her office at the house and wrote nonstop for months, only coming up for air to drink coffee, snack, and make love to me. It's not the passionate lovemaking we're used to, but I know she's still reeling from losing Harper and I know in time, she'll come back to me.

Jo's second book, *A Sister's Love*, publishes the following summer and she dedicates it to Harper, as she should. The story ends up being about a teenage girl who learns she has a sister and how they connected and grew close. There's some romance for the girl, but the story mainly centers around the sisters. And I know Jo wrote the story how she wished it would have ended. I think she did it so that if Harper read the book, she'd know we wanted her with us, even if we couldn't.

On Harper's seventeenth birthday, Jo buys another bookstore gift card, on the off chance we ever get to see her again. But she seems to be coming out of things and starts to smile again and laugh. She still has down days, but I think writing the book was cathartic for her and I know she hopes someday, Harper will find a way to make contact with us. We both hope for that.

PART TWO

TEN MONTHS LATER

CHAPTER FIFTEEN

JO

"Joanna, I know this hurts, but you have to push. Bear down for me. Right into your bottom." The doctor tells me to push, but all I can think is that as long as I don't, he's not really gone. He's still safe. He's still there.

But I can't fight the contractions that come, the pains persistent and relentless because of the drugs they gave me to induce labor. My body knows what to do at this point and I'm just along for the ride. The nurse beside me whispers what I'm sure are words of encouragement, but I don't hear them. I only hear my own screams as I deliver my stillborn son from my body.

I know he won't cry because I already know he's gone, but I still hold on to some shred of hope he'll draw breath and a squeal will come from his lungs.

But, of course, it doesn't. After he comes, they clean him up and ask me if I'd like to see him. I don't hesitate, and nod. I need to see his tiny face, his tiny hands, his tiny body. I need to memorize him to have the image of him always in my heart. The nurse wraps him in a blanket, same as they would any newborn, and brings him over to me.

He's perfect, except for his color, but I don't dwell on that. I examine his features, commit them to memory. I bring my nose to his hair and inhale, trying to memorize his scent. I run my fingers over his fine blonde hair and spend time with my son and know that Spence should be here.

"Spence!" I shoots bolt upright in bed with a gasp, tears in my eyes, my heart aching with the memory. Spence sits up and takes me into his arms. He knows without asking what the dream was about. I have the same one at least a few times a year.

"It's okay, Jo. I'm here. It's all right." He rubs my back and I cling to him as I cry.

After the dream, I'm never able to go back to sleep and once Spence drifts back off, I usually rise from our bed and go write. Because it's really all I have. Back when I drank, I would fix myself a drink and sit in the dark and get drunk trying to numb the pain. But I don't do that anymore.

Tonight, I don't get up. I let Spence hold me, even as he sleeps and wonder if I'll ever be past this. I want to be able to give him children. After seeing him with Zoey and Harper, I've always known he would be a good father. But a few months ago, when Jay and Delia welcomed baby Andrew into the world and we went to see him, I saw in his eyes that he wants it. Wants it bad. And it broke my heart.

He's never once brought up the subject of children with me. I told him when we first reconnected that I didn't know if I could ever go through another pregnancy because of what happened with Aaron. And part of me knows the likelihood of that kind of issue happening again are astronomical, but I'm still so afraid.

I was so broken for so many years after that. But I was also alone then, dealing with it all by myself. No one knew what I was going through. Not Spence, not Dad, especially not Jay, not even my best friends. I'm not alone now; I have Spence.

I love him so much and love can be stronger than fear, so I've been giving it more thought. And I know if Aaron—or whatever name his adoptive parents would've chosen—had been okay, I definitely would've wanted more children when I was ready. When I was older. I'd like to think that by now, we'd have a couple of them at least.

And so, tonight, I lie in bed feeling all my feelings about Aaron and his birth. The pain. The heartache. The anger. I let all that fear of it happening again wash over me. I imagine boxing up all the fear and heartache into a big ornate trunk and closing the lid. I imagine pushing the trunk into the very back of a closet and it getting covered up by other boxes. Boxes full of potential and happiness and hope. I take a deep breath and watch my husband, whom I've loved since I was twelve, as he sleeps and think, *I'm going to give you a child.*

When I wake up, Spence is already gone to work and I get out of bed and walk into the kitchen to see the coffee maker is still on. I pour myself a cup and sit on the couch and think more about the decision I made last night. I expect to feel worried or scared, and while there is an underlying current of fear, the hope pushes through all of it and I know I can do this.

Before I can lose my nerve, I call my gynecologist's office to make an appointment to have my IUD removed and get a full physical. They tell me they've had a cancelation for this afternoon if I could come then. I hesitate for only a moment and tell them I'll be there.

I spend the morning tidying up around the house and pulls some steaks out of the freezer to have for supper tonight. I write for a few hours, just brainstorming ideas for my next book, but I'm too keyed up to really focus and be able to work.

I shower and dress for my appointment and when I pull into the parking lot at the OB-GYN, I'm nervous and ready to get this over with. I think about how to tell Spence I'm ready. I figure I'll do it over supper tonight, and if I know him, he'll want to get started trying right away, which makes me smile.

After Harper left, I was so sad. Our lovemaking was more perfunctory, because we both needed the release, but it wasn't passionate for a while after that. Eventually, though, the passion returned and I'm thankful. I'm grateful for Spence's steadfastness and compassion and patience.

When I get checked in for my appointment, I wait anxiously for them to call my name. Although I'm only one in the waiting room for about twenty minutes, it seems like hours.

After I go through the routine of peeing in a cup and getting my height and weight documented, blood pressure and changes in medical history put in my file, they finally take me to a room and tell me to get undressed and put on a gown.

I sit on the exam table and wait for the doctor to enter. I read and reread all the posters on the walls until about five minutes later, there's a knock on the door and the doctor enters. She shakes my hand and offers me a warm grin. "Joanna, nice to meet you, I'm Dr. Brooks."

I smile. "Hello. Nice to meet you as well." She walks over to the sink and washes her hands and sits on a small stool facing me.

"So, I have in my notes you're wanting to get your IUD removed?"

"Yes, ma'am. I want to try to get pregnant."

"Oh, okay. Sure. And I saw in your file that you've had a previous pregnancy, so do have any concerns about your ability to get pregnant again?"

I shake my head. "No. My first pregnancy ended in a still-birth, and that was nine years ago. I don't have any reason to think I wouldn't be able to get pregnant again, I've just been very careful since then."

Her expression is compassionate. "I'm so sorry to hear about that. Okay. Well, we'll go ahead and get started and get you on your way."

She advises me to lie back and performs an internal exam and tells me there may be a slight pinch and cramping as the IUD is removed. The whole thing take about fifteen minutes and then she has me sit up.

"You may have some cramping and spotting for a few days, so you'll want to be aware of that. And you can take some ibuprofen if you have some discomfort."

"How soon after IUDs are removed does it typically take someone to get pregnant?" I ask.

"It's different for everyone. The type of IUD you had was non-hormonal and you've had your natural cycle the entire time you've had it, so you shouldn't have any issues with your body needing to balance out. Most women are able to conceive within a few months. But if it's been a year and you still haven't conceived, we may want to run some tests to rule out any kind of hormonal issues or anything like that."

I nod. "Okay. Thank you."

She smiles. "Hopefully, we'll see you back in a few months to go over prenatal care."

I blow out a breath. "Hopefully."

CHAPTER SIXTEEN

JO

By the time I get home, I know Spence will be arriving in about an hour, so I start supper. It will be simple and I'll have him grill the steaks, but I get some potatoes from the pantry and wash and dry them. I pierce the skin with a fork and rub them with olive oil and coat them in salt before wrapping them in foil and popping them in the oven.

I make a simple salad of baby greens, cucumbers, carrots, and tomatoes and when Spence comes in the door, I'm seasoning the steaks. He walks over to give me a kiss. "Hey, babe. Steaks? Perfect. Have you started the grill yet?"

"Nope. I was getting ready to do that. Want to go start it and then you can change out of your work clothes? You smell like a hospital."

"Yeah, I had to go visit a patient this afternoon. He'd had a minor stroke."

"Is he going to be okay?"

Spence nods. "Yeah, I was just there to go over his medical history and do my own exam on him. He should make a full recovery."

I smile. "That's great."

He goes out to the back porch and fires up the grill before heading to change into athletic shorts and a tee shirt. I'm washing my hands and he comes up behind me and wraps his arms around me and brushes a kiss just below my ear, sending a shiver down my spine. "I missed you today. How are feeling?"

I dry my hands and turn in his arms to face him and loop my arms around his waist. "I'm okay. I missed you, too." I press my lips to his and give him a deep kiss.

"Well, it sure seems like you missed me. You should miss me more often if that's the welcome I get when I come home."

I push him away and chuckle. "Go grill the steaks. I'm starving. I didn't get to eat lunch today and the potatoes will be done in just a little bit."

His brow furrows in concern. "Why didn't you eat lunch? That's not like you. You feeling all right? You know, after last night?"

I shrug, not wanting to tell him everything yet. "I'm fine. I just had a last minute appointment right in the middle of the day and I spent the morning cleaning house and writing and time got away from me."

"Okay, well, they won't take but just a few minutes." He walks out the door with the plate of steaks and I work to finish up the prep on the sides. I pull plates down and set the table and pour us glasses of sweet tea. I know he'd prefer beer, but we don't keep alcohol in the house for obvious reasons, so tea it is.

After we get done eating, Spence pushes back from the table. "Man, babe, the seasoning on that steak was perfect. Everything was so good."

"I'm glad. Want to watch a movie? I'll get the dishes cleaned up and we can chill."

"I'll help wash up. There's not that much. That way we can get done faster."

I nod. "Okay. The dishwasher's empty, so we really just have to rinse and load."

"Well, why don't I do them and you can just sit on the counter and let me look at you?"

"If you're offering, I'm not going to turn it down. Deal."

He chuckles and we take our plates to the kitchen and I put mine in the sink and hop up on the counter as he takes care of the dishes. Once he's done, he wipes his hands on a dish towel and comes over to stand in front of me. He nudges my knees apart and settles his hands on my hips. I pull him closer to me and wrap my arms around his neck and press my forehead to his and we just stay like that for a bit. After a few minutes, he asks, "What kind of appointment did you have today? I meant to ask earlier."

My heart begins to race. "Um, it was a doctor's appointment."

He pulls back, his face filled with concern. "Is everything okay, are you sick? You know you're married to a doctor, right?"

I chuckle. "You weren't the right kind of doctor today, babe. Sorry. I went to the gynecologist."

"Oh, well, I guess not. Everything all right? Or was it just your annual visit?"

"Everything's great. I had my IUD removed."

He nods. "Okay, did you decide you'd rather be on the pill or something? Did they replace it?"

I take his face in my hands and look into his eyes. "No. They didn't replace it. I asked them to remove it, Spence."

His brows press together in confusion. "Were you having some complication with it? Is everything okay?"

I nod, my expression relaxed. "I'm fine. More than fine," I say, my lips pulling into a soft smile.

His eyes search mine. "Jo, what are you not telling me?"

I take a deep breath. "I'm ready, Spence. I want—I want us to have a baby."

His breath hitches and he takes a step back. "What?"

"I'm ready. I want to give you a baby." My voice is soft and trembles a bit with my nerves, but I've never been more sure of anything in my life.

He swallows thickly and hope flashes in his eyes, but it's gone as quick as it comes and I hate that he doesn't feel like this is something he can hope for. "Babe, I told you, we don't have to. I'm okay. I'm sorry if you feel like I've pressured you. I know after Andrew was born I got really excited. But, I promise, I'm okay. I can't ask you to do this."

My heart aches with the earnestness in his voice and I take his face in my hands again. "Spence, I've given it a lot of thought. You've never pressured me. You've never even mentioned it. Even though I know how badly you want it. And I love you so much for that. But I'm okay. I've known for a long time you'd be a great dad. And watching you with Zoey and Harper and Andrew, I want that for you. I want that for us. I love you more than I'm scared of what will happen. And I know if Aaron had been okay, I would've wanted tons of babies with you. I'm ready. It's time."

Tears fill his eyes. "Jo, are you sure?" he asks, his voice barely above a whisper.

I nod. "Yeah. Because I know no matter what happens, I'm not alone this time. I have you, Spence, and I know even if the worst happens, we'll face it together."

He kisses me and smiles. "I don't know what to say."

"Well, I kinda hoped you wouldn't say anything, and would just take me to bed and put a baby in me."

He laughs. "You ain't gotta tell me twice." He steps back and I hop down off the counter. He pulls me to him and covers my mouth with his. His kiss is sweet and quickly grows deeper, stealing my breath and making need coil low in my belly.

When we break apart, my chest is heaving. "I take it, you like the idea?"

"I love it. And I love you. I know this wasn't an easy thing for you, Jo."

"Believe it or not, it was one of the easiest decisions I've ever made, Spence. Having Harper come into our lives opened my heart back up to the idea. She wasn't my child, but it sure felt like she was. I loved her like she was. And watching you with her and especially Andrew, I want that for us. I want to watch you be a dad. I kept Aaron from you. I don't want to keep anything else back from you. No matter what happens."

He huffs out a soft laugh. "You know, just when I think I've got you figured out, you surprise me in the best way possible. I can't wait to see you be a mom."

I raise an eyebrow. "Kind of hard to do that if you're still wearing pants, don't you think?"

He laughs. "Good point." He drops his shorts and I snort. "Now, let's go make a baby." He tugs me down the hall to our bedroom. When we get to our bed, he stops and his moss green eyes search mine. "Joanna, are you sure? I don't need this to be happy. I told you, you are enough. You'll always be enough."

Hearing him use my full name makes things feel more serious and I appreciate him checking with me, but I don't have doubts. I take his face in my hands. "Spencer Jackson, I love you. Thank you for being a man I want to have children with. Thank you for being so patient with me. You've waited long enough. I'm sure. I want this. Make love to me?"

He brings his mouth to mine and it's as though we've never kissed before, but it's the only thing we were made to do. It's hot and frantic and greedy. Spence's lips and tongue and hands are everywhere and in about thirty seconds, we're both naked and breathing hard.

I pull back from him and trail my fingers down his chest. "Do you remember that night at the bar?" I ask.

He appears to think back. "Are you talking about when we were still sneaking around?"

I nod. "Yeah. Do you remember that? How antsy you were? I thought for sure Jay was going to know something was up."

He kisses my neck. "I remember how jealous I got seeing you with that guy."

"It was really hot. I could tell you were jealous and I secretly loved it."

Spence's hand moves down my back to cup my ass. "I wanted to come over and deck that guy. I wanted to come over and kiss you so everyone knew you were mine. Because even then, I knew I loved you and the thought of seeing you with someone else made me so angry."

"You've got to admit, that quickie in the bathroom was some of the hottest sex we've ever had."

"Totally. When I read that part in the book and remembered it, I wanted to recreate it right then."

I bite my lip. "We could, you know?"

"What, recreate it?"

I nod and tilt my head toward the bathroom. "There's a sink in there. You could watch yourself in the mirror. You know you like that."

He gives me a lopsided smile and then laughs. "That time was hot, too. I think you got off on watching me."

"You're not wrong. I totally did." I walk into the bathroom and pull him with me and I lean against the sink. "Do you remember what you said that night? When you came into the bathroom?"

He runs his finger tips down my side making me shiver as

he bends and kisses my shoulder. "Yeah, I asked you if you remembered what I'd do to someone who touched what was mine. And that you were still mine until the end of summer." He slides his hand up my thigh and his thumb searches out my clit, causing me to let out a soft gasp.

My voice comes out breathy. "And do you remember what I said? I told you I wanted you to fuck me and make me forget about anyone else." His fingers slide into me and my head falls forward onto his chest.

Spence's voice is husky with need. "And do you remember what happened next?"

I nod. "Yeah, you put me up on the sink and fucked me right there in the bar." I hop up onto the sink and pull his mouth to mine. Spence pushes my knees apart and grips my hips and slams into me.

Except this time, I don't have to be quiet. I don't have to bite back the gasp that leaves my mouth. I lean back into the mirror as he lowers his mouth to my breast and continues his swift thrusts. My breathing begins to grow ragged as he flicks my nipple with his tongue and tugs it between his teeth.

After a moment, he pulls back and looks in the mirror as he takes me and I can't help but smile. I run my hand down his chest and abs and work my clit as my pleasure begins to mount. Spence blows out a breath. "Shit, babe, that's hot. You should see yourself."

"I'd rather watch you." I start to go over into my orgasm. "Don't stop. Just like that. Fuck, Spence. You feel so good." My climax grips me and I feel myself clench down as I cry out.

Spence grips the back of my neck and tangles his fingers in my hair and pulls my mouth to his. He lifts my leg to brace it on his arm as he drives deeper into me, the angle nearly causing me to come again. I hold tight to the edge of the counter as he starts to give into his own release. His cock jerks inside me a moment later with his final deep thrusts. He lets out a low grunt and then doesn't move for a bit. He just stands, leaning into me with his hands planted on either side of my hips, his face in my neck.

After a moment, I feel wetness on my neck and his shoulders start to shake. I try to push him back and he pulls me closer to him, his arms wrapped around my waist. I'm alarmed and worried. "Spence, what's wrong? Are you okay?" I grip the back of his neck. "Baby, talk to me. You're scaring me."

He finally raises his face and I see tears streaming down his cheeks and he presses his forehead to mine. "Nothing's wrong, Jo. I'm just really happy. Thank you."

I huff out a relieved laugh and wipe his tears away with my thumbs. "Baby, I haven't done anything yet. I know you're strong and virile, but I don't know that once is going to be enough to get me knocked up."

He laughs. "Still. This is a big deal. I love you. And you don't know, I might be that good. My boys are smart."

CHAPTER SEVENTEEN

SPENCE

So, once wasn't enough for Jo to get pregnant, but six weeks later, she woke up feeling nauseated and I'd noticed her breasts seemed to be fuller and very tender. I didn't want to get my hopes up, but when she brought home a pregnancy test, I was like a kid on Christmas morning while we waited for the results.

I've tried to keep my excitement in check, because I know as much as Jo says she wants this and I believe she does, this still has to be scary for her. But the fact she still wants to do it means the world to me.

As we sit on the side of the tub and I watch the timer on my phone slowly crawl to zero, I hold her hand and tell her that no matter what, we're fine; it's only been six weeks. We covered the test with a washcloth to not peek before it was time.

When the timer goes off, Jo puts her head down on her knees. "I can't look, Spence. You do it."

"Are you sure?"

"Yeah, I'm too nervous. Please?" Her voice is pleading.

I kiss the top of her head. "Okay." I take a deep breath and stand and walk over to the sink and pull the washcloth away and pick up the stick, but I don't look at the testing window just yet. It's a digital test, so it'll either say "pregnant" or "not pregnant". After steeling myself for whatever the result might be, I read it. *Pregnant.* My heart stops, but I don't react.

Jo looks up when I don't say anything. "What does it say?"

I feign nonchalance and shrug. "Well, that's okay."

She seems to deflate and her face falls. "Oh. Well. All right. There's always next month."

I keep my tone even. "I don't think I want to do that."

She looks confused. "Why, we knew it might take a little while. It's only been six weeks."

I can't hold back my smile anymore. "I'm just fucking with you, Jo. You're pregnant."

The color drains from her face. "Really? Spence, don't play." She holds out her hand and I give her the test. Her eyes fill with tears as she reads the results. "That wasn't nice. You can't mess with me like that."

I squat down in front of her and look into her eyes. "I'm sorry, babe."

Her blue eyes, always so beautiful, but now even more so with happy tears in them, search mine. "We're going to have a baby?"

I nod and press a kiss to her lips. "Yeah, we're going to have a baby, Jo."

She looks down and her breath hitches. "Spence, I'm scared."

I take her hands in mine. "I know you are. I'm here though, okay. You're not alone this time. We're in this together. No matter what, all right? I promise."

She nods. "Congratulations, Daddy."

I can't help but laugh. "You've never called me Daddy before. It's kinda kinky. I might like it."

She rolls her eyes and jabs me in the ribs. "Very funny. I'm never going to call you Daddy like that. Don't even think about it. But you're going to be a dad, Spence."

I take her face in my hands. "And you're going to be a mom, Jo."

Over the next several weeks, Jo is so nauseated and in the definite throes of morning sickness. Almost to the point that I'm concerned about her. She can't eat much at all and is so tired all the time, which I know is common, but still, I get worried.

Her obstetrician didn't want to see her until they thought she was at least six to eight weeks along, so I went with her to her first appointment and they decide to do an ultrasound to determine her due date. Jo's reaction to everything has been subdued, but I know it has to do with the past, so I try to temper my excitement. But inside, I am jumping up and down when they roll in the ultrasound machine. "Dr. Jackson, Joanna, how are we doing today?"

Jo blows out a breath and looks at me. "Please tell me there is a reason I am this sick. Like, it's twins or something, because I was nowhere near this sick the last time."

The ultrasound tech says, "Well, we can definitely see one way or the other on that."

Jo pulls her shirt up and unbuttons her jeans. The tech says the gel will be cold and goes through the spiel about what all measurements they'll do. He squirts the gel on her stomach and presses the wand into her abdomen. It takes him a moment to locate the baby, but then, there it is, plain as day. "There we go. Looks like it's just the one." He flips a switch and whooshing sounds play through a speaker.

My stomach turns over and I can't keep the awe out of my voice as I look down at Jo. "That's our baby, Jo."

She smiles. "Yeah, pretty cool, huh?"

I look back up at the tech. "How far along?"

"Let me do a quick measurement. Looks like about nine weeks. Probably sometime early March. I'll print these out for you to take with you."

We thank the tech as he hands us the photos and leaves. Jo wipes the gel off her belly and rights her clothes. "Well, a few more weeks and we can tell the family."

I nod. "Yep. You ready to go? Are you hungry? You've not really eaten anything today."

She frowns. "No. Nothing sounds good. Except maybe pizza."

I perk up at the thought that she actually wants to eat something for the first time in weeks. "What kind? Sausage and onions?"

She grows pale. "No onions. No sausage. Can we do cheese only? I don't know if I can do any toppings."

"Sure thing. We can order when we get home. How are you feeling other than nauseated?"

She chuckles and rolls her eyes. "Spence, honey, I love you, but you don't have to ask me how I am every five minutes. I'm okay. This is normal. I'm just really sick. It should pass in a few weeks. I honestly thought they were going to say it was twins just because of how sick I've been."

"There's always next time," I say and wiggle my eyebrows.

She laughs. "Let me get through this one first, okay?"

Jo finally eats really well when the pizza comes, which makes me feel better. As a doctor, I know everything she's experiencing is normal, but I feel like I will probably be on edge until the baby comes. I know that as her due date gets closer, Jo will likely grow more anxious, just based on her past pregnancy. So I'll happily take her nonchalance for right now.

CHAPTER EIGHTEEN

JO

As I throw up for what seems like the fifteenth time today, Spence holds my hair and rubs my back. "Remind me why I'm doing this again," I say as I sit on the bathroom floor with my forehead laying on the toilet seat.

"Because you're amazing. Because you're beautiful. Because you're strong. Tomorrow, I'll call your doctor to see if it's safe for you to take something for the nausea."

He brings me a wet washcloth and a glass of water and helps me off the floor. I sip the water and wipe my face. "Spence, I'm so tired." I know I sound as though I'm whining and at this point, I truly don't care. I'm so sick on a daily basis, I can hardly function.

He kisses my forehead. "I know, babe. Can I get you anything? Some crackers? Are you craving anything?"

Lord love him. He's been so sweet putting up with me and all my mood swings and complaints. "You're wonderful, you know that? But yes, can I have some shrimp lo mien? It's the only thing that sounds good to me right now."

I can see he's getting ready to say something about the sodium content, because he's a doctor and can't help himself, and I level him with a glare and he seems to reconsider. "Sure, babe. I'll take care of it. Let me go change and I'll run out. Anything else?"

"Thank you. The noodles should do it." He heads to the bedroom to change clothes and I sit on the couch. I'm getting ready to turn on the TV, when there's a knock at the door. It's almost eight PM, and I'm not expecting anyone, so I have no clue who it could be, but I still go answer the door.

When I do, my heart stops and I blink rapidly, sure I must be seeing things. It's Harper, but she looks terrible. She has a black eye and busted lip and I immediately want to murder whoever put their hands on her. I pull her into my arms and can't believe she's here in the flesh. "Harper! Oh my God." I can't hold back my tears at the sight of her.

"Hey, Jo." Her voice sounds tired, but she puts her arms around me and returns my embrace.

I pull her into the house and yell over my shoulder. "Spence, get out here." I take her over to the couch. "What are you doing here? What happened to you? Are you okay?"

Spence comes running. "What is it, Jo? Are you —." He stops when he sees Harper, his eyes going wide. "Harper!"

"Spence, check her over, she's hurt."

She dismisses my concern with a wave. "I'm fine. Really. I'm sorry I couldn't call before I just showed up. I didn't have your number."

Spence comes over to kneel down in front of Harper and examines her face. "That eye looks bad, kiddo. When did it happen?"

"A couple days ago."

"Harper, who did this to you?" I ask and I'm able to keep my rage out of my voice.

"Mom kicked me out. I was planning on leaving anyway,

but I hadn't saved up enough money yet. I'm sorry, but I didn't have anywhere else to go."

I wrap my arms around her more thankful than I've ever been in my life for making her memorize our address. "You know you're welcome with us. We would've always had you with us if we could. You said Maggie kicked you out? Did she hit you?"

Harper looks down at her knees. "Yeah. We got in a fight over her husband even though I didn't do anything. I mean, I did, but it was only a threat, I wouldn't have really done anything."

Spence says, "Okay, start at the top." He seems to think better of that statement and holds up his hand. "Actually, I was getting ready to go some supper for Jo, are you hungry? Chinese food?"

Harper's face turns green. "No Chinese."

"You love Chinese food," he replies, confused.

"Not right now I don't."

Understanding washes over me. "How far along?"

Harper flushes and looks down at her hands. "Eight weeks, give or take. I haven't been to see a doctor yet."

Even though I was expecting the answer she gives, Spence recovers faster than I do. "Well, what are you craving? You name it, I'll find it. I've gotten really good at tracking down whatever Jo's craving. I'm sure we can find something for you, too."

Her head snaps toward me. "You're pregnant?"

I give her a sheepish smile and nod. "Almost ten weeks."

Harper's expression morphs into one of joy. "Jo, that's amazing. Congratulations." Then she turns to Spence. "Tacos. Beef Tacos."

Spence nods. "On it. I'll be back."

I stand and pull her up with me. "Do you have any bags or anything?"

She shakes her head. "No, I was only able to get out with my backpack."

"That's all right, we'll get you squared away. Come with me." I show her to the guest room. "You can stay here. The bed has clean sheets." I take her face in my hands. "It's so good to see you, kid. I've missed you so much."

Tears fill her eyes. "I missed you guys, too. I was counting the days until I turned eighteen, because I was coming to find you."

I pull her into my arms. "You're here now. And you're safe. Do you want to take a shower or anything? Wash the road off? Speaking of which, how did you get here?"

"A shower would be great. Can we wait till Spence gets back to get into everything so I only have to tell the story once?"

"Sure, honey. I'll get you some clothes. Tomorrow, we can go shopping, okay?"

She nods. "Thanks, Jo."

"No thanks needed, Harper. You're family."

I go into my room and pull out a pair of leggings and a tee shirt and hand them over to her. "If you want to bring out your clothes, I'll wash them so you'll have your own clothes to wear out tomorrow. The bathroom's just through there." I gesture to the guest bath. "If you need anything, let me know."

She nods and goes in the bathroom and after a moment, I hear the shower start. I breathe a sigh of relief and send up a silent prayer of thanks that Harper is here now and Maggie can't hurt her anymore.

Harper's still in the shower when Spence gets back. He sets the food bags down and comes to sit next to me on the couch. "What did she tell you?"

"Nothing yet. I asked her some questions, but she said she

wanted to wait until you got back so she wouldn't have to get into everything more than once."

He nods. "I can't believe she's actually here."

"I know. I thought I was seeing things when I opened the door. I swear, I want to kill Maggie. Like, literally wrap my hands around her throat and choke the life out of her for hurting Harper. Her face looks awful."

Spence blows out a breath. "Yeah. I'll check on her later and make sure she doesn't have any other injuries."

We hear the bathroom door open, so we stop talking and get up to go into the kitchen. Harper comes in with her dirty clothes in her arms. "Where's the washer?"

Spence walks over to her. "I'll take those. The washer and dryer are downstairs. I'll get them started. Do you have anything else you'd like thrown in?"

Harper shakes her head and hands her clothes to Spence. "No, that's all I've got."

I gesture to the food bags. "Well, let's eat, shall we?"

She shrugs and we take our food over to the kitchen table. I also bring over a couple bottles of water and hand her one. "Thanks." I nod and we open the bags and I see that Spence got himself some food as well. He comes back up the stairs a few minutes later and sits with us at the table. Harper looks around as she opens her food wrapper. "Your house is really nice. Spence, this is the house you grew up in?"

"Yeah, it didn't look like this when my parents lived here, though. My mom has very different tastes than me. But I've always loved the house, so when my parents wanted to sell, I didn't think twice. Having Nick as a neighbor has been good, too."

"Nick is your dad, right, Jo?"

I nod. "Yep. It's a little weird living next door to my dad, but it's all right."

Spence rises to get a drink and comes back to sit at the table. "Harper, how did you get here, I didn't see a car out front."

She shakes her head. "I took a bus until I got to Knoxville and caught a taxi from there. I was just glad y'all were home. I'd run out of money and wouldn't have been able to get a motel or anything."

I ask, "What happened after you went back to Maggie? Catch us up on the last couple of years."

Harper takes a deep breath. "Well, when you told me they'd found my mom, and she was alive, I didn't want to go back. I really wanted to stay with you guys."

Nodding, I blink back the tears that burn my eyes knowing she wanted to stay with us as much as we wanted her to stay. "We wanted it, too, Harper. If we could've, we would've kept you. Please know that."

She nods. "Well, when I went back, Mom took my phone and smashed it and gave me a super old phone that didn't even have data. And I only had a computer at school that didn't have access to social media, so I didn't have any way to contact you guys. I think she knew I would try to find you.

"We'd moved across town, and Macon would come to visit me, but Mom found us in bed together and made it so he couldn't come see me anymore. She'd met a guy and they got married. He was a real creep, always looking at me and cornering me." When I start to say something, she holds up her hand. "Nothing ever really happened. He moved us to Atlanta, because that's where he was from and we lived in this really shitty apartment. But Mom thought he was just the best thing ever. And she stayed sober until we moved. But then she started drinking again.

"And I tried to never be home. I'd met this guy, Malachi, at school and we started hanging out and I would go to his place when Mom and Steve, that was her husband, were both home, because they'd get drunk and fight.

"Well, I'd been saving up and swiping money from Mom and Steve's wallets when they were passed out, just enough that they'd never notice it was gone. I know that's wrong, but I knew if I didn't figure out how to get out, I never would. And I had your address memorized, but not your phone numbers and didn't have a way to get in touch with y'all. Plus, I wasn't eighteen and I knew the state would just make me go back. So, my plan was that as soon as I turned eighteen and had just enough money to leave, I was out.

"And then, I found out I was pregnant a few days after my birthday. Happy birthday to me, right? I wasn't on anything, and Malachi said he'd pulled out, but well, that apparently doesn't work. I know, I was so stupid. Anyway, I told Mom I was pregnant and she called me a whore and said she wasn't raising any more babies. That if I was old enough to lay down with a guy and get pregnant, I was old enough to make it on my own.

"But I still didn't have enough money to leave, so I asked if I could stay a little bit longer. Mom said no and I went to my room to pack, because she was already drunk at that point and I didn't have a choice. I already had a bag mostly packed with all the money I'd swiped and some clothes.

"Steve came in and said he'd talk to her and got really close to me and said, 'we can work something out', and rubbed my arm. It was real creepy and grossed me out. I had a pair of scissors close by and I told him if he didn't get away from me, I'd cut off his dick and shove it down his throat.

"I went out and told Mom he was being creepy and he said I was making stuff up and she needed to shut me up. She came over to me and got in my face and said I needed to stop lying; wasn't me being a slut and getting myself knocked up enough?

She was so close to me, I could smell the beer on her breath, and it was making me really nauseous, so I pushed her back a little. You know, just to put some space between us. But because she was drunk, she was off balance already and when I pushed her, she stumbled. She must have thought I shoved her, because she came at me and backhanded me.

"Her wedding ring busted my lip and I wasn't expecting it when she hit me and I went flying across the room and hit my eye on the corner of a cabinet. Which, I guess is how I got the black eye. I also hit my hip on the counter, so it's bruised pretty bad, too. But after that, I ran. I grabbed my bag and ran. I went to Malachi's and stayed with him for the first night. I told him I was pregnant and I don't know what I expected from him, but he just told me to get rid of it. He said he had plans for his life and wasn't about to be tied down by a kid. I hadn't even decided what I wanted to do at that point, I just wanted him to know.

"So I asked him to give me a ride to the bus stop and asked him to help me buy a ticket and then took a taxi once I got here. So, yeah, that catches us up, I guess."

Spence and I share a look, but neither of us says anything. After a moment, I get up and pull Harper from her chair and give her a hug. "You should never have had to go through all that. I'm so sorry. I'm glad you came here. You're safe now."

She nods. "I know. That's all I could think about. I kept telling myself, 'if I can get to Jo and Spence, everything will be okay'. You guys were the only place I've ever really felt safe."

I can't fight back the tears threatening to spill. "And whatever you decide to do about the baby, we'll support you in that. Whatever you need."

"Thanks. I'm still not sure. I know I need to decide soon, but I'm just not sure."

Spence stands. "Harper, can I see your side? I want to make

sure there's nothing worse than just bruising." Harper pulls her tee shirt up a bit and leggings down just past her hip to reveal a deep purple bruise that runs the whole width of her side. Spence probes it gently and she winces. He says, "It doesn't look too bad. If you weren't pregnant, I'd tell you to take ibuprofen, but you're not really supposed to have it. Does it hurt?"

"Just when you press on it, otherwise, no." We sit back down, but after a minute, she says, "I think I'm just going to go to bed, if that's okay."

I pat her hand. "Of course. I'll see you in the morning. Let us know if you need anything, okay? Our room is right down from yours."

CHAPTER NINETEEN

SPENCE

After Harper heads off to bed, I run down to the basement to switch her clothes over to the dryer. When I come back up, Jo's putting all the food away in the fridge. "You not hungry anymore, babe? You hardly touched your food."

Jo shakes her head. "Lost my appetite." She comes over to me and wraps her arms around me. "Will you take me to bed and tuck me in? I know you'll probably stay up, but would you care to come cuddle me until I fall asleep?"

I smile and plant a kiss on her forehead. "Of course. Actually, all this excitement has me kinda worn out. I think I'll turn in as well. I'm just going to make sure the house is locked up. I'll be to bed in just a minute, okay?"

She nods and heads toward the bedroom. Five minutes later, after I've ensured all the doors are locked up tight, I go into our bathroom and shed my shorts and tee shirt and put them in the dirty clothes. I crawl in bed next to Jo and pull her to me. Her back is pressed against my chest and I brush a kiss across her shoulder.

"Spence?"

"Yeah, babe?"

Jo turns over so we're facing each other. "I'm sorry I've been so cranky lately. Thank you for putting up with me. I know I haven't been easy to live with the past few weeks."

I can't help but chuckle. "Babe, you're growing a person. That's hard work. I don't have to do anything except keep you happy. I'll take that over what you're going through."

She laughs. "Spoken like a man. Well, still, I feel bad because I've been so moody and you've been so sweet. And I know we haven't had sex much in the past few weeks, either, and I feel really bad about that."

"Jo, stop. You've got a lot going on. I know you don't feel good, I'm not going to pressure you or give you a hard time. I'm fine."

"Well, I'm not. I'm already going to have to give up sex for at least six weeks after this baby is born, I don't want to have to give it up now, too."

I huff out a soft laugh and pull her closer to me. "Believe me, babe, I'm more than willing, I just didn't want you to feel like you had to, knowing how bad you've been feeling."

She kisses my neck. "Would you be willing right now?"

"Now? I thought you were tired?" I ask, unable to hide my surprise.

Her hand trails down my stomach and into my boxers. "Well, I was, but I'm married to this extremely sexy man who I can't get enough of. So, for some reason, whenever he's around, I get this surge of energy. Just don't touch my boobs, they're still really tender."

"Yes, ma'am." I go on to show her all the ways I can touch her and bring her pleasure without once touching her breasts.

When I wake up, as usual, Jo is still out. I get up and throw on a pair of athletic shorts and socks and sneakers and go out into the living room to stretch before heading out the door for a run. As I walk into the room, I see Harper sitting on the couch with her knees drawn up, not doing anything.

"Hey, kiddo. What's up? You're up early."

She shrugs. "Couldn't sleep. A lot on my mind."

"I'm sure. Want to talk about anything? I know I'm not Jo, but I'm a pretty good listener. They trained me real well in med school."

She gives me a soft smile. "I know you are. I've never had a problem talking with you. I just don't know what to do. You know, about the baby and stuff."

I sit down beside her. "Well, you're the only one who can make that decision. Jo and I can't make it for you. Because no matter what option you choose, there are implications. Lifelong ones."

"What would you do, Spence?"

I let out an uncomfortable chuckle. "I'm definitely not the person to ask about that. I don't have a horse in the race."

"Yeah, but if you and Jo were young like me, what would you do?"

I look down and take a deep breath, not wanting her to know that we've been exactly in her position before, even if I was unaware at the time. "That would be a question for Jo. But even if it were the case, she'd be the one to make any decisions, even if I had opinions."

"Yeah, but as a guy, if a girl you'd been sleeping with told you she was pregnant, what would you want?"

"I guess it depends. Does the guy love the girl?"

She looks away. "No. Not love."

"Well, I think that can make a difference for what a guy might want to do. And, is he eighteen or is he older? What kind

of life does he have planned out? Can it make room for something like a baby? There are a lot of factors that go into decision
making in this sort of situation."

"But would you just tell a girl to 'get rid of it'? That just
seems like such a heartless thing to say."

"Yeah, teenage guys can be assholes. It was a really insensi-
tive thing to say. Sometimes people say things before thinking
and are more a fear response rather than what they truly feel.

"But, listen, Harper. What Jo said last night, about whatever you decide, we'll support you? That's the truth. If you
want to raise this baby, we'll help you. If you want to put it up
for adoption, we'll help you go through that. If you decide to
terminate, we'll take you to the appointment and make sure
you're okay. But you're the only one who can decide what you
want to do. We're here if you want to talk, but Jo and I aren't
going to to be able to make this decision for you. Because you're
the one who has to live with the decision, not us. And we may
know what we'd do in your shoes, but we're not you."

She takes a deep breath and nods. "Yeah. Thanks, Spence.
You really are a good listener. And good advice giver."

I stand. "Anytime. What are big brothers for? I'm going to
go for a run. Jo's still in bed, but your clothes are in the dryer
downstairs and they should be dry."

"Okay. Thanks."

I head out the door and start with a quick jog before
picking up the pace. The late summer humidity makes it difficult to breathe, even at this early hour, and after about four
miles, when I make it back to the house, I'm drenched with
sweat and very much looking forward to a shower.

Harper is still sitting on the couch, but has a cup of coffee
in her hand. She looks up at me. "Coffee's ready if you want
some."

"Thanks, I'll get some after my shower." I take off back

toward the bedroom and Jo is sitting up in bed drinking her coffee. I smile at her. "You got up and got coffee and came back to bed?"

She shakes her head. "No, Harper brought it in for me. I think if I get up, I'll probably want to puke, so I'm staying put for a few more minutes. Did you have a good run?"

"Yeah, it's humid as hell, though. Definitely felt sluggish today."

She quirks an eyebrow. "Well, you look like you had a good run. If I were not such a civilized person, I might want to come over and lick the sweat off your abs."

I can't help but laugh. "Yeah, but as soon as you smelled me, you'd probably get real nauseated, so it's probably best if I keep my distance."

"Very true. I'm going to to take Harper shopping today to get whatever she needs. I'll probably pick up some chicken and we can just do grilled chicken and veggies for supper."

"Sounds good." I come to sit on the edge of the bed. "I think she's struggling with what she wants to do. She asked me what we would do if we were younger." Jo's eyes go wide and I shake my head. "I didn't tell her anything, but you might want to. It might put things in perspective for her."

"Spence, if I tell her what happened to me, it becomes about me. And my story's not typical. I don't want to scare her."

"Well, I still think it might help her, knowing what you went through. Even if you leave out the scary bits."

"It's kinda hard not to tell the scary bits in my case. I'm not going to lie to her. If I tell her, I tell her all of it. But, like I said, I don't want to scare her. My story is scary. And it took me how long to even think about having kids after that?"

I stand. "I know, babe. But just think about it. I've gotta hustle or I'm going to be late for work."

She sighs and nods. "I will. Now, drop your drawers so I can watch you walk into the bathroom."

I do as requested and laugh when Jo whistles as I walk away.

CHAPTER TWENTY

JO

When I come out of the bedroom after taking a shower and getting dressed, I see Harper is sitting on the couch, wearing the clothes she had on yesterday. "Hey, kid. Did you already eat? I thought we could go out for breakfast. I'm actually hungry this morning, so I want to take advantage."

"I had some toast, but that was hours ago. I could eat." She sighs. "Do you think people will stare because of my face? I know I look like I went twelve rounds."

I come to sit beside her. "We can try to cover it with some makeup, but I don't know how well it will do. If anyone asks, you can just say, 'you should see the other guy' or something like that."

She gives me a soft smile. "Okay. I guess let's go."

We walk out the door and I lock the house before we climb into my car. "What store do you like to shop at for clothes?"

She shrugs. "I don't really have a preference. Most of my clothes come from Target, I think."

"Well, we can go there, or we can do Old Navy or American Eagle. Wherever you want. I need to get a few groceries, but other than that, today's all for you, sister. We can also swing by my dad's bookstore and pick out some books if you want."

Her eyes light up. "Can we?"

"Of course. I know you've gotta be jonesing. And I left a lot of my books in Jacksonville since I go down there to write sometimes. And Spence's collection is more sci-fi, so not exactly my cup of tea. I mainly read on my phone or iPad these days."

"Have you been back much? To Jacksonville?"

"A few times. Spence and I went there on our honeymoon. I know, not super glamorous or anything, but we already pay the mortgage on the condo, so we want to try to use it as much as we can. I went down to put the finishing touches on my second book and when I got the drafts back from editors. We'll probably go down before the baby comes, just to get away."

"I haven't gotten to read your second book yet. I knew if Mom saw it, she'd flip, so I didn't. I'm sorry. I would have otherwise."

I squeeze her shoulder. "That's okay. I've got copies at the house you're more than welcome to. I think you'll like it."

"And you're working on another one now, too, right? What's it going to be about?"

I blow out a breath. "Well, there will still be some romance, but it's got some mystery as well. There's a stalker."

"Ooh, sounds good. I can't wait to read it. I love getting to tell my friends that my big sister is a famous writer."

I chuckle. "Not exactly famous. I do all right. My second book was well received, so that made me feel good. And the advance and royalties that come in help pay for the condo, so that's always good.

"Spence wanted me to quit my day job so I could focus on writing full-time, but it's scary. I hate feeling like I'm relying on him to make all the money. What if, one day, the book ideas dry up? I mean, I guess I could always go back to work for a paper or something, but now with a baby coming, I don't want to do that. I like the freedom writing provides."

She nods. "Yeah. But you're super creative. You'll be fine. Hey, do you think I could get a job?"

"Sure, if you want. I can talk to my dad, see if he needs help at the store. He's always looking for good workers. I know you'd do a good job."

"Do you think it would be weird, me working for you dad? I mean, Maggie's my mom and she was married to your dad and I'm, at least partially, the reason they got divorced."

I shake my head. "No, it'll be fine. That was a long time ago. And besides, my dad's going to love you. He's not going to hold who your mother is against you. But what about school, you need to finish high school."

"How am I going to do that if I have a baby? I'm eighteen, I legally don't have to go. I can just work."

"Harper, how are you going to get into college or get a good job without at least a high school diploma. It's not going to happen. You deserve to go to college. Spence and I want to help you."

"Maybe I'll just get my GED. That way I can still work full-time."

"Sure, if that's what you want to do. I can help you study. But you're doing something, okay? And think about college. It's a great experience. And depending on what you want to do, it'll be necessary. I know before, when you were with us, you seemed interested in medicine. Is that still something you're into?"

Harper shrugs. "I think being a nurse would be good. I don't think I'd want to be a doctor; that's eight years of school. But nursing might be all right."

"Okay. Well, that's a great goal. We'll make sure you get

there. So," I ask, changing the subject, "do you still talk to Macon?"

Harper shakes her head. "No. After Mom ran him off and we moved, we lost touch. I still think about him, but I doubt he'd want to see me."

"Why do you say that? I'm sure he'd love to reconnect."

"He's in college now. He was planning on going to Duke. He's so smart and driven."

"Well, why don't you call him? Can't hurt, right?"

"And tell him what, that I'm a high school drop out who got knocked up and my mom kicked me out. Yeah, that's a real conversation starter."

I chuckle. "I don't know that I'd lead with all that. 'Hi' works, too. You never know."

She takes a deep breath. "I'm a mess, Jo. I wouldn't want him to see how bad things are."

"Well, you always said he was your best friend, right? Be his friend. I'm sure, as close as y'all were, you could be that to each other again."

"I don't know if I could see him if he's moved on. It might hurt too much. I mean, I know I slept with Malachi, but it was never serious. That was more just to not be at home and he was nice to me. I know that sounds bad, but I always thought about Macon."

I shake my head. "That doesn't sound bad to me. I get it. I was with guys after Spence and I still thought about him even after we broke up. All the time."

"Well, y'all are different. It's obvious to anyone who looks at you that you're so in love."

"Yeah, but when we broke up, I didn't want to love him anymore. I wanted to hate him. But I couldn't."

She frowns. "Why would you want to hate Spence? You've loved him since you were twelve."

"Well, just because you love someone doesn't mean that you can't hurt each other. I hurt him. He hurt me. We hurt each other. It happens. And it kept us apart for eight years."

"What happened?"

When I don't answer, Harper says, "I'm not fifteen anymore, Jo. You can tell me. I'm not a little girl."

"I know you're not. But part of it isn't my story. I did the things I did and Spence did the things he did and we both hurt one another. I don't want to paint him in a bad light, when it's not who he is anymore. And some things are best left between the people they happened to. Not that I don't think I can't trust you or anything, I know I can. But all of it was so long ago, I try not to think about it.

"Some things, I can't help but think about them, but others are better left in the past. I will say this, though, if I could go back, there are a lot of things I would change. I would have reached out to Spence and we would have had a lot more years together. So, if you still think about Macon, I say call him. The worst that happens is you find out once and for all it won't work. Trust me, it's better to know.

"Spence and I both spent years wondering and trying to make things work with other people when we both thought the one person we truly wanted hated us. It cost both of us so much happiness. I wouldn't wish that on anyone."

"Okay. Maybe I will."

CHAPTER TWENTY-ONE

SPENCE

As I come in the front door at home, I see Jo and Harper sitting on the couch laughing. It warms my heart to see both of them in such good spirits. "How are my two favorite girls? Did you put my credit card to work today?"

Jo jumps up and gives me a kiss. "It definitely got a work out. But I'll make it up to you later." She winks at me.

"Y'all, that's gross. I'm right here." Harper feigns disgust, but she's smiling.

"Sorry, Harp, what can I say, Jo finds me irresistible."

"Yeah, yeah." She sips a glass of water and turns back to the TV.

Jo follows me into the bedroom and as I change out of my khakis and polo, I say, "You seem to be feeling pretty good this evening."

She sighs. "Yeah, hopefully, the morning sickness is starting to subside. I was queasy this morning, but I've felt okay for the most part."

"Did y'all have a good time shopping and stuff? Harper get everything she needs?"

Jo nods. "Yeah. I invited Dad over for supper tonight. I hope that's okay. I want him to meet Harper. I'm going to talk to him about letting her work at the store. I think he'll be fine with it, but I still thought dinner would be nice."

"Sure. What about school? Harper needs to be in school, especially if she's going to go to college next year."

"She mentioned getting her GED, which I think is fine. Anymore, as long as you have good test scores and a GED, you can get in pretty much wherever. I know whatever she does is going to be dependent on what she does about the baby, but she's still got time."

"Not much. She only thinks she's eight weeks along. She might be further. She needs to see a doctor to be sure. And after a few more weeks, her options are going to be a lot more limited."

"I know. I'm going to call tomorrow to make her an appointment."

"So what else did y'all talk about today?"

"Not much. I asked her if she was still in contact with Macon. She said she still thinks about him, but he's in college at Duke, and she thinks she screwed things up with him. But I told her the worst that happens if she reaches out is that she finds out it won't work."

I wrap my arms around Jo's waist and pull her to me. "Better to know than wonder. Look at us, if either of us had reached out, we'd have been married years ago and could have been happier for a lot longer."

She smiles. "That's what I said. She mentioned even when she was with that Malachi guy, she thought about Macon. She acted like it was bad, but I told her it wasn't, because after we broke up, I'd still think about you when I was with other guys."

I nod. "Yeah. I would've preferred there be no other men or women, but that's what we get for being stubborn."

"Yep. We got to talking about our breakup because I'd said we both hurt each other, but I didn't get into specifics. Because that wasn't fair to you."

I shrug. "Yeah, but it's part of our story. It's what makes us, us. We can't change anything."

"I wish we could, though."

I brush a kiss across her lips. "Me, too. But we're happy now, so I say, we take the win."

"Deal." Jo bites he lip. "I still haven't told her about Aaron. If and when she decides what she wants to do, I'll tell her, but I don't want my story be a reason she does one thing or another."

"I get that. Well, I'm not going to tell her. It's not my story."

Jo brings her hand up to my face. "It should have been, though. I'm sorry."

I press my forehead to hers. "Babe, we can't keep hashing this out. Let's just be happy, okay? I know talking with Harper today probably dredged a lot of that up for you, but I'm okay. I love you. I love the life we have." I bring my hand down to her belly. "I love this little person we've created. And I love you for giving me this amazing gift."

Jo covers my hand with her own. "I love you, too. And this little peanut."

"Peanut, huh? Okay. I like it."

She shrugs. "We don't know if it's a boy or girl, so I figure peanut works for now."

"What time is your dad coming over?"

She looks over at the alarm clock. "In about a half-hour. Probably should start supper, huh? I mean, you should start supper, since everything's going on the grill."

I laugh. "Sure thing. You may also want to mention to Harper that we haven't told anyone you're pregnant yet, so she'll keep it quiet."

"Oh, yeah. I'll do that."

Right on time, Nick knocks on the door and Jo goes to answer. He enters and wraps his daughter in a big hug while I'm coming in from the back porch with a platter of chicken and vegetables. "Nick, good to see you." I set the dish down on the kitchen table and go over to shake my father-in-law's hand.

"Spencer, my boy. How's work?"

"Oh, you know. People come in sick, I try to make them better."

Jo goes down the hallway and a few minutes later, comes out, her arm around Harper. "Daddy, this is my sister, Harper. Harper, this is my dad, Nick."

Harper extends her hand to Nick, who I see notices her bruised face, but doesn't draw attention to it. He smiles and takes her hand. "Harper, so nice to finally meet you. I've heard so many great things about you. Joanna and Spencer speak very highly of you. I know they're happy to have you back in their lives."

Harper looks relieved by Nick's kind words. "I'm happy to be back. Jo's told me a lot about you as well. It's really cool that you own a bookstore. All the books you can read, I'm sure."

Nick chuckles. "You'd think that, and sometimes it is. But for the most part, it's like any other retail job with lots of cranky customers."

I interrupt. "Supper's done, if we want to take this conversation over to the table."

We all walk over to the table and I help Jo fix drinks for everyone. When we sit down, Nick and Harper are discussing the relevance of classic literature in today's society. After a few minutes, Nick says, "Wow, Joanna, you weren't joking. Harper is smart as a tack. Takes after her big sister."

Harper blushes with the compliment. "Thank you."

After supper, and Nick goes home, Harper is helping me clean up the dinner dishes so Jo can rest. Once we're done, we go sit on the couch. She says, "I was talking with Jo today."

"Yeah, she said y'all had some pretty good conversations."

She nods. "Yeah, she asked me about Macon and if we still talked and stuff."

"She mentioned that. How is Macon, do you think? Jo mentioned that you said he'd gone to Duke. That's a good school."

"Yeah. He's always wanted to go there. I've been giving it a lot of thought and I think I'll call him. Jo got me a phone today."

I give her an encouraging smile. "That'll be good. You never know, even if y'all just stay friends, you can't have too many of them."

She seems to consider my words. "I don't know if I could be just his friend. I mean, we were friends before we ever became more, but I love him, and it might hurt too much to see him with someone else."

I blow out a breath. "Yeah, it can. I know after Jo and I broke up and we reconnected, she'd told me she wasn't sure she could be in a relationship after everything that happened. She thought she was too damaged. But I told her I would still rather have her in my life as a friend, because it was better than nothing."

Harper's eyebrows scrunch in confusion. "Why would Jo be damaged? Because of what happened when y'all broke up? Can you tell me what happened? She wouldn't tell me. She said it wouldn't be fair to you, or whatever."

"It was partially what I did, but there was other stuff, too. But Jo will have to tell you about that when she's ready. That part of the story is hers to tell."

Harper rolls her eyes. "Y'all are so cryptic. I swear. Your story. Her story."

I shrug. "There were things we went through separately and things that we went through together, so yeah, her story and my story."

"Okay, so what's your part? Can you tell me?"

I take a deep breath and consider. "My part is not good. I was not a good guy. I was young, not that it's any excuse, because it's not. So, when Jo and I got together, how much do you know about that?"

She thinks for a minute. "I'm guessing it was a lot like Jo's book? It was only supposed to be for the summer?"

I nod. "Yeah. And because I was best friends with Jay, we thought it was better to keep things secret, because we knew we'd only be together over the summer and he'd be angry with me because my track record with women wasn't great. I wasn't willing to sacrifice my relationship with Jay at that time to be with Jo, so we were a secret. And it was only supposed to be casual.

"I'd never had a serious girlfriend before. Never needed or wanted one. Like I said, I wasn't a good guy. I was terrible, actually. But Jo knew that and was okay with it and was cool to keep things casual. But I fell for her. I wasn't supposed to, but it happened. And the day before she left for school, when it was supposed to be our last night, I told her I loved her and had for weeks.

"But Jo couldn't hear it. She said it wasn't fair to her to spring my feelings on her the day before she left, which it wasn't. I should've been honest as soon as I started having real feelings for her, because we'd agreed to that. But I was scared she'd want to break things off, so I didn't.

"And then she ran away and I was really hurt. I'd poured

out my heart to her and she'd run away, so I did a really stupid thing. Monumentally stupid. Unforgivably stupid."

Harper's expression is shocked. "You cheated? You told Jo you loved her and then cheated?"

I nod slowly and frown. "Yeah. I'm definitely not proud of my behavior. I was really hurt that I'd told Jo I loved her and she couldn't hear it. And I got drunk at a bar and hooked up with a girl. But there were other factors in play for Jo I didn't know about at the time. But she came the next morning to say she was just scared and she wanted to make it work. And the girl I'd brought home walked out of my bedroom."

She inhales sharply. "Oh, God. I bet Jo kicked your ass."

I let out a sad laugh. "I wish she would have. It probably would've hurt less. But after that, she wouldn't return my calls and she blocked my number. And when I saw her several months later, she was still hurt and I was hurt and then we didn't see each other again until her book signing. Because as scary as it was, I'd always promised her I would come. She didn't think I would, because she thought I hated her, but I keep my promises. And then we realized we still loved each other, so here we are now."

Harper's head tilts, a confused expression on her face. "But why were you hurt, if you were the one who cheated? Why would Jo think *you* hated *her*? I don't get it."

"And that's where Jo's story picks up. That's for her to tell. I know she'll tell you, but when she's ready. Don't push her. She's already decided she's got some things she wants you to know, but not yet."

"Wow. That's some story. So, did you really sing to Jo when you told her you loved her?"

I nod. "Yeah. Played the piano, too."

"Do you still play?"

"I hadn't in a long time. After Jo left, I wouldn't. But I did at our wedding and every once in a while, when I'm feeling extra romantic, I'll drag out the keyboard."

She smiles. "And you'll have to sing to the baby."

I nod. "Yeah, I guess I will."

CHAPTER TWENTY-TWO

JO

While I'm having my coffee a few days after the dinner where my dad and Harper met, she comes to sit next to me on the couch. "Hey, kid. What's on the agenda today?"

She smiles. "Sounds like you're feeling better."

I give her an excited grin. "Let's hope so. I'm *so* over throwing up."

"I'm going to work with your dad today. Thanks for getting me that job. It will be nice to have something to do."

"Sure. Tomorrow, though, you've got a doctor's appointment."

She blows out a breath. "Do you think they'll do an ultrasound?"

I nod. "Yeah, probably. Especially if you're not sure how far along you are. You still think you're about eight weeks? Is Malachi the only guy you were with?"

She nods. "Yeah. And we didn't start sleeping together until, like, four or five months ago, I think. But I've had a couple of periods."

"Okay, well, we'll just have to see, I guess. Do you have any questions about the appointment or anything?"

She bites her lip and tears fill her eyes. "I don't think I can raise this baby, Jo. I'm not ready to be a mom. I really do want to go to college. How can I do that if I have to work and take care of a baby?"

I pull her into my side and kiss the top of her head. "There's no shame in knowing you're not ready."

"But I know how bad the foster system is, I wouldn't wish that on any kid, especially mine."

"Well, if you decide to go the route of adoption, you can choose the baby's parents. That's the beauty of it. You get all these profiles to choose from and you can hang out with prospective parents and spend time with them to know if they're the right parents for your child. It's pretty cool actually. And you can choose an open adoption if you'd like the option to still have contact and see how they grow up. But, listen, whatever you decide is not going to be wrong. At all. You're the only one who knows what's right for you."

"Well, what do you think I should do?"

I blow out a breath. "I can't answer that, Harper. I'm not the one who has to live with your decision. You do." I swallow the lump that's formed in my throat and lift her chin to look at me. "I can tell you what I did, though."

She sits up, her expression confused. "What? What do you mean?"

"The summer I spent with Spence, I got pregnant."

The color drains from her face. "Really?"

"Yeah. And I wasn't ready to be a mom. I had dreams. I wanted to write. But I loved Spence, and I couldn't terminate, because even though I didn't want to be a mom, I knew that it was child we'd created in love. So I was going to put him up for adoption." I look down at my hands. "The morning I was supposed to leave for school—."

"When Spence had hooked up with a girl after he told you he loved you?"

I nod. "So, he's told you about that?"

"Yeah, but he said you thought he hated you, I don't get it. If he cheated on you, why would he hate you?"

"Well, the day we were planning on spending our last night together, was actually the day I found out I was pregnant. I was so overwhelmed with the news and then he told me he loved me and I got scared and left. But the next day, right before I was supposed to go back to school, I realized if there was no baby, I would have jumped at the chance to be with him, so I ran over here to tell him that. I was also going to tell him about the baby so we could decide together what to do.

"I'd put the ultrasound photo in a book and took it over. I walked in and set the book down on the coffee table and he came out and then, well, so did she. I didn't get to tell him about the baby, because I was so hurt by what he'd done. And then I blocked his number. But I remembered I'd left the book and ultrasound picture, so I thought he'd still find a way to get in touch with me.

"I'd still decided I was going to put the baby up for adoption, and had looked into families and things, and by Thanksgiving, I figured that Spence had already seen the ultrasound and didn't care, so I was even more hurt.

"I'd planned on hiding my pregnancy, and wasn't going to go home at Christmas because I was too big to hide it and I really couldn't face Spence, so I told my dad I had mono. But then, a few days before Christmas, I lost the baby."

Harper gasps and covers her mouth with her hand. "Jo. That's terrible. Was Spence with you, like Wes was with Hailey in the book?"

I shake my head. "No, he didn't know. I should have called him, but I couldn't. But then, he showed up on New Year's Eve at my dorm. He'd finally found the book and ultrasound at that point and flew down to talk about the baby."

Tears spring to my eyes and I blink them back and clear my throat. "But I was still in a lot of pain and super hormonal and emotional, I couldn't tell him what happened. I just told him there wasn't a baby anymore. So he assumed I'd had an abortion. And I let him believe it. At the time, I thought it would be easier for him to be angry or hate me than deal with the truth.

"And he didn't find out the truth until after he read my book and came to see me." I turn over my right wrist and show Harper my tattoo. "His name was Aaron Nicholas. After Spence and my dad. But for years and years, I was so depressed. I thought I had to feel it. Because even though I couldn't have done anything to prevent what happened—it was this fluke thing—I still felt like I deserved to carry the pain with me.

"And no one knew. Not Spence or Dad or Jay. Even my best friends didn't know. And so I told Spence before we decided to get back together that I couldn't promise I could give him children, because I didn't know if I'd be able to emotionally handle it after what happened to Aaron."

Harper blows out a breath. "But what changed? Was this pregnancy unplanned?"

I shake my head. "No, we were trying. And I'm still terrified, but honestly, it was you, Harper. You changed me."

She frowns in confusion. "Me? What did I do?"

I take her face in my hands. "You opened my heart back up to the thought of being a mother and made me realize that love is stronger than fear. You dropped into our lives and turned things upside down, but you showing up on my doorstep was one of the best things that ever happened to me. I know you're not my kid, but I love you like you are. And loving you made me realize I can be a mom. That I wanted to be a mom."

Harper's eyes fill with tears. "I don't know what to say, Jo."

"I'm only telling you all of this, because even knowing how things turned out, I wouldn't have done anything different. Seeing Aaron and getting to say goodbye to him, I wouldn't trade it for the world. But you have to do what's right for you. Every decision has consequences.

"I still carry Aaron's loss with me every day. I know I would've carried him with me if I'd given him up. I know I would've carried it with me if I had terminated. You'll carry it with you no matter what. You just have to figure out which decision will be the easiest to carry with you for the rest of your life.

"Now, my story is not typical. What happened to me was such a fluke thing, the likelihood of it happening is so astronomical. I didn't tell you any of it to scare you or sway your decision."

Harper nods. "Thank you for telling me. I guess after we go to the doctor tomorrow, I'll have to decide."

"And like I said, whatever you decide will be right for you. And that's all that matters. Don't let what I did sway you. *You* have to decide. And Spence and I will support whatever decision you make."

CHAPTER TWENTY-THREE

JO

Harper's knee jiggles nervously as we wait for the ultrasound tech to come in. She's already met with the obstetrician, so this is it for today. And then, it's just waiting for her to decide what she wants to do. The ultrasound tech, the same one who did mine a couple of weeks ago, come in with a smile. "Well, hello. I see you brought us someone new."

I chuckle. "This is my sister. I'm only here for moral support."

He looks down at Harper as she lies down on the table. "Sure. Harper Cole, is that correct?" Harper nods and raises her shirt. "Okay this gel might be a bit cold." He squirts the gel on to her stomach and then pulls out the wand.

Harper turns her head away from the screen and looks up into my eyes, her voice shaky. "I don't want to see, Jo. It might make it easier for me to decide if I don't see."

I squeeze her hand. "That's okay. I can look. You don't have to." I look up at the screen. "How far along?" The irony that Spence was in this same position a couple of weeks ago asking the exact same question is not lost on me.

The tech hits some keys to conduct measurements. "One second. Looks like it's about eighteen weeks."

Harper gasps but still doesn't look at the screen. "That can't be. Are you sure?"

The tech nods. "Yeah, according to the fetal measurements, you're about eighteen weeks, four days."

She closes her eyes and I see the tears well in them. Because she and I both know her window for options just narrowed drastically. I lean down to whisper in her ear. "It's okay. It's all going to be okay."

The tech offers to print the photos, but Harper declines and he steps out. I hand her a paper towel and she wipes the gel off and sits up, all the color drained from her face. I lift her chin. "It's fine. You're fine. Okay? We'll go home and talk through your options, all right?"

"Jo, I don't know how this is possible."

"You said you were with Malachi from about four months ago?"

"Yeah, and I mean, I guess it could have been farther back than that, but I didn't think so. But I wasn't with anyone else. Shit, Jo. What am I going to do?" Tears stream down her face and I pull her in for a hug.

"Like I said, you'll be okay. Let's go home, all right? We can talk about it there."

When we get home, Harper goes to lie down and process the information we've received. Spence comes home a little while later and sees me sitting on the couch not doing anything and sits down beside me. "What's with the face, babe? You look upset."

"I took Harper to the doctor today. She's farther along than she thought."

He looks surprised. "Really? How far along?"

"Eighteen weeks."

"Shit."

I blow out a breath. "Yeah. That's what we said. She said she must have been sleeping with Malachi longer than she originally thought. She said there wasn't anyone else."

"What does she want to do? She's going to have to decide, like, now. Legally, she's only got another week to terminate."

"I know. I don't know. I told her about Aaron yesterday."

His eyebrows go up. "How did she take that?"

I shrug. "You know her, she processes things on her own. She thanked me for telling her, but that was about it. I told her whatever she decided, we'd support it. She's lying down. I don't know how to help her, Spence."

He takes my hands and kisses the backs of them. "This is something she's going to have to decide on her own."

"I know. It still sucks, because she thought she had a lot more time."

He pulls me into his side. "Well, all we can do is be here for her, whatever she decides."

I nod. "Yeah. Sorry, but I haven't made supper. I was so thrown by Harper's appointment, I haven't even thought about it. Want to order pizza?"

"Sure, we can do that. Feel like any toppings?"

I think. "Yeah, sausage. No, mushrooms. No, bacon."

Spence laughs. "How about you decide and then tell me."

"Half sausage, half mushrooms."

"Okay. Fine. I'll order it. Then I'm going to take a shower."

I pull his face to mine. "How about before you do that, you give me a proper kiss. I've missed you today."

He smiles. "Well, Mrs. Jackson, I've missed you as well." He kisses me deeply and I wrap my arms around his neck and pull him down to the couch with me. His hand is traveling up the hem of my shirt when we hear Harper clear her throat. We both sit up as if we'd been caught doing something illicit. "Sorry, Harp."

She rolls her eyes and stands in front of us. "I'm used to y'all by now. Although I wouldn't like it, it wouldn't surprise me if I caught y'all naked in the kitchen."

Spence smirks and starts to say something, but I elbow him in the ribs. "Did you need something? We're going to order pizza for supper."

She takes a deep breath. "Yeah. I've decided what I want to do."

Spence and I both sit up straighter. I ask, "What have you decided?"

"I'm going to do adoption."

I nod. "Okay. Are you sure?"

She swallows and looks down. "Yeah. If I wasn't so far along, I might've decided to terminate, but knowing how big the baby is now and knowing that in a few weeks, it would be able to survive on its own outside the womb, it just feels wrong. And, Jo, what you said yesterday, about choosing the baby's parents, that struck me.

"Because if I could've chosen mine, I would've picked you guys. So if I can find parents for my baby who are half as great as you and Spence, I'll have done a good thing."

I try to swallow the lump that's formed in my throat. "Thanks, Harper, that means a lot."

"Yeah, well, you and Spence have been better parents to me in the short time I was with you than my mom has been for most of my whole life."

I stand and give her a hug. "I love you, kid. You know that?"

She nods. "I love you, too."

Spence stands. "Can I get in on this hug? I feel totally left out."

Harper laughs and we open our arms to pull Spence into a family hug.

———

Later on, while Spence and I lie in bed, my head is on his chest and he's rubbing my back. I say, "You better enjoy this while you can. Not too much longer until my belly is way far out and I won't be able to lay in your arms like this."

I feel him smile against the top of my head. "I cannot wait. I want to see you all big and pregnant and all belly. What do you think about what Harper said?"

"Which part?"

"About us being good parents to her and that's what made her want to choose adoption. Not going to lie, I had to fight back a little tear on that one."

I huff out a soft laugh. "Yeah, she's a sweet girl, that Harper. I think it's good. I don't think it's something she'll ever regret, so that's good."

"What if we did it?"

"Did what?"

"Adopt her baby?"

I sit up and turn on the lamp so I can see his face. "Spence, be serious. You know I'm pregnant, too, right? That's crazy."

He sits up. "Why is it crazy?"

"Because, it would pretty much be like having twins, except one is several weeks older. It's easy for you to say let's take on another baby, when you're going to be at work. I'd be the one here with both babies."

Spence takes my hand. "Just think about it, Jo. We could do this for Harper. She could stay in her child's life, but have her dreams. If you could've done something like this for Aaron, where you could have still been in his life, wouldn't you have wanted that?"

I tilt my head in annoyance, my voice low. "That's not fair, Spence. You can't bring him up when it suits your purpose."

"I'm not. I promise. But seriously, if you had it to do over, and you could choose someone in our family who could've raised Aaron so he could still be in our lives, would that not have been better than having a stranger raise him?"

I blow out a breath. "Yeah, probably, but it didn't work out like that. And besides, who's to say Harper even wants to be in this child's life. She may want to cut ties with the baby so she can move on with her life, unencumbered."

"All I'm saying is, we offer."

"Yeah, but she may feel pressured to do it, even if she doesn't want to, out of some sense of loyalty or feeling like she owes us something."

He nods. "Well, I still think we should think about it."

I roll my eyes and take his face in my hands. "What am I going to do with you? Damn superman. I need to think about this. Don't bring it up to her. I don't know if I can do two babies at once."

"You were the one who said you hoped it was twins when we went for the ultrasound."

I scoff. "That is not what I said. I said it would be a reason for me to be so sick. It's not the same thing at all."

"Jo, we could do this. I know we can. And we could love that baby. You know part of you wanted her to keep it so we could be in its life."

He's not wrong. I had hoped Harper would want to keep her baby and we could raise them together. "I have no doubts I could love it. I love Harper like she's mine. It's just a lot."

"Okay. So just think about it, that's all I'm asking. We've got time."

CHAPTER TWENTY-FOUR

SPENCE

Over the next several weeks, Harper really starts to show and we break the news to the family that Jo and I are expecting as well. Everyone is overjoyed, as expected, especially Nick. He is practically beaming.

Jo and I have discussed adopting Harper's baby at length, but she's not made her mind up yet. I'm hoping she'll come around to the idea, but I'm trying to be patient with her.

Harper works with Nick during the day and studies for her GED in the evenings, with plans to take her test in the spring and apply for college for next fall. We've told her we'd help her go to whatever school she chooses. I think Jo and I would both prefer she stay close and live at home, but we're not bringing it up with her. It really feels like she's ours most of the time, in spite of the fact she's only twelve years younger than Jo. It feels like she was always with us.

Jo and I are going to the doctor today to hopefully find out the sex of the baby, even though we're a few weeks from the official twenty-week mark. I told Jo I didn't care one way or the other to find out, but she wants to know, so we'll find out.

Harper is coming along as well and is really excited. She's chosen not to know what she's having, so we're respecting that as well.

Jo's belly is just starting to pop and I love talking to it at night when she's asleep. She makes fun of me, but I'm enjoying myself. I know there's a chance that this is the only pregnancy Jo will want to endure, so I'm trying to soak up every moment.

When we pull up at the doctor's office, we get some strange looks, what with me walking in with two pregnant women. People probably assume we're some sort of strange polygamists or something, but we just laugh it off. Jo gets signed in and we sit and wait for the nurse to call us back to the ultrasound room.

"Lunch after?" Jo asks. She's always hungry now, which is so much better than her being sick, so I'm happy to oblige her.

"Sure. What are you thinking?"

"Burgers. What say you, Harper?"

"Burgers are fine. Can we get milkshakes, too?"

Jo's eyes light up and she puts her hand on her belly. "Yes. Milkshakes. Baby wants a milkshake."

I can't help but laugh. "You know, this reminds me of that movie, *Father of the Bride* 2. Where the guy's wife and daughter are pregnant at the same time. He has to navigate all their cravings and try to survive."

Harper laughs. "Well, I guess that is kinda what it's like. You're the closest thing I've ever had to a dad, so sure."

Jo pipes up. "Except you are so much better looking than Steve Martin. I'd rather have your baby than his."

I chuckle. "Good to know, babe."

They call Jo's name and take us back to a dim room with large monitors on the wall. They tell Jo to get up on the exam table and pull her shirt up and pants down to her hips. They squirt the gel on and put the wand on her belly. I turn to Harper. "What do you think, Harper, boy or girl?"

She shakes her head but is smiling. "Nope. I'm not getting involved. Y'all are going to have to fight between yourselves on that one."

Jo's pretty sure it's a girl, and honestly, I have no clue, I just say boy to be contrarian. I look down at Jo and hold her hand. "You still think it's a girl, babe?"

She shrugs. "I don't know, this pregnancy has been a lot different than the last one, though, so that's the only reason I say girl."

The tech pipes up. "You're measuring perfectly at eighteen weeks. Everything looks great. You want to know the sex?"

Jo looks at the screen. "If it's possible. I know it might be a little early."

The tech types something on the screen above the profile of the baby. *I AM A GIRL.*

Jo and I exchange surprised looks. "Really? A girl?"

The tech smiles. "Yep. I mean, there's always room for error, but I'm about ninety percent sure. They can check and verify at your next ultrasound, but for now, we can say it's a girl."

I brush a kiss across Jo's lips. "A girl, babe. We're going to have a daughter."

"Spence, I didn't really care one way or another, you know that. I'm just excited."

The tech prints some photos out for us and we head out to go eat. Jo and Harper discuss nursery themes and names and I revel in the fact that I'm going to have a daughter. It just doesn't seem real.

While we're in bed later, Jo says, "You've been awful quiet this afternoon. You okay?"

I smile. "Oh, yeah. I'm fine. I just can't believe it's a girl. I'm going to be so wrapped around her finger." I lean down and kiss Jo's belly. "You hear that, little girl? This is your daddy."

Jo laughs. "I think you being wrapped around her finger is going to be pretty accurate." She winks. "It's safe to say that Harper and I both have you pretty well wrapped, too, don't you think?"

I kiss her. "You are not wrong, my dear. I'd do anything for the two of you."

Jo wiggles her eyebrows. "What would you do just for me, though?"

I kiss her neck. "Ooh, that's tough. There's a lot I'd do just for you."

"What about right this minute, what would you do for me?"

I slide my hand up her thigh. "Any special requests?"

Jo taps her chin, seeming to consider. "Hot mirror sex?"

My mouth falls open and I'm unable to hide my surprise. "Really?"

She nods. "Yeah, my boobs are huge and finally not so tender and my belly is not going to allow it too much longer, so yeah, hot mirror sex."

I kiss her and give her a wicked smile. "I have an even better idea."

"Oh, really? And what's that?"

I get up from the bed and pull her along. "I guess you'll just have to wait and see."

"Will I still get hot mirror sex?"

"Yes." I pull her into the bathroom with me and start the shower. "Step one," I say, turning back to her. "Strip."

She tugs her shirt over her head and drops her panties. I slide off my own shorts and once the water is hot, I help her step into the tub and climb in after her. I press Jo back against the wall of the shower and she asks, "And what's step two?"

I grip her face and kiss her deeply. "You stand there and let me worship you."

She chuckles. "Worship? Well, that sounds nice."

I move my mouth down her neck and shoulder. I lift her left arm and brush my lips across her skin, ending at her fingers, lifting each one to my lips and pressing a kiss into each of the fingertips. I turn her palm over and kiss it gently. I slowly come back up the underside of her arm before bringing my lips back to hers and repeating things down and back up her right arm.

I kiss every inch of her torso, focusing on her breasts because I've missed them so much and she's right, they're so much larger than they were. I flick my tongue over her nipples and draw them into my mouth, and Jo lets out a sharp exhale.

I move my mouth down her belly and fall to my knees and lift her left leg and start at her ankle and kiss my way up her leg, stopping at her hip. I do the same with her right leg, but I don't set it down. I rest it over my shoulder and look up at Jo. "Best hang on to something."

She smiles and rests her hand on top of my head as I slide my tongue up her pussy and settle in to work. Jo's fingers tangle in my hair and she gasps. Her right leg starts to slide so I wrap my arm around her thigh. I suck and lick and nip at her clit until she's grinding her pelvis against my face and panting. "Spence, please don't stop. I'm so close." I do as requested and a few minutes later, Jo cries out with a ragged gasp.

I trail my mouth back up her stomach and breasts and kiss her neck and whisper in her ear. "You still want mirror sex?"

She nods. "Yes, please. But first, I think you deserve a little worship, too." She steps forward and turns me so I'm against the wall. She kisses me and her hand trails down my stomach and grasps my cock, causing me to hiss. She strokes me slowly and I close my eyes and breathe. Jo's mouth moves down my neck and chest and abs and after a moment, I feel her take me in her mouth and I let out a groan. I reach down to tangle my fingers in her hair as her tongue flicks around the head and underside of my cock. My hips buck with the suction and I have to keep myself from thrusting deep.

My heart races and I'm struggling to breath and after a moment I tell Jo, "Babe. I'm close. If you want me inside you, you're going to have to stop." She pulls back and I help her stand. I turn off the shower, but don't bother grabbing a towel.

I make sure Jo gets out of the tub safely and walk her over to the sink and lean her against it and kiss her deeply as she snakes her arms around my neck. I trail my hands down her body and grip her ass, kneading the perfect roundness.

I break our kiss and turn her around to face the mirror and she plants her hands on the sink. I pull her hips back and brush a kiss across her shoulder blade. I grab my cock and slide the tip up and down her pussy. Jo huffs, "Stop teasing and fuck me."

I smirk. "Like this?" I slam into her and she gasps. She closes her eyes and nods. I pull almost completely out before driving into her again and again. I wrap my hand in Jo's hair and tug her head back. "You wanted to watch? Watch, Jo. Watch as I fuck this sweet cunt."

Her eyes catch mine in the mirror and they're hazy with need. Jo bites down on her bottom lip and a pleasant flush creeps into her face and chest. Her breasts swing with each thrust and I can't take my eyes off of them.

I'm not going to last much longer, so I reach around and work her clit and she jerks with the sensation. Her breathing grows ragged and she lets out a long moan as her pussy clenches around me, starting me into my own climax. My knees almost buckle as my orgasm crashes through me with a low grunt.

Jo and I stand up straight and her hand goes to her belly, a shocked look on her face and I'm suddenly alarmed. "Babe, you okay? What's wrong? Did I hurt you?"

She smiles and shakes her head. "No, I just felt the baby kick."

My mouth drops open and I can't keep the excitement out of my voice. "Show me."

"You won't be able to feel it yet. Probably a couple more weeks and you will."

I take her face in my hands and give her a light kiss. "I can't wait." I grab a towel and hand it to Jo and take one for myself as well.

We get dressed and climb back into bed and I turn off the light and spoon up next to Jo, my hand on her belly. "Spence?"

"Yeah, babe?"

"I think if Harper is open to letting us adopt her baby, I'm down."

"Really? What made up your mind?"

"It's like you said, that way she can still be a part of the baby's life if she wants. And we can do it. We've got enough love, right?"

I plant a kiss on her shoulder. "You know it."

Jo says, "She might not want to, though, you know that, right? She might decide it's too painful for her to see a child that biologically is hers everyday and hear that child call someone else Mom."

I nod. "I know. And if that's the case, I can respect it. But I'd still like to offer."

"Okay. Well, you have my support. We can do it."

"You're the best wife, you know that?"

"Eh, I'm probably just hormonal and fucked into submission."

I laugh and kiss her before falling asleep.

CHAPTER TWENTY-FIVE

JO

Over the next couple of weeks, Spence and I discuss how to broach the subject of adopting Harper's baby with her. Now that I've made up my mind, I'm fully on board. We decided we'll do it tonight over supper, so I'm making Harper's favorite food of the moment, lasagna.

When she gets home from working at the book store, she brings her GED study books to the kitchen table and while the lasagna is in the oven, I quiz her on the subject she's studying for the day.

"Guess what?" she says, after I finish grading her practice test.

"What?"

Her eyes are excited. "I finally called Macon."

I set the quiz and my pen down. "Yeah? How did it go?"

"It was great. We talked for almost an hour."

"Wow, Harp, that's awesome. So, what's he up to? Is he seeing anyone?"

She shakes her head. "No. And he wants to come see me

one weekend so we can hang out, but I haven't told him I'm pregnant."

"Wow. Well, he's more than welcome to visit. Are you going to tell him?"

"I mean, if he comes, I'm not going to be able to hide it. And maybe if I tell him I'm going to put the baby up for adoption, it won't make him hesitant to get back together if it goes that way."

I nod. "Yeah, that's true. And besides," I say with a smirk, "it's not like you can get more pregnant than you already are."

Harper blushes. "Jo! That's terrible. But very true." We both laugh.

After supper, once we've got the dishes cleaned up, we're sitting in the living room watching TV and I glance at Spence and nod and he turns off the television. "Harper?" Spence says, getting her attention.

She looks over at us and closes the book she's reading to give us her full attention. "Yeah?"

"There's something we wanted to talk with you about." He glances at me and I squeeze his hand in support. He looks back to Harper, his voice strong. "We wanted to offer to adopt your baby. You'd still be able to be a part of his or her life, as a big sister, if you want. But that way, you still get to pursue whatever dreams you have. If that's something you could see in your heart to allow, we'd be honored.

"But, if that's not something you can do, if you don't feel like you can be a part of your child's life, we completely respect that as well. We just wanted you to know we'd be happy to do it."

Harper looks back and forth between Spence and me.

"Y'all would do that? When you're getting ready to have your own baby? Why?"

I smile. "We love you, Harper. And we want you to be able to do whatever it is you want to do in life. But if you wanted to be a part of your baby's life, we want to make sure you get to do that, too. We would be his or her parents, but you'd be there. We have enough love. You showed us that. We'd love your baby, too."

Tears fill her eyes. "Are you sure? That's asking so much of you guys. You've already given me so much."

Spence says, "Harper, it's not asking. Like we said, we'd be honored. But we totally understand if you need time to think it over. It's a big decision."

She shakes her head. "I don't need to think about it. Yes. I'd love that. If you guys weren't already pregnant, I would have already brought it up. But I didn't want to burden y'all."

I can't fight my own tears. "Really, Harper? You'd let us be your child's parents?"

"Yes. It's perfect. Y'all are the best parents I know already. I'd love it if my baby could grow up in your family."

I stand and give Harper a hug. "We really do love you, kid. You know that?"

She nods and huffs a watery laugh. "Y'all are all right, too."

A couple of weeks later, Harper is preparing for Macon to come visit. She's so nervous, I feel like she's going to come out of her skin. "Harper, if you don't calm down, I'm going to scream. You're making me a nervous wreck. Macon will be here and you'll see him and it will be wonderful."

She laughs nervously. "I'm sorry, Jo. It's just that I haven't seen him in almost two years. What if he doesn't like the way I look? I'm huge."

"Honey, he knows you're pregnant. You're supposed to be big. But you look beautiful. He wouldn't be driving all this way if he didn't want to see you." I go to stand in front of her. "Now listen, I'm going to be a cool big sister and pretend I don't see when you sneak down to the basement to spend the night with him. But try to be covert. At least make it appear as though you're being sneaky." I wink. "That's half the fun."

She laughs. "Will do. Are you sure Spence is okay with Macon staying here?"

"Yes, of course. We liked Macon from what we saw. He's always been very respectful, and as long as things stay that way, he won't have any problems from us. Can I promise that Spence won't grill him about his future and plans and stuff? No? But that's only because he cares about you."

She nods. "I know he does. But, I have to admit, I'm so excited about seeing Macon. I've missed him so much."

"I know. I'm excited for you. But we'll all have supper together tonight and then y'all can do whatever. Spence and I will pretend you don't exist."

Harper hugs me. "You're the best."

There's a knock at the door and Harper gives me a wide smile. "Want me to answer it?" I ask.

She shakes her head. "No, I'll get it." I nod and go to stand beside the kitchen counter, out of the way.

Harper opens the door and for a moment, there's the adorable awkwardness of two people who share a history getting reacquainted. And I must admit, Macon could get it if I were a nineteen-year-old girl. He's very handsome and has filled out considerably in the past few years.

She welcomes him in and guides him over to me. "Macon, you remember my sister, Jo?"

I stick my hand out and he shakes it. "Nice to see you again, Jo. Thank you for welcoming me into your home. And for what you've done for Harper. I know she appreciates you and Spence for everything. And so do I."

"We love Harper. We're very pleased to have her here. Can I get you something to drink? We can sit and chat. I'd love to hear about your time at Duke."

"Sure, water would be fine, but you don't have to wait on me. Just show me to the glasses and I'll take care of myself. You and Harper shouldn't be up on your feet. Go relax."

I give Harper a smile and an impressed nod. "All right, well, come join us in a minute." I whisper to Harper, "He gets brownie points for that." She gives me a goofy grin. A moment later, Macon sits next to Harper on the sofa and they hold hands. I ask, "So, Macon, what's your major?"

"Biomedical Engineering. There's always a need for engineers in every field, but biomedical fascinates me."

"Wow, that's impressive. I bet you and Spence could have discussions at length about the medical field. How do you like Duke?"

"I love it. The campus is beautiful. I really like North Carolina." He looks over at Harper. "Tennessee's growing on me, too, though." I don't miss the blush that colors her cheeks.

"I bet your parents miss you. Do you get back to Florida much?"

"Only on the breaks. I'll go down at Christmas and spring break. Maybe Harper can join me for spring break. I know she might be too pregnant to travel at Christmas."

Harper smiles. "Maybe. That would be fun."

I stand. "Well, I'm going to go work for a bit and get out of your hair. Harper, why don't you show Macon to his room? Spence will be home in a couple hours and he's bringing

Chinese food home, so I'll probably be working. In my room. Until then."

Harper blushes. "Thanks, Jo. I think we're good."

I go in my room and try not to think about what the teenagers are doing in my basement, but honestly, Harper's happy, so who am I to stop her from having fun.

We enjoy a great evening hanging out with Macon and when Spence and I turn in, I hear Harper's bedroom door open and know she's going downstairs. Spence says, "I don't know how to feel about Harper having sex while we're in the house."

I laugh. "It's not like she's going to get pregnant again. Honestly, it's probably the safest time for her to do it. And they clearly still have feelings for each other. They're adorable."

He pulls me into his side. "Yeah, they are. He seems like a cool kid. Smart, too. Some of the stuff he was saying went over my head. I had to pretend I knew what he was talking about. But I'm going to look it up, so I'll actually know." After a beat, he asks, "Do you think she'll want to go to Duke? You know, to be with him?"

I shrug. "I don't know. I think if she did, she'd have to get some good financial aid and scholarships—Duke's expensive. And I know we want to help her, but out-of-state tuition at a private school? Whew. That's a lot. She's still not even sure what she wants to do yet. I'd rather her stay here and at least get a couple of years out of the way at a community college and then maybe move on."

He nods. "Yeah, that's one thought. She'd probably qualify for a lot of aid though, and she'll have a hell of an entrance essay. 'How I survived my alcoholic mother and a teenage pregnancy and let my sister adopt my baby'. It's got 'accepted' written all over it."

"You're not wrong. I guess we'll just have to see. Not to change the subject, but we need to start talking names. Harper's due in ten weeks. We'll need a boy and a girl name, since she's choosing not to find out."

Spence considers. "What about Lily?"

I scrunch up my face. "Wasn't the girl you were sorta serious with a few years ago named Lily?"

"Oh, yeah. Okay. Although, if we're not going with names of girls I've slept with, that's probably going to really limit us." He gives me a sheepish smile.

I playfully punch him in the ribs. "Trust me, I'm well acquainted with the fact that you have quite the body count. What about Clare?"

He considers. "Like from *The Time Traveler's Wife*? That could work. What about a middle name?"

"Harper," I say without hesitation.

"Perfect. So that's one girl's name. We might need another one. But Clare Harper Jackson. I love it. What about a boy's name? Have you given that any thought?"

"Oliver. Oliver Aaron."

Spence's eyes soften. "I love it. Little Ollie. It's adorable. I kind of hope Harper is having a boy. That way, we'd have one of each. Has Harper ever said what that Malachi guy looked like?"

"Not really. But I would imagine he's pretty good looking. Harp's got good taste. You saw Macon, right? Damn. For nineteen, he's quite handsome."

Spence laughs. "Easy there, cougar lady."

"Sorry, babe. It's all these pregnancy hormones. They've just got me a little extra *ready to go* all the time."

He quirks an eyebrow. "Oh, really? Well, allow me to do something about that." He slides his hand up my nightshirt.

"I thought we were discussing baby names?" I say, as I start to lie down with a smile on my face.

"We totally did." Spence's face register's surprise. "What was that?"

"Oh, were you able to feel that?" My hand goes to my belly and sure enough, the baby kicks. "I wasn't sure you'd be able to feel it yet. Since I've been feeling them for a few weeks, I hadn't noticed you can feel them from the outside yet."

His eyes light up. "Was that a kick?" When I nod, he abandons his pursuit to seduce me, in favor of concentrating on feeling my belly. I can't help but laugh. When it happens again, he looks up at me, a gleeful expression on his face. "That is so cool."

"Yeah, until she starts kicking up into my ribs, especially after she starts running out of room. You'll think it's real cool when I'm up every thirty minutes to pee."

He lays his cheek on my belly. "Don't listen to your mommy, little girl. You just keep kicking away."

My heart feels so full watching how excited he gets over everything. I know it would've been like this with Aaron as well, and I feel ashamed for holding this back from him for so long. I run my fingers through his hair as he continues to whisper to my belly. "Sing to her, babe."

He looks back at me. "I don't know what to sing."

"She's not going to care. But when she's born, she'll recognize your voice, and when you sing to her, it'll soothe her, because she's heard it all along." He considers for a minute and then starts singing "I Like Big Butts". I crack up. "That's not really what I had in mind, Spence."

He shrugs. "It's all I could think of in the moment. I do like big butts. Yours especially."

I feign offense. "My butt is not big."

He comes back up to my face and runs his thumb along my jaw. "No, it's not big, but I will say, it was one of the first things I noticed about you at the block party. And then when you got up into my Jeep in that mini skirt." He closes his eyes and smiles and sucks in a breath, as if remembering. "Damn. It was spectacular. I couldn't take my eyes off that fine ass."

I laugh. "Well, glad to know I made an impression."

He kisses me. "Definitely an impression."

CHAPTER TWENTY-SIX

SPENCE

A few days after Macon leaves to return to North Carolina, Harper seems really down, so I offer to take her for a driving lesson. She still doesn't have her driver's license; probably just one more thing Maggie thought would keep her held back. But Jo and I want her to be as independent as possible, especially once she starts college next year.

"Come on, Harper, take me on a drive." I jingle my keys and stand by the door.

She sighs. "I don't really feel like it, Spence."

I go over and tug her off the couch. "I know. You're sad because Macon's gone, but you can't sit around all the time. It's not good for you. You've got to get your hours in so you can get your license, and you're not going to do it by sitting on this couch. Let's go."

She huffs. "Fine. But we're stopping for coffee."

"Deal."

Once we get out on the road, I ask, "So, how much money have you saved up for your car? I know with all the hours you've been working at the bookstore, you've probably been able to put back quite a bit."

She nods. "Almost three grand. I spent a little bit on some books, but otherwise, I've been able to put back most of everything I've made. I still wish y'all would let me pay you rent or help with utilities or something."

"Nope. You're working hard and your priority right now is getting your GED and driver's license and getting into college. Jo and I were talking and we want to help you buy a car. If you've saved three thousand, we'll match it. It probably wouldn't be a super nice car or anything, but we'd make sure it was reliable."

Harper's eyes go wide. "Spence, no. You and Jo have already done too much for me. I'll get a car on my own."

"It's done. In fact, pull in over here. There's a car I saw online and wanted to check it out."

Harper narrows her eyes. "You're a sneaky bastard, you know that, Spence?"

I shrug. "Yeah, but you love me anyway." Once we've pulled in at the dealership and park, I see a salesman coming over and I pull up the ad on my phone to ask where the vehicle's located. He points it out and I thank him and promise to let him know if we need anything.

I pull Harper over to the car and gesture to it. "What do you think?"

She considers. "It's nice."

"Come on, sit in the driver's seat, see what you think. I've got a mechanic buddy I'll have come give it a once over if this is the one you want. But it's a great deal and it'll get good gas mileage for wherever you decide to go to school."

She sighs and then seems to get more excited and climbs behind the wheel. She has to move the seat back because of her belly, but she grips the wheel. "This is nice, Spence. What do you think?"

"I think it's a perfect car for a college student."

Harper eyes me suspiciously. "You've been looking at cars for a while haven't you? If I know you, you've pretty much already put this one on hold? How close am I, Superman?"

I stick my hands in my pockets and rock back on my heels. "I don't know what it is about you and Jo, but you're able to see through all my bullshit. Yes. A patient of mine owns the dealership and I've had him looking out for a couple months. So, what do you think? Will it do?"

Harper steps out of the car and shrugs. "Yeah, I guess it's all right." After a second, a wide grin comes across her face and she throws her arms around me. "I swear, you and Jo are too good to me. Thank you, Spence. This is perfect, actually."

I smile and return her hug. "Well, that's good. They're going to hold it here until you get your license and then we'll come pick it up."

She tugs my arm back toward my Jeep. "Well then, I guess I better get my hours in so I can come back and get my car."

I laugh. "All right. Let's go."

We drive around for another hour or so before stopping at a coffee shop to pick up iced coffees for us and Jo. Harper is chatting about Macon and how much he likes going to Duke. I ask, "So, where are you thinking you'll apply?"

She sighs. "I don't know. I think I want to go into nursing, but I can get that degree here. Macon showed me pictures of Duke's campus. It's beautiful, but I don't think I want to go away to school. Granted, it's not on the other side of the country, but it probably makes more sense for me to stay close. I can go to community college for a couple of years and then transfer. Try to get scholarships and stuff."

I nod. "You could definitely do that. Jo and I thought if you stayed local, you could move into the basement apartment and have your own space. It's got a full kitchen and you'd have your own entrance. I really loved living down there when I was in college. I barely saw my parents at all."

"Yeah, Macon and I liked being down there when he was in town. I cooked for us and stuff. It was nice."

"Well, whatever you decide, you know Jo and I support you. If you wanted to go away to school, we'd try to help out as much as we can and make sure you got all the financial aid you could."

"I know, y'all have been great." After a beat, she asks, "I've been meaning to ask, was there anything else we needed to do for the lawyers and the adoption and stuff?"

We'd gone to see a family lawyer to discuss the adoption of Harper's baby, but we've done everything we need to before the baby comes. We won't be able to do anything else until she gives birth and signs away her parental rights. Jo and I both know there's a chance Harper could change her mind and decide she wants to raise the baby after she sees it, and if that happens, we'll support her.

I shake my head. "Nope. Everything's done until after you give birth."

"Okay. Have you and Jo started talking about names?"

"Yeah. We have. We have one of each picked out, but if yours is a girl, we'll have to come up with another."

"What have you chosen?"

I shake my head. "It's a surprise. We're not telling anyone until after the baby's born. Either of them. But they're good."

"No fair."

"Sorry, kid. That's the way it is. So, how's the GED studying going?"

"Really good. I think I'm almost ready. I'd really like to test before I go into labor. That way, I don't have to worry about studying while I'm recovering."

I consider. "That's probably wise. You could probably do it. And you can take it more than once, right? If you need to."

She nods. "Yeah, but I think I could probably take it tomorrow if I needed to. Jo's been giving me those practice tests for weeks and I've aced them."

"Well, then go for it."

"I think I will. That way, I'm just done with it."

When we walk into the house, Jo is fixing supper and glances up at us. "What did Harper think about the car?"

Harper looks surprised. "You knew he was taking me to look at a car?"

"Well, duh. I figured it might get you out of your funk just a little." Jo smiles. "Did it work?"

Harper nods. "Yeah, definitely. Also, I'm going to go ahead and schedule my GED test for the next couple of weeks. I want to get it out of the way before the baby comes."

Jo nods. "Sounds good. You'll do fine. You've been acing your practice tests."

"Yeah." She sighs. "I think I'm going to go lie down for a bit and prop my feet up. My ankles are starting to swell a little."

I say, "Have a good rest. Holler if you need anything. We'll let you know when supper's finished."

She waves to me as she enters her room and shuts the door. I come over to Jo and give her a kiss. She asks, "So, did she figure out you'd already been looking at cars for her?"

I shake my head and huff out a laugh. "I swear, both of y'all are something else."

Jo rolls her eyes. "I told you she'd see through you. She's smart. She's my sister, after all."

"Yeah, yeah. I guess I better get used to all these smart ladies in my house." I place my hand on Jo's belly and kiss the side of her head. "We're going to have a third one here before long."

She nods. "Yep. Eighteen more weeks. It's flying by. Not going to lie though, I'm starting to get a little anxious."

I nod and turn her away from the vegetables she's chopping to face me and take her face in my hands. "It's completely understandable you'd feel that way. But you're fine. The baby's fine. Everything is going to be fine."

She lays her forehead on my chest. "Deep down, I think I know that, but my brain still wants to go to that place. I'm sorry."

I lift her face. "You have nothing to be sorry about. I knew this would probably get harder for you as the pregnancy progressed. I'm prepared to talk you off the ledge every day until this little girl is safe in our arms, okay?"

Jo bites her lip and nods. "Thank you. I'll try to keep my crazy contained, but I can't promise I'll be able to do it."

Changing the subject, I say, "Harper said she thinks she wants to stay close for college. Possibly community college for two years and then transfer. I told her she was more than welcome to the basement apartment."

She smiles and her eyes go wide in delighted surprise. "Really? That's great."

"Yeah, but I told her whatever she wanted to do, we'd get behind her on it." I walk over to the kitchen sink and wash my hands. "Okay, what can I help with? You should go rest. I know you've worked a lot today. You've got 'I wrote ten chapters' written all over your face."

Jo chuckles. "Actually, it was twelve. I'm just making a simple chicken soup. The veggies need to be sautéed, and then add the chicken and a box of broth and some seasonings. A few minutes before it's ready to serve, you add the egg noodles."

I nod. "Okay, I can do that. Go rest."

She kisses me. "You take good care of me, you know that?"

"It's mutual, babe. You go rest and I'll holler when supper's done."

CHAPTER TWENTY-SEVEN

JO

The next several weeks fly by as Harper grows nearer to her due date. She aces her GED exam and scores a thirty-four on her ACT test. She passes her driver's exam and moves into the basement so Spence and I can prepare one of the guest bedrooms as a nursery and she can have her own space. She also received early acceptance into the University of Tennessee on a full scholarship and we're so proud of her.

Macon has come to visit a couple of times for long weekends and they're adorable together. They take walks after lunch, in spite of the frigid January weather. Harper is planning on going to Florida to spend spring break with Macon and we've told them they can use the condo for the week. It's not like we'll be able to get down that way until at least April or May and with two babies, it'll probably be longer than that, so someone ought to be using it, right?

Both Harper's and my pregnancy have been picture perfect and up until this week, I've handled things really well. But in a few days, I'll be at the same gestation I was when I lost Aaron, so I'm on edge and feel as though I'm extra aware of my body and any little flutters or lack of them. But so far, so good. The baby has been extra active and I'm thankful.

Harper is due any day now and we're all antsy to get the show on the road. Poor Spence has dealt with both of our crankiness and the closer Harper gets to her due date, we watch her like she's a ticking bomb, ready to blow at any moment. We still don't know if she's having a boy or a girl, but we honestly don't care.

Today, we went to get a few last minute things we didn't receive from the shower Spence's mom threw us. Mainly an extra car seat. We have two of everything else. The nursery is gender neutral. We've gone with gray and navy blue with white accents. It's very modern and has become my favorite room in the house. I spend evenings sitting in the rocking chair with my hand on my belly, feeling her kick.

Part of me is a bit nervous Harper will change her mind, but I'm trying to keep the fear tamped down, because I know she has dreams and goals now and I really want her to achieve those.

Spence and I are lying in bed and I'm on my side, with him curled up behind me. His hand is resting on my belly. "Spence, I don't know how much bigger I can get. I'm already so huge."

He laughs. "You still have eight weeks. Plenty of time to get even bigger."

"What do you think she's going to look like?" We like to play this game where we give the baby features and then decide who gave the better description.

He thinks for a minute as he trails his hand up my belly. "Probably brown hair, green eyes. Her mommy's long legs."

"Her daddy has pretty long legs, too."

"Okay, so either way, she'll have long legs." He feels up under my ribs. "I think she's turned. This doesn't feel like a head."

"Yeah, her feet are in my ribs these days. That's good, though. That's what she's supposed to do."

"Oh, I know. I don't remember much from my rotation in OB-GYN, but I do remember they're supposed to come out head first." He kisses behind my ear.

"Don't be starting anything back there. I'm getting too big for all that."

He raises up on all fours and frames me with his arms and legs. "But I love you like this, babe. It just does something for me. You're so beautiful with my baby in your belly. And your boobs are huge."

I scoff. "You sure know how to charm a woman, you know that?" I reach up and touch his face and pull his mouth to mine and kiss him. "But, I'll tell you, it works for me. Although, I don't know how we're going to do this. For real, my belly is so big."

His hand slides up my thigh and he leans down to whisper in my ear. "You just lie there, just like that, and let me do all the work."

I shrug and chuckle. "Okay, I can do that." He tugs my panties down my hips and tosses them on the floor and kisses me. I wrap my arms around his neck and deepen the kiss until we're both breathing hard.

Spence kisses down my neck and slides his hand up my nightshirt to cup my breast, his thumb grazing my nipple and causing me to inhale sharply and making heat pool low in my belly. He lifts the hem of my shirt up until my breast is exposed and he draws it into his mouth, flicking his tongue over my nipple, making me moan. "There it is," Spence drawls, an easy smile curving his lips.

He drops down to his side behind me and I turn my head and pull his mouth to mine. His hand runs over my belly and down between my legs. He circles my clit lazily with the pad of one finger and kisses my neck. My pulse races and Spence chuckles. "Your heart rate is up." He leaves his mouth on my neck for a moment. "I'd say, it's up to at least ninety beats per minute. That's pretty high for a resting heart rate, Jo." His tone is playful.

My voice is breathy. "I'm definitely not resting. Those fingers of yours are putting in quite the workout." I huff out a soft gasp. "Fuck, that's sensitive."

"Your pussy is so swollen, babe. It's fucking sexy. Damn." He grinds himself against me and I can tell he definitely approves of his findings. He withdraws his hand to shuck his shorts and returns to his position behind me. I tilt my pelvis back to allow him easier access and he gently enters me from behind.

The penetration is shallow and his thrusts are easy and Spence's arm supports my leg. The angle from which he enters me perfectly hits my sweet spot and after only a few minutes, my orgasm starts to build. I reach down and pleasure my clit and cry out as my pussy clenches and my climax washes over me with a raspy exhale. Moments later, Spence joins me with his own shuddering release and soft grunt.

We lie there for a minute, his hand on my belly as the baby's elbows and knees roll across my belly as she stretches. He chuckles. "That is the strangest feeling."

I scoff. "You should feel it from the inside. It's wild." I sigh. "I have to pee. Help me up."

He jumps up and I curse his agility as he helps me sit up and stand. He picks my panties up off the floor and hands them to me as I waddle into the bathroom. Once I'm done and I'm on my way back to the bed, I see Spence putting on clothes. "What's going on?"

He looks up at me. "Harper's water just broke."

CHAPTER TWENTY-EIGHT

JO

My eyes go wide. "Really? Now?"

He nods. "Yeah, she just texted me from downstairs. I'm going to go down and walk her around the house. I figure it's easier than walking up the stairs, especially if she's having contractions."

"Okay, I'll get dressed and meet y'all in the car. Probably should take mine. It'll be easier for her to get in and out of. Don't forget her bag. I'll grab the diaper bag from the nursery."

Spence closes the distance between us and hugs me, both of us wanting to say the words, but don't dare. *One of our babies is going to be born tonight.* He hurries out the bedroom door and a few seconds later the door to the basement opens.

I dress quickly and make sure I've got all of our documents and the diaper bag and my purse before locking up the house and going to start the car.

A couple of minutes later, Harper and Spence come walking around the side of the house. They stop about ten feet from the car and I can see she's having a contraction. He supports her and when it passes, he helps her the rest of the way to the car. Once she's in, I ask, "How far apart?"

Spence gets behind the wheel and backs out of the driveway.

"About ten minutes. I thought it was only Braxton-Hicks, because they weren't too bad, until my water broke."

I nod. "Well, no turning back now, Harp. You ready?"

She huffs out an uncomfortable laugh. "Not in the least."

Spence is the picture of calm. "You're going to do just fine, Harper. You're tough. You've got this."

She scoffs. "That's easy for you to say, Spence. You don't have to push something the size of a Halloween pumpkin out of a hole the size of a softball."

I turn around to look at Harper. "Do you want me to call Macon? I know he wanted to come in and spend a couple days with you after to help with your recovery."

She shakes her head. "No, he's got labs this week. I'll call him when I get back home. I don't want him to worry and it mess up his grades."

Once we get to the hospital and get Harper checked in, she's put in a gown and hooked up to an IV and about twenty minutes later, her doctor comes in to assess the situation. "Harper, good to see you. Right on your due date. That's pretty impressive. I'll do a quick internal exam and then if you want, we can order the epidural; hopefully get you some rest before the show starts. How about that?"

She nods. "Yes, please."

Spence steps out while the doctor checks Harper's dilation. "Four centimeters. Good progress so far." The doctor catches sight of me. "Looks like you'll be here in a few weeks, too, right?"

I smile. "Eight, give or take."

Harper breathes through another pain. "This is my sister. She and her husband are going to adopt my baby."

The doctor's face registers surprise. "Well, that's something you don't hear every day. Congratulations. I'll go ahead and put those orders in for the epidural and tell Dad he can come back in. I'll be back after while."

I blow out a breath. "Harp, can I get you anything?"

She shakes her head. "I just can't believe it's time. I mean, I know it is, I'm totally ginormous and so ready to have my body back, but it's gone by so fast."

I nod. "Yeah. I know what you mean."

A few minutes later, Harper has another contraction and I watch the monitor and tell her when it starts to come down. "There, almost done now. Where is Spence? He should be back in here by now."

Spence comes back in a couple of minutes later. "Sorry, I was getting ice chips. I thought you might want some."

We sit and wait. And wait. And wait. One hour turns into four and then seven and then eleven. Harper is exhausted. Spence and I are beyond tired. We've taken turns sitting up with her. She did get a bit of rest after the epidural was put in, but since then, it's been pretty intermittent.

But finally, eleven-and-a-half hours after we've arrived at the hospital, Harper tells Spence to get the doctor. That she thinks it's time to push. "Jo?" Harper says through clenched teeth.

I turn to her. "Yeah, honey?"

Her breathing is ragged from exertion. "If I don't get to say it later, because I'm pretty sure I'll pass out after this is over, but thank you. So much. For everything. For being a good mom to me, which I know that's weird, cause you're not old enough, but still. You've been the best mom ever and I can't wait for this baby to have you as a mom, too."

I can't fight back the tears that threaten to spill. I brush the damp hair off her forehead. "Harper, you've been the best kid ever. Thank you for making me want to be a mom. We love you. And can't thank you enough for this amazing gift you're giving us. I know this wasn't an easy decision for you."

She shakes her head. "Easiest decision ever. I can't wait for this baby to meet his parents."

My mouth falls open in shock. "Harper, did you say, *his?*"

She smiles and winks. "Don't tell Spence. Let him be surprised to meet his son."

My breath catches. "Harper. Oh my goodness." I throw my arms around her and hug her.

"Jo, don't jostle me, I'm trying to keep this baby in until the doctor gets in here." We both laugh.

"Sorry," I say.

Spence comes back a moment later with the doctor on his heels. She comes over to the end of the bed and Spence comes up next to Harper's head and looks at her. "You want me to go? I don't want it to be weird for you."

Harper shakes her head. "No, stay."

The doctor pipes up. "Okay, folks, it's go time. Harper, on the next contraction, you're going to push, okay?"

She blows out a breath and nods.

Twenty minutes later, a perfect baby boy is delivered and I watch Spence's face morph from shock to joy and awe. The doctor places him on Harper's chest and the nurse begins to clean him up. Harper collapses back onto the bed, totally spent from her labor.

Once the baby is cleaned up and the cord is cut, they wrap

him in a blanket and place him in Harper's arms. She looks at him and smiles and then up and me and then Spence. "Spence, want to hold your son?"

His breath catches and he nods and takes the baby. Harper looks back at me. "What name did y'all pick out?"

"Oliver. Oliver Aaron." Her eyes soften. "That's beautiful, Jo. Welcome to the world, Oliver Aaron." She blows out a breath. "I'm tired, y'all."

I lean over the rail and kiss the top of her head. "You did good, kid. You going to help me get through mine in a few weeks?"

She huffs a laugh. "Sure thing, sis. Let me get a nap first." She lies back on the bed and closes her eyes.

Spence looks down at Harper. "Hey, Harp?"

She opens her eyes. "Yeah?"

"Thank you. Truly."

She smiles and closes her eyes.

I come around to stand next to Spence and look at Oliver. And even though I know he's nothing like Aaron, I'm still struck that this is what Spence would have looked like holding him. I lean my head on Spence's arm. "You look good with a baby, Spence."

He smiles. "He's beautiful, Jo. He's got yours and Harper's lips. And look at all this dark hair."

Over the next couple of days, Harper starts to feel better and signs the adoption papers while we're still in the hospital. When we get home, Spence helps her down to the apartment. While we were gone, my dad made several meals for Harper to have while she recovers.

We get Ollie settled and I waddle downstairs to check on Harper a few hours after we get back home. She's sitting up in bed and I go sit beside her. "How you doing, kid?"

"I'm still so tired, Jo. But I finally got to talk to Macon. He's going to come see me this weekend. He said he can't wait to take care of me." She rolls her eyes.

I smile. "That's sweet he wants to come take care of you."

"Yeah, I know. I really love him, Jo. He's a wonderful guy."

"He sure does seem like one. Can I get you anything? A drink or snack?"

She shakes her head. "Will you just sit with me for a little while? You think Spence will be okay with Ollie for a bit?"

I chuckle. "Are you kidding? He's not wanted to put him down since we got home."

I scoot up to the top of the bed and lean against the head-board and Harper leans into me. I wrap my arm around her and pull her to my side. "You okay?"

She nods, but has tears in her eyes. "Stupid hormones. I'm really happy you guys get to be Ollie's parents, but it's a little sad for me, not going to lie."

"I know it is. I understand. I'd be shocked if you were unaffected."

"Don't get me wrong, Jo, I'm am so beyond thankful, but it's hard. I know I'm going to get to do all the things I've dreamed about and it's all because of you and Spence, but I can't help but wish I was in a place where I could be his mom."

"I know, Harp. I really do. I won't tell you it gets easier, because I don't know if it does, but you'll still be such a huge part of his life. And he'll always know you are the reason he's here. We'll never keep that from him. And you'll be such a good sister-aunt to him. And your bond with him is going to be so special. I can feel it."

Harper drapes her arm across my belly and cries and I hold

her. Because I know that although this is truly what she
wanted, it's such a bittersweet thing. And I don't have any
words of wisdom for her. I can only be here for her in this
moment and love her and hope and pray that with time, the
hurt becomes less for her.

CHAPTER TWENTY-NINE

SPENCE

Seven weeks later, we find ourselves back at the hospital. Jo's contractions are five minutes apart and she's breathing like a champ. Nick came over to watch Ollie so Harper and I could be with Jo during her labor.

Jo looks at me. "Spence, this is the only time I'm doing this, you hear me? This sucks so bad."

Harper chuckles. "You should've gotten the epidural, Jo."

"Yeah, well, in the moment, I was trying to be stoic." I laugh and Jo shoots me a death glare and I stifle it. I wipe a damp cloth across Jo's brow and she blows out a breath. "Spence, after this, you are getting snipped. I'm done. Done. Got it?"

"Yes, dear."

She doubles over with another contraction. "Oh, fuck. It hurts so bad. Shit."

Harper's eyes go wide and she looks at me. "Wow, Spence, I don't think I've ever heard Jo say fuck before. It's serious."

I quirk a brow. "She does sometimes."

Harper snorts a laugh. "Seriously, Spence? Now is not the time for your juvenile humor."

Jo wraps her fist in my shirt and jerks me toward her. "Spence, I swear to all that is holy, if you don't shut up, I'm going to slug you. I love you, but I can't concentrate with all this noise."

I sober. "I'm sorry, babe. What do you need?"

She blows out a breath. "I think I need the doctor. I think it's time."

Harper goes out into the hall and I lean over and kiss Jo's head. "We're almost there, babe. Clare's almost here. You've got this. You are amazing and strong and awesome."

Jo's eyes snap to mine. "Spence. I don't know if I can do this. I know I wanted this, but I don't know if I can do this again. I'm so scared."

I take Jo's face in my hands. "This time is different. Clare is completely fine. You're going to help her come meet us. I can't imagine the emotions and feelings you're having right now and everything that's going through your mind. But remember what we said? It's different this time because we're together. No matter what. Do you remember that?"

She nods with tears in her eyes. "I'm just so scared, Spence."

"I know you are. But it's okay. We're almost to the best part. We get to hold our beautiful baby girl in our arms. You've got just a little bit more work to do to get her here, okay? But you're so strong and amazing. You've got this. I love you, Jo."

Jo's face blanches and her tone is fearful. "Spence, I don't feel so good."

"What is it, babe?"

"I don't know; I'm really lightheaded all of a sudden." The color drains from her face and I run to find someone and get to the end of the bed and freeze. Jo is hemorrhaging and there's a pool of dark red blood on the floor.

"Help! Someone!" I yell frantically and try to remember

my rotation during trauma, but nothing comes to mind. I'm totally blank. I look at the monitors. The baby's heart rate is dropping. Jo's stats are dropping as well and I know she's getting ready to lose consciousness. "Jo! Jo, stay with me, babe." I take her hand and squeeze it even as she passes out. My heart is pounding and after what seems like an eternity later, the doctor and some nurses come into the room.

The doctor checks Jo and says to the nurse, "Prep OR two for an emergency c-section." The nurses wheel Jo out and I struggle to breathe. Another nurse comes over to me. "Dr. Jackson, we're going to take Joanna into surgery. Dr. Brooks is going to do everything she can. I'll take you to the waiting room." She walks me out and Harper's coming toward me.

"What's going on, Spence?" I try to summon my skills as a physician to tell Harper what's going on, but knowing my wife and child are in danger has stripped away my ability to form words. Harper shakes me. "Spence. Answer me."

I finally snap out of it but can't hold back my tears. "Jo started hemorrhaging and they had to rush her into surgery."

Harper gasps. "Oh, God."

We sit and wait for what seems like eons. And when I can't sit, I pace. And then I sit and pray with my head in my hands. "Spence, you're making me nervous. Can you talk me through what's going on, please?"

I sit down and cry. "I don't know, Harper. I'm not a surgeon. And all I can think is that I wish I had become a surgeon, because at least then, I'd have some idea of what they're doing back there. But I don't. I'm useless." I look at Harper. "I can't lose them, Harper."

She comes to kneel in front of me. "Spence, Jo's a fighter. You know that. She'll be okay. She has to be." Her voice breaks on the last word.

Harper and I sit huddled together for a while, not speaking.

Both of us are afraid to say anything at this point because it seems there should've been some news by now. But every time someone comes out, it's not Jo's doctor and I begin to lose hope that we'll get any news at all.

I repeatedly check the time on my phone thinking hours will have passed, when it's only been minutes. But I know we've been out here close to two hours which seems like such a long time.

Finally, twenty minutes later, Jo's doctor comes out, her face utterly devoid of any emotion that would give anything away. Harper and I stand as she comes over. "Dr. Jackson," she addresses me.

"How are Jo and the baby?" My voice is pleading and Harper grips my hand.

Dr. Brooks smiles. "Your wife and daughter are both in stable condition. Joanna lost a lot of blood, and we had to do a blood transfusion during the operation, but she should make a full recovery. Your daughter is perfect. She aspirated a bit of meconium from the distress in utero, but she's doing fine now."

I take a full breath for the first time since I saw the pool of blood. "So, they're okay?" I can't hold back my tears.

Dr. Brooks nods. "Yes, they're going to be okay. Joanna will probably take a while to come out of the anesthesia, but if you want to come back with me, I can take you to the room where Joanna and the baby will be and we'll bring your daughter in."

Harper and I share a relieved hug and follow the doctor back.

We wait in a room that doesn't currently have a bed, and I remind myself that Jo will be brought into this room on a bed shortly. A nurse wheels in a hospital bassinet and my breath catches. I walk over and the nurse checks my wristband against the one on my daughter's ankle and then hands her over to me. I take her over and sit in a chair and examine her features.

Harper squats down. "Spence, she's beautiful. Look how chubby she is."

I look at Harper. "Jo has to be okay, right?"

She gives me a hopeful smile and nods. "Not a doubt in my mind, big brother. She's too stubborn and determined."

I can't help but laugh. "You're not wrong about that. You know, when Jo and I first hooked up, and this is probably TMI, but whatever, indulge me. I need to talk so I don't dwell on the fact Jo's not back in this room yet."

Harper chuckles. "Go for it. Who am I going to tell?"

"Anyway, I saw Jo walk down the stairs at the Christmas block party the first time she came home from college. Except I didn't know it was Jo. She knew me, of course, but she wouldn't tell me her name. She said I could have twenty questions to guess."

"But you weren't able to guess."

I shake my head. "No. But I was having a really good time, so I asked her if she wanted to go for a drive. And we went up to one of the overlooks as you drive up the mountains and we were talking. And then I kissed her and couldn't stop."

She wiggles her eyebrows. "Yeah, I read about that in Jo's book."

"But right up until the, you know, *moment*, she still wouldn't tell me her name. But, damn, was she persistent. And as we've established, I was not a good guy back then, so I didn't really need her name." I take a deep breath. "So, yeah, your sister is stubborn and determined, for sure."

I look down at my daughter who is sleeping peacefully and lift her head to my nose and breathe in her sweet baby smell. I look at Harper. "You want to hold your niece?"

She shakes her head. "I'll hold her after Jo does."

I nod. And then we wait. And wait some more.

CHAPTER THIRTY

JO

When I come to, I am in an inordinate amount of pain. I try to move, but everything hurts. My eyes slowly open and I try to bring everything into focus. "Spence?" My voice sounds hoarse.

"Jo? Hey, babe."

I swallow as his face comes into view. "The baby. How's the baby?" My mind is really fuzzy, but I try to focus on his words.

"She's fine, Jo. She's perfect. Can you sit up and you can see her? She's beautiful."

He helps me sit up and I feel his lips on my cheek. "Spence, I'm so groggy."

"I know, babe. It's the anesthesia and you lost a lot of blood. They had to transfuse you during the surgery."

"What happened?" I'm finally starting to come around and can hold my eyes open a bit more.

Spence takes my face and holds it so I can look him in the eyes. "You started hemorrhaging. They had to rush you in for a c-section. But you're fine. You're going to be really sore and you'll have a longer recovery, but you're fine."

"Can I see her? I don't think I can hold her; my arms don't work yet. Hold her up for me?" Spence walks over to the little bassinet and lifts a bundle into his arms. He brings her close to me. So close I can smell her sweet baby smell. "She's okay?" I can't hold back my tears.

"She's perfect. Ten fingers. Ten toes. Blonde hair. Nine pounds, two ounces."

I blow out a breath and see Harper sitting in a chair on the other side of the room. "Harper. You're still here?"

She jumps up and comes over to the bed. "Of course. Spence wouldn't tell me the baby's name. Said you could tell me yourself. I'm dying here, sis. What did you name this cutie?"

I take Harper's hand. "Her name is Clare. Clare Harper."

Harper's face registers surprise and her eyes fill with tears. "You named her after me?"

I smile. "Of course we did. You're the reason I wanted to have kids again after I lost Aaron. It was only right."

"Jo, I don't know what to say. I'm honored." She reaches over the bed rail and hugs me gingerly.

I turn back to Spence. "I think I'm ready to hold her now." He hands Clare over to me and ensures I'm secure before letting go. I look into my daughter's face and I'm struck. "God, Spence, she looks so much like Aaron. It's uncanny."

He smiles. "Really?"

I nod, my eyes filling with tears again. He leans down and presses his forehead to the side of my head, just above my ear. "You did good, babe. You sure make pretty babies."

I turn my face to kiss him. "Thank you, Spence. For all your patience with me and for this beautiful little girl. I love you."

EPILOGUE
JO — FOUR YEARS LATER

Spence, Ollie, Clare, Macon, and I sit in the stands at Neyland Stadium waiting to watch Harper walk across the stage and accept her Bachelor's Degree in nursing. When her name is called, we all cheer so loudly for her. Spence and I share proud glances because we feel like this is our victory, too.

As Harper steps off the stage, she waves to us and smiles, even from all the way down on the field and I have to fight to keep my emotions in check. I turn to Macon. "She did good."

"Yeah, she did. I'm so proud of her." He looks between Spence and me. "I know this is probably not the right time to do this, but it's really the only time I've been away from Harper and with y'all since I got into town. I want to ask Harper to marry me. And I know it would mean a lot to her if I had your blessing. She loves y'all so much."

"Macon, this is amazing. Duh, yes. Of course you have our blessing."

Spence claps him on the shoulder. "Welcome to the family."

Macon smiles. "If Harper says yes."

"Of course she's going to say yes. How are you going to do it? Do you have a big plan?"

"I was hoping we could borrow the condo in Jacksonville? I thought I'd do it on the beach at sunset. And Harper loves that place, so I thought it would be fitting."

Spence says. "Listen, what you do is, after she goes to sleep, you slip the ring on her finger and wait for her to notice after she wakes up."

I roll my eyes. "Macon, don't listen to him. Sunset is perfect and of course you can use the condo."

After the ceremony and we take the obligatory family photos with the graduate and we tell Harper and Macon good-bye, Spence, the kids, and I head home. It's almost their bedtime when we finally make it home, so we tag team a quick supper for them, then a bath and their bedtime routine. I read them a story and then Spence sings them a song and I love nothing more than standing in the doorway as he sits between the kids' beds and sings them to sleep.

Once Clare and Ollie have drifted off, we tiptoe out of their room and into the kitchen. "What do you want to do for supper?" Spence asks.

I shrug. "Want to toss in a frozen pizza and chill out and watch a movie?"

"Sounds good to me." He walks to the freezer, pulls out a pizza, unwraps it, and puts it in the oven before turning it on. I hop up on the counter and Spence comes to stand between my knees.

I wrap my arms around his neck. "Today was a good day."

He nods and plants his hands on either side of my hips on the counter. "Yes, it was. Our girl made it."

"I know. I'm so proud of her. And now, it looks like she'll be getting married. You know, we're too young to have a kid who's getting married."

He laughs. "Yeah, but it sure does feel like Harper's always been with us, doesn't it?"

I nod. "Yep. Hard to remember what our life was like before she was in it, huh?"

Spence brushes a kiss across my lips. "You did good, too, you know that?"

"I didn't do anything."

"Babe, you could have sent Harper away and never given her a second thought. But you didn't. You took her in and gave her a stable home. You loved her. You helped her grow. And even when it was out of your control, you tried to fight for her. You made it so she always knew she had a home, no matter what. You were a mother to her, even though your own mother abandoned you. You could have resented Harper for her mere existence, but you didn't. You were selfless and honest with her. Today is your victory, too.

"You helped her study for her GED and her ACT and fill out all her college forms. You made it so she could dream. You remember when we first met her and she said she probably wouldn't graduate high school. You helped her see her true potential."

"Spence, you convinced me to take Harper. I was seriously not going to do it. So you definitely get to take a big chunk of the credit in all of this, too."

He shrugs. "Well, if we drank, I would raise a glass to you, my wife."

"And I would raise a glass to you. But I guess raising those beautiful babies will have to be reward enough on its own."

He smiles sweetly. "It's a pretty great reward. They're a handful, but I wouldn't trade them for anything."

"Me, neither. I'm so thankful for them. I almost wouldn't mind having another one."

Spence's eyes snap to mine. "What?"

I shrug. "Might be nice and you love me pregnant."

His eyebrows go up. "Don't play, Jo. You know I do. I love your belly all big and round. It's fucking beautiful. Are you being serious right now? Because you know I'm always down for more babies. I love babies."

"Let's just say I'm really glad you didn't listen to me when I was in labor and told you that you had to go get a vasectomy. Because, yeah. I think I want one more. I feel like one is missing. And I know there's no replacing Aaron; that's not what I'm saying, but I still feel like maybe our family isn't complete."

Spence kisses the side of my neck. "So, when were you thinking you might like to *talk* about this a little bit more?"

"After the pizza? Because I'm starving."

He laughs. "Sure. Better eat up. If you recall, baby-making requires lots of energy for the copious amounts of sex we'll need to have."

I pull his face to mine and kiss him. "I'm sure all that sex will be such a hardship for you. I'll try to take it easy on you."

He pulls me to him for a tight hug. "Damn, Jo. I love you so much. How long do you think this happiness will last? Don't people normally stop feeling all mushy and stuff towards their spouse after a while?"

I brush his hair off his forehead. "Baby, I've loved and wanted you since I was twelve. It's never gone away. Pretty sure I'll love you and want you from now until forever."

ABOUT THE AUTHOR

For as long as she can remember, Rachael has been a voracious reader. At the age of eleven, she discovered her grandmother's stash of clench-cover romance novels and she was forever changed. A lover of many fictional men and one very non-fictional one, she strives to write real and emotional characters who always get their happily ever after. Rachael lives in East Tennessee with her husband and two sons on their family farm. When she's not tackling her endless TBR, she can be found drinking all the coffee in existence.

ALSO BY RACHAEL OGLE

Fake It Till You Fall (Fall Book One)

Fall Into Forever (Fall Book Two)

My Ada Mae (Knox County Book One)

Find Rachael Online

www.ingramcontent.com/pod-product-compliance
Lightning Source LLC
Chambersburg PA
CBHW020003120726
47903CB00004B/1115